each of these writers, as the title boldly states, modern legends in their genre. There isn't a misfire in the bunch, a rarity in anthologies, and very much a rarity in the fantasy field. This is a collection of grace, style, and substance.

"So if you are a follower of any of these series, you need this book. And if you've never tried modern fantasy, this is a wonderful place to be introduced to its masters."
—The Statesmen Journal (Salem, Oregon)

"This is an excellent way to visit old friends, or get clued in on some multivolumed epics." *—The Denver Post*

"A collection of short novels by some of the biggest names in fantasy, all set in their best-known secondary worlds. There are delights aplenty in this huge volume." *—Edmonton Journal*

"*Legends* more than lives up to its name. Its purpose is to bring us those writers who have created modern-day legends with such skill that they became what they created, and it does its job. To put it bluntly, everyone involved with this book did one hell of a job." *—Queen's College Quad*

"A fascinating assortment of short novels by fantasy's powerhouse authors, set in the most-loved world each created. Each tale stands alone, which is an added bonus for those readers who may not have read every series represented. Every tale in *Legends* is original, high-quality, and adds gloriously to the world in which it is set. Some are amusing and charming, others tragic, but all reflect the nobility of the human spirit."
—The Herald (Rock Hills, South Carolina)

"In addition to its obvious appeal to confirmed series readers, this tour de force serves as a superb introduction to the genre's most memorable sagas. A priority purchase." *—Liberty Journal*

"This is an altogether impressive volume, completely approachable. The illustrations and maps included throughout are certainly a lovely bonus, but quite unnecessary in a volume that sells itself by the fifth page and holds to its early promise all the way through." *—VOYA*

"An essential for every fantasy fan." *—SFX*

Legends

VOLUME 3

SHORT NOVELS BY THE MASTERS
OF MODERN FANTASY

edited by

ROBERT SILVERBERG

TOR ®

A TOM DOHERTY ASSOCIATES BOOK
NEW YORK

This is a work of fiction. All the characters and events portrayed in this book are either products of the author's imagination or are used fictitiously.

LEGENDS: VOLUME 3

Copyright © 1998 by Agberg, Ltd.

A Tor Book
Published by Tom Doherty Associates, LLC
175 Fifth Avenue
New York, NY 10010

www.tor.com

Tor® is a registered trademark of Tom Doherty Associates, LLC.

ISBN: 0-812-56664-5
Library of Congress Catalog Card Number: 98-23593

First edition: October 1998
First mass market edition: February 2000

Printed in the United States of America

0 9 8 7 6 5 4 3 2 1

CONTENTS

INTRODUCTION

❦

Here is a book of visions and miracles—the third volume in a set of three containing eleven rich, robust new stories by the best-known and most accomplished modern creators of fantasy, fiction, each one set in the special universe of the imagination that made that writer famous throughout the world.

Fantasy is the oldest branch of imaginative literature—as old as the human imagination itself. It is not difficult to believe that the same artistic impulse that produced the extraordinary cave paintings of Altamira and Chauvet, fifteen and twenty and even thirty thousand years ago, also probably produced astounding tales of gods and demons, of talismans and spells, of dragons and werewolves, of wondrous lands beyond the horizon—tales that fur-clad shamans recited to fascinated audiences around the campfires of Ice Age Europe. So, too, in torrid Africa, in the China of prehistory, in ancient India, in the Americas: everywhere, in fact, on and on back through time for thousands or even hundreds of thousands of years. I like to think that the storytelling impulse is universal—that there have been storytellers as long as there have been beings in this world that could be spoken of as ''human''—and that those storytellers have in particular devoted their skills and energies and talents, throughout our long evolutionary path, to the creation of extraordinary marvels and wonders.

We will never know, of course, what tales the Cro-Magnon storytellers told their spellbound audiences on those frosty nights in ancient France. But surely there were strong components of the fantastic in them. The evidence of the oldest stories that *have* survived argues in favor of that. If fantasy can be defined as literature that depicts the world beyond that of mundane reality, and mankind's struggle to assert dominance over that world, then the most ancient story that *has* come down to us—the Sumerian tale of the hero Gilgamesh, which dates from about 2500 B.C.—is fantasy, for its theme is Gilgamesh's quest for eternal life.

Homer's *Odyssey*, abounding as it does in shapeshifters and wizards and sorceresses, in Cyclopses and many-headed man-eating creatures, is rich with fantastic elements, too, as are any number of other Greek and Roman tales. As we come closer to our own times we meet the dread monster Grendel of the Anglo-Saxon *Beowulf*, the Midgard serpent and the dragon Fafnir and the apocalyptic Fenris-wolf of the Norse sagas, the hapless immortality-craving Dr. Faustus of German legend, the myriad enchanters of *The Thousand and One Nights,* the far-larger-than-life heroes of the Welsh *Mabinogion* and the Persian *Shah-Nameh*, and an infinity of other strange and wonderful creations.

Nor did the impulse toward the creation of the fantastic disappear as the modern era, the era of microscopes and telescopes, of steam engines and railway systems, of telegraphs and phonographs and electric light, came into being. Our fascination with the unseen and the unseeable did not end simply because so many things previously thought impossible now had become realities. What is more fantastic, after all, than having the sound of an entire symphony orchestra rise up out of a flat disk of plastic? Or to speak into a device that one holds in one's hand, and be heard and understood ten thousand miles away? But the same century that gave us the inventions of Thomas Alva Edison and Alexander Graham Bell gave us Lewis Carroll's two incomparable tales of Alice's adventures in other realities, H. Rider Haggard's innumerable novels of lost civilizations, and Mary Wollstonecraft Shelley's *Frankenstein*.

Nor did the twentieth century—the century of air travel and atomic energy, of television and computers, of open-heart surgery and sex-change operations—see us losing our taste for tales of the extraordinary. A host of machine-age fantasists—James Branch Cabell and A. Merritt and Lord Dunsany, E. R. Eddison and Mervyn Peake and L. Frank Baum, H. P. Lovecraft and Robert E. Howard and J. R. R. Tolkien, to name a few of the best-known ones—kept the world well supplied with wondrous tales of the fantastic.

One change of tone did occur in the twentieth century, though, with the rise to popularity of science fiction—the branch of fantasy that applies immense ingenuity to the task of making the impossible, or at least the implausible, seem altogether probable. As science fiction—which was given its essential nature well over a hundred years ago by Jules Verne and H. G. Wells, and developed in modern times by such writers as Robert A. Heinlein, Isaac Asimov, and Aldous Huxley—came to exert its immense appeal on the atomic-age reading public, "pure" fantasy fiction (that is, fantasy that makes no attempt at empirical explanation of its wonders) came to be thought of as something largely reserved for children, like myths and fairy tales.

The older kind of fantasy never disappeared, of course. But in the United States, at least, it went into eclipse for nearly fifty years. Science fiction, meanwhile, manifested itself to the reading public in the form of magazines with names like *Amazing Stories* and *Astounding Science Fiction* and readerships composed largely of boys and earnest young men with an interest in gadgets and scientific disputation. The only American magazine dealing in the material we define as fantasy fiction was *Weird Tales*, founded in 1923, but that magazine published not only fantasy but a great many other kinds of genre fiction that might not be thought of as fantasy today—tales of pure terror, for example, with no speculative content.

The separation between fantasy and science fiction is not always easy to locate, but some distinctions are fairly clear-cut, if not entirely rigid. Stories that deal with androids and robots, spaceships, alien beings, time machines, viruses from outer space, galactic empires, and the like usually can be described as science fiction. These are all matters that are *conceptually possible* within the framework of scientific law as we currently understand it. (Although such things as time machines and faster-than-light vehicles certainly stretch that framework to its limits, and perhaps beyond them.) Fantasy, meanwhile, uses as its material that which is *generally believed to be impossible or nonexistent* in our culture: wizards and warlocks, elves and goblins, werewolves and vampires, unicorns and enchanted princesses, efficacious incantations and spells.

Fantasy fiction per se did not have a real magazine of its own until 1939, when John W. Campbell, Jr., the foremost science-fiction editor of his time, brought *Unknown* (later called *Unknown Worlds*) into being in order to allow his writers greater imaginative latitude than his definitions of science fiction would permit. Many of the same writers who had turned Campbell's *Astounding Science Fiction* into the most notable magazine of its type yet published—Robert A. Heinlein, L. Sprague de Camp, Theodore Sturgeon, Lester del Rey, Jack Williamson—also became mainstays of *Unknown*, and the general structural approach was similar: postulate a far-out idea and develop all its consequences to a logical conclusion. The stories about being nasty to water gnomes or selling your soul to the devil wound up in *Unknown*; those about traveling in time or voyaging to distant planets were published in *Astounding*.

But *Unknown*, though it was cherished with great fondness by its readers and writers, never attained much of a public following, and when wartime paper shortages forced Campbell to choose between his two magazines in 1943, *Unknown* was swiftly killed, never to reappear. Postwar attempts by nostalgic ex-contributors to *Unknown* to recapture its special flavor were largely unsuccessful; H. L. Gold's *Beyond* lasted ten issues, Lester del Rey's *Fantasy Fiction* managed only four. Only *The Magazine of Fantasy,* edited by Anthony Boucher and J. Francis McComas, succeeded in establishing itself as a permanent entity, and even that magazine found it wisest to change its name to *Fantasy and Science Fiction* with its second issue. When science fiction became a fixture of paperback publishing in the 1950s, fantasy once again lagged behind: few fantasy novels were paperbacked, and most of them—Jack Vance's *The Dying Earth* and the early reprints of H. P. Lovecraft and Robert E. Howard are good examples—quickly vanished from view and became collector's items.

It all began to change in the late 1960s, when the sudden availability of paperback editions of J. R. R. Tolkien's *Lord of the Rings* trilogy (previously kept from paperback by an unwilling hardcover publisher) aroused a hunger for fantasy fiction in millions of readers that has, so far, been insatiable. Tolkien's books were such an emphatic commercial success that publishers rushed to find writers who could produce imitative trilogies, and the world was flooded with huge Hobbitesque novels, many of which sold in extraordinary quantities themselves. Robert Howard's *Conan* novels, once admired only by a small band of ardent cultists, began to win vast new readers about the same time. And a few years later Ballantine Books, Tolkien's paperback publisher, brought out an extraordinary series of books in its Adult Fantasy series, edited by Lin Carter, which made all the elegant classic masterpieces of such fantasists as E. R. Eddison, James Branch Cabell, Lord Dunsany, and Mervyn Peake available to modern readers. And, ever since, fantasy has been a dominant factor in modern publishing. What was a neglected stepsibling of science fiction fifty years ago is, today, an immensely popular genre.

In the wake of the great success of the Tolkien trilogy, newer writers have come along with their own deeply imagined worlds of fantasy, and have captured large and enthusiastic audiences themselves. In the late 1960s, Ursula Le Guin began her searching and sensitive Earthsea series, and Anne McCaffrey co-opted the ancient fantastic theme of the dragon for her Pern novels, which live on the borderline between fantasy and science fiction. Stephen King, some years later, won a readership of astounding magnitude by plumbing the archetypical fears of humanity and transforming them into powerful novels that occupied fantasy's darker terrain.

Terry Pratchett, on the other hand, has magnificently demonstrated the comic power of satiric fantasy. Such writers as Orson Scott Card and Raymond E. Feist have won huge followings for their Alvin Maker and Riftwar books. More recently, Robert Jordan's mammoth Wheel of Time series, George R. R. Martin's Song of Ice and Fire books, and Terry Goodkind's Sword of Truth tales have taken their place in the pantheon of modern fantasy, as has Tad Williams' Memory, Sorrow and Thorn series.

And here is the whole bunch of them, brought together in one huge three-volume collection in which fantasy enthusiasts can revel for weeks. A new Earthsea story, a new tale of Pern, a new Dark Tower adventure, a new segment in Pratchett's playful Discworld series, and all the rest that you'll find herein—there has never been a book like this before. Gathering such an elite collection of first-magnitude stars into a single volume has not been an easy task. My gratitude herewith for the special assistance of Martin H. Greenberg, Ralph Vicinanza, Stephen King, John Helfers, and Virginia Kidd, who in one way or another made my editorial task immensely less difficult than it otherwise would have been. And, too, although it goes without saying that I'm grateful to my wife, Karen, for her inestimable help in every phase of this intricate project, I think I'll say it anyway—not just because she's a terrific person, but because she came up with what unquestionably was the smartest idea of the whole enterprise.

—Robert Silverberg
December, 1997

THE WHEEL
OF TIME

Robert Jordan

The world of Robert Jordan's *The Wheel of Time* lies both in our future and our past, a world of kings and queens and Aes Sedai, women who can tap the True Source and wield the One Power, which turns the Wheel and drives the universe: a world where the war between the Light and the Shadow is fought every day.

At the moment of Creation, the Creator bound the Dark One away from the world of humankind, but more than three thousand years ago Aes Sedai, then both men and women, unknowingly bored into that prison outside of time. The Dark One was able to touch the world only lightly, and the hole was eventually sealed over, but the Dark One's taint settled on *saidin*, the male half of the Power. Eventually every male Aes Sedai went mad, and in the Breaking of the World they destroyed civilization and changed the very face of the earth, sinking mountains beneath the sea and bringing new seas where land had been.

Now only women bear the title Aes Sedai. Commanded by their Amyrlin Seat and divided into seven Ajahs named by color, they rule the great island city of Tar Valon, where their White Tower is located, and are bound by the Three Oaths, fixed into their bones with *saidar*, the female half of the Power: To speak no word that is not true, to make no weapon for one man to kill another, and never to use the One Power except as a weapon against Shadowspawn or in the last extreme of defending her own life, or that of her Warder or another sister.

Men still are born who can learn to channel the Power, or worse, who will channel one day whether they try to or not. Doomed to madness, destruction, and death by the taint on *saidin*, they are hunted down by Aes Sedai and gentled, cut off forever from the Power for the safety of the world. No man goes to this willingly. Even if they survive the hunt, they seldom survive long after gentling.

For more than three thousand years, while nations and empires rose and fell, nothing has been so feared as a man who can channel. But for all those three thousand years there have been the Prophecies of the Dragon, that the seals on the Dark One's prison will weaken and he will touch the world once more, and that the Dragon, who sealed up that hole, will be Reborn to face the Dark One again. A child, born in sight of Tar Valon on the slopes of Dragonmount, will grow up to be the Dragon Reborn, the only hope of humanity in the Last Battle—a man who can channel. Few people know more than scraps of the Prophecies, and few want to know more.

A world of kings and queens, nations and wars, where the White Tower rules only Tar Valon but even kings and queens are wary of Aes Sedai machinations. A world where the Shadow and the Prophecies loom together.

The present story takes place before the first volume of the series. The succeeding books should be read in order.

NEW SPRING

Robert Jordan

The air of Kandor held the sharpness of new spring when Lan returned to the lands where he had always known he would die. Trees bore the first red of new growth, and a few scattered wildflowers dotted winter-brown grass where shadows did not cling to patches of snow, yet the pale sun offered little warmth after the south, a gusting breeze cut through his coat, and gray clouds hinted at more than rain. He was almost home. Almost.

A hundred generations had beaten the wide road nearly as hard as the stone of the surrounding hills, and little dust rose, though a steady stream of ox-carts was leaving the morning farmers' markets in Canluum and merchant trains of tall wagons, surrounded by mounted guards in steel caps and bits of armor, flowed toward the city's high gray walls. Here and there the chains of the Kandori merchants' guild spanned a chest or an Arafellin wore bells, a ruby decorated this man's ear, a pearl brooch that woman's breast, but for the most part the traders' clothes were as subdued as their manner. A merchant who flaunted too much profit discovered it hard to find bargains. By contrast, farmers showed off their success when they came to town. Bright embroidery decorated the striding country men's baggy breeches, the women's wide trousers, their cloaks fluttering in the wind. Some wore colored ribbons in their hair, or a narrow fur collar. They might have been dressed for the coming Bel Tine dances and feasting. Yet country folk eyed strangers as warily as any guard, eyed them and hefted spears or axes and hurried along. The times carried an edge in Kandor, maybe all along the Borderlands. Bandits had sprung up like weeds this past year, and more troubles than usual out of the Blight. Rumor even spoke of a man who channeled the One Power, but then, rumor often did.

Leading his horse toward Canluum, Lan paid as little attention to the stares he and his companion attracted as he did to Bukama's scowls and carping. Bukama had raised him from the cradle, Bukama and other men now dead, and he could not recall seeing anything but a glower on that weathered face, even when Bukama spoke praise. This time his mutters were for a stone-bruised hoof that had him afoot, but he could always find something.

They did attract attention, two very tall men walking their mounts and a packhorse with a pair of tattered wicker hampers, their plain clothes worn and travel-stained. Their harness and weapons were well tended, though. A young man and an old, hair hanging to their shoulders and held back by a braided leather cord around the temples. The *hadori* drew eyes. Especially here in the Borderlands, where people had some idea what it meant.

"Fools," Bukama grumbled. "Do they think we're bandits? Do they think we mean to rob the lot of them, at midday on the high road?" He glared and shifted the sword at his hip in a way that brought considering stares from a number of merchants' guards. A stout farmer prodded his ox wide of them.

Lan kept silent. A certain reputation clung to Malkieri who still wore the *hadori*, though not for banditry, but reminding Bukama would only send him into a black humor for days. His mutters shifted to the chances of a decent bed that night, of a decent meal before. Bukama seldom complained when there actually was no bed or no food, only about prospects and the inconsequential. He expected little, and trusted to less.

Neither food nor lodging entered Lan's thoughts, despite the distance they had traveled. His head kept swinging north. He remained aware of everyone around him, especially those who glanced his way more than once, aware of the jingle of harness and the creak of saddles, the clop of hooves, the snap of wagon canvas loose on its hoops. Any sound out of place would shout at him. That had been the first lesson Bukama and his friends had imparted in his childhood: Be aware of everything, even when asleep. Only the dead could afford oblivion. Lan remained aware, but the Blight lay north. Still miles away across the hills, yet he could feel it, feel the twisted corruption.

Just his imagination, but no less real for that. It had pulled at him in the south, in Cairhien and Andor, even in Tear, almost five hundred leagues distant. Two years away from the Borderlands, his personal war abandoned for another, and every day the tug grew stronger. The Blight meant death to most men. Death and the Shadow, a rotting land tainted by the Dark One's breath, where anything at all could kill. Two tosses of a coin had decided where to begin anew. Four nations bordered the Blight, but his war covered the length of it, from the Aryth Ocean to the Spine of the World. One place to meet death was as good as another. He was almost home. Almost back to the Blight.

A drymoat surrounded Canluum's wall, fifty paces wide and ten deep, spanned by five broad stone bridges with towers at either end as tall as those that lined the wall itself. Raids out of the Blight by Trollocs and Myrddraal often struck much deeper into Kandor than Canluum, but none had ever made it inside the city's wall. The Red Stag waved above every tower. A proud man was Lord Varan, the High Seat of House Marcasiev; Queen Ethenielle did not fly so many of her own banners even in Chachin itself.

The guards at the outer towers, in helmets with Varan's antlered crest and the Red Stag on their chests, peered into the backs of wagons before allowing them to trundle onto the bridge, or occasionally motioned someone to push a hood further back. No more than a gesture was necessary; the law in every Borderland forbade hiding your face inside village or town, and no one wanted to be mistaken for one of the Eyeless trying to sneak into the city. Hard gazes followed Lan and Bukama onto the bridge. Their faces were clearly visible. And their *hadori*. No recognition lit any of those watching eyes, though. Two years was a long time in the Borderlands. A great many men could die in two years.

Lan noticed that Bukama had gone silent, always a bad sign, and cautioned him. "I never start trouble," the older man snapped, but he did stop fingering his sword hilt.

The guards on the wall above the open iron-plated gates and those on the bridge wore only back- and breast-plates for armor, yet they were no less watchful, especially of a pair of Malkieri with their hair tied back. Bukama's mouth grew tighter at every step.

"Al'Lan Mandragoran! The Light preserve us, we heard you were dead fighting the Aiel at the Shining Walls!" The exclamation came from a young guard, taller than the rest, almost as tall as Lan. Young, perhaps a year or two less than he, yet the gap seemed ten years. A lifetime. The guard bowed deeply, left hand on his knee. "*Tai'shar Malkier!*" True blood of Malkier. "I stand ready, Majesty."

"I am not a king," Lan said quietly. Malkier was dead. Only the war still lived. In him, at least.

Bukama was not quiet. "You stand ready for *what,* boy?" The heel of his bare hand struck the guard's breastplate right over the Red Stag, driving the man upright and back a step. "You cut your hair short and leave it unbound!" Bukama spat the words. "You're sworn to a Kandori lord! By what right do you claim to be Malkieri?"

The young man's face reddened as he floundered for answers. Other guards started toward the pair, then halted when Lan let his reins fall. Only that, but they knew his name, now. They eyed his bay stallion, standing still and alert behind him, almost as cautiously as they did him. A warhorse was a formidable weapon, and they could not know Cat Dancer was only half-trained yet.

Space opened up as people already through the gates hurried a little distance before turning to watch, while those still on the bridge pressed back. Shouts rose in both directions from people wanting to know what was holding traffic. Bukama ignored it all, intent on the red-faced guard. He had not dropped the reins of the packhorse or his yellow roan gelding.

An officer appeared from the stone guardhouse inside the gates, crested helmet under his arm, but one hand in a steel-backed gauntlet resting on his sword hilt. A bluff, graying man with white scars on his face, Alin Seroku had soldiered forty years along the Blight, yet his eyes widened slightly at the sight of Lan. Plainly he had heard the tales of Lan's death, too.

"The Light shine upon you, Lord Mandragoran. The son of el'Leanna and al'Akir, blessed be their memories, is always welcome." Seroku's eyes flickered toward Bukama, not in welcome. He planted his feet in the middle of the gateway. Five horsemen could have passed easily on either side, but he meant himself for a bar, and he was. None of the guards shifted a boot, yet every one had hand on sword hilt. All but the young man meeting Bukama's glares with his own. "Lord Marcasiev has commanded us to keep the peace strictly," Seroku went on, half in apology. But no more than half. "The city is on edge. All these tales of a man channeling are bad enough, but there have been murders in the street this last month and more, in broad daylight, and strange accidents. People whisper about Shadowspawn loose inside the walls."

Lan gave a slight nod. With the Blight so close, people always muttered of Shadowspawn when they had no other explanation, whether for a sudden death or unexpected crop failure. He did not take up Cat Dancer's reins, though. "We intend to rest here a few days before riding north."

For a moment he thought Seroku was surprised. Did the man expect pledges to keep the peace, or apologies for Bukama's behavior? Either would shame Bukama, now. A pity if the war ended here. Lan did not want to die killing Kandori.

His old friend turned from the young guard, who stood quivering, fists clenched at his sides. "All fault here is mine," Bukama announced to the air in a flat voice. "I had no call for what I did. By my mother's name, I will keep Lord Marcasiev's peace. By my mother's name, I will not draw sword inside Canluum's walls." Seroku's jaw dropped, and Lan hid his own shock with difficulty.

Hesitating only a moment, the scar-faced officer

stepped aside, bowing and touching sword hilt, then heart. "There is always welcome for Lan Mandragoran Dai Shan," he said formally. "And for Bukama Marenellin, the hero of Salmarna. May you both know peace, one day."

"There is peace in the mother's last embrace," Lan responded with equal formality, touching hilt and heart.

"May she welcome us home, one day," Seroku finished. No one really wished for the grave, but that was the only place to find peace in the Borderlands.

Face like iron, Bukama strode ahead pulling Sun Lance and the packhorse after him, not waiting for Lan. This was not well.

Canluum was a city of stone and brick, its paved streets twisting around tall hills. The Aiel invasion had never reached the Borderlands, but the ripples of war always diminished trade a long way from any battles, and now that fighting and winter were both finished, the city had filled with people from every land. Despite the Blight practically on the city's doorstep, gemstones mined in the surrounding hills made Canluum wealthy. And, strangely enough, some of the finest clockmakers anywhere. The cries of hawkers and shopkeepers shouting their wares rose above the hum of the crowd even away from the terraced market squares. Colorfully dressed musicians, or jugglers, or tumblers performed at every intersection. A handful of lacquered carriages swayed through the mass of people and wagons and carts and barrows, and horses with gold- or silver-mounted saddles and bridles picked their way through the throng, their riders' garb embroidered as ornately as the animals' tack and trimmed with fox or marten or ermine. Hardly a foot of street was left bare anywhere. Lan even saw several Aes Sedai, women with serene, ageless faces. Enough people recognized them on sight that they created eddies in the crowd, swirls to clear a way. Respect or caution, awe or fear, there were sufficient reasons for a king to step aside for a sister. Once you might have gone a year without seeing an Aes Sedai even in the Borderlands, but the sisters seemed to be everywhere since their old Amyrlin Seat died a few months earlier. Maybe it was those tales of a man channeling; they would not let him run free long, if he existed. Lan kept his eyes away from them. The *hadori* could be enough to attract the interest of a sister seeking a Warder.

Shockingly, lace veils covered many women's faces. Thin lace, sheer enough to reveal that they had eyes, and no one had ever heard of a female Myrddraal, but Lan had never expected law to yield to mere fashion. Next they would take down the oil lamps lining the streets and let the nights grow black. Even more shocking than the veils, Bukama looked right at some of those women and did not open his mouth. Then a jut-nosed man named Nazar Kurenin rode in front of Bukama's eyes, and he did not blink. The young guard surely had been born after the Blight swallowed Malkier, but Kurenin, his hair cut short and wearing a forked beard, was twice Lan's age. The years had not erased the marks of his *hadori* completely. There were many like Kurenin, and the sight of him should have set Bukama spluttering. Lan eyed his friend worriedly.

They had been moving steadily toward the center of the city, climbing toward the highest hill, Stag's Stand. Lord Marcasiev's fortress-like palace covered the peak, with those of lesser lords and ladies on the terraces below. Any threshold up there offered warm welcome for al'Lan Mandragoran. Perhaps warmer than he wanted now. Balls and hunts, with nobles invited from as much as fifty miles away, including from across the border with Arafel. People avid to hear of his "adventures." Young men wanting to join his forays into the Blight, and old men to compare their experiences there with his. Women eager to share the bed of a man whom, so fool stories claimed, the Blight could not kill. Kandor and Arafel were as bad as any southland at times; some of those women would be married. And there would be men like Kurenin, working to submerge memories of lost Malkier, and women who no longer adorned their foreheads with the *ki'sain* in pledge that they would swear their sons to oppose the Shadow while they breathed. Lan could ignore the false smiles while they named him al'Lan Dai Shan, diademed battle lord and uncrowned king of a nation betrayed while he was in his cradle. In his present mood, Bukama might do murder. Or worse, given his oaths at the gate. He would keep those to the death.

"Varan Marcasiev will hold us a week or more with ceremony," Lan said, turning down a narrower street that led away from the Stand. "With what we've heard of bandits and the like, he will be just as happy if I don't appear to make my bows." True enough. He had met the High Seat of House Marcasiev only once, years past, but he remembered a man given entirely to his duties.

Bukama followed without complaint about missing a palace bed or the feasts the cooks would prepare. It was worrying.

No palaces rose in the hollows toward the north wall, only shops and taverns, inns and stables and wagon yards. Bustle surrounded the factors' long warehouses, but no carriages came to the Deeps, and most streets were barely wide enough for carts. They were just as jammed with people as the wide ways, though, and every bit as noisy. Here, the street performers' finery was tarnished, yet they made up for it by being louder, and buyers and sellers alike bellowed as if trying to be heard in the next street. Likely some of the crowd were cutpurses, slipfingers, and other thieves, finished with a morning's business higher up or headed there for the afternoon. It would have been a wonder otherwise, with so many merchants in town. The second time unseen fingers brushed his coat in the crowd, Lan tucked his purse under his shirt. Any banker would advance him more against the Shienaran estate he had been granted on reaching manhood, but loss of the gold on hand meant accepting the hospitality of Stag's Stand.

At the first three inns they tried, slate-roofed cubes of gray stone with bright signs out front, the innkeepers had not a cubbyhole to offer. Lesser traders and merchants' guards filled them to the attics. Bukama began to mutter about making a bed in a hayloft, yet he never mentioned the feather mattresses and linens waiting on the Stand. Leaving their horses with ostlers at a fourth inn, The Blue Rose, Lan entered determined to find some place for them if it took the rest of the day.

Inside, a graying woman, tall and handsome, presided over a crowded common room where talk and laughter almost drowned out the slender girl singing to the music of her zither. Pipesmoke wreathed the ceiling beams, and the smell of roasting lamb floated from the kitchens. As soon as the innkeeper saw Lan and Bukama, she gave her blue-striped apron a twitch and strode toward them, dark eyes sharp.

Before Lan could open his mouth, she seized Bukama's ears, pulled his head down, and kissed him. Kandori women were seldom retiring, but even so it was a remarkably thorough kiss in front of so many eyes. Pointing fingers and snickering grins flashed among the tables.

"It's good to see you again, too, Racelle," Bukama murmured with a small smile when she finally released him. "I didn't know you had an inn here. Do you think—?" He lowered his gaze rather than meeting her eyes rudely, and that proved a mistake. Racelle's fist caught his jaw so hard that his hair flailed as he staggered.

"Six years without a word," she snapped. "Six years!" Grabbing his ears again, she gave him another kiss, longer this time. Took it rather than gave. A sharp twist of his ears met every attempt to do anything besides standing bent over and letting her do as she wished. At least she would not put a knife in his heart if she was kissing him. Perhaps not.

"I think Mistress Arovni might find Bukama a room somewhere," a man's familiar voice said dryly behind Lan. "And you, too, I suppose."

Turning, Lan clasped forearms with the only man in the room beside Bukama of a height with him, Ryne Venamar, his oldest friend except for Bukama.

The innkeeper still had Bukama occupied as Ryne led Lan to a small table in the corner. Five years older, Ryne was Malkieri too, but his hair fell in two long bell-laced braids, and morc silver bells lined the turned-down tops of his boots and ran up the sleeves of his yellow coat. Bukama did not exactly dislike Ryne—not exactly—yet in his present mood, only Nazar Kurenin could have had a worse effect.

While the pair of them were settling themselves on benches, a serving maid in a striped apron brought hot spiced wine. Apparently Ryne had ordered as soon as he saw Lan. Dark-eyed and full-lipped, she stared Lan up and down openly as she set his mug in front of him, then whispered her name, Lira, in his ear, and an invitation, if he was staying the night. All he wanted that night was sleep, so he lowered his gaze, murmuring that she honored him too much. Lira did not let him finish. With a raucous laugh, she bent to bite his car, hard, then announced that by tomorrow's sun she would have honored him till his knees would not hold him up. More laughter flared at the tables around them.

Ryne forestalled any possibility of righting matters, tossing her a fat coin and giving her a slap on the bottom to send her off. Lira offered him a dimpled smile as she slipped the silver into the neck of her dress, but she left sending smoky glances over her shoulder at Lan that made him sigh. If he tried to say no now, she might well pull a knife over the insult.

"So your luck still holds with women, too." Ryne's laugh had an edge. Perhaps he fancied her himself. "The Light knows, they can't find you handsome; you get uglier every year. Maybe I ought to try some of that coy modesty, let women lead me by the nose."

Lan opened his mouth, then took a drink instead of speaking. He should not have to explain, but Ryne's father had taken him to Arafel the year Lan turned ten. The man wore a single blade on his hip instead of two on his back, yet he was Arafellin to his toenails. He actually started conversations with women who had not spoken to him first. Lan, raised by Bukama and his friends in Shienar, had been surrounded by a small community who held to Malkieri ways.

A number of people around the room were watching their table, sidelong glances over mugs and goblets. A plump copper-skinned woman wearing a much thicker dress than Domani women usually did made no effort to hide her stares as she spoke excitedly to a fellow with curled mustaches and a large pearl in his ear. Probably wondering whether there would be trouble over Lira. Wondering whether a man wearing the *hadori* really would kill at the drop of a pin.

"I didn't expect to find you in Canluum," Lan said, setting the wine mug down. "Guarding a merchant train?" Bukama and the innkeeper were nowhere to be seen.

Ryne shrugged. "Out of Shol Arbela. The luckiest trader in Arafel, they say. Said. Much good it did him. We arrived yesterday, and last night footpads slit his throat two streets over. No return money for me this trip." He flashed a rueful grin and took a deep pull at his wine, perhaps to the memory of the merchant or perhaps to the lost half of his wages. "Burn me if I thought to see you here, either."

"You shouldn't listen to rumors, Ryne. I've not taken a wound worth mentioning since I rode south." Lan decided to twit Bukama if they did get a room, about whether it was already paid for and how. Indignation might take him out of his darkness.

"The Aiel," Ryne snorted. "I never thought *they* could put paid to you." He had never faced Aiel, of course. "I expected you to be wherever Edeyn Arrel is. Chachin, now, I hear."

That name snapped Lan's head back to the man across the table. "Why should I be near the Lady Arrel?" he demanded softly. Softly, but emphasizing her proper title.

"Easy, man," Ryne said. "I didn't mean . . ." Wisely, he abandoned that line. "Burn me, do you mean to say you haven't heard? She's raised the

Golden Crane. In your name, of course. Since the year turned, she's been from Fal Moran to Maradon, and coming back now.'' Ryne shook his head, the bells in his braids chiming faintly. "There must be two or three hundred men right here in Canluum ready to follow her. You, I mean. Some you'd not believe. Old Kurenin wept when he heard her speak. All ready to carve Malkier out of the Blight again.''

''What dies in the Blight is gone,'' Lan said wearily. He felt more than cold inside. Suddenly Seroku's surprise that he intended to ride north took on new meaning, and the young guard's assertion that he stood ready. Even the looks here in the common room seemed different. And Edeyn was part of it. Always she liked standing in the heart of the storm. ''I must see to my horse,'' he told Ryne, scraping his bench back.

Ryne said something about making a round of the taverns that night, but Lan hardly heard. He hurried through the kitchens, hot from iron stoves and stone ovens and open hearths, into the cool of the stable-yard, the mingled smells of horse and hay and woodsmoke. A graylark warbled on the edge of the stable roof. Graylarks came even before robins in the spring. Graylarks had been singing in Fal Moran when Edeyn first whispered in his ear.

The horses had already been stabled, bridles and saddles and packsaddle atop saddle blankets on the stall doors, but the wicker hampers were gone. Plainly Mistress Arovni had sent word to the ostlers that he and Bukama were being given accommodation.

There was only a single groom in the dim stable, a lean, hard-faced woman mucking out. Silently she watched him check Cat Dancer and the other horses as she worked, watched him begin to pace the length of the straw-covered floor. He tried to think, but Edeyn's name kept spinning though his head. Edeyn's face, surrounded by silky black hair that hung below her waist, a beautiful face with large dark eyes that could drink a man's soul even when filled with command.

After a bit the groom mumbled something in his direction, touching her lips and forehead, and hurriedly shoved her half-filled barrow out of the stable, glancing over her shoulder at him. She paused to shut the doors, and did that hurriedly, too, sealing him in shadow broken only by a little light from open hay doors in the loft. Dust motes danced in the pale golden shafts.

Lan grimaced. Was she that afraid of a man wearing the *hadori*? Did she think his pacing a threat? Abruptly he became aware of his hands running over the long hilt of his sword, aware of the tightness in his own face. Pacing? No, he had been in the walking stance called Leopard in High Grass, used when there were enemies on all sides. He needed calm.

Seating himself cross-legged on a bale of straw, he formed the image of a flame in his mind and fed emotion into it, hate, fear, everything, every scrap, until it seemed that he floated in emptiness. After years of practice, achieving *ko'di*, the oneness, needed less than a heartbeat. Thought and even his own body seemed distant, but in this state he was more aware than usual, becoming one with the bale beneath him, the stable, the scabbarded sword folded behind him. He could "feel" the horses, cropping at their mangers, and flies buzzing in the corners. They were all part of him. Especially the sword. This time, though, it was only the emotionless void that he sought.

From his belt pouch he took a heavy gold signet ring worked with a flying crane and turned it over and over in his fingers. The ring of Malkieri kings, worn by men who had held back the Shadow nine hundred years and more. Countless times it had been remade as time wore it down, always the old ring melted to become part of the new. Some particle might still exist in it of the ring worn by the rulers of Rhamdashar, that had lived before Malkier, and Aramaelle that had been before Rhamdashar. That piece of metal represented over three thousand years fighting the Blight. It had been his almost as long as he had lived, but he had never worn it. Even looking at the ring was a labor, usually. One he disciplined himself to every day. Without the emptiness, he did not think he could have done so today. In *ko'di*, thought floated free, and emotion lay beyond the horizon.

In his cradle he had been given four gifts. The ring in his hands and the locket that hung around his neck, the sword on his hip and an oath sworn in his name. The locket was the most precious, the oath the heaviest. "To stand against the Shadow so long as iron is hard and stone abides. To defend the Malkieri while one drop of blood remains. To avenge what cannot be defended." And then he had been anointed with oil and named Dai Shan, consecrated as the next King of Malkier, and sent away from a land that knew it would die. Twenty men began that journey; five survived to reach Shienar.

Nothing remained to be defended now, only a nation to avenge, and he had been trained to that from his first step. With his mother's gift at his throat and his father's sword in his hand, with the ring branded on his heart, he had fought to avenge Malkier from his sixteenth nameday. But never had he led men into the Blight. Bukama had ridden with him, and others, but he would not lead men there. That war was his alone. The dead could not be returned to life, a land any more than a man. Only, now, Edeyn Arrel wanted to try.

Her name echoed in the emptiness within him. A hundred emotions loomed like stark mountains, but he fed them into the flame until all was still. Until his heart beat time with the slow stamping of the stalled horses, and the flies' wings beat rapid counterpoint to his breath. She was his *carneira*, his first lover. A thousand years of tradition shouted that, despite the stillness that enveloped him.

He had been fifteen, Edeyn more than twice that, when she gathered the hair that had still hung to his waist in her hands and whispered her intentions. Women had still called him beautiful then, enjoying his blushes, and for half a year she had enjoyed parading him on her arm and tucking him into her bed. Until Bukama and the other men gave him the *hadori*. The gift of his sword on his tenth nameday had made him a man by custom along the Border, though years early for it, yet among Malkieri, that band of braided leather had been more important. Once that was tied around his head, he alone decided where he went, and when, and why. And the dark song of the Blight had become a howl that drowned every other sound. The oath that had murmured so long in his heart became a dance his feet had to follow.

Almost ten years past now that Edeyn had watched him ride away from Fal Moran, and been gone when he returned, yet he still could recall her face more clearly than that of any woman who had shared his bed since. He was no longer a boy, to think that she loved him just because she had chosen to become his first lover, yet there was an old saying among Malkieri men. *Your* carneira *wears part of your soul as a ribbon in her hair forever.* Custom strong as law made it so.

One of the stable doors creaked open to admit Bukama, coatless, shirt tucked raggedly into his breeches. He looked naked without his sword. As if hesitant, he carefully opened both doors wide before coming all the way in. "What are you going to do?" he said finally. "Racelle told me about . . . about the Golden Crane."

Lan tucked the ring away, letting emptiness drain from him. Edeyn's face suddenly seemed everywhere, just beyond the edge of sight. "Ryne says even Nazar Kurenin is ready to follow," he said lightly. "Wouldn't that be a sight to see?" An army could die trying to defeat the Blight. Armies had died trying. But the memories of Malkier already were dying. A nation was memory as much as land. "That boy at the gates might let his hair grow and ask his father for the *hadori*." People were forgetting, trying to forget. When the last man who bound his hair was gone, the last woman who painted her forehead, would Malkier truly be gone, too? "Why, Ryne might even get rid of those braids." Any trace of mirth dropped from his voice as he added, "But is it worth the cost? Some seem to think so." Bukama snorted, yet there had been a pause. He might be one of those who did.

Striding to the stall that held Sun Lance, the older man began to fiddle with his roan's saddle as though suddenly forgetting why he had moved. "There's always a cost for anything," he said, not looking up. "But there are costs, and costs. The Lady Edeyn . . ." He glanced at Lan, then turned to face him. "She was always one to demand every right and require the smallest obligation be met. Custom ties strings to you, and whatever you choose, she will use them like a set of reins unless you find a way to avoid it."

Carefully Lan tucked his thumbs behind his sword belt. Bukama had carried him out of Malkier tied to his back. The last of the five. Bukama had the right of a free tongue even when it touched Lan's *carneira*. "How do you suggest I avoid my obligations without shame?" he asked more harshly than he had intended. Taking a deep breath, he went on in a milder tone. "Come; the common room smells much better than this. Ryne suggested a round of the taverns tonight. Unless Mistress Arovni has claims on you. Oh, yes. How much will our rooms cost? Good rooms? Not too dear, I hope."

Bukama joined him on the way to the doors, his

face going red. "Not too dear," he said hastily. "You have a pallet in the attic, and I . . . ah . . . I'm in Racelle's rooms. I'd like to make a round, but I think Racelle. . . . I don't think she means to let me. . . . I. . . . Young whelp!" he growled. "There's a lass named Lira in there who's letting it be known you won't be using that pallet tonight, *or* getting much sleep, so don't think you can—!" He cut off as they walked into the sunlight, bright after the dimness inside. The graylark still sang of spring.

Six men were striding across the otherwise empty yard. Six ordinary men with swords at their belts, like any men on any street in the city. Yet Lan knew before their hands moved, before their eyes focused on him and their steps quickened. He had faced too many men who wanted to kill him not to know. And at his side stood Bukama, bound by oaths that would not let him raise a hand even had he been wearing his blade. If they both tried to get back inside the stable, the men would be on them before they could haul the doors shut. Time slowed, flowed like cool honey.

"Inside and bar the doors!" Lan snapped as his hand went to his hilt. "Obey me, armsman!"

Never in his life had he given Bukama a command in that fashion, and the man hesitated a heartbeat, then bowed formally. "My life is yours, Dai Shan," he said in a thick voice. "I obey."

As Lan moved forward to meet his attackers, he heard the bar drop inside with a muffled thud. Relief was distant. He floated in *ko'di*, one with the sword that came smoothly out of its scabbard. One with the men rushing at him, boots thudding on the hard-packed ground as they bared steel.

A lean heron of a fellow darted ahead of the others, and Lan danced the forms. Time like cool honey. The graylark sang, and the lean man shrieked as Cutting the Clouds removed his right hand at the wrist, and Lan flowed to one side so the rest could not all come at him together, flowed from form to form. Soft Rain at Sunset laid open a fat man's face and took his left eye, and a ginger-haired young splinter drew a gash across Lan's ribs with Black Pebbles on Snow. Only in stories did one man face six without injury. The Rose Unfolds sliced down a bald man's left arm, and ginger-hair nicked the corner of Lan's eye. Only in stories did one man face six and survive. He had known that from the start. Duty was a mountain, death a feather, and his duty was to Bukama, who had carried an infant on his back. For this moment he lived, though, so he fought, kicking ginger-hair in the head, dancing his way toward death, danced and took wounds, bled and danced the razor's edge of life. Time like cool honey, flowing from form to form, and there could only be one ending. Thought was distant. Death was a feather. Dandelion in the Wind slashed open the now one-eyed fat man's throat—he had barely paused when his face was ruined—and a fork-bearded fellow with shoulders like a blacksmith gasped in surprise as Kissing the Adder put Lan's steel through his heart.

And suddenly Lan realized that he alone stood, with six men sprawled across the width of the stableyard. The ginger-haired youth thrashed his heels on the ground one last time, and then only Lan of the seven still breathed. He shook blood from his blade, bent to wipe the last drops off on the blacksmith's too-fine coat, sheathed his sword as formally as if he were in the training yard under Bukama's eye.

Abruptly people flooded out of the inn, cooks and stablemen, maids and patrons shouting to know what all the noise was about, staring at the dead men in astonishment. Ryne was the very first, sword already in hand, his face blank as he came to stand by Lan. "Six," he muttered, studying the bodies. "You really do have the Dark One's own flaming luck."

Dark-eyed Lira reached Lan only moments before Bukama, the pair of them gently parting slashes in his clothes to examine his injuries. She shivered delicately as each was revealed, but she discussed whether an Aes Sedai should be sent for to give Healing and how much stitching was needed in as calm a tone as Bukama, and disparagingly dismissed his hand on the needle in favor of her own. Mistress Arovni stalked about, holding her skirts up out of patches of bloody mud, glaring at the corpses littering her stableyard, complaining in a loud voice that gangs of footpads would never be wandering in daylight if the Watch was doing its job. The Domani woman who had stared at Lan inside agreed just as loudly, and for her pains received a sharp command from the innkeeper to fetch them, along with a shove to start her on her way. It was a measure of Mistress Arovni's shock that she treated one of her patrons so, a measure of everyone's shock that the Domani woman went running without complaint. The innkeeper began organizing men to drag the bodies out of sight, still going on about footpads.

Ryne looked from Bukama to the stable as though he did not understand—perhaps he did not, at that—but what he said was, "Not footpads, I think." He pointed to the fellow who looked like a blacksmith. "That one listened to Edeyn Arrel when she was here, and he liked what he heard. One of the others did, too, I think." Bells chimed as he shook his head. "It's peculiar. The first she said of raising the Golden Crane was after we heard you were dead outside the Shining Walls. Your name brings men, but with you dead, she could be el'Edeyn." He spread his hands at the looks Lan and Bukama shot him. "I make no accusations," he said hastily. "I'd never accuse the Lady Edeyn of any such thing. I'm sure she is full of all a woman's tender mercy." Mistress Arovni gave a grunt like a fist, and Lira murmured half under her breath that the pretty Arafellin did not know much about women.

Lan shook his head. Edeyn might decide to have him killed if it suited her purposes, she might have left orders here and there in case the rumors about him proved false, but if she had, that was still no reason to speak her name in connection with this, especially in front of strangers.

Bukama's hands stilled, holding open a slash down Lan's sleeve. "Where do we go from here?" he asked quietly.

"Chachin," Lan said after a moment. There was always a choice, but sometimes every choice was grim. "You'll have to leave Sun Lance. I mean to depart at first light tomorrow." His gold would stretch to a new mount for the man.

"Six!" Ryne growled, sheathing his sword with considerable force. "I think I'll ride with you. I'd as soon not go back to Shol Arbela until I'm sure Ceiline Noreman doesn't lay her husband's death at my boots. And it will be good to see the Golden Crane flying again."

Lan nodded. To put his hand on the banner and abandon what he had promised himself all those years ago, or to stop her, if he could. Either way, he had to face Edeyn. The Blight would have been much easier.

Chasing after prophecy, Moiraine had decided by the end of the first month, involved very little adventure and a great deal of saddlesoreness and frustration. The Three Oaths still made her skin feel too tight. The wind rattled the shutters, and she shifted on the hard wooden chair, hiding impatience behind a sip of honeyless tea. In Kandor, comforts were kept to a minimum in a house of mourning. She would not have been overly surprised to see frost on the leaf-carved furniture or the metal clock above the cold hearth.

"It was all so strange, my Lady," Mistress Najima sighed, and for the tenth time hugged her daughters. Perhaps thirteen or fourteen, standing close to their mother's chair, Colar and Eselle had her long black hair and large blue eyes still full of loss. Their mother's eyes seemed big, too, in a face shrunken by tragedy, and her plain gray dress appeared made for a larger woman. "Josef was always careful with lanterns in the stable," she went on, "and he never allowed any kind of open flame. The boys must have carried little Jerid out to see their father at his work, and . . ." Another hollow sigh. "They were all trapped. How could the whole stable be ablaze so fast? It makes no sense."

"Little is ever senseless," Moiraine said soothingly, setting her cup on the small table at her elbow. She felt sympathy, but the woman had begun repeating herself. "We cannot always see the reason, yet we can take some comfort in knowing there is one. The Wheel of Time weaves us into the Pattern as it wills, but the Pattern is the work of the Light."

Hearing herself, she suppressed a wince. Those words required dignity and weight her youth failed to supply. If only time could pass faster. At least for the next five years or so. Five years should give her her full strength and provide all the dignity and weight she would ever need. But then, the agelessness that came after working long enough with the One Power would only have made her present task more difficult. The last thing she could afford was anyone connecting an Aes Sedai to her visits.

"As you say, my Lady," the other woman murmured politely, though an unguarded shift of pale eyes spoke her thoughts. This outlander was a foolish child. The small blue stone of a kesiera dangling from a fine golden chain onto Moiraine's forehead and a dark green dress with six slashes of color across the breast, far fewer than she was entitled to, made Mistress Najima think her merely a Cairhienin noblewoman, one of many wandering since the Aiel ruined Cairhien. A noblewoman of a minor House, named Alys not Moiraine, making sympathy calls in mourning for her own king, killed by the Aiel. The fiction was easy to maintain, though she did not mourn her uncle in the least.

Perhaps sensing that her thoughts had been too clear, Mistress Najima started up again, speaking quickly. "It's just that Josef was always so lucky, my Lady. Everyone spoke of it. They said if Josef Najima fell down a hole, there'd be opals at the bottom. When he answered the Lady Kareil's call to go fight the Aiel, I worried, but he never took a scratch. When camp fever struck, it never touched us or the children. Josef gained the Lady's favor without trying. Then it seemed the Light truly did shine on us. Jerid was born safe and whole, and the war ended, all in a matter of days, and when we came home to Canluum, the Lady gave us the livery stable for Josef's service, and . . . and . . ." She swallowed tears she would not shed. Colar began to weep, and her mother pulled her closer, whispering comfort.

Moiraine rose. More repetition. There was nothing here for her. Jurine stood, too, not a tall woman, yet almost a hand taller than she. Either of the girls could look her in the eyes. She had grown accustomed to that since leaving Cairhien. Forcing herself to take time, she murmured more condolences and tried to press a washleather purse on the woman as the girls brought her fur-lined cloak and gloves. A small purse. Obtaining coin meant visits to the bankers and a clear trail. Not that the Aiel had left her estates in a condition to provide much money for some years yet. And not that anyone was likely to be looking for her. Still, discovery might be decidedly unpleasant.

The woman's stiff-necked refusal to take the purse irritated Moiraine. No, that was not the real reason. She understood pride, and besides, Lady Kareil had provided. The real irritant was her own desire to be gone. Jurine Najima had lost her husband and three sons in one fiery morning, but her Jerid had been born in the wrong place by almost twenty miles. The search continued. Moiraine did not like feeling relief in connection with the death of an infant. Yet she did.

Outside under a gray sky, she gathered her cloak tightly. Ignoring the cold was a simple trick, but anyone who went about the streets of Canluum with open cloak would draw stares. Any outlander, at least, unless clearly Aes Sedai. Besides, not allowing the cold to touch you did not make you unaware of it. How these people could call this "new spring" without a hint of mockery was beyond her.

Despite the near-freezing wind that gusted over the rooftops, the winding streets were packed, requiring her to pick her way through a milling mass of people and carts and wagons. The world had certainly come to Canluum. A Taraboner with heavy mustaches pushed past her muttering a hasty apology, and an olive-skinned Altaran woman who scowled at Moiraine, then an Illianer with a beard that left his upper lip bare, a very pretty fellow and not too tall.

Another day she might have enjoyed the sight of him, in another city. Now, he barely registered. It was women she watched, especially those well dressed, in silks or fine woolens. If only so many were not veiled. Twice she saw Aes Sedai strolling through the crowds, neither a woman she had ever met. Neither glanced in her direction, but she kept her head down and stayed to the other side of the street. Perhaps she should put on a veil. A stout woman brushed by, features blurred behind lace. Sierin Vayu herself could have passed unrecognized at ten feet in one of those.

Moiraine shivered at the thought, ridiculous at it was. If the new Amrylin learned what she was up to. . . . Inserting herself into secret plans, unbidden and unannounced, would not go unpunished. No matter that the Amrylin who had made them was dead in her sleep and another woman sat on the Amrylin Seat. Being sequestered on a farm until the search was done was the least she could expect.

It was not just. She and her friend Siuan had helped gather the names, in the guise of offering assistance to any woman who had given birth during the days when the Aiel threatened Tar Valon itself. Of all the women involved in that gathering, just they two knew the real reason. They had winnowed those names for Tamra. Only children born outside the city's walls had really been important, though the promised aid went to every woman found, of course. Only boys born on the west bank of the River Erinin, boys who might have been born on the slopes of Dragonmount.

Behind her a woman shouted shrilly, angrily, and Moiraine jumped a foot before she realized it was a wagon driver, brandishing her whip at a hawker to hustle his pushcart of steaming meat pies out of her way. Light! A farm was the *least* she could expect! A few men around Moiraine laughed raucously at her leap, and one, a dark-faced Tairen in a striped cloak, made a rude joke about the cold wind curling under her skirts. The laughter grew.

Moiraine stalked ahead stiffly, cheeks crimson, hand tight on the silver hilt of her belt knife. Unthinking, she embraced the True Source, and the One Power flooded her with joyous life. A single glance over her shoulder was all she needed; with *saidar* in her, smells became sharper, colors truer. She could have counted the threads in the cloak the Tairen was letting flap while he laughed. She channeled fine flows of the Power, of Air, and the fellow's baggy breeches dropped to his turned-down boots, the laces undone. Bellowing, he snatched his cloak around him amid gales of renewed mirth. Let him see how *he* liked cold breezes and rowdy jokes!

Satisfaction lasted as long as it took to release the Source. Impetuous impulse and a quick temper had always been her downfall. Any woman able to channel would have seen her weaving if close enough, seen the glow of *saidar* surround her. Even those thin flows could have been felt at thirty paces by the weakest sister in the Tower. A fine way to hide.

Quickening her step, she put distance between herself and the incident. Too little too late, but all she could do now. She stroked the small book in her belt pouch, tried to focus on her task. With only one hand, keeping her cloak closed proved impossible. It whipped about in the wind, and after a moment, she let herself feel the knifing chill. Sisters who took on penances at every turn were foolish, yet a penance could serve many purposes, and maybe she needed a reminder. If she could not remember to be careful, she might as well return to the White Tower now and ask where to start hoeing turnips.

Mentally she drew a line through the name of Jurine Najima. Other names in the book already had real lines inked through them. The mothers of five boys born in the wrong place. The mothers of three girls. An army of almost two hundred thousand men had gathered to face the Aiel outside the Shining Walls, and it still astonished her how many women followed along, how many were with child. An older sister had had to explain. The war had not been short, and men who knew they might die tomorrow wanted to leave part of themselves behind. Women who knew their men might die tomorrow wanted that part of them to keep.

Hundreds had given birth during the key ten days, and in that sort of gathering, with soldiers from nearly every land, too often there was only rumor as to exactly where or when a child had been born. Or to where the parents had gone, with the war ended and the Coalition army melting away along with the Coalition. There were too many entries like "Saera Deosin. Husband Eadwin. From Murandy. A son?" A whole country to search, only a pair of names to go by, and no certainty the woman had borne a boy. Too many like "Kari al'Thor. From Andor? Husband Tamlin, Second Captain of the Il-lianer Companions, took discharge." That pair might have gone anywhere in the world, and there was doubt she had had a child at all. Sometimes only the mother was listed, with six or eight variations on the name of a home village that might lie in one of two or three countries. The list of those easy to find was growing shorter rapidly.

But the child had to be found. An infant who

would grow to manhood and wield the tainted male half of the One Power. Moiraine shuddered at the thought despite herself. That was why this search was so secret, why Moiraine and Siuan, still only Accepted when they learned of the child's birth by accident, had been shunted aside and kept in as much ignorance as Tamra could manage. This was a matter for experienced sisters. But who could she trust with the news that the birth of the Dragon Reborn had been Foretold, and more, that somewhere he already suckled at his mother's breast? Had she had the sort of nightmares that had wakened Moiraine and Siuan so many nights? Yet this boychild would grow to manhood and save the world, so the Prophecies of the Dragon said. If he was not found by a Red sister; the Red Ajah's main purpose was hunting down men who could channel, and Moiraine was sure Tamra had not trusted any of them, even with a child. Could a Red be trusted to remember that he would be humankind's salvation while remembering what else he would be? The day suddenly seemed colder to Moiraine, for remembering.

The inn where she had a small room was called The Gates of Heaven, four sprawling stories of green-roofed stone, Canluum's best and largest. Nearby shops catered to the lord and ladies on the Stand, looming behind the inn. She would not have stopped in it had there been another room to be found in the city. Taking a deep breath, she hurried inside. Neither the sudden warmth from fires on four large hearths nor the good smells of cooking from the kitchens eased her tight shoulders.

The common room was large, and every table beneath the bright red ceiling beams was taken. By plainly dressed merchants for the most part, and a sprinkling of well-to-do craftsfolk with rich embroidery covering colorful shirts or dresses. She hardly noticed them. No fewer than five sisters were staying at The Gates of Heaven, and all sat in the common room when she walked in. Master Helvin, the innkeeper, would always make room for an Aes Sedai even when he had to force other patrons to double up. The sisters kept to themselves, barely acknowledging one another, and people who might not have recognized an Aes Sedai on sight knew them now, knew enough not to intrude. Every other table was jammed, yet where any man sat with an Aes Sedai, it was her Warder, a hard-eyed man with a dangerous look about him however ordinary he might seem otherwise. One of the sisters sitting alone was a Red; Reds took no Warder.

Tucking her gloves behind her belt and folding her cloak over her arm, Moiraine started toward the stone stairs at the back of the room. Not too quickly, but not dawdling, either. Looking straight ahead. She did not need to see an ageless face or glimpse the golden serpent biting its own tail encircling a finger to know when she passed close to another sister. Each time, she felt the other woman's ability to channel, felt her strength. No one here matched her. She could sense their ability, and they could sense hers. Their eyes following her seemed the touch of fingers. Not quite grasping. None spoke to her.

Then, just as she reached the staircase, a woman did speak behind her. "Well, now. This is a surprise."

Turning quickly, Moiraine kept her face smooth with an effort as she made a brief curtsy suitable for a minor noblewoman to an Aes Sedai. To two Aes Sedai. She did not think she could have encountered two worse than this pair in sober silks.

The white wings in Larelle Tarsi's long hair emphasized her serene, copper-skinned elegance. She had taught Moiraine in several classes, as both novice and Accepted, and she had a way of asking the last question you wanted to hear. Worse was Merean Redhill, plump and so motherly that hair more gray than not, and gathered at the nape of her neck, almost submerged the agelessness of her features. She had been Mistress of Novices under Tamra, and she made Larelle seem blind when it came to discovering just what you most wanted to hide. Both wore their vine-embroidered shawls, Merean's fringed blue. Blue was Moiraine's Ajah, too. That might count for something. Or not. It was a surprise to see them together; she had not thought they particularly liked one another.

Both were stronger in the Power than she, unfortunately, though she would stand above them eventually, but the gap was only wide enough that she had to defer, not obey. In any case, they had no right to interfere in anything she might be doing. Custom held very strongly on that. Unless they were part of Tamra's search and had been told about her. An Amyrlin's commands superseded the strongest custom, or at least altered it. But if either said the wrong thing here, word that Moiraine Damodred was wandering about in disguise would spread with the sisters in the room, and it would reach the wrong ears as surely as peaches were poison. That was the way of the world. A summons back to Tar Valon would find her soon after. She opened her mouth hoping to forestall the chance, but someone else spoke first.

"No need trying that one," a sister alone at a table nearby said, twisting around on her bench. Felaana Bevaine, a slim yellow-haired Brown with a raspy voice, had been the first to corner Moiraine when she arrived. "Says she has no interest in going to the Tower. Stubborn as stone about it. Secretive, too. You would think we'd have heard about a wilder popping up in even a lesser Cairhienin House, but this child likes to keep to herself."

Larelle and Merean looked at Moiraine, Larelle arching a thin eyebrow, Merean apparently trying to suppress a smile. Most sisters disliked wilders, women who managed to survive teaching themselves to channel without going to the White Tower.

"It is quite true, Aes Sedai," Moiraine said carefully, relieved that someone else had laid a foundation. "I have no desire to enroll as a novice, and I will not."

Felaana fixed her with considering eyes, but she still spoke to the others. "Says she's twenty-two, but that rule has been bent a time or two. A woman says she's eighteen, and that's how she's enrolled. Unless it's too obvious a lie, anyway, and this girl—"

"Our rules were not made to be broken," Larelle said sharply, and Merean added in a wry voice, "I don't believe this young woman will lie about her age. She doesn't want to be a novice, Felaana. Let her go her way." Moiraine almost let out a relieved sigh.

Enough weaker than they to accept being cut off, Felaana still began to rise, plainly meaning to continue the argument. Halfway to her feet she glanced up the stairs behind Moiraine, her eyes widened, and abruptly she sat down again, focusing on her plate of black peas and onions as if nothing else in the world existed. Merean and Larelle gathered their shawls, gray fringe and blue swaying. They looked eager to be elsewhere. They looked as though their feet had been nailed to the floor.

"So this girl does not want to be a novice," said a woman's voice from the stairs. A voice Moiraine had heard only once, two years ago, and would never forget. A number of women were stronger than she, but only one could be as much stronger as this one. Unwillingly, she looked over her shoulder.

Nearly black eyes studied her from beneath a bun of iron-gray hair decorated with golden ornaments, stars and birds, crescent moons and fish. Cadsuane, too, wore her shawl, fringed in green. "In my opinion, girl," she said dryly, "you could profit from ten years in white."

Everyone had believed Cadsuane Melaidhrin dead somewhere in retirement until she reappeared at the start of the Aiel War, and a good many sisters probably wished her truly in her grave. Cadsuane was a legend, a most uncomfortable thing to have alive and staring at you. Half the tales about her came close to impossibility, while the rest were beyond it, even among those that had proof. A long-ago King of Tarabon winkled out of his palace when it was learned he could channel, carried to Tar Valon to be gentled while an army that did not believe chased after to attempt rescue. A King of Arad Doman and a Queen of Saldaea *both* kidnapped, spirited away in secrecy, and when Cadsuane finally released them, a war that had seemed certain simply faded away. It was said she bent Tower law where it suited her, flouted custom, went her own way and often dragged others with her.

"I thank the Aes Sedai for her concern," Moiraine began, then trailed off under that stare. Not a hard stare. Simply implacable. Supposedly even Amyrlins had stepped warily around Cadsuane over the years. It was whispered that she had actually *assaulted* an Amyrlin, once. Impossible, of course; she would have been executed! Moiraine swallowed and tried to start over, only to find she wanted to swallow again.

Descending the stair, Cadsuane told Merean and Larelle, "Bring the girl." Without a second glance, she glided across the common room. Merchants and craftsfolk looked at her, some openly, some from the corner of an eye, and Warders too, but every sister kept her gaze on her table.

Merean's face tightened, and Larelle sighed extravagantly, yet they prodded Moiraine after the bobbing golden ornaments. She had no choice but to go. At least Cadsuane could not be one of the women Tamra had called in; she had not returned to Tar Valon since that visit at the beginning of the war.

Cadsuane led them to one of the inn's private sitting rooms, where a fire blazed on the black stone hearth and silver lamps hung along the red wall panels. A tall pitcher stood near the fire to keep warm, and a lacquered tray on a small carved table held silver cups. Merean and Larelle took two of the brightly cushioned chairs, but when Moiraine put her cloak on a chair and started to sit, Cadsuane pointed to a spot in front of the other sisters. "Stand there, child," she said.

Making an effort not to clutch her skirt in fists, Moiraine stood as directed. Obedience had always been difficult for her. Until she went to the Tower at sixteen, there had been few people she had to obey. Most obeyed her.

Cadsuane circled the three of them slowly, once, twice. Merean and Larelle exchanged wondering frowns, and Larelle opened her mouth, but after one look at Cadsuane, closed it again. They assumed smooth-faced serenity; any watcher would have thought they knew exactly what was going on. Sometimes Cadsuane glanced at them, but the greater part of her attention stayed on Moiraine.

"Most new sisters," the legendary Green said abruptly, "hardly remove their shawls to sleep or bathe, but here you are without shawl or ring, in one of the most dangerous spots you could choose short of the Blight itself. Why?"

Moiraine blinked. A direct question. The woman

really did ignore custom when it suited her. She made her voice light. "New sisters also seek a Warder." Why was the woman singling her out in this manner? "I have not bonded mine, yet. I am told Bordermen make fine Warders." The Green sent her a stabbing look that made her wish she had been just a little less light.

Stopping behind Larelle, Cadsuane laid a hand on her shoulder. "What do you know of this child?"

Every girl in Larelle's classes had thought her the perfect sister and been intimidated by that cool consideration. They all had been afraid of her, and wanted to be her. "Moiraine was studious and a quick learner," she said thoughtfully. "She and Siuan Sanche were two of the quickest the Tower has ever seen. But you must know that. Let me see. She was rather too free with her opinions, and her temper, until we settled her down. As much as we did settle her. She and the Sanche girl had a continuing fondness for pranks. But they both passed for Accepted on the first try, and for the shawl. She needs seasoning, of course, yet she may make something of herself."

Cadsuane moved behind Merean, asking the same question, adding, "A fondness for . . . pranks, Larelle said. A troublesome child?"

Merean shook her head with a smile. None of the girls had wanted to be Merean, but everyone knew where to go for a shoulder to cry on or advice when you could not ask your closest friend. Many more girls visited her on their own than had been sent for chastisement. "Not troublesome, really," she said. "High-spirited. None of the tricks Moiraine played were mean, but they were plentiful. Novice and Accepted, she was sent to my study more often than any three other girls. Except for her pillow-friend Siuan. Of course, pillow-friends frequently get into tangles together, but with those two, one was never sent to me without the other. The last time the very night after passing for the shawl." Her smile faded into a frown very much like the one she had worn that night. Not angry, but rather disbelieving of the mischief young women could get up to. And a touch amused by it. "Instead of spending the night in contemplation, they tried to sneak mice into a sister's bed—Elaida a'Roihan—and were caught. I doubt any other women have been raised Aes Sedai while still too tender to sit from their last visit to the Mistress of Novices. Once the Three Oaths tightened on them, they needed cushions a week."

Moiraine kept her face smooth, kept her hands from knotting into fists, but she could do nothing about burning cheeks. That ruefully amused frown, as if she were still Accepted. She needed seasoning, did she? Well, perhaps she did, some, but still. And spreading out all these intimacies!

"I think you know all of me that you need to know," she told Cadsuane stiffly. How close she and Siuan had been was no one's business but theirs. And their punishments, *details* of their punishments. Elaida had been hateful, always pressing, demanding perfection whenever she visited the Tower. "If you are quite satisfied, I must pack my things. I am departing for Chachin."

She swallowed a groan before it could form. She still let her tongue go too free when her temper was up. If Merean or Larelle was part of the search, they must have at least part of the list in her little book. Including Jurine Najima here, the Lady Ines Demain in Chachin, and Avene Sahera, who lived in "a village on the high road between Chachin and Canluum." To strengthen suspicion, all she need do now was say she intended to spend time in Arafel and Shienar next.

Cadsuane smiled, not at all pleasantly. "You'll leave when I say, child. Be silent till you're spoken to. That pitcher should hold spiced wine. Pour for us."

Moiraine quivered. Child! She was no longer a novice. The woman could not order her coming and going. Or her tongue. But she did not protest. She walked to the hearth—stalked, really—and picked up the long-necked silver pitcher.

"You seem very interested in this young woman,

Cadsuane,'' Merean said, turning slightly to watch Moiraine pour. "Is there something about her we should know?"

Larelle's smile held a touch of mockery. Only a touch, with Cadsuane. "Has someone Foretold she'll be Amyrlin one day? I can't say that I see it in her, but then, I don't have the Foretelling."

"I might live another thirty years," Cadsuane said, putting out a hand for the cup Moiraine offered, "or only three. Who can say?"

Moiraine's eyes went wide, and she slopped hot wine over her own wrist. Merean gasped, and Larelle looked as though she had been struck in the forehead with a stone. Any Aes Sedai would spit on the table before referring to another sister's age or her own. Except that Cadsuane was not any Aes Sedai.

"A little more care with the other cups," she said, unperturbed by all the gaping. "Child?" Moiraine returned to the hearth still staring, and Cadsuane went on, "Meilyn is considerably older. When she and I are gone, that leaves Kerene the strongest." Larelle flinched. "Am I disturbing you?" Cadsuane's solicitous tone could not have been more false, and she did not wait for an answer. "Holding our silence about age doesn't keep people from knowing we live longer than they. Phaaw! From Kerene, it's a sharp drop to the next five. Five once this child and the Sanche girl reach their potential. And one of those is as old as I am and in retirement to boot.''

''Is there some point to this?'' Merean asked, sounding a little sick. Larelle pressed her hands against her middle, her face gray. They barely glanced at the wine Moiraine offered before gesturing it away, and she kept the cup, though she did not think she could swallow a mouthful.

Cadsuane scowled, a fearsome sight. ''No one has come to the Tower in a thousand years who could match me. No one to match Meilyn or Kerene in almost six hundred. A thousand years ago, there would have been fifty sisters or more who stood higher than this child. In another hundred years, though, she'll stand in the first rank. Oh, someone stronger may be found in that time, but there won't be fifty, and there may be none. We dwindle.''

''I don't understand,'' Larelle said sharply. She seemed to have gathered herself, and to be angry for her previous weakness. ''We are all aware of the problem, but what does Moiraine have to do with it? Do you think she can somehow make more girls come to the Tower, girls with stronger potential?'' Her snort said what she thought of that.

''I would regret her being wasted before she knows up from down. The Tower can't afford to lose her out of her own ignorance. Look at her. A pretty little doll of a Cairhienin noble.'' Cadsuane put a finger under Moiraine's chin, tilting it up. "Before you find a Warder like that, child, a brigand who wants to see what's in your purse will put an arrow through your heart. A footpad who'd faint at the sight of a sister in her sleep will crack your head, and you'll wake at the back of an alley minus your gold and maybe more. I suspect you'll want to take as much care choosing your first man as you do your first Warder."

Moiraine jerked back, spluttered with indignation. First her and Siuan, now this. There were things one talked about, and things one did not!

Cadsuane ignored her outrage. Calmly sipping her wine, she turned back to the others. "Until she does find a Warder to guard her back, it might be best to protect her from her own enthusiasm. You two are going to Chachin, I believe. She'll travel with you, then. I expect you not to let her out of your sight."

Moiraine found her tongue, but her protests did as much good as her indignation had. Merean and Larelle objected, too, just as vociferously. Aes Sedai did not need "looking after," no matter how new. They had interests of their own to look after. They did not make clear what those were—few sisters would have—but they plainly wanted no company. Cadsuane paid no attention to anything she did not want to hear, assumed they would do as she wished, pressed wherever they offered an opening. Soon the pair were twisting on their chairs and reduced to saying that they had only encountered each other the day before and were not sure they would be traveling on together. In any event, both meant to spend two or three days in Canluum, while Moiraine wanted to leave today.

"The child will stay until you leave," Cadsuane said briskly. "Good; that's done, then. I'm sure you two want to see to whatever brought you to Canluum. I won't keep you."

Larelle shifted her shawl irritably at the abrupt dismissal, then stalked out muttering that Moiraine would regret it if she got underfoot or slowed her reaching Chachin. Merean took it better, even saying she would look after Moiraine like a daughter, though her smile hardly looked pleased.

When they were gone, Moiraine stared at Cadsuane incredulously. She had never seen anything like it. Except an avalanche, once. The thing to do now was keep silent until she had a chance to leave without Cadsuane or the others seeing. Much the wisest thing. "I agreed to nothing," she said coolly. Very coolly. "What if I have affairs in Chachin that will not wait? What if I do not choose to wait here two or three days?" Perhaps she did need to learn to school her tongue a little more.

Cadsuane had been looking thoughtfully at the door that had closed behind Merean and Larelle, but

she turned a piercing gaze on Moiraine. "You've
worn the shawl five months, and you have affairs
that cannot wait? Phaaw! You still haven't learned
the first real lesson, that the shawl means you are
ready to truly begin learning. The second lesson is
caution. I know very well how hard that is to find
when you're young and have *saidar* at your finger-
tips and the world at your feet. As you think." Moiraine tried to fit a word in, but she might as well
have stood in front of that avalanche. "You will take
great risks in your life, if you live long enough. You
already take more than you know. Heed carefully
what I say. And do as I say. I will check your bed
tonight, and if you are not in it, I will find you and
make you weep as you did for those mice. You can
dry your tears afterward on that shawl you believe
makes you invincible. It does not."

Staring as the door closed behind Cadsuane,
Moiraine suddenly realized she still held the cup of
wine and gulped it dry. The woman was . . . formidable. Custom forbade physical violence against another sister, but Cadsuane had not sidestepped a hair
in her threat. She had said it right out, so by the
Three Oaths she meant it exactly. Incredible. Was it
happenstance that she had mentioned Meilyn Ar-
ganya and Kerene Nagashi? They were two of
Tamra's searchers. *Could* Cadsuane be another? Either way, she had very neatly cut Moiraine out of the

hunt for the next week or more. If she actually went with Merean and Larelle, at least. But why only a week? If the woman was part of the search. . . . If Cadsuane knew about her and Siuan. . . . If. . . . Standing there fiddling with an empty winecup was getting her nowhere. She snatched up her cloak.

A number of people looked around at her when she came out into the common room, some with sympathy in their eyes. Doubtless they were imagining what it must be like to be the focus of attention for three Aes Sedai, and they could not imagine any good in it. There was no commiseration on any sister's face. Felaana wore a pleased smile; she probably thought the Lady Alys' name as good as written in the novice book. Cadsuane was nowhere in sight, nor the other two.

Picking her way through the tables, Moiraine felt shaken. There were too many questions, and not an answer to be found. She wished Siuan were there; Siuan was very good at puzzles, and nothing shook her.

A young woman looked in at the door from the street, then jerked out of sight, and Moiraine missed a step. Wish for something hard enough, and you could think you saw it. The woman peeked in again, the hood of her cloak fallen atop the bundle on her back, and it really was Siuan, sturdy and handsome, in a plain blue dress that showed signs of hard travel. This time she saw Moiraine, but instead of rushing to greet her, Siuan nodded up the street and vanished again.

Heart climbing into her throat, Moiraine swept her cloak around her and went out. Down the street, Siuan was slipping through the traffic, glancing back at every third step. Moiraine followed quickly, worry growing.

Siuan was supposed to be six hundred miles away in Tar Valon, working for Cetalia Delarme, who ran the Blue Ajah's network of eyes-and-ears. She had let that secret slip while bemoaning her fate. The whole time they were novice and Accepted together Siuan had talked of getting out into the world, seeing the world, but Cetalia had taken her aside the day they received the shawl, and by that evening Siuan was sorting reports from men and women scattered through the nations. She had a mind that saw patterns others missed. Cetalia equaled Merean in the Power, and it would be another three or four years before Siuan gained enough strength to tell Cetalia she was leaving the job. There would be snow at Sunday before Cetalia let her go short of that. And the only other possibility for her being in Canluum. . . . Moiraine groaned, and when a big-eared fellow selling pins from a tray gave her a concerned look, she glared so hard that he started back.

It would be just like Sierin to send Siuan to bring her back, so their worry could feed on each other during the long ride. Sierin was a hard woman, without an ounce of mercy. An Amyrlin was supposed to grant indulgences and relief from penances on the day she was raised; Sierin had ordered two sisters birched and exiled three from the Tower for a year. She might well have told Siuan the penance she intended to impose. Moiraine shivered. Likely, Sierin would manage to combine Labor, Deprivation, Mortification of the Flesh, *and* Mortification of the Spirit.

A hundred paces from the inn, Siuan looked back once more, paused till she was sure that Moiraine saw her, then darted into an alley. Moiraine quickened her stride and followed.

Her friend was pacing beneath the still-unlit oil lamps that lined even this narrow, dusty passage. Nothing frightened Siuan Sanche, a fisherman's daughter from the toughest quarter in Tear, but fear glittered in those sharp blue eyes now. Moiraine opened her mouth to confirm her own fears about Sierin, but the taller woman spoke first.

"Tell me you've found him, Moiraine. Tell me the Najima boy's the one, and we can hand him to the Tower with a hundred sisters watching, and it's done."

A hundred sisters? "No, Siuan." This did not

sound like Sierin. "What is the matter?"

Siuan began to weep. Siuan, who had a lion's heart and had never let a tear fall until after they left Merean's study. Throwing her arms around Moiraine, she squeezed hard. She was trembling. "They're all dead," she mumbled. "Aisha and Kerene, Valera and Ludice and Meilyn. They say Aisha and her Warder were killed by bandits in Murandy. Kerene supposedly fell off a ship in the Alguenya during a storm and drowned. And Meilyn . . . Meilyn . . ."

Moiraine hugged her, making soothing sounds. And staring past Siuan's shoulder in consternation. They had learned five of the women Tamra had selected, and all five were dead. "Meilyn was . . . hardly young," she said slowly. She was not sure she could have said it at all if Cadsuane had not spoken so openly. Siuan gave a startled jerk, and she made herself go on. "Neither were any of the others, even Kerene." Close to two hundred was not young even for Aes Sedai. "And accidents do happen. Bandits. Storms." She was having a hard time making herself believe. *All* of them?

Siuan pushed herself away. "You don't understand. Meilyn!" Grimacing, she scrubbed at her eyes. "Fish guts! I'm not making this clear. Get hold of yourself, you bloody fool!" That last was growled to herself. Merean and others had gone to a great deal of trouble to clean up Siuan's language, but she had reverted the moment the shawl was on her shoulders. Guiding Moiraine to an upended cask with no bung, she sat her down. "You won't want to be standing when you hear what I have to say. For that matter, I bloody well don't want to be standing myself."

Dragging a crate with broken slats from further up the alley, she settled on it, fussing with her skirts, peering toward the street, muttering about people looking in as they passed. Her reluctance did little to soothe Moiraine's stomach. It seemed to do little for Siuan's, either. When she started up again, she kept pausing to swallow, like a woman who wanted to sick up.

"Meilyn returned to the Tower almost a month ago. I don't know why. She didn't say where she had been, or where she was going, but she only meant to stay a few nights. I . . . I'd heard about Kerene the morning Meilyn came, and the others before that. So I decided to speak to her. Don't look at me that way! I know how to be cautious!" "Cautious" was a word Moiraine had never thought to apply to Siuan. "Anyway, I sneaked into her rooms and hid under the bed. So the servants wouldn't see me when they turned down her sheets." Siuan grunted sourly. "I fell asleep under there. Sunrise woke me, and her bed hadn't been slept in. So I sneaked out and went down to the second sitting of breakfast. And while I was spooning my porridge, Chesmal Emry came in to . . . She . . . She announced that Meilyn had been found in her bed, that she'd died during the night.'' She finished in a rush and sagged, staring at Moiraine.

Moiraine was very glad to be sitting. Her knees would not have supported a feather. She had grown up amid *Daes Dae'mar*, the scheming and plotting that dominated Cairhienin life, the shades of meaning in every word, every action. There was too much here for shadings. Murder had been done. ''The Red Ajah?'' she suggested finally. A Red might kill a sister she thought intended to protect a man who could channel.

Siuan snorted. ''Meilyn didn't have a mark on her, and Chesmal would have detected poison, or smothering, or . . . That means the Power, Moiraine. Could even a Red do that?'' Her voice was fierce, but she pulled the bundle around from her back, clutching it on her lap. She seemed to be hiding behind it. Still, there was less fear on her face than anger, now. ''Think, Moiraine. Tamra supposedly died in her sleep, too. Only we know Meilyn didn't, no matter where she was found. First Tamra, then the others started dying. The only thing that makes sense is that someone noticed her calling sisters in and wanted to know why badly enough that they bloody risked putting the Amyrlin Seat herself to the question. They had to have something to hide to do that, something they'd risk anything to keep hidden. They killed her to hide it, to hide what they'd done, and then they set out to kill the rest. Which means they don't want the boy found, not alive. They don't want the Dragon Reborn at the Last Battle. Any other way to look at it is tossing the slop bucket into the wind and hoping for the best.''

Unconsciously, Moiraine peered toward the mouth of the alley. A few people walking by glanced in, but none more than once. No one paused at seeing them seated there. Some things were easier to speak of when you were not too specific. ''The Amyrlin'' had been put to the question; ''she'' had been killed. Not Tamra, not a name that brought up the familiar, determined face. ''Someone'' had murdered her. ''They'' did not want the Dragon Reborn found. Murder with the Power certainly violated the Three Oaths, even for . . . for those Moiraine did not want to name any more than Siuan did.

Forcing her face to smoothness, forcing her voice to calm, she forced the words out. ''The Black Ajah.'' Siuan flinched, then nodded, glowering.

Any sister grew angry at the suggestion there was a secret Ajah hidden inside the others, dedicated to the Dark One. Most sisters refused to listen. The White Tower had stood for the Light for over three thousand years. But some sisters did not deny the Black straight out. Some believed. Very few would admit it even to another sister, though. Moiraine did not want to admit it to herself.

Siuan plucked at the ties on her bundle, but she went on in a brisk voice. "I don't think they have our names—Tamra never really thought us part of it—else I'd have had an 'accident,' too. Just before I left, I slipped a note with my suspicions under Sierin's door. Only, I didn't know how much to trust her. The Amyrlin Seat! I wrote with my left hand, but I was shaking so hard, no one could recognize my writing if I'd used my right. Burn my liver! Even if we knew who to trust, we have bilge water for proof."

"Enough for me. If they know everything, all the women Tamra chose, there may be none left except us. We will have to move fast if we have a hope of finding the boy first." Moiraine tried for a vigorous tone, too. It was gratifying that Siuan only nodded. She would not give up for all her talk of shaking, and she never considered that Moiraine might. Most gratifying. "Perhaps they know us, and perhaps not. Perhaps they think they can leave two new sisters for last. In any case, we cannot trust anyone but ourselves." Blood drained from her face. "Oh, Light! I just had an encounter at the inn, Siuan."

She tried to recall every word, every nuance, from

the moment Merean first spoke. Siuan listened with a distant look, filing and sorting. "Cadsuane could be one of Tamra's chosen," she agreed when Moiraine finished. "Or she could be Black Ajah." She barely hesitated over the words. "Maybe she's just trying to get you out of the way until she can dispose of you without rousing suspicion. The trouble is, any of them could be either." Leaning across her bundle, she touched Moiraine's knee. "Can you bring your horse from the stable without being seen? I have a good mount, but I don't know if she can carry both of us. We should be hours from here before they know we're gone."

Moiraine smiled in spite of herself. She very much doubted the good mount. Her friend's eye for horseflesh was no better than her seat in the saddle, and sometimes Siuan fell off nearly before the animal moved. The ride north must have been agony. And full of fear. "No one knows you are here at all, Siuan," she said. "Best if it stays so. You have your book? Good. If I remain until morning, I will have a day's start on them instead of hours. You go on to Chachin now. Take some of my coin." By the state of Siuan's dress, she had spent the last part of that trip sleeping under bushes. A fisherman's daughter had no estates to provide gold. "Start looking for the Lady Ines, and I will catch you up there."

It was not that easy, of course. Siuan had a stubborn streak as wide as the Erinin. Quite aside from that, as novice and Accepted it had been the fisherman's daughter who led, not the king's niece, something that had startled Moiraine at first, until she realized that it felt natural somehow. Siuan had been born to lead.

"I have enough for my needs," she grumbled, but Moiraine insisted on handing her half the coins in her purse, and when Moiraine reminded her of their pledge during their first months in the Tower, that what one owned belonged to the other as well, she muttered, "We swore we'd find beautiful young princes to bond, too, and marry them besides. Girls say all sort of silly things. You watch after yourself, now. You leave me alone in this, and I'll wring your neck."

Embracing to say goodbye, Moiraine found it hard to let go. An hour ago, her worries had been whether she might be stuck away on a farm, or at worse birched. Now. . . . The Black Ajah She wanted to empty her stomach. If only she had Siuan's courage. Watching Siuan slip down the alley adjusting that bundle on her back again, Moiraine wished she were Green. Only Greens bonded more than one Warder, and she would have liked at least three or four to guard her back right then.

Walking back up the street, she could not help

looking at everyone she passed, man or woman. If the Black Ajah—her stomach twisted every time she thought that name—if they were involved, then ordinary Darkfriends were, too. No one denied that some misguided people believed the Dark One would give them immortality, people who would kill and do every sort of evil to gain that hoped-for reward. And if any sister could be Black Ajah, anyone she met could be a Darkfriend. She hoped Siuan remembered that.

As she approached The Gates of Heaven, a sister appeared in the inn's doorway. Part of a sister, at least; all she could see was an arm with a fringed shawl over it. A tall man who had just come out, his hair in two belled braids, turned back to speak for a moment, but the shawl-draped arm gestured peremptorily, and he strode past Moiraine wearing a scowl. She would not have thought twice of it if not for thinking about the Black Ajah and Darkfriends. The Light knew, Aes Sedai did speak to men, and some did more than speak. She had been thinking of Darkfriends, though. And Black sisters. If only she could have made out the color of that fringe. She hurried the last thirty-odd paces frowning.

Merean and Larelle were seated together by themselves near the door, both still wearing their shawls. Few sisters did that except for ceremony, or for show. Both women were watching Cadsuane go into that private sitting room, followed by a pair of gray-haired men who looked as hard as last year's oak. She still wore her shawl, too, with the white Flame of Tar Valon bright on her back. It could have been any of them. Cadsuane might be looking for another Warder; Greens always seemed to be looking. Moiraine did not know whether Merean and Larelle had Warders. The fellow's scowl might have been for hearing he did not measure up. There were a hundred possible explanations, and she put the man out of her head. The sure dangers were real enough without inventing more.

Before she was three steps into the common room, Master Helvin bustled up in a green-striped apron, a bald man nearly as wide as he was tall, and handed her a new irritation. With three more Aes Sedai stopping at his inn, he need to shuffle the beds, as he put it. The Lady Alys would not mind sharing hers, certainly, under the circumstances. Mistress Palan was a most pleasant woman.

Haesel Palan was a rug merchant from Murandy with the lilt of Lugard in her voice. Moiraine heard more of it than she wanted from the moment she stepped into the small room that had been hers alone. Her clothes had been moved from the wardrobe to pegs on the wall, her comb and brush displaced from the washstand for Mistress Palan's. The plump woman might have been diffident with "Lady Alys," but not with a wilder who everybody said was off in the morning to become a novice in the White Tower. She lectured Moiraine on the duties of a novice, all of it wrong. She followed Moiraine down to dinner and gathered other traders of her acquaintance at the table, every woman of them eager to share what she knew of the White Tower. Which was nothing at all. They shared it in great detail, though. Moiraine thought to escape by retiring early, but Mistress Palan appeared almost as soon as she had her dress off and talked until she dropped off to sleep.

It was not an easy night. The bed was narrow, the woman's elbows sharp and her feet icy despite thick blankets that trapped the warmth of the small stove under the bed. The rainstorm that had threatened all day broke, wind and thunder rattling the shutters for hours. Moiraine doubted she could have slept in any event. Darkfriends and the Black Ajah danced in her head. She saw Tamra being dragged from her sleep, dragged away to somewhere secret and tortured by women wielding the Power. Sometimes the women wore Merean's face, and Larelle's, and Cadsuane's, and every sister's she had ever seen. Sometimes Tamra's face became her own.

When the door creaked slowly open in the dark hours of morning, Moiraine embraced the Source in a flash. *Saidar* filled her to the point where the sweetness and joy came close to pain. Not as much of the Power as she would be able to handle in another year, much less five, yet a hair more would burn the ability out of her now, or kill her. One was as bad as the other, but she wanted to draw more, and not just because the Power always made you want more.

Cadsuane put her head in. Moiraine had forgotten her promise, her threat. Cadsuane saw the glow, of course, could feel how much she held. "Fool girl" was all the woman said before leaving.

Moiraine counted to one hundred slowly, then swung her feet out from under the covers. Now was as good a time as any. Mistress Palan heaved onto her side and began to snore. Channeling Fire, Moiraine lit one of the lamps and dressed hurriedly. A riding dress, this time. Reluctantly she decided to abandon her saddlebags along with everything else she had to leave behind. Anyone who saw her moving about might not think too much of it even this time of the morning, but not if she had saddlebags over her shoulder. All she took was what she could fit into the pockets sewn inside her cloak, little more than some spare stockings and a clean shift. Mistress Palan was still snoring as she closed the door behind her.

The skinny groom on night duty was startled to

see her with the sky just beginning to turn gray, but a silver penny had him knuckling his forehead and saddling her bay mare. She regretted leaving her packhorse behind, but not even a fool noble—she heard the fellow mutter that—would take a pack animal for a morning jaunt. Climbing into Arrow's high-cantled saddle, she gave the man a cool smile instead of the second penny he would have received without the comment, and rode slowly out into damp, empty streets. Just out for a ride, however early. It looked to be a good day. The sky looked rained out, for one thing, and there was little wind.

The lamps were still lit all along the streets and alleys, leaving no more than the palest shadow anywhere, yet the only people to be seen were the Night Watch's patrols and the Lamplighters, heavily armed as they made their rounds to make sure no lamp went out. A wonder that people could live so close to the Blight that a Myrddraal could step out of any dark shadow. No one went out in the night, though. Not in the Borderlands.

Which was why she was surprised to see that she was not the first to reach the western gates. Slowing Arrow, she stayed well back from the three very large men waiting with a packhorse behind their mounts. Their attention was all on the barred gates, with now and again a word shared with the gate guards. They barely glanced at her. The lamps here showed their faces clearly. A grizzled old man and a hard-faced young one wearing braided leather cords tied around their heads. Malkieri? She thought that was what that meant. The third was an Arafellin with belled braids. The same fellow she had seen leaving The Gates of Heaven.

By the time the bright sliver of sunrise allowed the gates to be swung open, several merchants' trains had lined up to depart. The three men were first through, but Moiraine let a train of a dozen wagons behind eight-horse teams rumble ahead of her before she followed across the bridge and onto the road through the hills. She kept the three in sight, though. They were heading in the same direction so far, after all.

They moved quickly, good riders who barely shifted a rein, but a trot suited her. The more distance she put between herself and Cadsuane, the better. The merchants' wagons fell back out of sight long before they reached the first village near midday, a small cluster of tile-roofed stone houses around a tiny inn on a forested hill slope. Moiraine paused long enough to ask whether anyone knew a woman named Avene Sahcra. The answer was no, and she galloped on, not slowing until the three men appeared on the hard-packed road ahead, their horses still in that ground-eating pace. Maybe they knew nothing more than the name of the sister the

Arafellin had spoken to, but anything at all she learned about Cadsuane or the other two would be to the good.

She formulated several plans for approaching them, and discarded each. Three men on a deserted forest road could well decide that a young woman alone was a good opportunity, especially if they were what she feared. Handling them presented no problem, if it came to it, but she wanted to avoid that. Woods gave way to scattered farms, and farms faded to more woods. A red-crested eagle soared overhead and became a shape against the descending sun.

As her shadow stretched out behind her, she decided to forget the men and find a place to sleep. With luck she might see more farms soon, and if a little silver did not bring a bed, a hayloft would have to do.

Ahead, the three men stopped, conferring for a moment; then one took the packhorse and turned aside into the forest. The others dug in their heels and galloped on.

Moiraine stared after them. The Arafellin was one of the pair rushing off, but if they were traveling together, maybe he had mentioned meeting an Aes Sedai to his companion. And one man would certainly be less trouble than three, if she was careful. Riding to where rider and packhorse had vanished, she dismounted.

Tracking was a thing most ladies left to their huntsmen, but she had taken an interest in the years when climbing trees and getting dirty had seemed equal fun. Broken twigs and kicked winter-fall leaves left a trail a child could have followed. A hundred paces or so into the forest, she spotted a pond in a hollow through the trees. The fellow had already unsaddled and hobbled his bay—a fine-looking animal—and was setting the packsaddle on the ground. It was the younger of the Malkieri. He looked even larger, this close. Unbuckling his sword belt, he sat down facing the pond, laid sword and belt beside him, and put his hands on his knees. He seemed to be staring off across the water, still glittering through the late-afternoon shadows. He did not move a muscle.

Moiraine considered. Plainly he had been left to make camp. The others would come back. A question or two would not take long, though. And if he was unnerved a little—say at finding a woman suddenly standing right behind him—he might answer before he thought. Tying Arrow's reins to a low branch, she gathered her cloak and skirts and moved forward as silently as possible. A low hummock stood humped up behind him, and she stepped up onto that. Added height could help. He was a very tall man. And it might help if he found her with her belt knife in one hand and his sword in the other.

Channeling, she whisked the scabbarded blade from his side. Every little bit of shock she could manage for him—

He moved faster than thought. Her grasp closed on the scabbard, and he uncoiled, whirling, one hand clutching the scabbard between hers, the other seizing the front of her dress. Before she could think to channel, she was flying through the air. She had just time to see the pond coming up at her, just time to shout something, she did not know what, and then she struck the surface flat, driving all the wind out of her, struck with a great splash and sank. The water was *freezing! Saidar* fled in her shock.

Floundering to her feet, she stood up to her waist in the icy water, coughing, wet hair clinging to her face, sodden cloak dragging at her shoulders. Furiously she twisted around to confront her attacker, furiously embraced the Source once more. The test for the shawl required channeling with absolute calm under great stress, and far worse than this had been done to her then. She turned, prepared to knock him down and drub him till he squealed!

He stood shaking his head and frowning at the spot where she had stood, a long stride from where he had sat. When he deigned to notice her, he came to the edge of the pond and bent to stretch out a hand. "Unwise to try separating a man from his sword," he said, and after a glance at the colored slashes on her dress, added, "My Lady." Hardly an apology. His startlingly blue eyes did not quite meet hers. If he was hiding mirth . . . !

Muttering under her breath, she splashed awkwardly to where she could take his outstretched hand in both of hers . . . and heaved with all of her might. Ignoring icy water tickling down your ribs was not easy, and if she was wet, so would he be, and without any need to use the . . .

He straightened, raised his arm, and she came out of the water dangling from his hand. In consternation she stared at him until her feet touched the ground and he backed away.

"I'll start a fire and hang up blankets so you can dry yourself," he murmured, still not meeting her gaze.

He was as good as his word, and by the time the other men appeared, she was standing beside a small fire surrounded by blankets dug from his pack-saddles and hung from branches. She had no need of the fire for drying, of course, or the privacy. The proper weave of Water had taken every drop from her hair and clothes while she stayed in them. As well he did not see that, though. And she did appreciate the flame's warmth. Anyway, she had to stay inside the blankets long enough for the man to think she had used the fire as he intended. She very definitely held on to *saidar*.

The other men arrived, full of questions about whether "she" had followed into the woods. They had known? Men watched for bandits in these times, but they had noticed a lone woman and decided she was following them? It seemed suspicious.

"A Cairhienin, Lan? I suppose you've seen a Cairhienin in her skin, but I never have." That certainly caught her ear, and with the Power filling her, so did another sound. Steel whispering on leather. A sword leaving its sheath. Preparing several weaves that would stop the lot of them in their tracks, she made a crack in the blankets to peek out.

To her surprise, the man who had dunked her— Lan?—stood with his back to her blankets. He was the one with sword in hand. The Arafellin, facing him, looked surprised. "You remember the sight of the Thousand Lakes, Ryne," Lan said coldly. "Does a woman need protection from your eyes?"

For a moment, she thought Ryne was going to draw despite the blade already in Lan's hand, but the older man, a much battered, graying fellow though as tall as the others, calmed matters, took the other two a little distance away with talk of some game called "sevens." A strange game it seemed to be. Lan and Ryne sat cross-legged facing one another, their swords sheathed, then without warning drew, each blade flashing toward the other man's throat, stopping just short of flesh. The older man pointed to Ryne, they sheathed swords, and then did it again. For as long as she watched, that was how it went. Perhaps Ryne had not been as overconfident as he seemed.

Waiting inside the blankets, she tried to recall what she had been taught of Malkier. Not a great deal, except as history. Ryne remembered the Thousand Lakes, so he must be Malkieri, too. There had been something about distressed women. Now that she was with them, she might as well stay until she learned what she could.

When she came out from behind the blankets, she was ready. "I claim the right of a woman alone," she told them formally. "I travel to Chachin, and I ask the shelter of your swords." She also pressed a fat silver coin into each man's hand. She was not really sure about this ridiculous "woman alone" business, but silver caught most men's attention. "And two more each, paid in Chachin."

The reactions were not what she expected. Ryne glared at the coin as he turned it over in his fingers. Lan looked at his without expression and tucked it into his coat pocket with a grunt. She had given them some of her last Tar Valon marks, she realized, but Tar Valon coins could be found anywhere, along with those of every other land.

Bukama, the grizzled man, bowed with his left hand on his knee. "Honor to serve, my Lady," he said. "To Chachin, my life before yours." His eyes were also blue, and they, too, would not quite meet hers. She hoped he did not turn out to be a Darkfriend.

Learning anything proved to be difficult. Impossible. First the men were busy setting up camp, tending the horses, making a larger fire. They did not seem eager to face a new spring night without that. Bukama and Lan barely said a word over a dinner of flatbread and dried meat that she tried not to wolf down. Her stomach remembered all too well that she had not eaten that day. Ryne talked and was quite charming, really, with a dimple in his cheek when he smiled, and a sparkle in his blue eyes, but he gave no opening for her to mention The Gates of Heaven or Aes Sedai. When she finally inquired why he was going to Chachin, his face turned sad.

"Every man has to die somewhere," he said softly, and went off to make up his blankets.

Lan took the first watch, sitting cross-legged not far from Ryne, and when Bukama doused the fire and rolled himself up in his blankets near Lan, she wove a ward of Spirit around each man. Flows of Spirit she could hold on to sleeping, and if any of them moved in the night, the ward would wake her without alerting them. It meant waking every time they changed guard, but there was nothing for it. Her own blankets lay well away from the men, and as she was lying down, Bukama murmured something she could not catch. She heard Lan's reply plainly enough.

"I'd sooner trust an Aes Sedai, Bukama. Go to sleep."

All the anger she had tamped down flared up. The man threw her into an icy pond, he did not apologize, he . . . ! She channeled, Air and Water weaving with a touch of Earth. A thick cylinder of water rose from the surface of the pond, stretching up and up in the moonlight, arching over. Crashing down on the fool who was so free with his tongue!

Bukama and Ryne bounded to their feet with oaths, but she continued the torrent for a count of ten before letting it end. Freed water splashed down across the campsite. She expected to see a sodden, half-frozen man ready to learn proper respect. He *was* dripping wet, a few small fish flopping around his feet. He was standing on his feet. With his sword out.

"Shadowspawn?" Ryne said in a disbelieving tone, and atop him, Lan said, "Maybe! Guard the woman, Ryne! Bukama, take west; I'll take east!"

"Not Shadowspawn!" Moiraine snapped, stopping them in their tracks. They stared at her. She wished she could see their expressions better in the moonshadows, but those cloud-shifting shadows aided her, too, cloaking her in mystery. With an effort she gave her voice every bit of cool Aes Sedai serenity she could muster. "It is unwise to show anything except respect to an Aes Sedai, Master Lan."

"Aes Sedai?" Ryne whispered. Despite the dim light, the awe on his face was clear. Or maybe it was fear.

No one else made a sound, except for Bukama's grumbles as he shifted his bed away from the mud. Ryne spent a long time moving his blankets in silence, giving her small bows whenever she glanced his way. Lan made no attempt to dry off. He started to choose a new spot for his watch, then stopped and sat back where he had been, in the mud and water. She might have thought it a gesture of humility, only he glanced at her, very nearly meeting her eyes this time. If that was humility, kings were the most humble men on earth.

She wove her wards around them again, of course. If anything, revealing herself only made it more necessary. She did not go to sleep for quite a while, though. She had a great deal to think about. For one thing, none of the men had asked *why* she was following them. The man had been on his *feet*! When she drifted off, she was thinking of Ryne, strangely. A pity if he was afraid of her, now. He was charming, and she did not mind a man wanting to see her unclothed, only his telling others about it.

* * *

Lan knew the ride to Chachin would be one he would rather forget, and it met his expectations. It stormed twice, freezing rain mixed with ice, and that was the least. Bukama was angry that he refused to make proper pledge to the diminutive woman who claimed to be Aes Sedai, but Bukama knew the reasons and did not press. He only grumbled whenever he thought Lan could hear; Aes Sedai or not, a decent man followed certain forms. As if he did not share Lan's reasons. Ryne twitched and peered wide-eyed at her, fetched and trotted and offered up compliments on "skin of snowy silk" and the "deep, dark pools of her eyes" like a courtier on a leash. He seemed unable to decide between besotted and terrified, and he let her see both. That would have been bad enough, but Ryne was right; Lan had seen a Cairhienin in her skin, more than one, and they had all tried to mesh him in a scheme, or two, or three. Over one particularly memorable ten days in the south of Cairhien, he had almost been killed six times and nearly married twice. A Cairhienin *and* an Aes Sedai? There could be no worse combination.

This Alys—she told them to call her Alys, which he doubted as much as the Great Serpent ring she produced, especially after she tucked it back into her belt pouch and said no one must know she was Aes

Sedai—this "Alys" had a temper. Normally, he did not mind that, cold or hot, in man or woman. Hers was ice. That first night he had sat in the wet to let her know he would accept what she had done. If they were to travel together, better to end it with honors even, as she must see it. Except that she did not.

They rode hard, never stopping long in a village and sleeping under the stars most nights, since no one had the coin for inns, not for four people with horses. He slept when he could. The second night she remained awake till dawn and made sure he did as well, with sharp flicks of an invisible switch whenever he nodded off. The third night, sand somehow got inside his clothes and boots, a thick coating of it. He had shaken out what he could and ridden covered in grit the next day. The fourth night. . . . He could not understand how she managed to make ants crawl into his smallclothes, or make them all bite at once. It had been her doing for sure. She was standing over him when his eyes shot open, and she seemed surprised that he did not cry out. Clearly, she wanted some response, some reaction, but he could not see what. Surely not the pledge of protection. Bukama's sufficed, and besides, she had given them money. The woman did not know insult when she offered it.

When they had first seen her behind them, outpacing the merchant trains and the shield of their guards, Bukama had offered a reason for a woman alone to follow three men. If six swordsmen could not kill a man in daylight, perhaps one woman could in darkness. Bukama had not mentioned Edeyn, of course. In truth, it plainly could not be that, or he would be dead instead of uncomfortable, yet Alys herself never made any explanation, however much Bukama waited for one. Edeyn might set a woman to watch him, thinking he would be less on his guard. So Lan watched her. But the only suspicious thing he saw, if it could be called that, was that she asked questions whenever they came to a village, always away from him and the others, and she went silent if they came too near. Two days from Canluum, she stopped asking, though. Perhaps she had found an answer in the market village called Ravinda, but if so, she did not seem happy about it. That night she discovered a patch of blisterleaf near their campsite, and to his shame, he almost lost his temper.

If Canluum was a city of hills, Chachin was a city of mountains. The three highest rose almost a mile even with their peaks sheared off short, and all glittered in the sun with colorful glazed tile roofs and tile-covered palaces. Atop the tallest of those the Aesdaishar Palace shone brighter than any other in red and green, the prancing Red Horse flying above its largest dome. Three towered ringwalls surrounded the city, as did a deep drymoat a hundred paces wide spanned by two dozen bridges, each with a fortress hulking at its mouth. The traffic was too great here, and the Blight too far away, for the guards with the Red Horse on their chests to be so diligent as in Canluum, but crossing the Bridge of Sunrise amid tides of wagons and people flowing both ways still took some little while. Once inside, Lan wasted no time drawing rein.

"We are within the walls of Chachin," he told the woman. "The pledge has been kept. Keep your coin," he added coldly when she reached for her purse.

Ryne immediately started going on about giving offense to Aes Sedai and offering her smiling apologies, while Bukama rumbled about men with the manners of pigs. The woman herself gazed at Lan with so little expression, she might even have been what she claimed. A dangerous claim if untrue. And if true . . .

Whirling Cat Dancer, he galloped up the street scattering people afoot and some mounted. Bukama and Ryne caught him up before he was halfway up the mountain to the Aesdaishar. If Edeyn was in Chachin, she would be there. Wisely, Bukama and Ryne held their silence.

The palace filled the flattened mountaintop completely, an immense, shining structure of domes and high balconies covering fifty hides, a small city to itself. The great bronze gates, worked with the Red Horse, stood open beneath a red-tiled arch, and once Lan identified himself—as Lan Mandragoran, not al'Lan—the guards' stiffness turned to smiling bows. Servants in red-and-green came running to take the horses and show each man to rooms befitting his station. Bukama and Ryne each received a small room above one of the barracks. Lan was given three rooms draped in silk tapestries, with a bedchamber that overlooked one of the palace gardens, two square-faced serving women to tend him, and a lanky young fellow to run errands.

A little careful questioning of the servants brought answers. Queen Ethenielle was making a progress through the heartland, but Brys, the Prince Consort, was in residence. As was the Lady Edeyn Arrel. The women smiled when they said that; they had known what he wanted from the first.

He washed himself, but let the women dress him. Just because they were servants was no reason to insult them. He had one white silk shirt that did not show too much wear, and a good black silk coat embroidered along the sleeves with golden bloodroses among their hooked thorns. Bloodroses for loss and remembrance. Then he set the women outside to guard his door and sat to wait. His meetings with Edeyn must be public, with as many people around as possible.

A summons came from her, to her chambers, which he ignored. Courtesy demanded he be given time to rest from his journey, yet it seemed a very long time before the invitation to join Brys came, brought by the *shatayan*. A stately, graying woman with a presence to match any queen, she had charge of all the palace servants, and it was an honor to be conducted by her personally. Outsiders needed a guide to find their way anywhere in the Palace. His sword remained on the lacquered rack by the door. It would do him no good here, and would insult Brys besides, indicating that he thought he needed to protect himself.

He expected a private meeting first, but the *shatayan* took him to a columned hall full of people. Soft-footed servants moved through the crowd offering spiced wine to Kandori lords and ladies in silks embroidered with House sigils, and folk in fine woolens worked with the sigils of the more important guilds. And to others, too. Lan saw men wearing the *hadori* he knew had not worn it these ten years or more. Women with hair still cut at the shoulders and higher wore the small dot of the *ki'sain* painted on their foreheads. They bowed at his appearance, and made deep curtsies, those men and women who had decided to remember Malkier.

Prince Brys was a stocky, rough-hewn man in his middle years who looked more suited to armor than his green silks, though in truth he was accustomed to either. Brys was Ethenielle's Swordbearer, the general of her armies, as well as her consort. He caught Lan's shoulders, refusing to allow him to bow.

"None of that from the man who twice saved my life in the Blight, Lan." Brys laughed. "Besides, your coming seems to have rubbed some of your luck off on Diryk. He fell from a balcony this morning, a good fifty feet, without breaking a bone." He motioned his second son, a handsome dark-eyed boy of eight in a coat like his, to come forward. A large bruise marred the side of the boy's head, and he moved with the stiffness of other bruises, but he made a formal bow spoiled only somewhat by a wide grin. "He should be at his lessons," Brys confided, "but he was so eager to meet you, he'd have forgotten his letters and cut himself on a sword." Frowning, the boy protested that he would never cut himself.

Lan returned the lad's bow with equal formality, then had to put up with a deluge of questions. Yes, he had fought Aiel, in the south and on the Shienaran marches, but they were just men, if dangerous, not ten feet tall; they did veil their faces before killing, but they did not eat their dead. No, the White

Tower was not as high as a mountain, though it was taller than anything made by men that Lan had ever seen, even the Stone of Tear. Given a chance, the boy would have drained him dry about the Aiel, and the wonders of the great cities in the south like Tar Valon and Far Madding. Likely, he would not have believed that Chachin was as big as either of those.

"Lord Mandragoran will fill your head to your heart's content later," Brys told the boy. "There is someone else he must meet now. Off with you to Mistress Tuval and your books."

Edeyn was exactly as Lan remembered. Oh, ten years older, with touches of white streaking her temples and a few fine lines at the corners of her eyes, but those large dark eyes gripped him. Her *ki'sain* was still the white of a widow, and her hair still hung in black waves below her waist. She wore a red silk gown in the Domani style, clinging and little short of sheer. She was beautiful, but even she could do nothing here.

For a moment she merely looked at him, cool and considering, when he made his bow. "It would have been . . . easier had you come to me," she murmured, seeming not to care whether Brys heard. And then, shockingly, she knelt gracefully and took his hands in hers. "Beneath the Light," she announced in a strong, clear voice, "I, Edeyn ti Gemallen Arrel, pledge fealty to al'Lan Mandragoran, Lord of the

Seven Towers, Lord of the Lakes, the true Blade of Malkier. May he sever the Shadow!'' Even Brys looked startled. A moment of silence held while she kissed Lan's fingers; then cheers erupted on every side. Cries of ''The Golden Crane!'' and even ''Kandor rides with Malkier!''

The sound freed him to pull his hands loose, to lift her to her feet. ''My Lady,'' he began in a tight voice.

''What must be, will be,'' she said, putting a hand over his lips. And then she faded back into the crowd of those who wanted to cluster around him, congratulate him—who would have pledged fealty on the spot had he let them.

Brys rescued him, drawing him off to a long, stone-railed walk above a two-hundred-foot drop to the roofs below. It was known as a place Brys went to be private, and no one followed. Only one door let onto it, no window overlooked, and no sound from the palace intruded. ''What will you do?'' the older man asked simply as they walked.

''I do not know,'' Lan replied. She had won only a skirmish, but he felt stunned at the ease of it. A formidable opponent, the woman who wore part of his soul in her hair.

For the rest they spoke quietly of hunting and bandits and whether this past year's flare-up in the Blight might die down soon. Brys regretted withdrawing his army from the war against the Aiel, but there had been no alternative. They talked of the rumors about a man who could channel—every tale had him in a different place; Brys thought it another jak o' the mists and Lan agreed—and of the Aes Sedai who seemed to be everywhere, for what reason no one knew. Ethenielle had written him that two sisters had caught a woman pretending to be Aes Sedai in a village along her progression. The woman could channel, but that did her no good. The two real Aes Sedai flogged her squealing through the village, making her confess her crime to every last man and woman who lived there. Then one of the sisters carried her off to Tar Valon for her true punishment, whatever that might be. Lan found himself hoping that Alys had not lied about being Aes Sedai.

He hoped to avoid Edeyn the rest of the day, too, but when he was guided back to his rooms, she was there, waiting languorously in one of the gilded chairs. The servants were nowhere to be seen.

"You are no longer beautiful, I fear, sweetling," she said when he came in. "I think you may even be ugly when you are older. But I always enjoyed your eyes more than your face. And your hands."

He stopped still gripping the door handle. "My Lady, not two hours gone you swore—" She cut him off.

"And I will obey my king. But a king is not a king, alone with his *carneira*. I brought your *daori*. Bring it to me."

Unwillingly, his eyes followed her gesture to a flat lacquered box on a small table beside the door. Lifting the hinged lid took as much effort as lifting a boulder. Coiled inside lay a long cord woven of hair. He could recall every moment of the morning after their first night, when she took him to the women's quarters of the Royal Palace in Fal Moran and let ladies and servants watch as she cut his hair at his shoulders. She even told them what it signified. The women had all been amused, making jokes as he sat at Edeyn's feet to weave the *daori* for her. Edeyn kept custom, but in her own way. The hair felt soft and supple; she must have had it rubbed with lotions every day.

Crossing the floor slowly, he knelt before her and held out his *daori* stretched between his hands. "In token of what I owe to you, Edeyn, always and forever." If his voice did not hold the fervor of that first morning, surely she understood.

She did not take the cord. Instead, she studied him. "I knew you had not been gone so long as to forget our ways," she said finally. "Come."

Rising, she grasped his wrist and drew him to the windows overlooking the garden ten paces below. Two servants were spreading water from buckets, and a young woman was strolling along a slate path in a blue dress as bright as any of the early flowers that grew beneath the trees.

"My daughter, Iselle." For a moment, pride and affection warmed Edeyn's voice. "Do you remember her? She is seventeen, now. She hasn't chosen her *carneira*, yet"—young men were chosen by their *carneira*; young women chose theirs—"but I think it time she married anyway."

He vaguely recalled a child who always had servants running, the blossom of her mother's heart, but his head had been full of Edeyn, then. "She is as beautiful as her mother, I am sure," he said politely. He twisted the *daori* in his hands. She had too much advantage as long as he held it, all advantage, but she had to take it from him. "Edeyn, we must talk." She ignored that.

"Time you were married, too, sweetling. Since none of your female relatives is alive, it is up to me to arrange."

He gasped at what she seemed to be suggesting. At first he could not believe. "*Iselle?*" he said hoarsely. "*Your* daughter?" She might keep custom in her own way, but this was scandalous. "I'll not be reined into something so shameful, Edeyn. Not by you, or by this." He shook the *daori* at her, but she only looked at it and smiled.

"Of course you won't be reined, sweetling. You

are a man, not a boy. Yet you do keep custom," she mused, running a finger along the cord of hair quivering between his hands. "Perhaps we do need to talk."

But it was to the bed that she led him.

Moiraine spent most of the day asking discreet questions at inns in the rougher parts of Chachin, where her silk dress and divided skirts drew stares from patrons and innkeepers alike. One leathery fellow wearing a permanent leer told her that his establishment was not for her and tried to escort her to a better, while a round-faced, squinting woman cackled that the evening trade would have a tender pretty like her for dinner if she did not scurry away quick, and a fatherly old man with pink cheeks and a joyous smile was all too eager for her to drink the spiced wine he prepared out of her sight. There was nothing for it but to grit her teeth and move on. That was the sort of place Siuan had liked to visit when they were allowed a rare trip into Tar Valon as Accepted, cheap and unlikely to be frequented by sisters, but none had a blue-eyed Tairen staying under any name. Cold daylight began to settle toward yet another icy night.

She was walking Arrow through lengthening shadows, eyeing darknesses that moved suspiciously in an alley and thinking that she would have to give up for today, when Siuan came bustling up from behind.

"I thought you might look down here when you came," Siuan said, taking her elbow to hurry her along. "Let's get inside before we freeze." She eyed those shadows in the alley, too, and absently fingered her belt knife as if using the Power could not deal with any ten of them. Well, not without revealing themselves. Perhaps it was best to move quickly. "Not the quarter for you, Moiraine. There are fellows around here would bloody well have you for dinner before you knew you were in the pot. Are you laughing or choking?"

Siuan, it turned out, was at a most respectable inn called The Evening Star, which catered to merchants of middling rank, especially women unwilling to be bothered by noise or rough sorts in the common room. A pair of bull-shouldered fellows made sure there was none of that. Siuan's room was tidy and warm, if not large, and the innkeeper, a lean woman with an air of brooking little nonsense, made no objections to Moiraine joining Siuan. So long as the extra for two was paid.

While Moiraine was hanging her cloak on a peg, Siuan settled cross-legged on the not-very-wide bed. She seemed invigorated since Canluum. A goal always made Siuan bubble with enthusiasm. "I've had a time, Moiraine, I tell you. That fool horse nearly beat me to death getting here. The Creator made people to walk or go by boat, not be bounced around. I suppose the Sahera woman wasn't the one, or you'd be jumping like a spawning redtail. I found Ines Demain almost right off, but not where *I* can reach her. She's a new widow, but she did have a son, for sure. Named him Rahien because she saw the dawn come up over Dragonmount. Talk of the streets. Everybody thinks it a fool reason to name a child.''

''Avene Sahera's son was born a week too early and thirty miles from Dragonmount,'' Moiraine said when Siuan paused for breath. She pushed down a momentary thrill. Seeing dawn over the mountain did not mean the child had been born on it. There was no chair or stool, nor room for one, so she sat on the end of the bed. ''If you have found Ines and her son, Siuan, why is she out of reach?'' The Lady Ines, it turned it out, was in the Aesdaishar Palace, where Siuan could have gained entry easily as Aes Sedai and otherwise only if the Palace was hiring servants.

The Aesdaishar Palace. ''We will take care of that in the morning,'' Moiraine sighed. It meant risk, yet the Lady Ines had to be questioned. No woman Moiraine had found yet had been able to *see* Dragonmount when her child was born. ''Have you seen any sign of . . . of the Black Ajah?'' She had to get used to saying that name.

Instead of answering immediately, Siuan frowned at her lap and fingered her skirt. "This is a strange city, Moiraine," she said finally. "Lamps in the streets, and women who fight duels, even if they do deny it, and more gossip than ten men full of ale could spew. Some of it interesting." She leaned forward to put a hand on Moiraine's knee. "Everybody's talking about a young blacksmith who died of a broken back a couple of nights ago. Nobody expected much of him, but this last month or so he turned into quite a speaker. Convinced his guild to take up money for the poor who've come into the city, afraid of the bandits, folks not connected to a guild or House."

"Siuan, what under the Light—"

"Just listen, Moiraine. He collected a lot of silver himself, and it seems he was on his way to the guild house to turn in six or eight bags of it when he was killed. Fool was carrying it all by himself. The point is, there wasn't a bloody coin of it taken, Moiraine. And he didn't have a mark on him, aside from his broken back."

They shared a long look; then Moiraine shook her head. "I cannot see how to tie that to Meilyn or Tamra. A blacksmith? Siuan, we can go mad thinking we see Black sisters everywhere."

"We can die from thinking they aren't there," Siuan replied. "Well. Maybe we can be silverpike in the nets instead of grunters. Just remember sil-verpike go to the fish-market, too. What do you have in mind about this Lady Ines?''

Moiraine told her. Siuan did not like it, and this time it took most of the night to make her see sense. In truth, Moiraine almost wished Siuan would talk her into trying something else. But Lady Ines had seen dawn over Dragonmount. At least Ethenielle's Aes Sedai advisor was with her in the south.

Morning was a whirlwind of activity, little of it satisfying. Moiraine got what she wanted, but not without having to bite her tongue. And Siuan started up again. Arguments Moiraine had dealt with the night before cropped up anew. Siuan did not like being argued out of what she thought was right. She did not like Moiraine taking all the risks. A bear with a sore tooth would have been better company. Even that fellow Lan!

A near-dawn visit to a banker's counting house produced gold—after the stern-eyed woman used an enlarging glass to study the Cairhienin banker's seal at the bottom of the letter-of-rights Moiraine presented. An enlarging glass! At least the letter it-self was only a little blurred from its immersion in that pond. Mistress Noallin did not bother to hide her surprise when the pair of them began distributing purses of gold beneath their cloaks.

''Is Chachin so lawless two women are not safe

by daylight?'' Moiraine asked her civilly. ''I think our business is done. You may have your man show us out.'' She and Siuan clinked when they moved.

Outside, Siuan muttered that even that blacksmith must have staggered, loaded down like a mule. And who could have broken his back that way? Whatever the reason, it must be the Black Ajah. An imposing woman with ivory combs in her hair heard enough of that to give a start, then hike her skirts to her knees and run, leaving her two gaping servants to scramble after her through the crowd. Siuan flushed but remained defiantly unrepentant.

A slim seamstress with a haughty air informed Moiraine that what she wanted was easily done. At end of the month, perhaps. A great many ladies had ordered new gowns. A king was visiting in the Aesdaishar Palace. The King of Malkier!

''The last King of Malkier died twenty-five years ago, Mistress Dorelmin,'' Moiraine said, spilling thirty gold crowns on the receiving table. Silene Dorelmin eyed the fat coins greedily, and her eyes positively shone when she was told there would be as much again when the dresses were done. ''But I will keep six coins from the second thirty for each day it takes.'' Suddenly it seemed that the dresses could be finished sooner than a month after all. Much sooner.

"Did you see what that skinny trull was wearing?" Siuan said as they left. "You should have your dresses made like that, ready to fall off. You might as well enjoy men looking at you if you're going to lay your fool head on the chopping block."

Moiraine performed a novice exercise, imaging herself a rosebud in stillness, opening to the sun. As always, it brought calm. She would crack a tooth if she kept grinding them. "There is no other way, Siuan. Do you think the innkeeper will hire out one of her strongarms?" The King of *Malkier?* Light! The woman must have thought her a complete fool!

At midmorning two days after Moiraine arrived in Chachin, a yellow-lacquered carriage driven by a fellow with shoulders like a bull arrived at the Aesdaishar Palace, with two mares tied behind, a fine-necked bay and a lanky gray. The Lady Moiraine Damodred, colored slashes marching from the high neck of her dark blue gown to below her knees, was received with all due honor. The name of House Damodred was known, if not hers, and with King Laman dead, any Damodred might ascend to the Sun Throne. If another House did not seize it. She was given suitable apartments, three rooms looking north across the city toward higher, snowcapped peaks, and assigned servants who rushed about unpacking the lady's brass-bound chests and pouring hot scented water for the lady to wash. No one but the servants so much as glanced at Suki, the Lady Moiraine's maid.

"All right," Siuan muttered when the servants finally left them alone in the sitting room, "I admit I'm invisible in this." Her dark gray dress was fine wool, but entirely plain except for collar and cuffs banded in Damodred colors. "You, though, stand out like a High Lord pulling oar. Light, I nearly swallowed my tongue when you asked if there were any sisters in the Palace. I'm so nervous I'm starting to get light-headed. It feels hard to breathe."

"It is the altitude," Moiraine told her. "You will get used to it. Any visitor would ask about Aes Sedai; you could see, the servants never blinked." She had held her breath, however, until she heard the answer. One sister would have changed everything. "I do not know why I must keep telling you. A royal palace is not an inn; 'You may call me Lady Alys' would satisfy no one, here. That is fact, not opinion. I must be myself." The Three Oaths allowed you to say whatever you believed was true even if you could not prove it, as well as to dodge around truth; only words you knew to be a lie would not come off of your tongue. "Suppose you make use of that invisibility and see what you can learn about the Lady Ines. I would be pleased if we leave as soon as possible."

Tomorrow, that would be, without causing insult

and talk. Siuan was right. Every eye in the Palace would be on the outland noblewoman from the House that had started the Aiel War. Any Aes Sedai who came to the Aesdaishar would hear of her immediately, and any Aes Sedai who passed through Chachin might well come. Siuan was right; she was standing on a pedestal like a target, and without a clue as to who might be an archer. Tomorrow, early.

Siuan slipped out, but returned quickly with bad news. The Lady Ines was in seclusion, mourning her husband. "He fell over dead in his breakfast porridge ten days ago," Siuan reported, dropping onto a sitting-room chair and hanging an arm over the back. Lessons in deportment were something else forgotten once the shawl was hers. "A much older man, but it seems she loved him. She's been given ten rooms and a garden on the south side of the palace; her husband was a close friend to Prince Brys." Ines would remain to herself a full month, seeing no one but close family. Her servants only came out when absolutely necessary.

"She will see an Aes Sedai," Moiraine sighed. Not even a woman in mourning would refuse to see a sister.

Siuan bolted to her feet. "Are you mad? The Lady Moiraine Damodred attracts enough attention. Moiraine Damodred Aes Sedai might as well send out riders! I thought the idea was to be gone before anyone outside the Palace knows we were here!''

One of the servingwomen came in just then, to announce that the *shatayan* had arrived to escort Moiraine to Prince Brys, and was startled to find Suki standing over her mistress and stabbing a finger at her.

''Tell the *shatayan* I will come to her,'' Moiraine said calmly, and as soon as the wide-eyed woman curtsied and backed out, she rose to put herself on a more equal footing, hard enough with Siuan even when one had all the advantage. ''What else do you suggest? Remaining almost two weeks till she comes out will be as bad, and you cannot befriend her servants if they are secluded with her.''

''They may only come out for errands, Moiraine, but I think I can get myself invited inside.''

Moiraine started to say that might take as long as the other, but Siuan took her firmly by the shoulders and turned her around, eyeing her up and down critically. ''A lady's maid is supposed to make sure her mistress is properly dressed,'' she said, and gave Moiraine a push toward the door. ''Go. The *shatayan* is waiting for you. And with any luck, a young footman named Cal is waiting for Suki.''

The *shatayan* indeed was waiting, a tall handsome woman, wrapped in dignity and frosty at being made to wait. Her hazel eyes could have chilled wine. Any queen who got on the wrong side of a *shatayan* was a fool, so Moiraine made herself pleasant as the woman escorted her through the halls. She thought she made some progress in melting that frost, but it was difficult to concentrate. A young footman? She did not know whether Siuan had ever been with a man, but surely she would not just to reach Ines' servants! Not a *footman*!

Statues and tapestries lined the hallways, most surprising for what she knew of the Borderlands. Marble carvings of women with flowers or children playing, silk weavings of fields of flowers and nobles in gardens and only a few hunting scenes, without a single battle shown anywhere. At intervals along the halls arched windows looked down into many more gardens than she expected, too,. and flagged courtyards, sometimes with a splashing marble fountain. In one of those, she saw something that pushed questions about Siuan and a footman to the back of her mind.

It was a simple courtyard, without fountain or columned walk, and men stood in rows along the walls watching two others, stripped to the waist and fighting with wooden practice swords. Ryne and Bukama. It was fighting, if in practice; blows landed on flesh hard enough for her to hear the thuds. All landed by Ryne. She would have to avoid them, and Lan, if he was there too. He had not bothered to hide his doubts, and he might raise questions she did not dare have asked. Was she Moiraine or Alys? Worse, was she Aes Sedai or a wilder pretending? Questions that would be discussed in the streets by the next night, for any sister to hear, and that last was one any sister would investigate. Fortunately, three wandering soldiers would hardly be present anywhere she was.

Prince Brys, a solid, green-eyed man, greeted her intimately in a large room paneled red and gold. Two of the Prince's married sisters were present with their husbands, and one of Ethenielle's with hers, the men in muted silks, the women in bright colors belted high beneath their breasts. Liveried servants offered sweetmeats and nuts. Moiraine thought she might get a sore neck from looking up; the shortest of the women was taller than Siuan, and they all stood very straight. Their necks would have bent a little for a sister, men's and women's alike, but they knew themselves the equals of the Lady Moiraine.

The talk ranged from music and the best musicians among the nobles at court to the rigors of travel, from whether rumors of a man who could channel might be true to why so many Aes Sedai seemed to be about, and Moiraine found it difficult to maintain the expected light wittiness. She cared little for music and less for whoever played the instruments; in Cairhien, musicians were hired and forgotten. Everyone knew that travel was arduous, with no assurance of beds or decent food at the end of the day's twenty or thirty miles, and that was when the weather was good. Obviously some of the sisters were about because of rumors about the man, and others to tighten ties that might have loosened during the Aiel War, to make sure thrones and Houses understood they were still expected to meet their obligations to the Tower, both public and private. If an Aes Sedai had not come to the Aesdaishar yet, one soon would, reason enough for her to make heavy going of idle chat. That and thinking about other reasons for sisters to be wandering. The men put a good face on it, but she thought the women found her particularly dull.

When Brys' children were brought in, Moiraine felt a great relief. Having his children introduced to her was a sign of acceptance to his household, but more, it signaled the end of the audience. The eldest son, Antol, was in the south with Ethenielle as heir, leaving a lovely green-eyed girl of twelve named Jarene to lead in her sister and four brothers, formally aligned by age, though in truth the two youngest boys were still in skirts and carried by nursemaids. Stifling her impatience to find out what Siuan had learned, Moiraine complimented the children on their behavior, encouraged them at their lessons. They must think her as dull as their elders did. Something a little less flat.

"And how did you earn your bruises, my Lord Diryk?" she asked, hardly listening to the boy's soberly delivered story of a fall. Until . . .

"My father says it was Lan's luck I wasn't killed, my Lady," Diryk said, brightening out of his formality. "Lan is the King of Malkier, and the luckiest man in the world, and the best swordsman. Except for my father, of course."

"The King of Malkier?" Moiraine said, blinking. Diryk nodded vigorously and began explaining in a rush of words about Lan's exploits in the Blight and the Malkieri who had come to the Aesdaishar to follow him, until his father motioned him to silence.

"Lan is a king if he wishes it, my Lady," Brys said. A very odd thing to say, and his doubtful tone made it odder. "He keeps much to his rooms"— Brys sounded troubled about that, too—"but you will meet him before you—My Lady, are you well?"

"Not very," she told him. She had hoped for another meeting with Lan Mandragoran, planned for it, but not here! Her stomach was trying to twist into knots. "I myself may keep to my rooms for a few days, if you will forgive me."

He would, of course, and everyone was full of regret at missing her company and sympathy for the strain traveling must have put on her. Though she did hear one of the women murmur that southlanders must be very delicate.

A pale-haired young woman in green-and-red was waiting to show Moiraine back to her rooms. Elis bobbed a curtsy every time she spoke, which meant she bobbed quite often in the beginning. She had been told of Moiraine's "faintness," and she asked every twenty paces whether Moiraine wished to sit and catch her breath, or have cool damp cloths brought to her rooms, or hot bricks for her feet, or smelling salts, or a dozen more sure cures for "a light head," until Moiraine curtly told her to be quiet. The fool girl led on in silence, face blank.

Moiraine cared not at a whit whether the woman was offended. All she wanted right then was to find Siuan with good news. With the boy in her arms, born on Dragonmount, and his mother packed to travel would be best of all. Most of all, though, she wanted herself out of the halls before she ran into Lan Mandragoran.

Worrying about him, she rounded a corner behind the serving girl and came face-to-face with Merean, blue-fringed shawl looped over her arms. The *shatayan* herself was guiding Merean, and behind the motherly-looking sister came a train of servants, one woman carrying her red riding gloves, another her fur-trimmed cloak, a third her dark velvet hat. Pairs of men bore wicker pack hampers that could have been carried by one, and others had arms full of flowers. An Aes Sedai received more honor than a mere lady, however high her House.

Merean's eyes narrowed at the sight of Moiraine. "A surprise to see you here," she said slowly. "By your dress, I take it you've given over your disguise? But no. Still no ring, I see."

Moiraine was so startled at the woman's sudden appearance that she hardly heard what Merean said. "Are you alone?" she blurted.

For a moment Merean's eyes became slits. "Larelle decided to go her own way. South, I believe. More, I don't know."

"It was Cadsuane I was thinking of," Moiraine said, blinking in surprise. The more she had thought about Cadsuane, the more she had become convinced the woman must be Black Ajah. What surprised her was Larelle. Larelle had seemed bent on reaching Chachin, and without delay. Of course, plans could change, but suddenly Moiraine realized something that should have been obvious. Black sisters could lie. It was impossible—the Oaths *could* not be broken!—yet it had to be.

Merean moved close to Moiraine, and when Moiraine took a step back, she followed. Moiraine held herself erect, but she still came no higher than the other woman's chin. "Are you so eager to see Cadsuane?" Merean said, looking down at her. Her voice was pleasant, her smooth face comforting, but her eyes were cold iron. Abruptly glancing at the servants, she seemed to realize they were not alone. The iron faded, but it did not disappear. "Cadsuane was right, you know. A young woman who thinks she knows more than she does can land herself in very deep trouble. I suggest you be very still and very quiet until we can talk." Her gesture for the *shatayan* to lead on was peremptory, and the dignified woman leaped to obey. A king or queen might find themselves in a *shatayan*'s bad graces, but never an Aes Sedai.

Moiraine stared after Merean until she vanished around a corner far down the corridor. Everything Merean had just said could have come from one of Tamra's chosen. Black sisters could lie. Had Larelle changed her mind about Chachin? Or was she dead somewhere, like Tamra and the others? Suddenly Moiraine realized she was smoothing her skirts. Stilling her hands was easy, but she could not stop herself trembling faintly.

Elis was staring at her with her mouth open. "You're Aes Sedai, too!" the woman squeaked, then gave a jump, taking Moiraine's wince for a grimace. "I won't say a word to anyone, Aes Sedai," she said breathlessly. "I swear, by the Light and my father's grave!" As if every person behind Merean had not heard everything she had. They would not hold their tongues.

"Take me to Lan Mandragoran's apartments," Moiraine told her. What was true at sunrise could change by noon, and so could what was necessary. She took the Great Serpent ring from her pouch and put it on her right hand. Sometimes, you had to gamble.

After a long walk, mercifully in silence, Elis rapped at a red door and announced to the gray-haired woman who opened it that the Lady Moiraine Damodred Aes Sedai wished to speak with King al'Lan Mandragoran. The woman had added her own touches to what Moiraine told her. King, indeed! Shockingly, the reply came back that Lord Mandragoran had no wish to speak with any Aes Sedai. The gray-haired woman looked scandalized, but closed the door firmly.

Elis stared at Moiraine wide-eyed. "I can show my Lady Aes Sedai to her own rooms now," she said uncertainly, "if—" She squeaked when Moiraine pushed open the door and went in.

The gray-haired servingwoman and another a little younger leaped up from where they had been sitting, apparently darning shirts. A bony young man scrambled awkwardly to his feet beside the fireplace, looking to the women for instruction. They simply stared at Moiraine until she raised a questioning eyebrow. Then the gray-haired woman pointed to one of the two doors leading deeper into the apartments.

The door she pointed to led to a sitting room much like Moiraine's own, but all of the gilded chairs had been moved back against the walls and the flowered carpets rolled up. Shirtless, Lan was practicing the sword in the cleared area. A small golden locket swung at his neck as he moved, his blade a blur. Sweat covered him, and more scars than she expected on a man so young. Not to mention a number of half-healed wounds crossed by dark stitches. He spun gracefully out of the forms to face her, the point of his sword grounding on the floor tiles. He still did not quite meet her gaze, in that strange way he and Bukama had. His hair hung damply, clinging to his face despite the leather cord, but he was not breathing hard.

"You," he growled. "So you are Aes Sedai *and* a Damodred today. I've no time for your games, Cairhienin. I am waiting for someone." Cold blue eyes flickered to the door behind her. Oddly, what appeared to be a cord woven of hair was tied around the inner handle in an elaborate knot. "She will not be pleased to find another woman here."

"Your lady love need have no fear of me," Moiraine told him dryly. "For one thing, you are much too tall, and for another, I prefer men with at least a modicum of charm. And manners. I came for your help. There was a pledge made, and held since the War of the Hundred Years, that Malkier would ride when the White Tower called. I *am* Aes Sedai, and I call you!''

"You know the hills are high, but not how they lie,'' he muttered as if quoting some Malkieri saying. Stalking across the room away from her, he snatched up his scabbard and sheathed the sword forcefully. "I'll give you your help, if you can answer a question. I've asked Aes Sedai over the years, but they wriggled away from answering like vipers. If you are Aes Sedai, answer it.''

"If I know the answer, I will.'' She would not tell him again that she was what she was, but she embraced *saidar*, and moved one of the gilded chairs out into the middle of the floor. She could not have lifted the thing with her hands, yet it floated easily on flows of Air, and would have had it been twice as heavy. Sitting, she rested her hands on crossed knees where the golden serpent on her finger was plain. The taller person had an advantage when both stood, but someone standing must feel they were being judged by someone sitting, especially an Aes Sedai.

He did not seem to feel anything of the kind. For the first time since she had met him, he met her eyes directly, and his stare was blue ice. "When Malkier died,'' he said in tones of quiet steel, "Shienar and Arafel sent men. They could not stop the flood of Trollocs and Myrddraal, yet they came. Men rode from Kandor, and even Saldaea. They came too late, but they came.'' Blue ice became blue fire. His voice did not change, but his knuckles grew white gripping his sword. ''For nine hundred years we rode when the White Tower called, but where was the Tower when Malkier died? If you are Aes Sedai, answer me that!''

Moiraine hesitated. The answer he wanted was Sealed to the Tower, taught to Accepted in history lessons yet forbidden to any except initiates of the Tower. But what was a penance alongside what she faced? ''Over a hundred sisters were ordered to Malkier,'' she said more calmly than she felt. By everything she had been taught, she should *ask* a penance for what she had told him already. ''Even Aes Sedai cannot fly, however. They were too late.'' By the time the first had arrived, the armies of Malkier were already broken by endless hordes of Shadowspawn, the people fleeing or dead. The death of Malkier had been hard and blood-soaked, and fast. ''That was before I was born, but I regret it deeply. And I regret that the Tower decided to keep their effort secret.'' Better that the Tower be thought to have done nothing than to have it known Aes Sedai had tried and failed. Failure was a blow to stature, and mystery an armor the Tower needed. Aes Sedai had reasons of their own for what they did, and for what they did not do, and those reasons were known only to Aes Sedai. "That is as much answer as I can give. More than I should have, more than any other sister ever will, I think. Will it suffice?"

For a time he simply looked at her, fire slowly fading to ice once more. His eyes fell away. "Almost, I can believe," he muttered finally, without saying what he almost believed. He gave a bitter laugh. "What help can I give you?"

Moiraine frowned. She very much wanted time alone with this man, to bring him to heel, but that had to wait. "There is another sister in the Palace. Merean Redhill. I need to know where she goes, what she does, who she meets." He blinked, but did not ask the obvious questions. Perhaps he knew he would get no answers, but his silence was still pleasing.

"I have been keeping to my rooms the past few days," he said, looking at the door again. "I do not know how much watching I can do."

In spite of herself, she sniffed. The man promised help, then looked anxiously for his lady. Perhaps he was not what she had thought. But he was who she had. "Not you," she told him. Her visit here would be known throughout the Aesdaishar soon, if it was not already, and if he was noticed spying on Merean. . . . That could be disaster even if the woman was as innocent as a babe. "I thought you might ask one of the Malkieri I understand have gathered here to follow you. Someone with a sharp eye and a close tongue. This must be done in utter secrecy.''

''No one follows me,'' he said sharply. Glancing at the door once more, he suddenly seemed weary. He did not slump, but he moved to the fireplace and propped his sword beside it with the care of a tired man. Standing with his back to her, he said, ''I will ask Bukama and Ryne to watch her, but I cannot promise for them. That is all I can do for you.''

She stifled a vexed sound. Whether it was all he could do or all he would, she had no leverage to force him. ''Bukama,'' she said. ''Only him.'' Going by how he had behaved around her, Ryne would be too busy staring at Merean to see or hear anything. That was if he did not confess what he was doing the moment Merean looked at him. ''And do not tell him why.''

His head whipped around, but after a moment he nodded. And again he did not ask the questions most people would have. Telling him how to get word to her, by notes passed to her maid Suki, she hoped she was not making a grave mistake.

Back in her own rooms, she discovered just how quickly news had spread. In the sitting room, Siuan was offering a tray of sweetmeats to a tall, full-mouthed young woman in pale green silk, little older than a girl, with black hair that fell well below her hips and a small blue dot painted on her forehead about where the stone of Moiraine's kesiera hung. Siuan's face was smooth, but her voice was tight as she made introductions. The Lady Iselle quickly showed why.

"Everyone in the Palace is saying you are Aes Sedai," she said, eyeing Moiraine doubtfully. She did not rise, much less curtsy, or even incline her head. "If that is so, I need your assistance. I wish to go to the White Tower. My mother wants me to marry. I would not mind Lan as my *carneira* if Mother were not already his, but when I marry, I think it will be one of my Warders. I will be Green Ajah." She frowned faintly at Siuan. "Don't hover, girl. Stand over there until you are needed." Siuan took up a stance by the fireplace, back stiff and arms folded beneath her breasts. No real servant would have stood so—or frowned so—but Iselle no longer noticed her. "Do sit down, Moiraine," she went on with a smile, "and I will tell you what I need of you. If you *are* Aes Sedai, of course."

Moiraine stared. Invited to take a chair in her own sitting room. This silly child was certainly a suitable match for Lan when it came to arrogance. Her *carneira*? That meant "first" in the Old Tongue, and plainly something else here. Not what it seemed to, of course; even these Malkieri could not be that peculiar! Sitting, she said dryly, "Choosing your Ajah should at least wait until I test you to see whether there is any point in sending you to the Tower. A few minutes will determine whether you can learn to channel, and your potential strength if you—'' The girl blithely broke in.

''Oh, I was tested years ago. The Aes Sedai said I would be very strong. I told her I was fifteen, but she learned the truth. I don't see why I could not go to the Tower at twelve if I wanted. Mother was furious. She has always said I was to be Queen of Malkier one day, but that means marrying Lan, which I would not want even if mother weren't his *carneira*. When you tell her you are taking me to the Tower, she will have to listen. Everyone knows that Aes Sedai take any woman they want for training, and no one can stop them.'' That full mouth pursed. ''You *are* Aes Sedai, aren't you?''

Moiraine performed the rosebud exercise. ''If you want to go to Tar Valon, then go. I certainly do not have time to escort you. You will find sisters there about whom you can have no doubts. Suki, will you show the Lady Iselle out? No doubt she does not wish to delay in setting off before her mother catches her.''

The chit was all indignation, of course, but Moiraine wanted only to see the back of her, and Siuan very nearly pushed her out into the corridor.

''That one,'' Siuan said as she came back dusting

her hands, "won't last a month if she can equal Cadsuane." The Tower clung like iron bands to any woman who had the smallest chance of earning the shawl, but those who could not or would not learn did find themselves put out, and channeling was only part of what had to be learned.

"Sierin herself can toss her from the top of the Tower for all I care," Moiraine snapped. "Did you learn anything?"

It seemed that Siuan had learned that the young footman knew how to kiss, a revelation that did not even pinken her cheeks, and aside from that, nothing whatsoever. Surprisingly, learning that Moiraine had approached Lan upset her more than Merean's appearance.

"Skin me and salt me if you don't take idiot risks, Moiraine. A man who claims the throne of a dead country is nine kinds of fool. He could be flapping his tongue about you right this minute to anybody who'll bloody listen! If Merean learns you're having her watched. . . . Burn me!"

"He is many kinds of fool, Siuan, but I do not think he ever 'flaps his tongue.' Besides, 'you cannot win if you will not risk a copper,' as you always tell me your father used to say. We have no choice but to take risks. With Merean here, time may be running out. You must reach the Lady Ines as quickly as you can."

"I'll do what I can," Siuan muttered, and stalked out squaring her shoulders as if for a struggle. But she was smoothing her skirt over her hips, too.

Night had long since fallen and Moiraine was trying to read by lamplight when Siuan returned. Moiraine set her book aside; she had been staring at the same page for the past hour. This time, Siuan did have news, delivered while digging through the dresses and shifts Mistress Dorelmin had made.

For one thing, she had been approached on her way back to Moiraine's rooms by "a gristly old stork" who asked if she was Suki, then told her Merean had spent almost the entire day with Prince Brys before retiring to her apartments for the night. No clue there to anything. More important, Siuan had been able to bring up Rahien in casual conversation with Cal. The footman had not been with the Lady Ines when the boy was born, but he did know the day, one day after the Aiel began their retreat from Tar Valon. Moiraine and Siuan shared a long look over that. One day after Gitara Moroso had made her Foretelling of the Dragon's Rebirth and dropped dead from the shock of it. Dawn over the mountain, and born during the ten days before a sudden thaw melted the snow. Gitara had specifically mentioned the snow.

"Anyway," Siuan went on, beginning to make a bundle of clothes and stockings, "I led Cal to believe I'd been dismissed from your service for spilling wine on your dress, and he's offered me a bed with the Lady Ines' servants. He thinks he might be able to get me a place with his Lady.'' She snorted with amusement, then caught Moiraine's eyes and snorted again, more roughly. "It isn't *his* bloody bed, Moiraine. And if it was, well, he has a gentle manner and the prettiest brown eyes you've ever seen. One of these days, you're going to find yourself ready to do more than dream about some man, and I hope I'm there to see it!''

"Do not talk nonsense,'' Moiraine told her. The task in front of them was too important to spare thoughts for men. In the way Siuan meant, at least. Merean had spent all day with Brys? Without going near Lady Ines? One of Tamra's chosen or Black Ajah, that made no sense, and it went beyond credibility to believe Merean was not one or the other. She was missing something, and that worried her. What she did not know could kill her. Worse, it could kill the Dragon Reborn in his cradle.

Lan slipped through the corridors of the Aesdaishar alone, using every bit of the skill he had learned in the Blight, avoiding the eyes of passersby. His own servingwomen took Edeyn's commands ahead of his, now, as though they believed that some part of Malkieri ways. She might have told them it was. He expected that anyone in the Aesdaishar wearing livery would tell Edeyn where to find him. He thought he knew where he was, now. Despite previous visits, he had gotten lost twice, without a guide. He felt a fool for wearing his sword. Steel was no use in this battle.

A flicker of movement made him flatten himself against the wall behind a statue of a woman clad in clouds, her arms full of flowers. Just in time. Two women came out of the crossing corridor ahead, pausing in close conversation. Iselle and the Aes Sedai, Merean. He was as still as the stone he hid behind.

He did not like skulking, but while Edeyn was untying the knot in his *daori* that had kept him penned for two days she had made it clear that she intended to announce his marriage to Iselle soon. Bukama had been right. Edeyn used his *daori* like reins, and he did not believe she would stop just because he married her daughter. The only thing to do when faced by an opponent you could not defeat was run, and he wanted to.

At a sharp motion from Merean, Iselle nodded eagerly and went back the way they had come. For a moment Merean watched her go, face unreadable in Aes Sedai serenity. Then, surprisingly, she followed, gliding in a way that made Iselle look awkward.

Lan did not waste time wondering what Merean was up to, any more than he had in wondering why Moiraine wanted her watched. A man could go mad trying to puzzle out Aes Sedai. Which Moiraine really must be, or Merean would have her howling up and down the corridors. Waiting long enough for the pair to be out of sight again, he moved quietly to the corner and peeked. They were both gone, so he hurried on. Aes Sedai were no concern of his today. He had to talk to Bukama.

Running would end Edeyn's schemes of marriage. If he avoided her long enough, she would find another husband for Iselle. Running would end Edeyn's dream of reclaiming Malkier; her support would fade like mist under a noon sun once people learned he was gone. Running would end many dreams. The man who had carried an infant tied to his back had a right to dreams, though. Duty was a mountain, but it had to be carried.

Ahead lay a long flight of broad, stone-railed stairs. He turned to start down, and suddenly he was falling. He just had time to go limp, and then he was bounding from step to step, tumbling head over heels, landing on the tiled floor at the bottom with a crash that drove the last remaining air from his lungs. Spots shimmered in front of his eyes. He struggled to breathe, to push himself up.

Servants appeared from nowhere, helping him

dizzily to his feet, all exclaiming over his luck in not killing himself in such a fall, asking whether he wanted to see one of the Aes Sedai for Healing. Frowning up the stairway, he murmured replies, anything in hope of making them go away. He thought he might be as bruised as he had ever been in his life, but bruises went away, and the last thing he wanted at that moment was a sister. Most men would have fought that fall and been lucky to end with half their bones broken. Something had jerked his ankles up there. Something had hit him between the shoulders. There was only one thing it could have been, however little sense it made. An Aes Sedai had tried to kill him.

"Lord Mandragoran!" A stocky man in the striped coat of a palace guard skidded to a halt and nearly fell over trying to bow while still moving. "We've been looking for you everywhere, my Lord!" he panted. "It's your man, Bukama! Come quickly, my Lord! He may still be alive!"

Cursing, Lan ran behind the guard, shouting for the man to go faster, but he was too late. Too late for the man who had carried an infant. Too late for dreams.

Guards crowding a narrow passage just off one of the practice yards squeezed back to let Lan through. Bukama lay facedown, blood pooled around his mouth, the plain wooden hilt of a dagger rising from the dark stain on the back of his coat. His staring eyes looked surprised. Kneeling, Lan closed those eyes and murmured a prayer for the last embrace of the mother to welcome Bukama home.

"Who found him?" he asked, but he barely heard the jumbled replies about who and where and what. He hoped Bukama was reborn in a world where the Golden Crane flew on the wind, and the Seven Towers stood unbroken, and the Thousand Lakes shone like a necklace beneath the sun. How could he have let anyone get close enough to do this? Bukama could *feel* steel being unsheathed near him. Only one thing was sure. Bukama was dead because Lan had tangled him in an Aes Sedai's schemes.

Rising, Lan began to run. Not away from, though. Toward. And he did not care who saw him.

The muffled crash of the door in the anteroom and outraged shouts from the servingwomen lifted Moiraine from the chair where she had been waiting. For anything but this. Embracing *saidar*, she started from the sitting room, but before she reached the door, it swung open. Lan shook off the liveried women clinging to his arms, shut the door in their faces, and put his back to it, meeting Moiraine's startled gaze. Purpling bruises marred his face, and he moved as if he had been beaten. From outside came silence. Whatever he intended, they would be sure she could handle it.

Absurdly, she found herself fingering her belt knife. With the Power she could wrap him up like a child, however large he was, and yet. . . . He did not glare. There certainly was no fire in those eyes. She wanted to step back. No fire, but death seared cold. That black coat suited him with its cruel thorns and stark gold blossoms.

"Bukama is dead with a knife in his heart," he said calmly, "and not an hour gone, someone tried to kill me with the One Power. At first I thought it must be Merean, but the last I saw of her, she was trailing after Iselle, and unless she saw me and wanted to lull me, she had no time. Few see me when I do not want to be seen, and I don't think she did. That leaves you."

Moiraine winced, and only in part for the certainty in his tone. She should have known the fool girl would go straight to Merean. "You would be surprised how little escapes a sister," she told him. Especially if the sister was filled with *saidar*. "Perhaps I should not have asked Bukama to watch Merean. She is very dangerous." She *was* Black Ajah; Moiraine was certain of that, now. Sisters might make painful examples of people caught snooping, but they did not kill them. But what to do about her? Certainty was not proof, surely not that would stand up before the Amyrlin Seat. And if Sierin herself was Black. . . . Not a worry she could do anything about now. What was the woman doing wasting any time at all with Iselle? "If you care for the girl, I suggest you find her as quickly as possible and keep her away from Merean."

Lan grunted. "All Aes Sedai are dangerous. Iselle is safe enough for the moment; I saw her on my way here, hurrying somewhere with Brys and Diryk. Why did Bukama die, Aes Sedai? What did I snare him in for you?"

Moiraine flung up a hand for silence, and a tiny part of her was surprised when he obeyed. The rest of her thought furiously. Merean with Iselle. Iselle with Brys and Diryk. Merean had tried to kill Lan. Suddenly she saw a pattern, perfect in every line; it made no sense, but she did not doubt it was real. "Diryk told me you are the luckiest man in the world," she said, leaning toward Lan intently, "and for his sake, I hope he was right. Where would Brys go for absolute privacy? Somewhere he would not be seen or heard." It would have to be a place he felt comfortable, yet isolated.

"There is a walk on the west side of the Palace," Lan said slowly; then his voice quickened. "If there is danger to Brys, I must rouse the guards." He was already turning, hand on the door handle.

"No!" she said. She still held the Power, and she prepared a weave of Air to seize him if necessary. "Prince Brys will not appreciate having his guards burst in if Merean is simply talking to him.''

"And if she is not talking?" he demanded.

"We have no proof of anything against her, Lan. Suspicions against the word of an Aes Sedai." His head jerked angrily, and he growled something about Aes Sedai that she deliberately did not hear. "Take me to this walk, Lan. Let Aes Sedai deal with Aes Sedai. And let us hurry." If Merean did any talking, Moiraine did not expect her to talk for long.

Hurry Lan surely did, long legs flashing as he ran. All Moiraine could do was gather her skirts high and run after him, ignoring the stares and murmurs of servants and others in the corridors, thanking the Light that the man did not outpace her. She let the Power fill her as she ran, till sweetness and joy bordered pain, and tried to plan what she would do, what she could do, against a woman considerably stronger than she, a woman who had been Aes Sedai more than a hundred years before her own great-grandmother was born. She wished she were not so afraid. She wished Siuan were with her.

The mad dash led through glittering state chambers, along statuary-lined hallways, and suddenly they were into the open, the sounds of the Palace left behind, on a long stone-railed walk twenty paces wide with a vista across the city roofs far below. A cold wind blew like a storm. Merean was there, surrounded by the glow of *saidar*, and Brys and Diryk, standing by the rail, twisting futilely against bonds and gags of Air. Iselle was frowning at the Prince and his son, and surprisingly, farther down the walk stood a glowering Ryne.

". . . and I could hardly bring Lord Diryk to you without his father," Iselle was saying petulantly. "I *did* make sure no one knows, but why—?"

Weaving a shield of Spirit, Moiraine hurled it at Merean with every shred of the Power in her, hoping against hope to cut the woman off from the Source. The shield struck and splintered. Merean was too strong, drawing too near her capacity.

The Blue sister—the Black sister—did not even blink. "You did well enough killing the spy, Ryne," she said calmly as she wove a gag of Air to stop up Iselle's mouth and bonds that held the girl stiff and wide-eyed. "See if you can make certain of the younger one this time. You did say you are a better swordsman."

Everything seemed to happen at once. Ryne rushed forward, scowling, the bells in braids chiming. Lan barely got his own sword out in time to meet him. And before the first clash of steel on steel, Merean struck at Moiraine with the same weave she herself had used, but stronger. In horror Moiraine realized that Merean might have sufficient strength remaining to shield her even while she was embracing as much of *saidar* as she could. Frantically she struck out with Air and Fire, and Merean grunted as severed flows snapped back into her. In the brief interval, Moiraine tried to slice the flows holding Diryk and the others, but before her weave touched Merean's, Merean sliced hers instead, and this time Merean's attempted shield actually touched her before she could cut it. Moiraine's stomach tried to tie itself in a knot.

"You appear too often, Moiraine," Merean said as though they were simply chatting. She looked as if there were no more to it, serene and motherly, not in the slightest perturbed. "I fear I must ask you how, and why." Moiraine just managed to sever a weave of Fire that would have burned off her clothes and perhaps most of her skin, and Merean smiled, a mother amused at the mischief young women get up to. "Don't worry, child. I'll Heal you to answer my questions."

If Moiraine had had any lingering doubts that Merean was Black Ajah, that weave of Fire would have ended them. In the next moments she had more proof, weavings that made sparks dance on her dress and her hair rise, weavings that left her gasping for air that was no longer there, weavings she could not recognize yet was sure would leave her broken and bleeding if they settled around her, if she failed to cut them. . . .

When she could, she tried again and again to cut

the bonds holding Diryk and the others, to shield Merean, even to knock her unconscious. She knew she fought for her life—she would die if the other woman won, now or after Merean's questioning— but she never considered that loophole in the Oaths that held her. She had questions of her own for the woman, and the fate of the world might rest on the answers. Unfortunately, most of what she could do was defend herself, and that always on the brink. Her stomach *was* in a knot, and trying to make another. Holding three people bound, Merean was still a match for her, and maybe more. If only Lan could distract the woman.

A hasty glance showed how unlikely that was. Lan and Ryne danced the forms, their blades like whirlwinds, but if there was a hair between their abilities, it rested with Ryne. Blood fanned down the side of Lan's face.

Grimly, Moiraine bore down, not even sparing the bit of concentration necessary to ignore the cold. Shivering, she struck at Merean, defended herself and struck again, defended and struck. If she could manage to wear the woman down, or . . .

"This is taking too long, don't you think, child?" Merean said. Diryk floated into the air, struggling against the bonds he could not see as he drifted over the railing. Brys' head twisted, following his son, and his mouth worked around his unseen gag.

"No!" Moiraine screamed. Desperately, she flung out flows of Air to drag the boy back to safety. Merean slashed them even as she released her own hold on him. Wailing, Diryk fell, and white light exploded in Moiraine's head.

Groggily she opened her eyes, the boy's fading shriek still echoing in her mind. She was on her back on the stone walk, her head spinning. Until that cleared, she had as much chance of embracing *saidar* as a cat did of singing. Not that it made any difference, now. She could see the shield Merean was holding on her, and even a weaker woman could maintain a shield once in place. She tried to rise, fell back, managed to push up on an elbow.

Only moments had passed. Lan and Ryne still danced their deadly dance to the clash of steel. Brys was rigid for more than his bonds, staring at Merean with such implacable hate it seemed he might break free on the strength of his rage. Iselle was trembling visibly, snuffling and weeping and staring wide-eyed at where the boy had fallen. Where Diryk had fallen. Moiraine made herself think the boy's name, flinched to recall his grinning enthusiasm. Only moments.

"You will hold a moment for me, I think," Merean said, turning from Moiraine. Brys rose from the walk. The stocky man's face never changed, never stopped staring hatred at Merean.

Moiraine struggled to her knees. She could not channel. She had no courage left, no strength. Only determination. Brys floated over the railing. Moiraine tottered to her feet. Determination. That look of pure hate etched on his face, Brys fell, never making a sound. This had to end. Iselle lifted into the air, writhing frantically, throat working in an effort to scream past her gag. It had to end now! Stumbling, Moiraine drove her belt knife into Merean's back, blood spurting over her hands.

They fell to the paving stones together, the glow around Merean vanishing as she died, the shield on Moiraine vanishing. Iselle screamed, swaying where Merean's bonds had let her drop, atop the stone railing. Pushing herself to move, Moiraine scrambled across Merean's corpse, seized one of Iselle's flailing hands in hers just as the girl's slippers slid off into open air.

The jolt pulled Moiraine belly-down across the railing, staring down at the girl held by her blood-slick grip above a drop that seemed to go on forever. It was all Moiraine could do to hold them where they were, teetering. If she tried to pull the girl up, they would both go over. Iselle's face was contorted, her mouth a rictus. Her hand slipped in Moiraine's grasp. Forcing herself to calm, Moiraine reached for the Source and failed. Staring down at those distant rooftops did not help her whirling head. Again she tried, but it was like trying to scoop up water with spread fingers. She would save one of the three, though, if the most useless of them. Fighting dizziness, she strove for *saidar*. And Iselle's hand slid out of her bloody fingers. All Moiraine could do was watch her fall, hand still stretched up as if she believed someone might still save her.

An arm pulled Moiraine away from the railing.

"Never watch a death you don't have to," Lan said, setting her on her feet. His right arm hung at his side, a long slash laying open the blood-soaked sleeve and the flesh beneath, and he had other injuries besides the gash on his scalp that still trickled red down his face. Ryne lay on his back ten paces away, staring at the sky in sightless surprise. "A black day," Lan muttered. "As black as ever I've seen."

"A moment," she told him, her voice unsteady. "I am too dizzy to walk far, yet." Her knees wavered as she walked to Mercan's body. There would be no answers. The Black Ajah would remain hidden. Bending, she withdrew her belt knife and cleaned it on the traitor's skirts.

"You are a cool one, Aes Sedai," Lan said flatly.

"As cool as I must be," she told him. Diryk's scream rang in her ears. Iselle's face dwindled below her. "It seems Ryne was wrong as well as a Darkfriend. You were better than he."

Lan shook his head slightly. "He was better. But he thought I was finished, with only one arm. He never understood. You surrender after you're dead."

Moiraine nodded. Surrender after you are dead. Yes.

It took a little while for her head to clear enough that she could embrace the Source again, and she had to put up with Lan's anxiety to let the *shatayan* know that Brys and Diryk were dead before word came that their bodies had been found on the roof-tops. Understandably, he seemed less eager to inform the Lady Edeyn of her daughter's death. Moiraine was anxious about time, too, if not for the same reasons. She Healed him as soon as she was able. He gasped in shock as the complex weaves of Spirit, Air, and Water knit up his wounds, flesh writhing together into unscarred wholeness. Like anyone who had been Healed, he was weak after-ward, weak enough to catch his breath leaning on the stone rail. He would run nowhere for a while.

Carefully Moiraine floated Merean's body over that rail and down a little, close to the stone of the mountain. Flows of Fire, and flame, enveloped the Black sister, flame so hot there was no smoke, only a shimmering in the air, and the occasional crack of a splitting rock.

"What are you—?" Lan began, then changed it to, "Why?"

Moiraine let herself feel the rising heat, currents of air fit for a furnace. "There is no proof she was Black Ajah, only that she was Aes Sedai." The White Tower needed its armor of secrecy again, more than it had when Malkier died, but she could not tell him that. Not yet. "I cannot lie about what happened here, but I can be silent. Will you be silent, or will you do the Shadow's work?"

"You are a very hard woman," he said finally. That was the only answer he gave, but it was enough.

"I am as hard as I must be," she told him. Diryk's scream. Iselle's face. There was still Ryne's body to dispose of, and the blood. As hard as she must be.

Next dawn found the Aesdaishar in mourning, white banners flying from every prominence, the servants with long white cloths tied to their arms. Rumors in the city already talked of portents foretelling the deaths, comets in the night, fires in the sky. People had a way of folding what they saw into what they knew and what they wanted to believe. The disappearance of a simple soldier, and even of an Aes Sedai, escaped notice alongside grief.

Returning from destroying Merean's belongings— after searching in vain for any clue to other Black sisters—Moiraine stepped aside for Edeyn Arrel, who glided down the corridor in a white gown, her hair cut raggedly short. Whispers said she intended to retire from the world. Moiraine thought she already had. The woman's staring eyes looked haggard and old. In a way, they looked much as her daughter's did, in Moiraine's mind.

When Moiraine entered her apartments, Siuan leaped up from a chair. It seemed weeks since Moiraine had seen her. "You look like you reached into the bait well and found a fangfish," she growled. "Well, it's no surprise. I always hated mourning when I knew the people. Anyway, we can go whenever you're ready. Rahien was born in a farmhouse almost two miles from Dragonmount. Merean hasn't been near him, as of this morning. I don't suppose she'll harm him on suspicion even if she is Black."

Not the one. Somehow, Moiraine had almost expected that. "Merean will not harm anyone, Siuan. Put that mind of yours to a puzzle for me." Settling in a chair, she began with the end, and hurried through despite Siuan's gasps and demands for more detail. It was almost like living it again. Getting to what had led her to that confrontation was a relief. "She wanted Diryk dead most of all, Siuan; she killed him first. And she tried to kill Lan. The only thing those two had in common was luck. Diryk survived a fall that should have killed him, and everyone says Lan is the luckiest man alive or the

Blight would have killed him years ago. It makes a pattern, but the pattern looks crazy to me. Maybe your blacksmith is even part of it. And Josef Najima, back in Canluum, for all I know. He was lucky, too. Puzzle it out for me if you can. I think it is important, but I cannot see how.''

Siuan strode back and forth across the room, kicking her skirt and rubbing her chin, muttering about ''men with luck'' and ''the blacksmith rose suddenly'' and other things Moiraine could not make out. Suddenly she stopped dead and said, ''She never went near Rahien, Moiraine. The Black Ajah knows the Dragon was Reborn, but they don't bloody know *when*! Maybe Tamra managed to keep it back, or maybe they were too rough and she died before they could pry it out of her. That has to be it!'' Her eagerness turned to horror. ''Light! They're killing any man or boy who *might* be able to channel! Oh, burn me, thousands could die, Moiraine. Tens of thousands.''

It did make a terrible sense. Men who could channel seldom knew what they were doing, at least in the beginning. At first, they often just seemed to be lucky. Events favored them, and frequently, like the blacksmith, they rose to prominence with unexpected suddenness. Siuan was right. The Black Ajah had begun a slaughter.

''But they do not know to look for a boychild,''

Moiraine said. As hard as she had to be. "An infant will show no signs." Not until he was sixteen at the earliest. No man on record had begun channeling before that, and some not for ten years or more later. "We have more time than we thought. Not enough to be careless, though. Any sister can be Black. I think Cadsuane is. They know others are looking. If one of Tamra's searchers locates the boy and they find her with him, or if they decide to question one of them instead of killing her as soon as it is convenient . . ." Siuan was staring at her. "We still have the task," Moiraine told her.

"I know," Siuan said slowly. "I just never thought. Well, when there's work to do, you haul nets or gut fish." That lacked her usual force, though. "We can be on our way to Arafel before noon."

"You go back to the Tower," Moiraine said. Together, they could search no faster than one could alone, and if they had to be apart, what better place for Siuan than working for Cetalia Delarme, seeing the reports of all the Blue Ajah eyes-and-ears? The Blue was a small Ajah, but every sister said it had a larger network than any other. While Moiraine hunted for the boy, Siuan could learn what was happening in every land, and knowing what she was looking for, she could spot any sign of the Black Ajah or the Dragon Reborn.

Siuan truly could see sense when it was pointed out to her, though it took some effort this time, and when she agreed, she did it with a poor grace.

"Cetalia will use me to caulk drafts for running off without leave," she grumbled. "Burn me! Hung out on a drying rack in the Tower! Moiraine, the politics are enough to make you sweat buckets in midwinter! I hate it!" But she was already pawing through the trunks to see what she could take with her for the ride back to Tar Valon. "I suppose you warned that fellow Lan. Seems to me, he deserves it, much good it'll do him. I heard he rode out an hour ago, heading for the Blight, and if that doesn't kill him—Where are you going?"

"I have unfinished business with the man," Moiraine said over her shoulder. She had made a decision about him the first day she knew him, and she intended to keep it.

In the stable where Arrow was kept, silver marks tossed like pennies got the mare saddled and bridled almost while the coins were still in air, and she scrambled onto the animal's back without a care that her skirts pushed up to bare her legs above the knee. Digging her heels in, she galloped out of the Aesdaishar and north through the city, making people leap aside and once setting Arrow to leap cleanly over an empty wagon with a driver too slow to move out of her way. She left a tumult of shouts and shaken fists behind.

On the road north from the city, she slowed enough to ask wagon drivers heading the other way whether they had seen a Malkieri on a bay stallion, and was more than a little relieved the first time she got a yes. The man could have gone in fifty directions after crossing the moat bridge. And with an hour's lead. . . . She would catch him if she had to follow him into the Blight!

"A Malkieri?" The skinny merchant in a dark blue cloak looked startled. "Well, my guards told me there's one up there." Twisting on his wagon seat, he pointed to a grassy hill a hundred paces off the road. Two horses stood in plain sight at the crest, one a packhorse, and the thin smoke of a fire curled into the breeze.

Lan barely looked up when she dismounted. Kneeling beside the remains of a small fire, he was stirring the ashes with a long twig. Strangely, the smell of burned hair hung in the air. "I had hoped you were done with me," he said.

"Not quite yet," she told him. "Burning your future? It will sorrow a great many, I think, when you die in the Blight."

"Burning my past," he said, rising. "Burning memories. A nation. The Golden Crane will fly no more." He started to kick dirt over the ashes, then hesitated and bent to scoop up damp soil and pour it out of his hands almost formally. "No one will sorrow for me when I die, because those who would are dead already. Besides, all men die.''

"Only fools choose to die before they must. I want you to be my Warder, Lan Mandragoran.''

He stared at her unblinking, then shook his head. "I should have know it would be that. I have a war to fight, Aes Sedai, and no desire to help you weave White Tower webs. Find another.''

"I fight the same war as you, against the Shadow. Merean was Black Ajah.'' She told him all of it, from Gitara's Foretelling in the presence of the Amyrlin Seat and two Accepted to what she and Siuan had reasoned out. For another man, she would have left most unsaid, but there were few secrets between Warder and Aes Sedai. For another man, she might have softened it, but she did not believe hidden enemies frightened him, not even when they were Aes Sedai. "You said you burned your past. Let the past have its ashes. This is the same war, Lan. The most important battle yet in that war. And this one, you can win.''

For a long time he stood staring north, toward the Blight. She did not know what she would do if he refused. She had told him more than she would have anyone but her Warder.

Suddenly he turned, sword flashing out, and for an instant she thought he meant to attack her. Instead he sank to his knees, the sword lying bare across his hands. "By my mother's name, I will draw as you say 'draw' and sheathe as you say 'sheathe.' By my mother's name, I will come as you say 'come' and go as you say 'go.' " He kissed the blade and looked up at her expectantly. On his knees, he made any king on a throne look meek. She would have to teach him some humility for his own sake. And for a pond's sake.

"There is a little more," she said, laying hands on his head.

The weave of Spirit was one of the most intricate known to Aes Sedai. It wove around him, settled into him, vanished. Suddenly she was aware of him, in the way that Aes Sedai were of their Warders. His emotions were a small knot in the back of her head, all steely hard determination, sharp as his blade's edge. She knew the muted pain of old injuries, tamped down and ignored. She would be able to draw on his strength at need, to find him however far away he was. They were bonded.

He rose smoothly, sheathing his sword, studying her. "Men who weren't there call it the Battle of the Shining Walls," he said abruptly. "Men who were, call it the Blood Snow. No more. They know it was a battle. On the morning of the first day, I led nearly five hundred men. Kandori, Saldaeans, Domani. By evening on the third day, half were dead or wounded. Had I made different choices, some of those dead would be alive. And others would be dead in their places. In war, you say a prayer for your dead and ride on, because there is always another fight over the next horizon. Say a prayer for the dead, Moiraine Sedai, and ride on.''

Startled, she came close to gaping. She had forgotten that the bond's flow worked both ways. He knew her emotions, too, and apparently could reason out hers far better than she could his. After a moment, she nodded, though she did not know how many prayers it would take to clear her mind.

Handing her Arrow's reins, he said, ''Where do we ride first?''

''Back to Chachin,'' she admitted. ''And then Arafel, and . . .'' So few names remained that were easy to find. ''The world, if need be. We win this battle, or the world dies.''

Side by side they rode down the hill and turned south. Behind them the sky rumbled and turned black, another late storm rolling down from the Blight.

EARTHSEA

Ursula K. Le Guin

The Inner Archipelago of Earthsea

To the West Reach ←

To the Kargad Lands →

GONT

EA
EBRA
ORA-NEA

TOR-HEVEN

HAVNOR
Mt. On

ESKEL

Havnor Great Port

WAY
Kember-mouth

OMER

FELK WAY

ARK

Shelieth

HOSK

The Inmost Sea

ILIEN

VISS

KAMERY

Thwil

The Closed Sea

UNY

The East Reach

WATHORT

NAMIEN

UKL

The island world of Earthsea is inhabited by human beings and by dragons. The dragons are aloof and dangerous creatures, whose native tongue is the Language of the Making. Some events and stories (in *Tehanu*) suggest that there was a time when dragons and human beings were all one kind, but they have long been divided and unfriendly. Among the human beings, magic is a gift with which some people are born, but which must also be learned as an art or science. Essential to the practice of magic is learning at least some words of the Language of the Making, in which things are given their true names. By learning the true name, the witch or wizard gains power over the thing or the person.

Power, of course, may be used for good or for ill.

A Wizard of Earthsea opens on Gont Island. Ged, a young peasant boy with a great gift of magic, goes to the School for Wizards on Roke Island. There, attempting to prove his superiority to another boy, he brings a shadow-being from the realm of the dead into the world of the living. This shadow hunts him through the islands, driving him always toward danger and evil. At last, guided by his old teacher Ogion, he turns on it, and pursues it on a desperate course that leads him out of the world across the barrier of death. There Ged and his shadow, confronting each other, find that they are one; and thus Ged's being is healed and made whole.

The Tombs of Atuan is set on one of the four islands of the Kargish people, whose language and customs are different from those of the Archipelagans. A child named Tenar is taken from her parents, renamed Arha, "the Eaten One," and trained as the High Priestess of the Tombs, an ancient desert sanctuary in Atuan, where only women and eunuchs may come. When she is near the end of her training, she comes upon a stranger, a man, in the underground Labyrinth, the heart of the sacred place. This is Ged, now a powerful wizard, seeking the missing half of the Ring of Erreth-Akbe, on which is engraved the broken Rune of Peace. The young priestess's duty is to kill him. Talking with her prisoner, she begins to see that she herself is a prisoner in the Tombs, bound by a meaningless and cruel ritual. Ged gives her back her true name, Tenar. As he has freed her, she frees him: she leads him out of the Labyrinth, and the two escape with the reunited Ring of Peace. Tenar is honored in Havnor, the City of the Kings of Earthsea, but Ged will take her to live and study with his old master Ogion, on Gont.

In *The Farthest Shore*, Ged, now Archmage of Roke and the most powerful man in the Archipelago, goes with young Arren, Prince of Enlad, on a quest to find why magic seems to be losing its power. After strange adventures far in the south, they are led to the dragons' islands; and on Selidor, the westernmost of them all, their quest takes them into the realm of death, the dry land of darkness. There they find the wizard Cob, who, desiring immortality for himself, has breached the wall between life and death. Ged takes Cob's power from him and closes the wound in the world, but it takes all his own power to do so. Arren, who will inherit the throne of Earthsea, empty for five centuries, leads him back into life. The dragon Kalessin carries them both to Roke, where Ged salutes Arren as king; then Kalessin bears him home to Gont Island.

Tehanu, though written seventeen years after *The Farthest Shore*, takes up the story where it ended. Tenar of the Tombs did not stay with Ogion but married a farmer, Flint, had two children, and has lived these thirty years as a farm woman. Dying, Ogion sends for her. She stays on at the old mage's house after his death. With her is her adopted daughter. This girl, Therru, who was raped and burned and left for dead by the men who traveled with her mother, is a silent child full of fear and uncomprehended power. The dragon brings Ged to Gont. Worn out and ill, having lost all his powers of magic, Ged is full of shame, and hides even from Arren, who comes seeking him. Aspen, a disciple of Cob, brews evil magic on Gont; Handy, one of the men who abused the child Therru, keeps hanging around. The young king takes Tenar back to her husband's farm. There Handy and the others try to get at Tenar and the child; Ged comes in time to help her fight them off. That winter Ged stays with Tenar at the farm, and though he has lost his power as a mage, he finds at last his power as a sexual human being. In the spring, Aspen lures Ged and Tenar back to Ogion's house, and since they cannot work magic they have no defense against him. He humiliates and is about to kill them. Now the disfigured, powerless child Therru finds her true name, Tchanu, and her own power. She summons the dragon Kalessin in the dragons' speech, the Language of the Making. The dragon destroys Aspen, and greets

Therru as a daughter. She will live with Ged and Tenar now, but will live with the dragons later: "I give you my child," Kalessin says to Ged, "as you will give me yours."

DRAGONFLY

⌇〰⌇

Ursula K. Le Guin

1. Iria

Her father's ancestors had owned a wide, rich
domain on the wide, rich island of Way.
Claiming no title or court privilege in the days of
the kings, through all the dark years after Maharion
fell they held their land and people with firm hands,
putting their gains back into the land, upholding
some sort of justice, and fighting off petty tyrants.
As order and peace returned to the Archipelago under the sway of the wise men of Roke, for a while
yet the family and their farms and villages pros-
pered. That prosperity and the beauty of the mead-
ows and upland pastures and oak-crowned hills
made the domain a byword, so that people said, "as

fat as a cow of Iria," or, "as lucky as an Irian."
The masters and many tenants of the domain added
its name to their own, calling themselves Irian. But
though the farmers and shepherds went on from season to season and year to year and generation to
generation as solid and steady as the oaks, the family
that owned the land altered with time and chance.

A quarrel between brothers over their inheritance
divided them. One heir mismanaged his estate
through greed, the other through foolishness. One
had a daughter who married a merchant and tried to
run her estate from the city, the other had a son
whose sons quarreled again, redividing the divided
land. By the time the girl called Dragonfly was born,
the domain of Iria, though still one of the loveliest
regions of hill and field and meadow in all Earthsea,
was a battleground of feuds and litigations. Farm-
lands went to weeds, farmsteads went unroofed,
milking sheds stood unused, and shepherds followed
their flocks over the mountain to better pastures. The
old house that had been the center of the domain
was half in ruins on its hill among the oaks.

Its owner was one of four men who called themselves Master of Iria. The other three called him
Master of Old Iria. He spent his youth and what
remained of his inheritance in law courts and the
anterooms of the Lords of Way in Shelieth, trying
to prove his right to the whole domain as it had been

a hundred years ago. He came back unsuccessful and embittered and spent his age drinking the hard red wine from his last vineyard and walking his boundaries with a troop of ill-treated, underfed dogs to keep interlopers off his land.

He had married while he was in Shelieth, a woman no one at Iria knew anything about, for she came from some other island, it was said, somewhere in the west, and she never came to Iria, for she died in childbirth there in the city. When he came home he had a three-year-old daughter with him. He turned her over to the housekeeper and forgot about her. When he was drunk sometimes he remembered her. If he could find her, he made her stand by his chair or sit on his knees and listen to all the wrongs that had been done to him and to the house of Iria. He cursed and cried and drank and made her drink, too, pledging to honor her inheritance and be true to Iria. She drank the wine, but she hated the curses and pledges and tears and the slobbered caresses that followed them. She escaped, if she could, and went down to the dogs and the horses and the cattle, and swore to them that she would be loyal to her mother, whom nobody knew or honored or was true to, except herself.

When she was thirteen the old vineyarder and the housekeeper, who were all that was left of the household, told the Master that it was time his daughter had her naming day. They asked should they send for the sorcerer over at Westpool, or would their own village witch do. The Master of Iria fell into a screaming rage. "A village witch? A hex-hag to give Irian's daughter her true name? Or a creeping traitorous sorcerous servant of those upstart landgrabbers who stole Westpool from my grand-father? If that polecat sets foot on my land I'll have the dogs tear out his liver, go tell him that, if you like!" And so on. Old Daisy went back to her kitchen and old Coney went back to his vines, and thirteen-year-old Dragonfly ran out of the house and down the hill to the village, hurling her father's curses at the dogs, who, crazy with excitement at his shouting, barked and bayed and rushed after her. "Get back, you black-hearted bitch!" she yelled. "Home, you crawling traitor!" And the dogs fell silent and went sidling back to the house with their tails down.

Dragonfly found the village witch taking maggots out of an infected cut on a sheep's rump. The witch's use-name was Rose, like a great many women of Way and other islands of the Hardic Archipelago. People who have a secret name that holds their power the way a diamond holds light may well like their public name to be ordinary, common, like other people's names.

Rose was muttering a rote spell, but it was her

hands and her little short sharp knife that did most of the work. The ewe bore the digging knife patiently, her opaque, amber, slotted eyes gazing into silence; only she stamped her small left front foot now and then, and sighed. Dragonfly peered close at Rose's work. Rose brought out a maggot, dropped it, spat on it, and probed again. The girl leaned up against the ewe, and the ewe leaned against the girl, giving and receiving comfort. Rose extracted, dropped, and spat on the last maggot, and said, "Just hand me that bucket now." She bathed the sore with salt water. The ewe sighed deeply and suddenly walked out of the yard, heading for home. She had had enough of medicine. "Bucky!" Rose shouted. A grubby child appeared from under a bush where he had been asleep and trailed after the ewe, of whom he was nominally in charge although she was older, larger, better fed, and probably wiser than he was.

"They said you should give me my name," said Dragonfly. "Father fell to raging. So that's that."

The witch said nothing. She knew the girl was right. Once the Master of Iria said he would or would not allow a thing he never changed his mind, priding himself on his intransigeance, since only weak men said a thing and then unsaid it.

"Why can't I give myself my own true name?" Dragonfly asked, while Rose washed the knife and her hands in the salt water.

"Can't be done."

"Why not? Why does it have to be a witch or a sorcerer? What do you *do*?"

"Well," Rose said, and dumped out the salt water on the bare dirt of the small front yard of her house, which, like most witches' houses, stood somewhat apart from the village. "Well," she said, straightening up and looking about vaguely as if for an answer, or a ewe, or a towel. "You have to know something about the power, see," she said at last, and looked at Dragonfly with one eye. Her other eye looked a little off to the side. Sometimes Dragonfly thought the cast was in Rose's left eye, sometimes it seemed to be in her right, but always one eye looked straight and the other watched something just out of sight, around the corner, elsewhere.

"Which power?"

"The one," Rose said. As suddenly as the ewe had walked off, she went into her house. Dragonfly followed her, but only to the door. Nobody entered a witch's house uninvited.

"You said I had it," the girl said into the reeking gloom of the one-roomed hut.

"I said you have a strength in you, a great one," the witch said from the darkness. "And you know it too. What you are to do I don't know, nor do you. That's to find. But there's no such power as to name yourself."

"Why not? What's more yourself than your own true name?"

A long silence.

The witch emerged with a soapstone drop-spindle and a ball of greasy wool. She sat down on the bench beside her door and set the spindle turning. She had spun a yard of greybrown yarn before she answered.

"My name's myself. True. But what's a name, then? It's what another calls me. If there was no other, only me, what would I want a name for?"

"But," said Dragonfly and stopped, caught by the argument. After a while she said, "So a name has to be a gift?"

Rose nodded.

"Give me my name, Rose," the girl said.

"Your dad says not."

"I say to."

"He's the Master here."

"He can keep me poor and stupid and worthless, but he can't keep me nameless!"

The witch sighed, like the ewe, uneasy and constrained.

"Tonight," Dragonfly said. "At our spring, under Iria Hill. What he doesn't know won't hurt him." Her voice was half coaxing, half savage.

"You ought to have your proper name day, your feast and dancing, like any young 'un," the witch said. "It's at daybreak a name should be given. And then there ought to be music and feasting and all. Not sneaking about at night and no one knowing . . ."

"I'll know. How do you know what name to say, Rose? Does the water tell you?"

The witch shook her iron-grey head once. "I can't tell you." Her "can't" did not mean "won't." Dragonfly waited. "It's the power, like I said. It comes just so." Rose stopped her spinning and looked up with one eye at a cloud in the west; the other looked a little northward of the sky. "You're there in the water, together, you and the child. You take away the child-name. People may go on using that name for a use-name, but it's not her name, nor ever was. So now she's not a child, and she has no name. So then you wait. You open your mind up, like. Like opening the doors of a house to the wind. So it comes. Your tongue speaks it, the name. Your breath makes it. You give it to that child, the breath, the name. You can't think of it. You let it come to you. It must come through you to her it belongs to. That's the power, the way it works. It's all like that. It's not a thing you do. You have to know how to let it do. That's all the mastery."

"Mages can do more than that," the girl said.

"Nobody can do more than that," said Rose.

Dragonfly rolled her head round on her neck,

stretching till the vertebrae cracked, stretching out her long arms and legs restlessly. "Will you?" she said.

Rose nodded once.

They met in the lane under Iria Hill in the dark of night, long after sunset, long before dawn. Rose made a dim glow of werelight so that they could find their way through the marshy ground around the spring without falling in a sinkhole among the reeds. In the cold darkness under a few stars and the black curve of the hill, they stripped and waded into the shallow water, their feet sinking deep in velvet mud. The witch touched the girl's hand, saying, "I take your name, child. You are no child. You have no name."

It was utterly still.

In a whisper the witch said, "Woman, be named. You are Irian."

For a moment longer they held still; then the night wind blew across their naked shoulders, and shivering, they waded out, dried themselves as well as they could, struggled barefoot and wretched through the sharp-edged reeds and tangling roots, and found their way back to the lane. And there Dragonfly spoke in a ragged, raging whisper: "How could you name me that!"

The witch said nothing.

"It isn't right. It isn't my true name! I thought

my name would make me be me. But this makes it worse. You got it wrong. You're only a witch. You did it wrong. It's *his* name. He can have it. He's so proud of it, his stupid domain, his stupid grandfather. I don't want it. I won't have it. It isn't me. I still don't know who I am. I'm not Irian!'' She fell silent abruptly, having spoken the name.

The witch still said nothing. They walked along in the darkness side by side. At last, in a placating, frightened voice, Rose said, ''It came so . . .''

''If you ever tell it to anyone I'll kill you,'' Dragonfly said.

At that, the witch stopped walking. She hissed like a cat. ''*Tell* anyone?''

Dragonfly stopped too. She said after a moment, ''I'm sorry. But I feel like—I feel like you betrayed me.''

''I spoke your true name. It's not what I thought it would be. And I don't feel easy about it. As if I'd left something unfinished. But it is your name. If it betrays you, then that's the truth of it.'' Rose hesitated and then spoke less angrily, more coldly: ''If you want the power to betray me, Irian, I'll give you that. My name is Etaudis.''

The wind had come up again. They were both shivering, their teeth chattering. They stood face-to-face in the black lane, hardly able to see where the other was. Dragonfly put out her groping hand and

met the witch's hand. They put their arms round
each other in a fierce, long embrace. Then they hurried on, the witch to her hut near the village, the
heiress of Iria up the hill to her ruinous house, where
all the dogs, who had let her go without much fuss,
received her back with a clamor and racket of bark-
ing that woke everybody for a halfmile round except
the Master, sodden drunk by his cold hearth.

2. Ivory

The Master of Iria of Westpool, Birch, didn't own
the old house, but he did own the central and richest
lands of the old domain. His father, more interested
in vines and orchards than in quarrels with his relatives, had left Birch a thriving property. Birch hired
men to manage the farms and wineries and cooper-
age and cartage and all, while he enjoyed his wealth.
He married the timid daughter of the younger
brother of the Lord of Wayfirth, and took infinite
pleasure in thinking that his daughters were of noble
blood. The fashion of the time among the nobility
was to have a wizard in their service, a genuine wizard with a staff and a grey cloak, trained on the Isle
of the Wise, and so the Master of Iria of Westpool
got himself a wizard from Roke. He was surprised
how easy it was to get one, if you paid the price.

The young man, called Ivory, did not actually have his staff and cloak yet; he explained that he was to be made wizard when he went back to Roke. The Masters had sent him out in the world to gain experience, for all the classes in the School cannot give a man the experience he needs to be a wizard. Birch looked a little dubious at this, and Ivory reassured him that his training on Roke had equipped him with every kind of magic that could be needed in Iria of Westpool on Way. To prove it, he made it seem that a herd of deer ran through the dining hall, followed by a flight of swans, who marvellously soared through the south wall and out through the north wall; and lastly a fountain in a silver basin sprang up in the center of the table, and when the Master and his family cautiously imitated their wizard and filled their cups from it and tasted it, it was a sweet golden wine. "Wine of the Andrades," said the young man with a modest, complacent smile. By then the wife and daughters were entirely won over. And Birch thought the young man was worth his fee, although his own silent preference was for the dry red Fanian of his own vineyards, which got you drunk if you drank enough, while this yellow stuff was just honeywater.

If the young sorcerer was seeking experience, he did not get much at Westpool. Whenever Birch had guests from Kembermouth or from neighboring domains, the herd of deer, the swans, and the fountain of golden wine made their appearance. He also worked up some very pretty fireworks for warm spring evenings. But if the managers of the orchards and vineyards came to the Master to ask if his wizard might put a spell of increase on the pears this year or maybe charm the black rot off the Fanian vines on the south hill, Birch said, "A wizard of Roke doesn't lower himself to such stuff. Go tell the village sorcerer to earn his keep!" And when the youngest daughter came down with a wasting cough, Birch's wife dared not trouble the wise young man about it, but sent humbly to Rose of Old Iria, asking her to come in by the back door and maybe make a poultice or sing a chant to bring the girl back to health. Ivory never noticed that the girl was ailing, nor the pear trees, nor the vines. He kept himself to himself, as a man of craft and learning should. He spent his days riding about the countryside on the pretty black mare that his employer had given him for his use when he made it clear that he had not come from Roke to trudge about on foot in the mud and dust of country byways.

On his rides, he sometimes passed an old house on a hill among great oaks. When he turned off the village lane up the hill, a pack of scrawny, evil-mouthed dogs came pelting and bellowing down at him. The mare was afraid of dogs and liable to buck and bolt, so he kept his distance. But he had an eye for beauty, and liked to look at the old house dreaming away in the dappled light of the early summer afternoons.

He asked Birch about the place. "That's Iria," Birch said—"Old Iria, I mean to say. I own the house by rights. But after a century of feuds and fights over it, my granddad let the place go to settle the quarrel. Though the Master there would still be quarreling with me if he didn't keep too drunk to talk. Haven't seen the old man for years. He had a daughter, I think."

"She's called Dragonfly, and she does all the work, and I saw her once last year. She's tall, and as beautiful as a flowering tree," said the youngest daughter, Rose, who was busy crowding a lifetime of keen observation into the fourteen years that were all she was going to have for it. She broke off, coughing. Her mother shot an anguished, yearning glance at the wizard. Surely he would hear that cough, this time? He smiled at young Rose, and the mother's heart lifted. Surely he wouldn't smile so if Rose's cough was anything serious?

"Nothing to do with us, that lot at the old place," Birch said, displeased. The tactful Ivory asked no more. But he wanted to see the girl as beautiful as a flowering tree. He rode past Old Iria regularly. He tried stopping in the village at the foot of the hill to

ask questions, but there was nowhere to stop and
nobody would answer questions. A wall-eyed witch
took one look at him and scuttled into her hut. If he
went up to the house he would have to face the pack
of hellhounds and probably a drunk old man. But it
was worth the chance, he thought; he was bored out
of his wits with the dull life at Westpool, and was
never slow to take a risk. He rode up the hill till the
dogs were yelling around him in a frenzy, snapping
at the mare's legs. She plunged and lashed out her
hoofs at them, and he kept her from bolting only by
a staying-spell and all the strength in his arms. The
dogs were leaping and snapping at his own legs
now, and he was about to let the mare have her head
when somebody came among the dogs shouting
curses and beating them back with a strap. When he
got the lathered, gasping mare to stand still, he saw
the girl as beautiful as a flowering tree. She was very
tall, very sweaty, with big hands and feet and mouth
and nose and eyes, and a head of wild dusty hair.
She was yelling, "Down! Back to the house, you
carrion, you vile sons of bitches!" to the whining,
cowering dogs.

Ivory clapped his hand to his right leg. A dog's
tooth had ripped his breeches at the calf, and a
trickle of blood came through.

"Is she hurt?" the woman said. "Oh, the traitorous vermin!" She was stroking down the mare's

right foreleg. Her hands came away covered with blood-streaked horse sweat. "There, there," she said. "The brave girl, the brave heart." The mare put her head down and shivered all over with relief. "What did you keep her standing there in the middle of the dogs for?" the woman demanded furiously. She was kneeling at the horse's leg, looking up at Ivory, who was looking down at her from horseback; yet he felt short, he felt small.

She did not wait for an answer. "I'll walk her up," she said, standing up, and put out her hand for the reins. Ivory saw that he was supposed to dismount. He did so, asking, "Is it very bad?" and peering at the horse's leg, seeing only bright, bloody foam.

"Come on then, my love," the young woman said, not to him. The mare followed her trustfully. They set off up the rough path round the hillside to an old stone and brick stableyard, empty of horses, inhabited only by nesting swallows that swooped about over the roofs calling their quick gossip.

"Keep her quiet," said the young woman, and left him holding the mare's reins in this deserted place. She returned after some time lugging a heavy bucket, and set to sponging off the mare's leg. "Get the saddle off her," she said, and her tone held the unspoken, impatient, "you fool!" Ivory obeyed, half annoyed by this crude giantess and half intrigued. She did not put him in mind of a flowering tree at all, but she was in fact beautiful, in a large, fierce way. The mare submitted to her absolutely. When she said, "Move your foot!" the mare moved her foot. The woman wiped her down all over, put the saddle blanket back on her, and made sure she was standing in the sun. "She'll be all right," she said. "There's a gash, but if you'll wash it with warm salt water four or five times a day, it'll heal clean. I'm sorry." She said the last honestly, though grudgingly, as if she still wondered how he could have let his mare stand there to be assaulted, and she looked straight at him for the first time. Her eyes were clear orange-brown, like dark topaz or amber. They were strange eyes, right on a level with his own.

"I'm sorry too," he said, trying to speak carelessly, lightly.

"She's Irian of Westpool's mare. You're the wizard, then?"

He bowed. "Ivory, of Havnor Great Port, at your service. May I—"

She interrupted. "I thought you were from Roke."

"I am," he said, his composure regained. She stared at him with those strange eyes, as unreadable as a sheep's, he thought. Then she burst out: "You lived there? You studied there? Do you know the Archmage?"

"Yes," he said with a smile. Then he winced and stooped to press his hand against his shin for a moment.

"Are you hurt too?"

"It's nothing," he said. In fact, rather to his annoyance, the cut had stopped bleeding. The woman's gaze returned to his face.

"What is it—what is it like—on Roke?"

Ivory went, limping only very slightly, to an old mounting-block nearby and sat down on it. He stretched his leg, nursing the torn place, and looked up at the woman. "It would take a long time to tell you what Roke is like," he said. "But it would be my pleasure."

The man's a wizard, or nearly," said Rose the witch, "a Roke wizard! You must not ask him questions!" She was more than scandalized, she was frightened.

"He doesn't mind," Dragonfly reassured her. "Only he hardly ever really answers."

"Of course not!"

"Why of course not?"

"Because he's a wizard! Because you're a woman, with no art, no knowledge, no learning!"

"You could have taught me! You never would!"

Rose dismissed all she had taught or could teach with a flick of the fingers.

"Well, so I have to learn from him," said Dragonfly.

"Wizards don't teach women. You're besotted."

"You and Broom trade spells."

"Broom's a village sorcerer. This man is a wise man. He learned the High Arts at the Great House on Roke!"

"He told me what it's like," Dragonfly said. "You walk up through the town, Thwil Town. There's a door opening on the street, but it's shut. It looks like an ordinary door." The witch listened, unable to resist the lure of secrets revealed and the contagion of passionate desire. "And a man comes when you knock, an ordinary-looking man. And he gives you a test. You have to say a certain word, a password, before he'll let you in. If you don't know it, you can never go in. But if he lets you in, then from inside you see that the door is entirely different—it's made out of horn, with a tree carved on it, and the frame is made out of a tooth, one tooth of a dragon that lived long, long before Erreth-Akbe, before Morred, before there were people in Earthsea. There were only dragons, to begin with. They found the tooth on Mount Onn, in Havnor, at the center of the world. And the leaves of the tree are carved so thin that the light shines through them, but the door's so strong that if the Doorkeeper shuts it no spell could ever open it. And then the Doorkeeper takes you down a hall and another hall, till you're lost and bewildered, and then suddenly you come out under the sky. In the Court of the Fountain, in the very deepest inside of the Great House. And that's where the Archmage would be, if he was there. . . .''

"Go on," the witch murmured.

"That's all he really told me, yet," said Dragonfly, coming back to the mild, overcast spring day and the infinite familiarity of the village lane, Rose's front yard, her own seven milch-ewes grazing on Iria Hill, the bronze crowns of the oaks. "He's very careful how he talks about the Masters."

Rose nodded.

"But he told me about some of the students."

"No harm in that, I suppose."

"I don't know," Dragonfly said. "To hear about the Great House is wonderful, but I thought the people there would be—I don't know. Of course, they're mostly just boys when they go there. But I thought they'd be . . .'' She gazed off at the sheep on the hill, her face troubled. "Some of them are really bad and stupid," she said in a low voice. "They get into the School because they're rich. And they study there just to get richer. Or to get power."

"Well, of course they do," said Rose, "that's what they're there for!"

"But power—like you told me about—that isn't

the same as making people do what you want, or pay you—"

"Isn't it?"

"No!"

"If a word can heal, a word can wound," the witch said. "If a hand can kill, a hand can cure. It's a poor cart that goes only one direction."

"But on Roke, they learn to use power well, not for harm, not for gain."

"Everything's for gain some way, I'd say. People have to live. But what do I know? I make my living doing what I know how to do. But I don't meddle with the great arts, the perilous crafts, like summoning the dead," and Rose made the hand-sign to avert the danger spoken of.

"Everything's perilous," Dragonfly said, gazing now through the sheep, the hill, the trees, into still depths, a colorless, vast emptiness like the clear sky before sunrise.

Rose watched her. She knew she did not know who Irian was or what she might be. A big, strong, awkward, ignorant, innocent, angry woman, yes. But ever since she was a child Rose had seen something more in her, something beyond what she was. And when Irian looked away from the world like that, she seemed to enter that place or time or being beyond herself, utterly beyond Rose's knowledge. Then Rose feared her, and feared for her.

"You take care," the witch said, grim. "Everything's perilous, right enough, and meddling with wizards most of all."

Through love, respect, and trust, Dragonfly would never disregard a warning from Rose; but she was unable to see Ivory as perilous. She didn't understand him, but the idea of fearing him, him personally, was not one she could keep in mind. She tried to be respectful, but it was impossible. She thought he was clever and quite handsome, but she didn't think much about him, except for what he could tell her. He knew what she wanted to know and little by little he told it to her, and then it was not really what she had wanted to know, but she wanted to know more. He was patient with her, and she was grateful to him for his patience, knowing he was much quicker than she. Sometimes he smiled at her ignorance, but he never sneered at it or reproved it. Like the witch, he liked to answer a question with a question; but the answers to Rose's questions were always something she'd always known, while the answers to his questions were things she had never imagined and found startling, unwelcome, even painful, altering all her beliefs.

Day by day, as they talked in the old stableyard of Iria, where they had fallen into the habit of meeting, she asked him and he told her more, though reluctantly, always partially; he shielded his Masters, she thought, trying to defend the bright image of Roke, until one day he gave in to her insistence and spoke freely at last.

"There are good men there," he said. "Great and wise the Archmage certainly was. But he's gone. And the Masters . . . Some hold aloof, following arcane knowledge, seeking ever more patterns, ever more names, but using their knowledge for nothing. Others hide their ambition under the grey cloak of wisdom. Roke is no longer where power is in Earthsea. That's the Court in Havnor, now. Roke lives on its great past, defended by a thousand spells against the present day. And inside those spell-walls, what is there? Quarreling ambitions, fear of anything new, fear of young men who challenge the power of the old. And at the center, nothing. An empty courtyard. The Archmage will never return."

"How do you know?" she whispered.

He looked stern. "The dragon bore him away."

"You saw it? You saw that?" She clenched her hands, imagining that flight.

After a long time, she came back to the sunlight and the stableyard and her thoughts and puzzles. "But even if he's gone," she said, "surely some of the Masters are truly wise?"

When he looked up and spoke it was with a hint of a melancholy smile. "All the mystery and wisdom of the Masters, when it's out in the daylight, doesn't amount to so much, you know. Tricks of the trade—wonderful illusions. But people don't want to believe that. They want the mysteries, the illusions. Who can blame them? There's so little in most lives that's beautiful or worthy."

As if to illustrate what he was saying, he had picked up a bit of brick from the broken pavement, and tossed it up in the air, and as he spoke it fluttered about their heads on delicate blue wings, a butterfly. He put out his finger and the butterfly lighted on it. He shook his finger and the butterfly fell to the ground, a fragment of brick.

"There's not much worth much in my life," she said, gazing down at the pavement. "All I know how to do is run the farm, and try to stand up and speak truth. But if I thought it was all tricks and lies even on Roke, I'd hate those men for fooling me, fooling us all. It can't be lies. Not all of it. The Archmage did go into the labyrinth among the Hoary Men and come back with the Ring of Peace. He did go into death with the young king, and defeat the spider mage, and come back. We know that on the word of the king himself. Even here, the harpers came to sing that song, and a teller came to tell it. . . ."

Ivory nodded gravely. "But the Archmage lost all his power in the land of death. Maybe all magery was weakened then."

"Rose's spells work as well as ever," she said stoutly.

Ivory smiled. He said nothing, but she knew how petty the doings of a village witch appeared to him, who had seen great deeds and powers. She sighed and spoke from her heart—"Oh, if only I wasn't a woman!"

He smiled again. "You're a beautiful woman," he said, but plainly, not in the flattering way he had used with her at first, before she showed him she hated it. "Why would you be a man?"

"So I could go to Roke! And see, and learn! Why, why is it only men can go there?"

"So it was ordained by the first Archmage, centuries ago," said Ivory. "But . . . I too have wondered."

"You have?"

"Often. Seeing only boys and men, day after day, in the Great House and all the precincts of the School. Knowing that the townswomen are spellbound from so much as setting foot on the fields about Roke Knoll. Once in years, perhaps, some great lady is allowed to come briefly into the outer courts. . . . Why is it so? Are all women incapable of understanding? Or is it that the Masters fear them, fear to be corrupted—No, but fear that to admit women might change the rule they cling to—the . . . purity of that rule—"

"Women can live chaste as well as men can," Dragonfly said bluntly. She knew she was blunt and coarse where he was delicate and subtle, but she did not know any other way to be.

"Of course," he said, his smile growing brilliant. "But witches aren't always chaste, are they? . . . Maybe that's what the Masters are afraid of. Maybe celibacy isn't as necessary as the Rule of Roke teaches. Maybe it's not a way of keeping the power pure, but of keeping the power to themselves. Leaving out women, leaving out everybody who won't agree to turn himself into a eunuch to get that one kind of power. . . . Who knows? A she-mage! Now that would change everything, all the rules!"

She could see his mind dance ahead of hers, taking up and playing with ideas, transforming them as he had transformed brick into butterfly. She could not dance with him, she could not play with him, but she watched him in wonder.

"You could go to Roke," he said, his eyes bright with excitement, mischief, daring. Meeting her almost pleading, incredulous silence, he insisted— "You could. A woman you are, but there are ways to change your seeming. You have the heart, the courage, the will of a man. You could enter the Great House. I know it."

"And what would I do there?"

"What all the students do. Live alone in a stone

cell and learn to be wise! It might not be what you dream it to be, but that, too, you'd learn."

"I couldn't. They'd know. I couldn't even get in. There's the Doorkeeper, you said. I don't know the word to say to him."

"The password, yes. But I can teach it to you."

"You can? Is it allowed?"

"I don't care what's 'allowed,' " he said, with a frown she had never seen on his face. "The Archmage himself said, *Rules are made to be broken.* Injustice makes the rules, and courage breaks them. I have the courage, if you do!"

She looked at him. She could not speak. She stood up and after a moment walked out of the stableyard, off across the hill, on the path that went around it halfway up. One of the dogs, her favorite, a big, ugly, heavy-headed hound, followed her. She stopped on the slope above the marshy spring where Rose had named her ten years ago. She stood there; the dog sat down beside her and looked up at her face. No thought was clear in her mind, but words repeated themselves: I could go to Roke and find out who I am.

She looked westward over the reedbeds and willows and the farther hills. The whole western sky was empty, clear. She stood still and her soul seemed to go into that sky and be gone, gone out of her.

There was a little noise, the soft clipclop of the black mare's hoofs, coming along the lane. Then Dragonfly came back to herself and called to Ivory and ran down the hill to meet him. "I will go," she said.

He had not planned or intended any such adventure, but crazy as it was, it suited him better the more he thought about it. The prospect of spending the long grey winter at Westpool sank his spirits like a stone. There was nothing here for him except the girl Dragonfly, who had come to fill his thoughts. Her massive, innocent strength had defeated him absolutely so far, but he did what she pleased in order to have her do at last what he pleased, and the game, he thought, was worth playing. If she ran away with him, the game was as good as won. As for the joke of it, the notion of actually getting her into the School on Roke disguised as a man, there was little chance of pulling it off, but it pleased him as a gesture of disrespect to all the piety and pomposity of the Masters and their toadies. And if somehow it succeeded, if he could actually get a woman through that door, even for a moment, what a sweet revenge it would be!

Money was a problem. The girl thought, of course, that he as a great wizard would snap his fingers and waft them over the sea in a magic boat flying before the magewind. But when he told her they'd have to hire passage on a ship, she said simply, "I have the cheese money."

He treasured her rustic sayings of that kind. Sometimes she frightened him, and he resented it. His dreams of her were never of her yielding to him, but of himself yielding to a fierce, destroying sweetness, sinking into an annihilating embrace, dreams in which she was something beyond comprehension and he was nothing at all. He woke from those dreams shaken and shamed. In daylight, when he saw her big, dirty hands, when she talked like a yokel, a simpleton, he regained his superiority. He only wished there were someone to repeat her sayings to, one of his old friends in the Great Port who would find them amusing. " 'I have the cheese money,' " he repeated to himself, riding back to Westpool, and laughed. "I do indeed," he said aloud. The black mare flicked her ear.

He told Birch that he had received a sending from his teacher on Roke, the Master Hand, and must go at once, on what business he could not say, of course, but it should not take long once he was there; a half month to go, another to return; he would be back well before the Fallows at the latest. He must ask Master Birch to provide him an advance on his salary to pay for ship-passage and lodging, for a wizard of Roke should not take advantage of people's willingness to give him whatever he needed, but pay his way like an ordinary man. As Birch agreed with this, he had to give Ivory a purse for his journey. It was the first real money he had had in his pocket for years: ten ivory counters carved with the Otter of Shelieth on one side and the Rune of Peace on the other in honor of King Lebannen. "Hello, little namesakes," he told them when he was alone with them. "You and the cheese money will get along nicely."

He told Dragonfly very little of his plans, largely because he made few, trusting to chance and his own wits, which seldom let him down if he was given a fair chance to use them. The girl asked almost no questions. "Will I go as a man all the way?" was one. "Yes," he said, "but only disguised. I won't put a semblance-spell on you till we're on Roke Island."

"I thought it would be a spell of Change," she said.

"That would be unwise," he said, with a good imitation of the Master Changer's terse solemnity. "If need be, I'll do it, of course. But you'll find wizards very sparing of the great spells. For good reason."

"The Equilibrium," she said, accepting all he said in its simplest sense, as always.

"And perhaps because such arts have not the

power they once had," he said. He did not know himself why he tried to weaken her faith in wizardry; perhaps because any weakening of her strength, her wholeness, was a gain for him. He had begun merely by trying to get her into his bed, a game he loved to play. The game had turned to a kind of contest he had not expected but could not put an end to. He was determined now not to win her, but to defeat her. He could not let her defeat him. He must prove to her and himself that his dreams were meaningless.

Quite early on, impatient with wooing her massive physical indifference, he had worked up a charm, a sorcerer's seduction-spell of which he was contemptuous even as he made it, though he knew it was effective. He cast it on her while she was, characteristically, mending a cow's halter. The result had not been the melting eagerness it had produced in girls he had used it on in Havnor and Thwil. Dragonfly had gradually become silent and sullen. She ceased asking her endless questions about Roke and did not answer when he spoke. When he very tentatively approached her, taking her hand, she struck him away with a blow to the head that left him dizzy. He saw her stand up and stride out of the stableyard without a word, the ugly hound she favored trotting after her. It looked back at him with a grin.

She took the path to the old house. When his ears stopped ringing he stole after her, hoping the charm was working and that this was only her particularly uncouth way of leading him at last to her bed. Nearing the house, he heard crockery breaking. The father, the drunkard, came wobbling out looking scared and confused, followed by Dragonfly's loud, harsh voice—"Out of the house, you drunken, crawling traitor! You foul, shameless lecher!"

"She took my cup away," the Master of Iria said to the stranger, whining like a puppy, while his dogs yammered around him. "She broke it."

Ivory departed. He did not return for two days. On the third day he rode experimentally past Old Iria, and she came striding down to meet him. "I'm sorry, Ivory," she said, looking up at him with her smoky orange eyes. "I don't know what came over me the other day. I was angry. But not at you. I beg your pardon."

He forgave her gracefully. He did not try a love-charm on her again.

Soon, he thought now, he would not need one. He would have real power over her. He had finally seen how to get it. She had given it into his hands. Her strength and her willpower were tremendous, but fortunately she was stupid, and he was not.

Birch was sending a carter down to Kembermouth with six barrels of ten-year-old Fanian ordered by the wine merchant there. He was glad to send his wizard along as bodyguard, for the wine was valuable, and though the young king was putting things to rights as fast as he could, there were still gangs of robbers on the roads. So Ivory left Westpool on the big wagon pulled by four big carthorses, jolting slowly along, his legs dangling. Down by Jackass Hill an uncouth figure rose up from the wayside and asked the carter for a lift. "I don't know you," the carter said, lifting his whip to warn the stranger off, but Ivory came round the wagon and said, "Let the lad ride, my good man. He'll do no harm while I'm with you."

"Keep an eye on him then, master," said the carter.

"I will," said Ivory, with a wink at Dragonfly. She, well disguised in dirt and a farmhand's old smock and leggings and a loathsome felt hat, did not wink back. She played her part even while they sat side by side dangling their legs over the tailgate, with six great halftuns of wine jolting between them and the drowsy carter, and the drowsy summer hills and fields slipping slowly, slowly past. Ivory tried to tease her, but she only shook her head. Maybe she was scared by this wild scheme, now she was embarked on it. There was no telling. She was solemnly, heavily silent. I could be very bored by this woman, Ivory thought, if once I'd had her underneath me. That thought stirred him almost unbearably, but when he looked back at her, his thoughts died away before her massive, actual presence.

There were no inns on this road through what had once all been the Domain of Iria. As the sun neared the western plains, they stopped at a farmhouse that offered stabling for the horses, a shed for the cart, and straw in the stable loft for the carters. The loft was dark and stuffy and the straw musty. Ivory felt no lust at all, though Dragonfly lay not three feet from him. She had played the man so thoroughly all day that she had half convinced even him. Maybe she'll fool the old men after all! he thought, and grinned at the thought, and slept.

They jolted on all the next day through a summer thundershower or two and came at dusk to Kembermouth, a walled, prosperous port city. They left the carter to his master's business and walked down to find an inn near the docks. Dragonfly looked about at the sights of the city in a silence that might have been awe or disapproval or mere stolidity. "This is a nice little town," Ivory said, "but the only city in the world is Havnor." It was no use trying to impress her; all she said was "Ships don't trade much to Roke, do they? Will it take a long time to find one to take us, do you think?"

"Not if I carry a staff," he said.

She stopped looking about and strode along in

thought for a while. She was beautiful in movement, bold and graceful, her head carried high.

"You mean they'll oblige a wizard? But you aren't a wizard."

"That's a formality. We senior sorcerers may carry a staff when we're on Roke's business. Which I am."

"Taking me there?"

"Bringing them a student—yes. A student of great gifts!"

She asked no more questions. She never argued; it was one of her virtues.

That night, over supper at the waterfront inn, she asked with unusual timidity in her voice, "Do I have great gifts?"

"In my judgment, you do," he said.

She pondered—conversation with her was often a slow business—and said, "Rose always said I had power, but she didn't know what kind. And I . . . I know I do, but I don't know what it is."

"You're going to Roke to find out," he said, raising his glass to her. After a moment she raised hers and smiled at him, a smile so tender and radiant that he said spontaneously, "And may what you find be all you seek!"

"If I do, it will be thanks to you," she said. In that moment he loved her for her true heart, and would have forsworn any thought of her but as his companion in a bold adventure, a gallant joke.

They had to share a room at the crowded inn with two other travelers, but Ivory's thoughts were perfectly chaste, though he laughed at himself a little for it.

Next morning he picked a sprig of an herb from the kitchen garden of the inn and spelled it into the semblance of a fine staff, coppershod and his own height exactly. "What is the wood?" Dragonfly asked, fascinated, when she saw it, and when he answered with a laugh, "Rosemary," she laughed too. They set off along the wharves, asking for a ship bound south that might take a wizard and his Prentice to the Isle of the Wise, and soon enough they found a heavy trader bound for Wathort, whose master would carry the wizard for goodwill and the Prentice for half price. Even half price was half the cheese money, but they would have the luxury of a cabin, for *Sea Otter* was a decked, two-masted ship.

As they were talking with her master a wagon drew up on the dock and began to unload six familiar halftun barrels. "That's ours," Ivory said, and the ship's master said, "Bound for Hort Town," and Dragonfly said softly, "From Iria."

She glanced back at the land then. It was the only time he ever saw her look back.

The ship's weatherworker came aboard just before they sailed, no Roke wizard but a weatherbeaten fellow in a worn sea-cloak. Ivory flourished his staff a little in greeting him. The sorcerer looked him up and down and said, "One man works weather on this ship. If it's not me, I'm off."

"I'm a mere passenger, Master Bagman. I gladly leave the winds in your hands."

The sorcerer looked at Dragonfly, who stood straight as a tree and said nothing.

"Good," he said, and that was the last word he spoke to Ivory.

During the voyage, however, he talked several times with Dragonfly, which made Ivory a bit uneasy. Her ignorance and trustfulness could endanger her and therefore him. What did she and the bagman talk about? he asked, and she answered, "What is to become of us."

He stared.

"Of all of us. Of Way, and Felkway, and Havnor, and Wathort, and Roke. All the people of the islands. He says that when King Lebannen was to be crowned, last autumn, he sent to Gont for the old Archmage to come crown him, and he wouldn't come. And there was no new archmage. So he took the crown himself. And some say that's wrong, and he doesn't rightly hold the throne. But others say the king himself is the new archmage. But he isn't a wizard, only a king. So others say the dark years will come again, when there was no rule of justice, and wizardry was used for evil ends."

After a pause Ivory said, "That old weather-worker says all this?"

"It's common talk, I think," said Dragonfly, with her grave simplicity.

The weatherworker knew his trade, at least. *Sea Otter* sped south; they met summer squalls and choppy seas, but never a storm or a troublesome wind. They put off and took on cargo at ports on the north shore of O, at Ilien, Leng, Kamery, and O Port, and then headed west to carry the passengers to Roke. And facing the west Ivory felt a little hollow at the pit of his stomach, for he knew all too well how Roke was guarded. He knew neither he nor the weatherworker could do anything at all to turn the Roke-wind if it blew against them. And if it did, Dragonfly would ask why? Why did it blow against them?

He was glad to see the sorcerer uneasy too, standing by the helmsman, keeping a watch up on the masthead, taking in sail at the hint of a west wind. But the wind held steady from the north. A thunder-squall came pelting on that wind, and Ivory went down to the cabin, but Dragonfly stayed up on deck. She was afraid of the water, she had told him. She could not swim; she said, "Drowning must be a horrible thing—Not to breathe the air—" She had shuddered at the thought. It was the only fear she had ever shown of anything. But she disliked the low, cramped cabin, and had stayed on deck every day and slept there on the warm nights. Ivory had not tried to coax her into the cabin. He knew now that coaxing was no good. To have her he must master her; and that he would do, if only they could come to Roke.

He came up on deck again. It was clearing, and as the sun set the clouds broke all across the west, showing a golden sky behind the high dark curve of a hill.

Ivory looked at that hill with a kind of longing hatred.

"That's Roke Knoll, lad," the weatherworker said to Dragonfly, who stood beside him at the rail. "We're coming into Thwil Bay now. Where there's no wind but the wind they want."

By the time they were well into the bay and had let down the anchor it was dark, and Ivory said to the ship's master, "I'll go ashore in the morning."

Down in their tiny cabin Dragonfly sat waiting for him, solemn as ever but her eyes blazing with excitement. "We'll go ashore in the morning," he repeated to her, and she nodded, acceptant. She said, "Do I look all right?"

He sat down on his narrow bunk and looked at her sitting on her narrow bunk; they could not face each other directly, as there was no room for their knees. At O Port she had bought herself a decent shirt and breeches, at his suggestion, so as to look a more probable candidate for the School. Her face was windburned and scrubbed clean. Her hair was braided and the braid clubbed, like Ivory's. She had got her hands clean, too, and they lay flat on her thighs, long strong hands, like a man's.

"You don't look like a man," he said. Her face fell. "Not to me. You'll never look like a man to me. But don't worry. You will to them."

She nodded, with an anxious face.

"The first test is the great test, Dragonfly," he said. Every night as he lay alone in this cabin he had planned this conversation. "To enter the Great House: to go through that door."

"I've been thinking about it," she said, hurried and earnest. "Couldn't I just tell them who I am? With you there to vouch for me—to say even if I am a woman, I have some gift—and I'd promise to take the vow and make the spell of celibacy, and live apart if they wanted me to—"

He was shaking his head all through her speech. "No, no, no, no. Hopeless. Useless. Fatal!"

"Even if you—"

"Even if I argued for you. They won't listen. The Rule of Roke forbids women to be taught any High Art, any word of the Language of the Making. It's always been so. They will not listen. So they must be shown! And we'll show them, you and I. We'll teach them. You must have courage, Dragonfly. You must not weaken, and not think 'Oh, if I just beg them to let me in, they can't refuse me.' They can, and will. And if you reveal yourself, they will punish you. And me.'' He put a ponderous emphasis on the last word, and inwardly murmured, ''Avert.''

She gazed at him from her unreadable eyes, and finally said, ''What must I do?''

''Do you trust me, Dragonfly?''

''Yes.''

''Will you trust me entirely, wholly—knowing that the risk I take for you is greater even than your risk in this venture?''

''Yes.''

''Then you must tell me the word you will speak to the Doorkeeper.''

She stared. ''But I thought you'd tell it to me— the password.''

''The password he will ask you for is your true name.''

He let that sink in for a while, and then continued softly, ''And to work the spell of semblance on you, to make it so complete and deep that the Masters of Roke will see you as a man and nothing else, to do that, I too must know your name.'' He paused again. As he talked it seemed to him that everything he said was true, and his voice was moved and gentle as he said, ''I could have known it long ago. But I chose not to use those arts. I wanted you to trust me enough to tell me your name yourself.''

She was looking down at her hands, clasped now on her knees. In the faint reddish glow of the cabin lantern her lashes cast very delicate, long shadows on her cheeks. She looked up, straight at him. ''My name is Irian,'' she said.

He smiled. She did not smile.

He said nothing. In fact he was at a loss. If he had known it would be this easy, he could have had her name and with it the power to make her do whatever he wanted, days ago, weeks ago, with a mere pretense at this crazy scheme—without giving up his salary and his precarious respectability, without this sea voyage, without having to go all the way to Roke for it! For he saw the whole plan now was folly. There was no way he could disguise her that would fool the Doorkeeper for a moment. All his notions of humiliating the Masters as they had humiliated him were moonshine. Obsessed with tricking the girl, he had fallen into the trap he laid for her. Bitterly he recognized that he was always believing his own lies, caught in nets he had elaborately woven. Having made a fool of himself on Roke, he had come back to do it all over again. A great, desolate anger swelled up in him. There was no good, no good in anything.

''What's wrong?'' she asked. The gentleness of

her deep, husky voice unmanned him, and he hid his face in his hands, fighting against the shame of tears.

She put her hand on his knee. It was the first time she had ever touched him. He endured it, the warmth and weight of her touch that he had wasted so much time wanting.

He wanted to hurt her, to shock her out of her terrible, ignorant kindness, but what he said when he finally spoke was "I only wanted to make love to you."

"You did?"

"Did you think I was one of their eunuchs? That I'd castrate myself with spells so I could be holy? Why do you think I don't have a staff? Why do you think I'm not at the School? Did you believe everything I said?"

"Yes," she said. "I'm sorry." Her hand was still on his knee. She said, "We can make love if you want."

He sat up, sat still.

"What are you?" he said to her at last.

"I don't know. It's why I wanted to come to Roke. To find out."

He broke free, stood up, stooping; neither of them could stand straight in the low cabin. Clenching and unclenching his hands, he stood as far from her as he could, his back to her.

"You won't find out. It's all lies, shams. Old men

playing games with words. I wouldn't play their games, so I left. Do you know what I did?'' He turned, showing his teeth in a rictus of triumph. ''I got a girl, a town girl, to come to my room. My cell. My little stone celibate cell. It had a window looking out on a back street. No spells—you can't make spells with all their magic going on. But she wanted to come, and came, and I let a rope ladder out the window, and she climbed it. And we were at it when the old men came in! I showed 'em! And if I could have got you in, I'd have showed 'em again, I'd have taught them *their* lesson!''

''Well, I'll try,'' she said.

He stared.

''Not for the same reasons as you,'' she said, ''but I still want to. And we came all this way. And you know my name.''

It was true. He knew her name: Irian. It was like a coal of fire, a burning ember in his mind. His thought could not hold it. His knowledge could not use it. His tongue could not say it.

She looked up at him, her sharp, strong face softened by the shadowy lantern-light. ''If it was only to make love you brought me here, Ivory,'' she said, ''we can do that. If you still want to.''

Wordless at first, he simply shook his head. After a while he was able to laugh. ''I think we've gone on past . . . that possibility . . .''

She looked at him without regret, or reproach, or shame.

"Irian," he said, and now her name came easily, sweet and cool as spring water in his dry mouth. "Irian, here's what you must do to enter the Great House . . ."

3. Azver

He left her at the corner of the street, a narrow, dull, somehow sly-looking street that slanted up between featureless walls to a wooden door in a higher wall. He had put his spell on her, and she looked like a man, though she did not feel like one. She and Ivory took each other in their arms, because after all they had been friends, companions, and he had done all this for her. "Courage!" he said, and let her go. She walked up the street and stood before the door. She looked back then, but he was gone.

She knocked.

After a while she heard the latch rattle. The door opened. An ordinary-looking middle-aged man stood there. "What can I do for you?" he said. He did not smile, but his voice was pleasant.

"You can let me into the Great House, sir."

"Do you know the way in?" His almond-shaped

eyes were attentive, yet seemed to look at her from miles or years away.

"This is the way in, sir."

"Do you know whose name you must tell me before I let you in?"

"My own, sir. It is Irian."

"Is it?" he said.

That gave her pause. She stood silent. "It's the name the witch Rose of my village on Way gave me, in the spring under Iria Hill," she said at last, standing up and speaking truth.

The Doorkeeper looked at her for what seemed a long time. "Then it is your name," he said. "But maybe not all your name. I think you have another."

"I don't know it, sir."

After another long time she said, "Maybe I can learn it here, sir."

The Doorkeeper bowed his head a little. A very faint smile made crescent curves in his cheeks. He stood aside. "Come in, daughter," he said.

She stepped across the threshold of the Great House.

Ivory's spell of semblance dropped away like a cobweb. She was and looked herself.

She followed the Doorkeeper down a stone passageway. Only at the end of it did she think to turn back to see the light shine through the thousand leaves of the tree carved in the high door in its bone-white frame.

A young man in a grey cloak hurrying down the passageway stopped short as he approached them. He stared at Irian; then with a brief nod he went on. She looked back at him. He was looking back at her.

A globe of misty, greenish fire drifted swiftly down the corridor at eye level, apparently pursuing the young man. The Doorkeeper waved his hand at it, and it avoided him. Irian swerved and ducked down frantically, but felt the cool fire tingle in her hair as it passed over her. The Doorkeeper looked round, and now his smile was wider. Though he said nothing, she felt he was aware of her, concerned for her. She stood up and followed him.

He stopped before an oak door. Instead of knocking he sketched a little sign or rune on it with the top of his staff, a light staff of some greyish wood. The door opened as a resonant voice behind it said, "Come in!"

"Wait here a little, if you please, Irian," the Doorkeeper said, and went into the room, leaving the door wide open behind him. She could see bookshelves and books, a table piled with more books and inkpots and writings, two or three boys seated at the table, and the grey-haired, stocky man the Doorkeeper spoke to. She saw the man's face change, saw his eyes shift to her in a brief, startled gaze, saw him question the Doorkeeper, low-voiced, intense.

They both came to her. "The Master Changer of Roke: Irian of Way," said the Doorkeeper.

The Changer stared openly at her. He was not as tall as she was. He stared at the Doorkeeper, and then at her again.

"Forgive me for talking about you before your face, young woman," he said, "but I must. Master Doorkeeper, you know I'd never question your judgment, but the Rule is clear. I have to ask what moved you to break it and let her come in."

"She asked to," said the Doorkeeper.

"But—" The Changer paused.

"When did a woman last ask to enter the School?"

"They know the Rule doesn't allow them."

"Did you know that, Irian?" the Doorkeeper asked her, and she said, "Yes, sir."

"So what brought you here?" the Changer asked, stern, but not hiding his curiosity.

"Master Ivory said I could pass for a man. Though I thought I should say who I was. I will be as celibate as anyone, sir."

Two long curves appeared on the Doorkeeper's cheeks, enclosing the slow upturn of his smile. The Changer's face remained stern, but he blinked, and after a little thought said, "I'm sure—yes—It was definitely the better plan to be honest. What Master did you speak of?"

"Ivory," said the Doorkeeper. "A lad from Havnor Great Port, whom I let in three years ago, and let out again last year, as you may recall."

"Ivory! That fellow that studied with the Hand?—Is he here?" the Changer demanded of Irian, wrathily. She stood straight and said nothing.

"Not in the School," the Doorkeeper said, smiling.

"He fooled you, young woman. Made a fool of you by trying to make fools of us."

"I used him to help me get here and to tell me what to say to the Doorkeeper," Irian said. "I'm not here to fool anybody, but to learn what I need to know."

"I've often wondered why I let the boy in," said the Doorkeeper. "Now I begin to understand."

At that the Changer looked at him, and after pondering said soberly, "Doorkeeper, what have you in mind?"

"I think Irian of Way may have come to us seeking not only what she needs to know, but also what we need to know." The Doorkeeper's tone was equally sober, and his smile was gone. "I think this may be a matter for talk among the nine of us."

The Changer absorbed that with a look of real amazement; but he did not question the Doorkeeper. He said only, "But not among the students."

The Doorkeeper shook his head, agreeing.

"She can lodge in the town," the Changer said, with some relief.

"While we talk behind her back?" .

"You won't bring her into the Council Room?" the Changer said in disbelief.

"The Archmage brought the boy Arren there."

"But—But Arren was King Lebannen—"

"And who is Irian?"

The Changer stood silent, and then he said quietly, with respect, "My friend, what is it you think to do, to learn? What is she, that you ask this for her?"

"Who are we," said the Doorkeeper, "that we refuse her without knowing what she is?"

A woman," said the Master Summoner.

Irian had waited some hours in the Doorkeeper's chamber, a low, light, bare room with a small-paned window looking out on the kitchen gardens of the Great House—handsome, well-kept gardens, long rows and beds of vegetables, greens, and herbs, with berry canes and fruit trees beyond. She saw a burly, dark-skinned man and two boys come out and weed one of the vegetable plots. It eased her mind to watch their careful work. She wished she could help them at it. The waiting and the strangeness were very difficult. Once the Doorkeeper came in, bringing her a plate with cold meat and bread and scallions, and she ate because he told her to eat, but chewing and swallowing was hard work. The gardeners went away and there was nothing to watch out the window but the cabbages growing and the sparrows hopping, and now and then a hawk far up in the sky, and the wind moving softly in the tops of tall trees, on beyond the gardens.

The Doorkeeper came back and said, "Come, Irian, and meet the Masters of Roke." Her heart began to go at a carthorse gallop. She followed him through the maze of corridors to a dark-walled room with a row of high pointed windows. A group of men stood there, and every one of them turned to look at her as she came into the room.

"Irian of Way, my lords," said the Doorkeeper. They were all silent. He motioned her to come farther into the room. "The Master Changer you have met," he said. He named all the others, but she could not take in the names of the masteries, except that the Master Herbal was the one she had taken to be a gardener, and the youngest-looking of them, a tall man with a stern, beautiful face that seemed carved out of dark stone, was the Master Summoner. It was he who spoke, when the Doorkeeper was done. "A woman," he said.

The Doorkeeper nodded once, mild as ever.

"This is what you brought the Nine together for? This and no more?"

"This and no more," said the Doorkeeper.

"Dragons have been seen flying above the Inmost Sea. Roke has no Archmage, and the islands no true-crowned king. There is real work to do," the Summoner said, and his voice too was like stone, cold and heavy. "When will we do it?"

There was an uncomfortable silence, as the Doorkeeper did not speak. At last a slight, bright-eyed man who wore a red tunic under his grey wizard's cloak said, "Do you bring this woman into the House as a student, Master Doorkeeper?"

"If I did, it would be up to you all to approve or disapprove," said he.

"Do you?" asked the man in the red tunic, smiling a little.

"Master Hand," said the Doorkeeper, "she asked to enter as a student, and I saw no reason to deny her."

"Every reason," said the Summoner.

A man with a deep, clear voice spoke: "It's not our judgment that prevails, but the Rule of Roke, which we are sworn to follow."

"I doubt the Doorkeeper would defy it lightly," said one of them Irian had not noticed till he spoke, though he was a big man, white-haired, rawboned, and crag-faced. Unlike the others, he looked at her as he spoke. "I am Kurremkarmerruk," he said to her. "As the Master Namer here, I make free with names, my own included. Who named you, Irian?''

"The witch Rose of our village, lord," she answered, standing straight, though her voice came out high-pitched and rough.

"Is she misnamed?" the Doorkeeper asked the Namer.

Kurremkarmerruk shook his head. "No. But . . ."

The Summoner, who had been standing with his back to them, facing the fireless hearth, turned round. "The names witches give each other are not our concern here," he said. "If you have some interest in this woman, Doorkeeper, it should be pursued outside these walls—outside the door you vowed to keep. She has no place here nor ever will. She can bring only confusion, dissension, and further weakness among us. I will speak no longer and say nothing else in her presence. The only answer to conscious error is silence."

"Silence is not enough, my lord," said one who had not spoken before. To Irian's eyes he was very strange-looking, having pale reddish skin, long pale hair, and narrow eyes the color of ice. His speech was also strange, stiff and somehow deformed. "Silence is the answer to everything, and to nothing," he said.

The Summoner lifted his noble, dark face and looked across the room at the pale man, but did not speak. Without a word or gesture he turned away again and left the room. As he walked slowly past Irian, she shrank back from him. It was as if a grave had opened, a winter grave, cold, wet, dark. Her breath stuck in her throat. She gasped a little for air. When she recovered herself she saw the Changer and the pale man both watching her intently.

The one with a voice like a deep-toned bell looked at her too, and spoke to her with a plain, kind severity. "As I see it, the man who brought you here meant to do harm, but you do not. Yet being here, Irian, you do us and yourself harm. Everything not in its own place does harm. A note sung, however well sung, wrecks the tune it isn't part of. Women teach women. Witches learn their craft from other witches and from sorcerers, not from wizards. What we teach here is in a language not for women's tongues. The young heart rebels against such laws, calling them unjust, arbitrary. But they are true laws, founded not on what we want, but on what is. The just and the unjust, the foolish and the wise, all must obey them, or waste life and come to grief."

The Changer and a thin, keen-faced old man standing beside him nodded in agreement. The Master Hand said, "Irian, I am sorry. Ivory was my pupil. If I taught him badly, I did worse in sending him away. I thought him insignificant, and so harmless. But he lied to you and beguiled you. You must not feel shame. The fault was his, and mine."

"I am not ashamed," Irian said. She looked at them all. She felt that she should thank them for their courtesy but the words would not come. She nodded stiffly to them, turned round, and strode out of the room.

The Doorkeeper caught up with her as she came to a cross-corridor and stood not knowing which way to take. "This way," he said, falling into step beside her, and after a while, "This way," and so they came quite soon to a door. It was not made of horn and ivory. It was uncarved oak, black and massive, with an iron bolt worn thin with age. "This is the back door," the mage said, unbolting it. "Medra's Gate, they used to call it: I keep both doors." He opened it. The brightness of the day dazzled Irian's eyes. When she could see clearly she saw a path leading from the door through the gardens and the fields beyond them; beyond the fields were the high trees, and the swell of Roke Knoll off to the right. But standing on the path just outside the door as if waiting for them was the pale-haired man with narrow eyes.

"Patterner," said the Doorkeeper, not at all surprised.

"Where do you send this lady?" said the Patterner in his strange speech.

"Nowhere," said the Doorkeeper. "I let her out as I let her in, at her desire."

"Will you come with me?" the Patterner said to Irian.

She looked at him and at the Doorkeeper and said nothing.

"I don't live in this House. In any house," the Patterner said. "I live there. The Grove. —Ah," he said, turning suddenly. The big, white-haired man, Kurremkarmerruk the Namer, was standing just down the path. He had not been standing there until the other mage said "Ah." Irian stared from one to the other in blank bewilderment.

"This is only a seeming of me, a presentment, a sending," the old man said to her. "I don't live here either. Miles off." He gestured northward. "You might come there when you're done with the Patterner here. I'd like to learn more about your name." He nodded to the other two mages and was not there. A bumblebee buzzed heavily through the air where he had been.

Irian looked down at the ground. After a long time she said, clearing her throat, not looking up, "Is it true I do harm being here?"

"I don't know," said the Doorkeeper.

"In the Grove is no harm," said the Patterner. "Come on. There is an old house, a hut. Old, dirty. You don't care, eh? Stay awhile. You can see." And he set off down the path between the parsley and the bush-beans. She looked at the Doorkeeper; he smiled a little. She followed the pale-haired man.

They walked a half mile or so. The knoll rose up full in the western sun on their right. Behind them the School sprawled grey and many-roofed on its lower hill. The grove of trees towered before them now. She saw oak and willow, chestnut and ash, and tall evergreens. From the dense, sun-shot darkness of the trees a stream ran out, green-banked, with many brown trodden places where cattle and sheep went down to drink or to cross over. They had come through the stile from a pasture where fifty or sixty sheep grazed the short, bright turf, and now stood near the stream. "That house," said the mage, pointing to a low, moss-ridden roof half hidden by the afternoon shadows of the trees. "Stay tonight. You will?"

He asked her to stay, he did not tell her to. All she could do was nod.

"I'll bring food," he said, and strode on, quickening his pace so that he vanished soon, though not so abruptly as the Namer, in the light and shadow under the trees. Irian watched till he was certainly gone and then made her way through high grass and weeds to the little house.

It looked very old. It had been rebuilt and rebuilt again, but not for a long time. Nor had anyone lived in it for a long time, from the feel of it. But it was a pleasant feeling, as if those who had slept there

had slept peacefully. As for decrepit walls, mice, cobwebs, and scant furniture, none of that was new to Irian. She found a bald broom and swept out a bit. She unrolled her blanket on the plank bed. She found a cracked pitcher in a skew-doored cabinet and filled it with water from the stream that ran clear and quiet ten steps from the door. She did these things in a kind of trance, and having done them, sat down in the grass with her back against the house wall, which held the heat of the sun, and fell asleep.

When she woke, the Master Patterner was sitting nearby, and a basket was on the grass between them.

"Hungry? Eat," he said.

"I'll eat later, sir. Thank you," said Irian.

"I am hungry now," said the mage. He took a hardboiled egg from the basket, cracked, shelled, and ate it.

"They call this the Otter's House," he said. "Very old. As old as the Great House. Everything is old, here. We are old—the Masters."

"You're not," Irian said. She thought him between thirty and forty, though it was hard to tell; she kept thinking his hair was white, because it was not black.

"But I came far. Miles can be years. I am Kargish, from Karego. You know?"

"The Hoary Men!" said Irian, staring openly at him. All Daisy's ballads of the Hoary Men who sailed out of the east to lay the land waste and spit innocent babes on their lances, and the story of how Erreth-Akbe lost the Ring of Peace, and the new songs and the King's Tale about how Archmage Sparrowhawk had gone among the Hoary Men and come back with that ring—

"Hoary?" said the Patterner.

"Frosty. White," she said, looking away, embarrassed.

"Ah." Presently he said, "The Master Summoner is not old." And she got a sidelong look from those narrow, ice-colored eyes.

She said nothing.

"I think you feared him."

She nodded.

When she said nothing, and some time had passed, he said, "In the shadow of these trees is no harm. Only truth."

"When he passed me," she said in a low voice, "I saw a grave."

"Ah," said the Patterner.

He had made a little heap of bits of eggshell on the ground by his knee. He arranged the white fragments into a curve, then closed it into a circle. "Yes," he said, studying his eggshells, then, scratching up the earth a bit, he neatly and delicately buried them. He dusted off his hands. Again his glance flicked to Irian and away.

"You have been a witch, Irian?"

"No."

"But you have some knowledge."

"No. I don't. Rose wouldn't teach me. She said she didn't dare. Because I had power but she didn't know what it was."

"Your Rose is a wise flower," said the mage, unsmiling.

"But I know I have—I have something to do, to be. That's why I wanted to come here. To find out. On the Isle of the Wise."

She was getting used to his strange face now and was able to read it. She thought that he looked sad. His way of speaking was harsh, quick, dry, peaceable. "The men of the Isle are not always wise, eh?" he said. "Maybe the Doorkeeper." He looked at her now, not glancing but squarely, his eyes catching and holding hers. "But there. In the wood. Under the trees. There is the old wisdom. Never old. I can't teach you. I can take you into the Grove." After a minute he stood up. "Yes?"

"Yes," she said uncertainly.

"The house is all right?"

"Yes—"

"Tomorrow," he said, and strode off.

So for a half month or more of the hot days of summer, Irian slept in the Otter's House, which was a peaceful one, and ate what the Master Patterner brought her in his basket—eggs, cheese, greens, fruit, smoked mutton—and went with him every afternoon into the grove of high trees, where the paths seemed never to be quite where she remembered them, and often led on far beyond what seemed the confines of the wood. They walked there in silence, and spoke seldom when they rested. The mage was a quiet man. Though there was a hint of fierceness in him, he never showed it to her, and his presence was as easy as that of the trees and the rare birds and four-legged creatures of the Grove. As he had said, he did not try to teach her. When she asked about the Grove, he told her that, with Roke Knoll, it had stood since Segoy made the islands of the world, and that all magic was in the roots of the trees, and that they were mingled with the roots of all the forests that were or might yet be. "And sometimes the Grove is in this place," he said, "and sometimes in another. But it is always."

She had never seen where he lived. He slept wherever he chose to, she imagined, in these warm summer nights. She asked him where the food they ate came from; what the School did not supply for itself, he said, the farmers round about provided, considering themselves well recompensed by the protections the Masters set on their flocks and fields and orchards. That made sense to her. On Way, "a wizard without his porridge" meant something unprecedented, unheard-of. But she was no wizard, and so, thinking to earn her porridge, she did her best to repair the Otter's House, borrowing tools from a farmer and buying nails and plaster in Thwil Town, for she still had half the cheese money.

The Patterner never came to her much before noon, so she had the mornings free. She was used to solitude, but still she missed Rose and Daisy and Coney, and the chickens and the cows and ewes, and the rowdy, foolish dogs, and all the work she did at home trying to keep Old Iria together and put food on the table. So she worked away unhurriedly every morning till she saw the mage come out from the trees with his sunlight-colored hair shining in the sunlight.

Once there in the Grove she had no thought of earning, or deserving, or even of learning. To be there was enough, was all.

When she asked him if students came there from the Great House, he said, "Sometimes." Another time he said, "My words are nothing. Hear the leaves." That was all he said that could be called teaching. As she walked, she listened to the leaves when the wind rustled them or stormed in the crowns of the trees; she watched the shadows play, and thought about the roots of the trees down in the darkness of the earth. She was utterly content to be there. Yet always, without discontent or urgency, she felt that she was waiting. And that silent expectancy was deepest and clearest when she came out of the shelter of the woods and saw the open sky.

Once, when they had gone a long way and the trees, dark evergreens she did not know, stood very high about them, she heard a call—a horn blowing, a cry?—remote, on the very edge of hearing. She stood still, listening toward the west. The mage walked on, turning only when he realized she had stopped.

"I heard—" she said, and could not say what she had heard.

He listened. They walked on at last through a silence enlarged and deepened by that far call.

She never went into the Grove without him, and it was many days before he left her alone within it. But one hot afternoon when they came to a glade among a stand of oaks, he said, "I will come back here, eh?" and walked off with his quick, silent step, lost almost at once in the dappled, shifting depths of the forest.

She had no wish to explore for herself. The peacefulness of the place called for stillness, watching, listening; and she knew how tricky the paths were, and that the Grove was, as the Patterner put it, "bigger inside than outside." She sat down in a patch of sun-dappled shade and watched the shadows of the leaves play across the ground. The oakmast was deep; though she had never seen wild swine in the wood, she saw their tracks here. For a moment she caught the scent of a fox. Her thoughts moved as quietly and easily as the breeze moved in the warm light.

Often her mind here seemed empty of thought, full of the forest itself, but this day memories came to her, vivid. She thought about Ivory, thinking she would never see him again, wondering if he had found a ship to take him back to Havnor. He had told her he'd never go back to Westpool; the only place for him was the Great Port, the King's City, and for all he cared the island of Way could sink in the sea as deep as Soléa. But she thought with love of the roads and fields of Way. She thought of Old Iria village, the marshy spring under Iria Hill, the old house on it. She thought about Daisy singing ballads in the kitchen, winter evenings, beating out the time with her wooden clogs; and old Coney in the vineyards with his razor-edge knife, showing her how to prune the vine "right down to the life in it"; and Rose, her Etaudis, whispering charms to ease the pain in a child's broken arm. I have known wise people, she thought. Her mind flinched away from remembering her father, but the motion of the leaves and shadows drew it on. She saw him drunk, shouting. She felt his prying, tremulous hands on her. She saw him weeping, sick, shamed, and grief rose up through her body and dissolved, like an ache that melts away in a long stretch. He was less to her than the mother she had not known.

She stretched, feeling the ease of her body in the warmth, and her mind drifted back to Ivory. She had had no one in her life to desire. When the young wizard first came riding by so slim and arrogant, she wished she could want him; but she didn't and couldn't, and so she had thought him spell-protected. Rose had explained to her how wizards' spells worked "so that it never enters your head nor theirs, see, because it would take from their power, they say." But Ivory, poor Ivory, had been all too unprotected. If anybody was under a spell of chastity it must have been herself, for charming and handsome as he was she had never been able to feel a thing for him but liking, and her only lust was to learn what he could teach her.

She considered herself, sitting in the deep silence of the Grove. No bird sang; the breeze was down; the leaves hung still. Am I ensorcelled? Am I a sterile thing, not whole, not a woman? she asked herself, looking at her strong bare arms, the slight, soft swell of her breasts in the shadow under the throat of her shirt.

She looked up and saw the Hoary Man come out of a dark aisle of great oaks and come toward her across the glade.

He stopped in front of her. She felt herself blush, her face and throat burning, dizzy, her ears ringing. She sought words, anything to say, to turn his attention away from her, and could find nothing at all. He sat down near her. She looked down, as if studying the skeleton of a last-year's leaf by her hand.

What do I want? she asked herself, and the answer came not in words but throughout her whole body and soul: the fire, a greater fire than that, the flight, the flight burning—

She came back into herself, into the still air under the trees. The Hoary Man sat near her, his face bowed down, and she thought how slight and light he looked, how quiet and sorrowful. There was nothing to fear. There was no harm.

He looked over at her.

"Irian," he said, "do you hear the leaves?"

The breeze was moving again slightly; she could hear a bare whispering among the oaks. "A little," she said.

"Do you hear the words?"

"No."

She asked nothing and he said no more. Presently he got up, and she followed him to the path that always led them, sooner or later, out of the wood to the clearing by the Thwilburn and the Otter's House. When they came there, it was late afternoon. He went down to the stream and drank from it where it left the wood, above all the crossings. She did the same. Then sitting in the cool, long grass of the bank, he began to speak.

"My people, the Kargs, they worship gods. Twin gods, brothers. And the king there is also a god. But before that and after are the streams. Caves, stones, hills. Trees. The earth. The darkness of the earth."

"The Old Powers," Irian said.

He nodded. "There, women know the Old Powers. Here too, witches. And the knowledge is bad—eh?"

When he added that little questioning "eh?" or "neh?" to the end of what had seemed a statement it always took her by surprise. She said nothing.

"Dark is bad," said the Patterner. "Eh?"

Irian drew a deep breath and looked at him eye to eye as they sat there. " 'Only in dark the light,' " she said.

"Ah," he said. He looked away so that she could not see his expression.

"I should go," she said. "I can walk in the Grove, but not live there. It isn't my—my place. And the Master Chanter said I did harm by being here."

"We all do harm by being," said the Patterner.

He did as he often did, made a little design out of whatever lay to hand: on the bit of sand on the riverbank in front of him he set a leaf-steam, a grass-blade, and several pebbles. He studied them and re-arranged them. "Now I must speak of harm," he said.

After a long pause he went on. "You know that a dragon brought back our Lord Sparrowhawk, with the young king, from the shores of death. Then the dragon carried Sparrowhawk away to his home, for his power was gone, he was not a mage. So presently the Masters of Roke met to choose a new Archmage, here, in the Grove, as always. But not as always.

"Before the dragon came, the Summoner too had returned from death, where he can go, where his art can take him. He had seen our lord and the young king there, in that country across the wall of stones. He said they would not come back. He said Lord Sparrowhawk had told him to come back to us, to life, to bear that word. So we grieved for our lord.

"But then came the dragon, Kalessin, bearing him living.

"The Summoner was among us when we stood on Roke Knoll and saw the Archmage kneel to King Lebannen. Then, as the dragon bore our friend away, the Summoner fell down.

"He lay as if dead, cold, his heart not beating, yet he breathed. The Herbal used all his art, but could not rouse him. 'He is dead,' he said. 'The breath will not leave him, but he is dead.' So we mourned him. Then, because there was dismay among us, and all my patterns spoke of change and danger, we met to choose a new Warden of Roke, an Archmage to guide us. And in our council we set the young king in the Summoner's place. To us it seemed right that he should sit among us. Only the Changer spoke against it at first, and then agreed.

"But we met, we sat, and we could not choose. We said this and said that, but no name was spoken. And then I . . ." He paused awhile. "There came on me what my people call the *eduevanu*, the other breath. Words came to me and I spoke them. I said, *Hama Gondun!*—And Kurremkarmerruk told them this in Hardic: 'A woman on Gont.' But when I came back to my own wits, I could not tell them what that meant. And so we parted with no Archmage chosen.

"The king left soon after, and the Master Windkey went with him. Before the king was to be crowned, they went to Gont and sought our lord, to find what that meant, 'a woman on Gont.' Eh? But they did not see him, only my countrywoman Tenar of the Ring. She said she was not the woman they sought. And they found no one, nothing. So Lebannen judged it to be a prophecy yet to be fulfilled. And in Havnor he set his crown on his own head.

"The Herbal, and I too, judged the Summoner dead. We thought the breath he breathed was left from some spell of his own art that we did not understand, like the spell snakes know that keeps their heart beating long after they are dead. Though it seemed terrible to bury a breathing body, yet he was cold, and his blood did not run, and no soul was in him. That was more terrible. So we made ready to bury him. And then, by his grave, his eyes opened. He moved, and spoke. He said, 'I have summoned myself again into life, to do what must be done.' "

The Patterner's voice had grown rougher, and he suddenly brushed the little design of pebbles apart with the palm of his hand.

"So when the Windkey returned, we were nine again. But divided. For the Summoner said we must meet again and choose an Archmage. The king had had no place among us, he said. And 'a woman on Gont,' whoever she may be, has no place among the men on Roke. Eh? The Windkey, the Chanter, the Changer, the Hand, say he is right. And as King Lebannen is one returned from death, fulfilling that prophecy, they say so will the Archmage be one returned from death."

"But—" Irian said, and stopped.

After a while the Patterner said, "That art, summoning, you know, is very . . . terrible. It is . . . always danger. Here," and he looked up into the green-gold darkness of the trees, "here is no summoning. No bringing back across the wall. No wall."

His face was a warrior's face, but when he looked into the trees it was softened, yearning.

"So," he said, "now he makes you his reason for our meeting. But I will not go to the Great House. I will not be summoned."

"He won't come here?"

"I think he will not walk in the Grove. Nor on Roke Knoll. On the Knoll, what is, is so."

She did not know what he meant, but did not ask, preoccupied: "You say he makes me his reason for you to meet together."

"Yes. To send away one woman, it takes nine mages." He very seldom smiled, and when he did it was quick and fierce. "We are to meet to uphold the Rule of Roke. And so to choose an Archmage."

"If I went away—" She saw him shake his head. "I could go to the Namer—"

"You are safer here."

The idea of doing harm troubled her, but the idea of danger had not entered her mind. She found it inconceivable. "I'll be all right," she said. "So the Namer, and you— and the Doorkeeper?—"

"—do not wish Thorion to be Archmage. Also the Master Herbal, though he digs and says little." He saw Irian staring at him in amazement. "Thorion the Summoner speaks his true name," he said. "He died, eh?"

She knew that King Lebannen used his true name

openly. He too had returned from death. Yet that the Summoner should do so continued to shock and disturb her as she thought about it.

"And the . . . the students?"

"Divided also."

She thought about the School, where she had been so briefly. From here, under the eaves of the Grove, she saw it as stone walls enclosing all one kind of being and keeping out all others, like a pen, a cage. How could any of them keep their balance in a place like that?

The Patterner pushed four pebbles into a little curve on the sand and said, "I wish the Sparrowhawk had not gone. I wish I could read what the shadows write. But all I can hear the leaves say is Change, change. . . . Everything will change but them." He looked up into the trees again with that yearning look. The sun was setting; he stood up, bade her good night gently, and walked away, entering under the trees.

She sat on awhile by the Thwilburn. She was troubled by what he had told her and by her thoughts and feelings in the Grove, and troubled that any thought or feelings could have troubled her there. She went to the house, set out her supper of smoked meat and bread and summer lettuce, and ate it without tasting it. She roamed restlessly back down the streambank to the water. It was very still and warm in the late dusk, only the largest stars burning through a milky overcast. She slipped off her sandals and put her feet in the water. It was cool, but veins of sunwarmth ran through it. She slid out of her clothes, the man's breeches and shirt that were all she had, and slipped naked into the water, feeling the push and stir of the current all along her body. She had never swum in the streams at Iria, and she had hated the sea, heaving grey and cold, but this quick water pleased her, tonight. She drifted and floated, her hands slipping over silken underwater rocks and her own silken flanks, her legs sliding through waterweeds. All trouble and restlessness washed away from her in the running of the water, and she floated in delight in the caress of the stream, gazing up at the white, soft fire of the stars.

A chill ran through her. The water ran cold. Gathering herself together, her limbs still soft and loose, she looked up and saw on the bank above her the black figure of a man.

She stood straight up in the water.

"Get out!" she shouted. "Get away, you traitor, you foul lecher, or I'll cut the liver out of you!" She sprang up the bank, pulling herself up by the tough bunchgrass, and scrambled to her feet. No one was there. She stood afire, shaking with rage. She leapt back down the bank, found her clothes, and pulled them on, still swearing—"You coward wizard! You traitorous son of a bitch!"

"Irian?"

"He was here!" she cried. "That foul heart, that Thorion!" She strode to meet the Patterner as he came into the starlight by the house. "I was bathing in the stream, and he stood there watching me!"

"A sending—only a seeming of him. It could not hurt you, Irian."

"A sending with eyes, a seeming with seeing! May he be—" She stopped, at a loss suddenly for the word. She felt sick. She shuddered, and swallowed the cold spittle that welled in her mouth.

The Patterner came forward and took her hands in his. His hands were warm, and she felt so mortally cold that she came close up against him for the warmth of his body. They stood so for a while, her face turned from him but their hands joined and their bodies pressed close. At last she broke free, straightening herself, pushing back her lank wet hair. "Thank you," she said. "I was cold."

"I know."

"I'm never cold," she said. "It was him."

"I tell you, Irian, he cannot come here, he cannot harm you here."

"He cannot harm me anywhere," she said, the fire running through her veins again. "If he tries to, I'll destroy him."

"Ah," said the Patterner.

She looked at him in the starlight, and said, "Tell

me your name—not your true name—only what I
can call you. When I think of you."

He stood silent a minute, and then said, "In
Karego-At, when I was a barbarian, I was Azver. In
Hardic, that is a banner of war."

"Thank you," she said.

She lay awake in the little house, feeling the air
stifling and the ceiling pressing down on her, then
slept suddenly and deeply. She woke as suddenly
when the east was just getting light. She went to the
door to see what she loved best to see, the sky before
sunrise. Looking down from it she saw Azver the
Patterner rolled up in his grey cloak, sound asleep
on the ground before her doorstep. She withdrew
noiselessly into the house. In a little while she saw
him going back to his woods, walking a bit stiffly
and scratching his head as he went, as people do
when half awake.

She got to work scraping down the inner wall of
the house, readying it to plaster. But before the sun
was in the windows, there was a knock at her open
door. Outside was the man she had thought was a
gardener, the Master Herbal, looking solid and
stolid, like a brown ox, beside the gaunt, grim-faced
old Namer.

She came to the door and muttered some kind of
greeting. They daunted her, these Masters of Roke,

and also their presence meant that the peaceful time
was over, the days of walking in the silent summer
forest with the Patterner. That had come to an end
last night. She knew it, but she did not want to know
it.

"The Patterner sent for us," said the Master
Herbal. He looked uncomfortable. Noticing a clump
of weeds under the window, he said, "That's velver.
Somebody from Havnor planted it here. Didn't
know there was any on the island." He examined it
attentively, and put some seedpods into his pouch.

Irian was studying the Namer covertly but equally
attentively, trying to see if she could tell if he was
what he had called a sending or was there in flesh
and blood. Nothing about him appeared insubstan-
tial, but she thought he was not there, and when he
stepped into the slanting sunlight and cast no
shadow, she knew it.

"Is it a long way from where you live, sir?" she
asked.

He nodded. "Left myself halfway," he said. He
looked up; the Patterner was coming toward them,
wide awake now.

He greeted them and asked, "The Doorkeeper
will come?"

"Said he thought he'd better keep the doors,"
said the Herbal. He closed his many-pocketed pouch
carefully and looked around at the others. "But I

don't know if he can keep a lid on the anthill.''

"'What's up?" said Kurremkarmerruk. "I've been reading about dragons. Not paying attention. But all the boys I had studying at the Tower left."

"Summoned," said the Herbal, dryly.

"So?" said the Namer, more dryly.

"I can tell you only how it seems to me," the Herbal said, reluctant, uncomfortable.

"Do that," the old mage said.

The Herbal still hesitated. "This lady is not of our council," he said at last.

"She is of mine," said Azver.

"She came to this place at this time," the Namer said. "And to this place, at this time, no one comes by chance. All any of us knows is how it seems to us. There are names behind names, my Lord Healer."

The dark-eyed mage bowed his head at that, and said, "Very well," evidently with relief at accepting their judgment over his own. "Thorion has been much with the other Masters, and with the young men. Secret meetings, inner circles. Rumors, whispers. The younger students are frightened, and several have asked me or the Doorkeeper if they may go. And we'd let them go. But there's no ship in port, and none has come into Thwil Bay since the one that brought you, lady, and sailed again next day for Wathort. The Windkey keeps the Roke-wind against all. If the king himself should come, he could not land on Roke."

"Until the wind changes, eh?" said the Patterner.

"Thorion says Lebannen is not truly king, since no Archmage crowned him."

"Nonsense! Not history!" said the old Namer. "The first Archmage came centuries after the last king. Roke ruled in the kings' stead."

"Ah," said the Patterner. "Hard for the housekeeper to give up the keys when the owner comes home."

"The Ring of Peace is healed," said the Herbal, in his patient, troubled voice, "the prophecy is fulfilled, the son of Morred is crowned, and yet we have no peace. Where have we gone wrong? Why can we not find the balance?"

"What does Thorion intend?" asked the Namer.

"To bring Lebannen here," said the Herbal. "The young men talk of 'the true crown.' A second coronation, here. By the Archmage Thorion."

"Avert!" Irian blurted out, making the sign to prevent word from becoming deed. None of the men smiled, and the Herbal belatedly made the same gesture.

"How does he hold them all?" the Namer said. "Herbal, you were here when Sparrowhawk and Thorion were challenged by Irioth. His gift was as great as Thorion's, I think. He used it to use men, to control them wholly. Is that what Thorion does?"

"I don't know," the Herbal said. "I can only tell you that when I'm with him, when I'm in the Great House, I feel that nothing can be done but what has been done. That nothing will change. Nothing will grow. That no matter what cures I use, the sickness will end in death." He looked around at them all like a hurt ox. "And I think it is true. There is no way to regain the Equilibrium but by holding still. We have gone too far. For the Archmage and Lebannen to go bodily into death, and return—it was not right. They broke a law that must not be broken. It was to restore the law that Thorion returned."

"What, to send them back into death?" the Namer said, and the Patterner, "Who is to say what is the law?"

"There is a wall," the Herbal said.

"That wall is not as deep rooted as my trees," said the Patterner.

"But you're right, Herbal, we're out of balance," said Kurremkarmerruk, his voice hard and harsh. "When and where did we begin to go too far? What have we forgotten, turned our back on, overlooked?"

Irian looked from one to the other.

"When the balance is wrong, holding still is not good. It must get more wrong," said the Patterner. "Until—" He made a quick gesture of reversal with his open hands, down going up and up down.

"What's more wrong than to summon oneself back from death?" said the Namer.

"Thorion was the best of us all—a brave heart, a noble mind." The Herbal spoke almost in anger. "Sparrowhawk loved him. So did we all."

"Conscience caught him," said the Namer. "Conscience told him he alone could set things right. To do it, he denied his death. So he denies life."

"And who shall stand against him?" said the Patterner. "I can only hide in my woods."

"And I in my tower," said the Namer. "And you, Herbal, and the Doorkeeper, are in the trap, in the Great House. The walls we built to keep all evil out. Or in, as the case may be."

"We are four against him," said the Patterner.

"They are five against us," said the Herbal.

"Has it come to this," the Namer said, "that we stand at the edge of the forest Segoy planted and talk of how to destroy one another?"

"Yes," said the Patterner. "What goes too long unchanged destroys itself. The forest is forever because it dies and dies and so lives. I will not let this dead hand touch me. Or touch the king who brought us hope. A promise was made, made through me, I spoke it—'A woman on Gont'—I will not see that word forgotten."

"Then should we go to Gont?" said the Herbal, caught in Azver's passion. "Sparrowhawk is there."

"Tenar of the Ring is there," said Azver.

"Maybe our hope is there," said the Namer.

They stood silent, uncertain, trying to cherish hope.

Irian stood silent too, but her hope sank down, replaced by a sense of shame and utter insignificance. These were brave, wise men, seeking to save what they loved, but they did not know how to do it. And she had no share in their wisdom, no part in their decisions. She drew away from them, and they did not notice. She walked on, going toward the Thwilburn where it ran out of the wood over a little fall of boulders. The water was bright in the morning sunlight and made a happy noise. She wanted to cry but she had never been good at crying. She stood and watched the water, and her shame turned slowly into anger.

She came back toward the three men, and said, "Azver."

He turned to her, startled, and came forward a little.

"Why did you break your Rule for me? Was it fair to me, who can never be what you are?"

Azver frowned. "The Doorkeeper admitted you because you asked," he said. "I brought you to the Grove because the leaves of the trees spoke your name to me before you ever came here. *Irian*, they said, *Irian*. Why you came I don't know, but not by chance. The Summoner too knows that.''

"Maybe I came to destroy him.''

He looked at her and said nothing.

"Maybe I came to destroy Roke.''

His pale eyes blazed then. "Try!''

A long shudder went through her as she stood facing him. She felt herself larger than he was, larger than she was, enormously larger. She could reach out one finger and destroy him. He stood there in his small, brave, brief humanity, his mortality, defenseless. She drew a long, long breath. She stepped back from him.

The sense of huge strength was draining out of her. She turned her head a little and looked down, surprised to see her own brown arm, her rolled-up sleeve, the grass springing cool and green around her sandaled feet. She looked back at the Patterner and he still seemed a fragile being. She pitied and honored him. She wanted to warn him of the peril he was in. But no words came to her at all. She turned round and went back to the streambank by the little falls. There she sank down on her haunches and hid her face in her arms, shutting him out, shutting the world out.

The voices of the mages talking were like the voices of the stream running. The stream said its

words and they said theirs, but none of them were
the right words.

4. Irian

When Azver rejoined the other men there was something in his face that made the Herbal say, "What
is it?"

"I don't know," he said. "Maybe we should not
leave Roke."

"Probably we can't," said the Herbal. "If the
Windkey locks the winds against us . . ."

"I'm going back to where I am," Kurremkarmerruk said abruptly. "I don't like leaving myself
about like an old shoe. I'll join you this evening."
And he was gone.

"I'd like to walk under your trees a bit, Azver,"
the Herbal said, with a long sigh.

"Go on, Deyala. I'll stay here." The Herbal went
off. Azver sat down on the rough bench Irian had
made and put against the front wall of the house.
He looked upstream at her, crouching motionless on
the bank. Sheep in the field between them and the
Great House blatted softly. The morning sun was
getting hot.

His father had named him Banner of War. He had
come west, leaving all he knew behind him, and had

learned his true name from the trees of the Immanent Grove, and become the Patterner of Roke. All this year the patterns of the shadows and the branches and the roots, all the silent language of his forest, had spoken of destruction, of transgression, of all things changed. Now it was upon them, he knew. It had come with her.

She was in his charge, in his care, he had known that when he saw her. Though she came to destroy Roke, as she had said, he must serve her. He did so willingly. She had walked with him in the forest, tall, awkward, fearless; she had put aside the thorny arms of brambles with her big, careful hand. Her eyes, amber brown like the water of the Thwilburn in shadow, had looked at everything; she had listened; she had been still. He wanted to protect her and knew he could not. He had given her a little warmth when she was cold. He had nothing else to give her. Where she must go she would go. She did not understand danger. She had no wisdom but her innocence, no armor but her anger. Who are you, Irian? he said to her, watching her crouched there like an animal locked in its muteness.

His friend came back from the woods and sat down beside him on the bench awhile. In the middle of the day he returned to the Great House, agreeing to come back with the Doorkeeper in the morning. They would ask all the other Masters to meet with them in the Grove. "But *he* won't come," Deyala said, and Azver nodded.

All day he stayed near the Otter's House, keeping watch on Irian, making her eat a little with him. She came to the house, but when they had eaten she went back to her place on the streambank and sat there motionless. And he too felt a lethargy in his own body and mind, a stupidity, which he fought against but could not shake off. He thought of the Summoner's eyes, and then it was he that felt cold, cold through, though he was sitting in the full heat of the summer's day. We are ruled by the dead, he thought. The thought would not leave him.

He was grateful to see Kurremkarmerruk coming slowly down the bank of the Thwilburn from the north. The old man waded through the stream barefoot, holding his shoes in one hand and his tall staff in the other, snarling when he missed his footing on the rocks. He sat down on the near bank to dry his feet and put his shoes back on. "When I go back to the Tower," he said, "I'll ride. Hire a carter, buy a mule. I'm old, Azver."

"Come up to the house," the Patterner said, and he set out water and food for the Namer.

"Where's the girl?"

"Asleep." Azver nodded toward where she lay, curled up in the grass above the little falls.

The heat of the day was beginning to lessen and

the shadows of the Grove lay across the grass, though the Otter's House was still in sunlight. Kurremkarmerruk sat on the bench with his back against the house wall, and Azver on the doorstep.

"We've come to the end of it," the old man said out of silence.

Azver nodded, in silence.

"What brought you here, Azver?" the Namer asked. "I've often thought of asking you. A long, long way to come. And you have no wizards in the Kargish lands, I think."

"No. But we have the things wizardry is made of. Water, stones, trees, words . . ."

"But not the words of the Making."

"No. Nor dragons."

"Never?"

"Only in some very, very old tales. Before the gods were. Before men were. Before men were men, they were dragons."

"Now that is interesting," said the old scholar, sitting up straighter. "I told you I was reading about dragons. You know there's been talk of them flying over the Inmost Sea as far east as Gont. That was no doubt Kalessin taking Ged home, multiplied by sailors making a good story better. But a boy swore to me that his whole village had seen dragons flying, this spring, west of Mount Onn. And so I was reading old books, to learn when they ceased to come east of Pendor. And in one I came on your story, or something like it. That men and dragons were all one kind, but they quarreled. Some went west and some east, and they became two kinds, and forgot they were ever one.''

"We went farthest east," Azver said. "But do you know what the leader of an army is, in my tongue?''

"*Erdan*,'' said the Namer promptly, and laughed. "Drake. Dragon. . . .''

After a while he said, "I could chase an etymology on the brink of doom. . . . But I think, Azver, that that's where we are. We won't defeat him.''

"He has the advantage," Azver said, very dry.

"He does. So. . . . So therefore, admitting it unlikely, admitting it impossible—if we did defeat him—if he went back into death and left us here alive—what would we do? What comes next?''

After a long time, Azver said, "I have no idea.''

"Your leaves and shadows tell you nothing?''

"Change, change," said the Patterner. "Transformation.''

He looked up suddenly. The sheep, who had been grouped near the stile, were scurrying off, and someone was coming along the path from the Great House.

"A group of young men," said the Herbal, breathless, as he came to them. "Thorion's army.

Coming here. To take the girl. To send her away."
He stood and drew breath. "The Doorkeeper was
speaking with them when I left. I think—"

"Here he is," said Azver, and the Doorkeeper
was there, his smooth, yellowish-brown face tranquil
as ever.

"I told them," he said, "that if they went out
Medra's Gate this day, they'd never go back through
it into a house they knew. Some of them were for
turning back, then. But the Windkey and the Chanter
urged them on. They'll be along soon."

They could hear men's voices in the fields east of
the Grove.

Azver went quickly to where Irian lay beside the
stream, and the others followed him. She roused up
and got to her feet, looking dull and dazed. They
were standing around her, a kind of guard, when the
group of thirty or more men came past the little
house and approached them. They were mostly older
students; there were five or six wizard's staffs
among the crowd, and the Master Windkey led
them. His thin, keen old face looked strained and
weary, but he greeted the four mages courteously by
their titles. They greeted him, and Azver took the
word—"Come into the Grove, Master Windkey,"
he said, "and we will wait there for the others of
the Nine."

"First we must settle the matter that divides us,"
said the Windkey.

"That is a stony matter," said the Namer.

"The woman with you defies the Rule of Roke," the Windkey said. "She must leave. A boat is waiting at the dock to take her, and the wind, I can tell you, will stand fair for Way."

"I have no doubt of that, my lord," said Azver, "but I doubt she will go."

"My Lord Patterner, will you defy our Rule and our community, that has been one so long, upholding order against the forces of ruin? Will it be you, of all men, who break the pattern?"

"It is not glass, to break," Azver said. "It is breath, it is fire."

It cost him a great effort to speak.

"It does not know death," he said, but he spoke in his own language, and they did not understand him. He drew closer to Irian. He felt the warmth of her body. She stood staring, in that animal silence, as if she did not understand any of them.

"Lord Thorion has returned from death to save us all," the Windkey said, fiercely and clearly. "He will be Archmage. Under his rule Roke will be as it was. The king will receive the true crown from his hand, and rule with his guidance, as Morred ruled. No witches will defile sacred ground. No dragons will threaten the Inmost Sea. There will be order, safety, and peace."

None of the mages answered him. In the silence,

the men with him murmured, and a voice among them said, "Let us have the witch."

"No," Azver said, but could say nothing else. He held his staff of willow, but it was only wood in his hand. Of the four of them, only the Doorkeeper moved and spoke. He took a step forward, looking from one young man to the next and the next. He said, "You trusted me, giving me your names. Will you trust me now?"

"My lord," said one of them with a fine, dark face and a wizard's oaken staff, "we do trust you, and therefore ask you to let the witch go, and peace return."

Irian stepped forward before the Doorkeeper could answer.

"I am not a witch," she said. Her voice sounded high, metallic, after the men's deep voices. "I have no art. No knowledge. I came to learn."

"We do not teach women here," said the Windkey. "You know that."

"I know nothing," Irian said. She stepped forward again, facing the mage directly. "Tell me who I am."

"Learn your place, woman," the mage said with cold passion.

"My place," she said, slowly, the words dragging—"my place is on the hill. Where things are what they are. Tell the dead man I will meet him there."

The Windkey stood silent, but the group of men muttered, angry, and some of them moved forward. Azver came between her and them, her words releasing him from the paralysis of mind and body that had held him. "Tell Thorion we will meet him on Roke Knoll," he said. "When he comes, we will be there. Now come with me," he said to Irian. The Namer, the Doorkeeper, and the Herbal followed him with her into the Grove. There was a path for them. But when some of the young men started after them, there was no path.

"Come back," the Windkey said to the men.

They turned back, uncertain. The low sun was still bright on the fields and the roofs of the Great House, but inside the wood it was all shadows.

"Witchery," they said, "sacrilege, defilement."

"Best come away," said the Master Windkey, his face set and somber, his keen eyes troubled. He set off back to the School, and they straggled after him, arguing and debating in frustration and anger.

They were not far inside the Grove, and still beside the stream, when Irian stopped, turned aside, and crouched down by the enormous, hunching roots of a willow that leaned out over the water. The four mages stood on the path.

"She spoke with the other breath," Azver said.

The Namer nodded.

DRAGONFLY

"So we must follow her?" the Herbal asked.

This time the Doorkeeper nodded. He smiled faintly and said, "So it would seem."

"Very well," said the Herbal, with his patient, troubled look; and he went aside a little, and knelt to look at some small plant or fungus on the forest floor.

Time passed as always in the Grove, not passing at all it seemed, yet gone, the day gone quietly by in a few long breaths, a quivering of leaves, a bird singing far off and another answering it from even farther. Irian stood up slowly. She did not speak, but looked down the path, and then walked down it. The four men followed her.

They came out into the calm, open evening air. The west still held some brightness as they crossed the Thwilburn and walked across the fields to Roke Knoll, which stood up before them in a high dark curve against the sky.

"They're coming," the Doorkeeper said. Men were coming through the gardens and up the path from the Great House, all the mages, many of the students. Leading them was Thorion the Summoner, tall in his grey cloak, carrying his tall staff of bone-white wood, about which a faint gleam of werelight hovered.

Where the two paths met and joined to wind up to the heights of the Knoll, Thorion stopped and stood waiting for them. Irian strode forward to face him.

"Irian of Way," the Summoner said in his deep, clear voice, "that there may be peace and order, and for the sake of the balance of all things, I bid you now leave this island. We cannot give you what you ask, and for that we ask your forgiveness. But if you seek to stay here you forfeit forgiveness, and must learn what follows on transgression."

She stood up, almost as tall as he, and as straight. She said nothing for a minute and then spoke out in a high, harsh voice. "Come up onto the hill, Thorion," she said.

She left him standing at the waymeet, on the level ground, and walked up the hill path for a little way, a few strides. She turned and looked back down at him. "What keeps you from the hill?" she said.

The air was darkening around them. The west was only a dull red line, the eastern sky was shadowy above the sea.

The Summoner looked up at Irian. Slowly he raised his arms and the white staff in the invocation of a spell, speaking in the tongue that all the wizards and mages of Roke had learned, the language of their art, the Language of the Making: "Irian, by your name I summon you and bind you to obey me!"

She hesitated, seeming for a moment to yield, to come to him, and then cried out, "I am not only Irian!"

At that the Summoner ran up toward her, reaching out, lunging at her as if to seize and hold her. They were both on the hill now. She towered above him impossibly, fire breaking forth between them, a flare of red flame in the dusk air, a gleam of red-gold scales, of vast wings—then that was gone, and there was nothing there but the woman standing on the hill path and the tall man bowing down before her, bowing slowly down to earth, and lying on it.

Of them all it was the Herbal, the healer, who was the first to move. He went up the path and knelt down by Thorion. "My lord," he said, "my friend."

Under the huddle of the grey cloak his hands found only a huddle of clothes and dry bones and a broken staff.

"This is better, Thorion," he said, but he was weeping.

The old Namer came forward and said to the woman on the hill, "Who are you?"

"I do not know my other name," she said. She spoke as he had spoken, as she had spoken to the Summoner, in the Language of the Making, the tongue the dragons speak.

She turned away and began to walk on up the hill.

"Irian," said Azver the Patterner, "will you come back to us?"

She halted and let him come up to her. "I will, if you call me," she said.

She reached out and touched his hand. He drew his breath sharply.

"Where will you go?" he said.

"To those who will give me my name. In fire not water. My people."

"In the west," he said.

She said, "Beyond the west."

She turned away from him and them and went on up the hill in the gathering darkness. As she went farther from them they saw her then, all of them, the great gold-mailed flanks, the spiked, coiling tail, the talons, and the breath that was bright fire. On the crest of the knoll she paused awhile, her long head turning to look slowly round the Isle of Roke, gazing longest at the Grove, only a blur of darkness in darkness now. Then with a rattle like the shaking of sheets of brass the wide, vaned wings opened and the dragon sprang up into the air, circled Roke Knoll once, and flew.

A curl of fire, a wisp of smoke drifted down through the dark air.

Azver the Patterner stood with his left hand holding his right hand, which her touch had burnt. He looked down at the men who stood silent at the foot of the hill, staring after the dragon. "Well, my friends," he said, "what now?"

Only the Doorkeeper answered. He said, "I think we should go to our house, and open its doors."

MEMORY, SORROW AND THORN

Tad Williams

THE DRAGONBONE CHAIR (1988)
STONE OF FAREWELL (1990)
TO GREEN ANGEL TOWER (1993)

Tad Williams' trilogy takes place all across the lands
of Osten Ard, from the marshes of the southern
Wran to Yiqanuc, the icy northern home of the
trolls, but its heart is in the great high keep known
as the Hayholt.

The story begins when the death of Prester John,
the powerful human king who has been the castle's
master for many years, and who has extended his
empire out from Erkynland to rule nearly all the
nations of Osten Ard, sets in motion a falling-out
between his royal sons—a war that eventually
brings the entire world to the edge of actual extinc-
tion as the undead immortal Ineluki exploits the con-
flict for his own purposes. Among those caught up

in this vast apocalyptic struggle are the scullion Simon Snowlock; Miriamele, the daughter of one of the royal brothers; Binabik the troll; the mysterious witch woman known as Geloë; and several members of Ineluki's own Sithi—the near-immortal people he once gave his life to protect.

Five centuries before Prester John's era, in the failing days of his race's multimillennial empire, Ineluki had been the lord of the Hayholt, known then by its ancient name of Asu'a. As mortals besieged his castle, he had cast a terrible spell, a final and suicidal attempt to defeat the human upstarts. Ineluki and his followers had died in the conflagration, and Asu'a had been largely destroyed, but the mortals who survived merely rebuilt on the ruins of the Sithi's great keep, making it their own. Several mortal kings of different lands claimed the castle over the centuries, among them the Heron King, Holly King, and Fisher King of Osten Ard's legends, but none ever held it long until Prester John began his storied reign.

THE BURNING MAN

❦

Tad Williams

Years and years later, I still start up in the deepest part of night with his agonized face before me. And always, in these terrible dreams, I am helpless to ease his suffering.

I will tell the tale then, in hope the last ghosts may be put to rest, if such a thing can even happen in this place where there are more ghosts than living souls. But you will have to listen closely—this is a tale that the teller herself does not fully understand.

I will tell you of Lord Sulis, my famous stepfather.

I will tell you what the witch foretold to me.

I will tell you of the love that I had and I lost.

I will tell you of the night I saw the burning man.

* * *

Tellarin gifted me with small things, but they were not small to me. My lover brought me sweetmeats, and laughed to see me eat them so greedily.

"Ah, little Breda," he told me. "It is strange and wonderful that a mere soldier should have to smuggle honeyed figs to a king's daughter." And then he kissed me, put his rough face against me and kissed me, and that was a sweeter thing than any fig that God ever made.

But Sulis was not truly a king, nor was I his true daughter.

Tellarin was not wrong about everything. The gladness I felt when I saw my soldier or heard him whistling below the window was strange and wonderful indeed.

My true father, the man from whose loins I sprang, died in the cold waters of the Kingslake when I was very small. His companions said that a great pikefish became caught in the nets and dragged my father Ricwald to a drowning death, but others whispered that it was his companions themselves who murdered him, then weighted his body with stones.

Everyone knew that my father would have been gifted with the standard and spear of Great Thane when all the thanes of the Lake People next met.

His father and uncle had both been Great Thane before him, so some whispered that God had struck down my poor father because one family should not hold power so long. Others believed that my father's companions on the boat had simply been paid shame-gold to drown him, to satisfy the ambition of one of the other families.

I know these things only from my mother Cynethrith's stories. She was young when my father died, and had two small children—me, not yet five years old, and my brother Aelfric, two years my elder. Together we went to live in the house of my father's father because we were the last of his line, and among the Lake People of Erkynland it was blood of high renown. But it was not a happy house. Godric, my grandfather, had himself been Great Thane for twice ten years before illness ended his rule, and he had high hopes that my father would follow him, but after my father died, Godric had to watch a man from one of the other families chosen to carry the spear and standard instead. From that moment, everything that happened in the world only seemed to prove to my grandfather that the best days of Erkynland and the Lake People had passed.

Godric died before I reached seven years, but he made those years between my father's death and his own very unhappy ones for my mother, with many complaints and sharp rebukes at how she managed the household and how she raised Aelfric and me, his dead son's only children. My grandfather spent much time with Aelfric, trying to make him the kind of man who would bring the spear and standard back to our family, but my brother was small and timid— it must have been clear he would never rule more than his own household. This Godric blamed on my mother, saying she had taught the boy womanish ways.

Grandfather was less interested in me. He was never cruel to me, only fierce and short-spoken, but he was such a frightening figure, with bristling white beard, growling voice, and several missing fingers, that I could never do anything but shrink from him. If that was another reason he found little savor in life, then I am sorry for it now.

In any case, my mother's widowhood was a sad, bitter time for her. From mistress of her own house, and wife of the Great Thane, she now became only one of three grown daughters in the house of a sour old man, for one of my father's sisters had also lost her husband, and the youngest had been kept at home, unmarried, to care for her father in his dotage.

I believe that had even the humblest of fishermen courted my mother, she would have looked upon him kindly, as long as he had a house of his own and no living relatives. But instead a man who has made the entire age tremble came to call.

*   *   *

"What is he like?" Tellarin once asked me. "Tell me about your stepfather."

"He is your lord and commander." I smiled. "What can I tell you that you do not know?"

"Tell me what he says when he is in his house, at his table, what he does." Tellarin looked at me then, his long face suddenly boyish and surprised. "Hah! It feels like sacrilege even to wonder!"

"He is just a man," I told him, and rolled my eyes. Such silly things men feel about other men—that this one is so large and important, while they themselves are so small! "He eats, he sleeps, he breaks wind. When my mother was alive, she used to say that he took up more room in a bed than any three others might, because he thrashed so, and talked aloud in his sleep." I made my stepfather sound ordinary on purpose, because I did not like it when Tellarin seemed as interested in him as he was in me.

My Nabbanai soldier became serious then. "How it must have grieved him when your mother died. He must have loved her very much."

As if it had not grieved me! I resisted the temptation to roll my eyes again, and instead told him, with all the certainty of youth, "I do not think he loved her at all."

* * *

My mother once said that when my stepfather and his household first appeared across the meadowlands, riding north toward the Kingslake, it was as though the heavenly host itself had descended to earth. Trumpets heralded their approach, drawing people from every town as though to witness a pilgrimage passing, or the procession of a saint's relic. The knights' armor and lances were polished to a sparkle, and their lord's heron crest gleamed in gold thread on all the tall banners. Even the horses of the Nabban-men were larger and prouder than our poor Erkynlandish ponies. The small army was followed by sheep and cattle in herds, and by dozens and dozens of wagons and oxcarts, a train so vast that their rutted path is still visible on the face of the land three score years later.

I was a child, though, and saw none of it—not then. Within my grandfather's hall, I heard only rumors, things whispered by my aunts and my mother over their sewing. The powerful lord who had come was a Nabbanai nobleman, they reported, called by many Sulis the Apostate. He claimed that he came in peace, and wanted only to make a home for himself here beside the Kingslake. He was an exile from his own country—a heretic, some claimed, driven forth by the Lector under threat of excommunication because of his impertinent questions about the life of Usires Aedon, our blessed Ransomer. No, he had been forced from his home by the conniving of the escritors, said others. Angering a churchman is like treading on a serpent, they said.

Mother Church still had an unsolid grip on Erkynland in those days, and even though most had been baptized into the Aedonite faith, very few of the Lake People trusted the Sancellan Aedonitis. Many called it ''that hive of priests,'' and said that its chief aim was not God's work, but increasing its own power.

Many still think so, but they no longer speak ill of the church where strangers can hear them.

I know far more of these things today than I did when they happened. I understand much and much, now that I am old and everyone in my story is dead. Of course, I am not the first to have traveled this particular sad path. Understanding always comes too late, I think.

Lord Sulis had indeed fallen out with the Church, and in Nabban the Church and the state were so closely tied, he had made an enemy of the Imperator in the Sancellan Mahistrevis as well, but so powerful and important was the family of my stepfather-to-be that he was not imprisoned or executed, but instead strongly encouraged to leave Nabban. His countrymen thought he took his household to Erkynland because any nobleman could be king in that backward country—my country—but Sulis had his own reasons, darker and stranger than anyone could guess. So it was that he had brought his entire household, his knights and kerns and all their women and children, a small city's worth of folk, the shores of the Kingslake.

For all the sharpness of their swords and strength of their armor, the Nabbanai treated the Lake People with surprising courtesy, and for the first weeks there was trade and much good fellowship between their camp and our towns. It was only when Lord Sulis announced to the thanes of the Lake People that he meant to settle in the High Keep, the deserted castle on the headlands, that the Erkynlanders became uneasy.

Huge and empty, the domain only of wind and shadows, the High Keep had looked down on our lands since the beginnings of the oldest tales. No one remembered who had built it—some said giants, but some swore the fairy-folk had built it themselves. The Northmen from Rimmersgard were said to have held it for a while, but they were long gone, driven out by a dragon from the fortress the Rimmersmen had stolen from the Peaceful Ones. So many tales surrounded that castle! When I was small, one of my mother's bondwomen told me that it was now the haunt of frost-witches and restless ghosts. Many a night I had thought of it standing deserted on the windy clifftop, only a half-day's ride away, and frightened myself so that I could not sleep.

The idea of someone rebuilding the ruined fortress made the thanes uneasy, but not only for fear of waking its spirits. The High Keep held a powerful position, perhaps an impregnable one—even in their crumbling condition, the walls would be almost impossible to storm if armed men held them. But the thanes were in a difficult spot. Though the men of the Lake People might outnumber those of Sulis, the heron knights were better armed, and the discipline of Nabbanai fighting men was well known—a half-legion of the Imperator's Sea Wolves had slaughtered ten times that number of Thrithingsmen in a battle just a few years before. And Osweard, the new Great Thane, was young and untested as a war leader. The lesser thanes asked my grandfather Godric to lend his wisdom, to speak to this Nabbanai lord and see what he could grasp of the man's true intention.

So it was that Lord Sulis came to my grandfather's steading, and saw my mother for the first time.

When I was a little girl, I liked to believe that Sulis fell in love with my mother Cynethrith the moment he saw her, as she stood quietly behind her father-in-law's chair in Godric's great hall. She was beautiful, that I know—before my father died, all the people of the household used to call her Ricwald's Swan, because of her long neck and white shoulders. Her hair was a pale, pale gold, her eyes as green as the summer Kingslake. Any ordinary man would have loved her on sight. But "ordinary" must be the least likely of all the words that could be used to describe my stepfather.

When I was a young woman, and falling in love myself for the first time, I knew for certain that Sulis could not have loved her. How could anyone who loved have been as cold and distant as he was? As heavily polite? Aching then at the mere thought of Tellarin, my secret beloved, I knew that a man who acted as my stepfather had acted toward my mother could not feel anything like love.

Now I am not so sure. So many things are different when I look at them now. In this extremity of age, I am farther away, as though I looked at my own life from a high hilltop, but in some ways it seems I see things much more closely.

Sulis was a clever man, and could not have failed to notice how my grandfather Godric hated the new Great Thane—it was in everything my grandfather said. He could not speak of the weather without mentioning how the summers had been warmer and the winters shorter in the days when he himself had been Great Thane, and had his son been allowed to succeed him, he as much as declared, every day would have been the first day of Maia-month. Seeing this, Sulis made compact with the bitter old man, first by the gifts and subtle compliments he gave him, but soon in the courting of Godric's daughter-in-law as well.

While my grandfather became more and more impressed by this foreign nobleman's good sense, Sulis made his master stroke. Not only did he offer a bride price for my mother—for a widow!—that was greater than would have been paid even for the virgin daughter of a ruling Great Thane, a sizable fortune of swords and proud Nabban horses and gold plate, but Sulis told Godric that he would even leave my brother and myself to be raised in our grandfather's house.

Godric had still not given up all hope of Aelfric, and this idea delighted him, but he had no particular use for me. My mother would be happier, both men eventually decided, if she were allowed to bring at least one of her children to her new home on the headlands.

Thus it was settled, and the powerful foreign lord married into the household of the old Great Thane.

Godric told the rest of the thanes that Sulis meant only good, that by this gesture he had proved his honest wish to live in peace with the Lake People. There were priests in Sulis' company who would cleanse the High Keep of any unquiet spirits, Godric explained to the thanes—as Sulis himself had assured my grandfather—and thus, he argued, letting Sulis take the ancient keep for his own would bring our folk a double blessing.

What Osweard and the lesser thanes thought of this, I do not know. Faced with Godric's enthusiasm, with the power of the Nabbanai lord, and perhaps even with their own secret shame in the matter of my father's death, they chose to give in. Lord Sulis and his new bride were gifted with the deserted High Keep, with its broken walls and its ghosts.

Did my mother love her second husband? I cannot answer that any better than I can say what Sulis felt, and they are both so long dead that I am now the only living person who knew them both. When she first saw him in the doorway at Godric's house, he would certainly have been the light of every eye. He was not young—like my mother, he had already lost a spouse, although a decade had passed since his widowing, while hers was still fresh—but he was a great man from the greatest city of all. He wore a mantle of pure white over his armor, held at the shoulder by a lapis badge of his family's heron crest. He had tucked his helmet under his arm when he entered the hall and my mother could see that he had very little hair, only a fringe of curls at the back of his head and over his ears, so that his forehead gleamed in the firelight. He was tall and strongly made, his unwhiskered jaw square, his nose wide and prominent. His strong, heavy features had a deep and contemplative look, but also a trace of sadness—almost, my mother once told me, the sort of face she thought God Himself might show on the Day of Weighing-Out.

He frightened her and he excited her—both of these things I know from the way she spoke of that first meeting. But did she love him, then or in the days to come? I cannot say. Does it matter? So many years later, it is hard to believe that it does.

Her time in her father-in-law's house had been hard, though. Whatever her deepest feelings about him, I do not doubt that she was happy to wed Sulis.

In the month that my mother died, when I was in my thirteenth year, she told me that she believed Sulis had been afraid to love her. She never explained this—she was in her final weakness, and it was difficult for her to speak—and I still do not know what she meant.

The next to the last thing she ever said to me made even less sense. When the weakness in her chest was so terrible that she would lose the strength to breathe for long moments, she still summoned the strength to declare, "I am a ghost."

She may have spoken of her suffering—that she felt she only clung to the world, like a timid spirit that will not take the road to Heaven, but lingers ever near the places it knew. Certainly her last request made it clear that she had grown weary of the circles of this world. But I have wondered since if there might be some other meaning to her words. Did she mean that her own life after my father's death had been nothing more than a ghost-life? Or did she perhaps intend to say that she had become a shade in her own house, something that waited in the dark, haunted corridors of the High Keep for her second husband's regard to give it true life—a regard that would never come from that silent, secret-burdened man?

My poor mother. Our poor, haunted family!

I remember little of the first year of my mother's marriage to Lord Sulis, but I cannot forget the day we took possession of our new home. Others had gone before us to make our arrival as easeful as possible—I know they had, because a great tent had already been erected on the green in the Inner Bailey, which was where we slept for the first months—but to the child I was, it seemed we were riding into a place where no mortals had ever gone. I expected witches or ogres around every corner.

We came up the cliff road beside the Kingslake until we reached the curtain wall and began to circle the castle itself. Those who had gone before had hacked a crude road in the shadow of the walls, so we had a much easier passage than we would have only days earlier. We rode in a tunnel cut between the wall and forest. Where the trees and brush had not been chopped away, the Kingswood grew right to the castle's edge, striving with root and tendril to breach the great stones of the wall.

At the castle's northern gate we found nothing but a cleared place on the hillside, a desolation of tree stumps and burn-blackened grass—the thriving town of Erkynchester that today sprawls all around the castle's feet had not even been imagined. Not all the forest growth had been cleared. Vines still clung to the pillars of the shattered gatehouse, rooted in the cracks of the odd, shiny stone which was all that remained of the original gateway, hanging in great braids across the opening to make a tangled, living arbor.

"Do you see?" Lord Sulis spread his strong arms as if he had designed and crafted the wilderness himself. "We will make our home in the greatest and oldest of all houses."

As he led her across that threshold and into the ruins of the ancient castle, my mother made the sign of the Tree upon her breast.

I know many things now that I did not know on the first day we came to the High Keep. Of all the many tales about the place, some I now can say are false, but others I am now certain are true. For one thing, there is no question that the Northmen lived here. Over the years I have I found many of their coins, struck with the crude "F" rune of their King Fingil, and they also left the rotted remains of their wooden longhouses in the Outer Bailey, which my stepfather's workmen found during the course of other diggings. So I came to realize that if the story of the Northmen living here was a true one, it stood to reason that the legend of the dragon might also be true, as well as the terrible tale of how the Northmen slaughtered the castle's immortal inhabitants.

But I did not need such workaday proofs as coins or ruins to show me that our home was full of unquiet ghosts. That I learned for myself beyond all dispute, on the night I saw the burning man.

Perhaps someone who had grown up in Nabban or one of the other large cities of the south would not have been so astonished by their first sight of the High Keep, but I was a child of the Lake People.

Before that day, the largest building I had ever approached was the great hall of our town, where the thanes met every spring—a building that could easily have been hidden in any of several parts of the High Keep and then never discovered again. On that first day, it was clear to me that the mighty castle could only have been built by giants.

The curtain wall was impressive enough to a small girl—ten times my own height and made of huge, rough stones that I could not imagine being hauled into place by anything smaller than the grandest of ogres—but the inner walls, in the places where they still stood, were not just vast but also beautiful. They were shaped of shining white stone that had been polished like jewelry, the blocks of equal size to those of the outer wall but with every join so seamless that from a distance each wall appeared to be a single thing, a curving piece of ivory or bone erupting from the hillside.

Many of the keep's original buildings had been burned or torn down, some so that the men from Rimmersgard could pillage the stones to build their own tower, squat as a barrel but very tall. In any other place the Northmen's huge construction would have loomed over the whole landscape and would certainly have been the focus of my amazement. But in any other place, there would not have been the Angel Tower.

I did not know its name then—in fact, it had no name, since the shape at its very peak could scarcely be seen—but the moment I saw it I knew there could be nothing else like it on earth, and for once childish exaggeration was correct. Its entrance was blocked by piles of rubble the Northmen had never finished clearing, and much of the lower part of its façade had cracked and fallen away in some unimaginable cataclysm, so that its base was raw stone, but it still thrust into the sky like a great white fang, taller than any tree, taller than anything mortals have ever built.

Excited but also frightened, I asked my mother whether the tower might not fall down on us. She tried to reassure me, saying it had stood for a longer time than I could imagine, perhaps since before there had even been people living beside the Kingslake, but that only made me feel other, stranger things.

The last words my mother ever spoke to me were "Bring me a dragon's claw."

I thought at first that in the final hours of her illness she was wandering in her thoughts back to our early days at the castle.

The story of the High Keep's dragon, the creature who had driven out the last of the Northmen, was so old it had lost much of its power to frighten, but it was still potent to a little girl. The men of my

stepfather's company used to bring me bits of polished stone—I learned after a while that they were
shards of crumbled wall carvings from the oldest
parts of the castle—and tell me, "See, here is a broken piece of the great red dragon's claw. He lives
down in the caves below the castle, but sometimes
at night he comes up to sniff around. He is sniffing
for little girls to eat!"

The first few times, I believed them. Then, as I
grew older and less susceptible, I learned to scorn
the very idea of the dragon. Now that I am an old
woman, I am plagued by dreams of it again. Sometimes even when I am awake, I think I can sense it
down in the darkness below the castle, feel the moments of restlessness that trouble its long, deep
sleep.

So on that night long ago, when my dying mother
told me to bring her a dragon's claw, I thought she
was remembering something from our first year in
the castle. I was about to go look for one of the old
stones, but her bondwoman Ulca—what the Nabbanai called her handmaiden or body servant—told
me that was not what my mother wanted. A dragon's
claw, she explained to me, was a charm to help those
who suffered find the ease of a swift death. Ulca had
tears in her eyes, and I think she was Aedonite
enough to be troubled by the idea, but she was a
sensible young woman and did not waste time ar-

guing the right or wrong of it. She told me that the
only way I could get such a thing swiftly would
be from a woman named Xanippa who lived in the
settlement that had sprung up just outside the High
Keep's walls.

I was barely into womanhood, but I felt very
much a child. The idea of even such a short journey
outside the walls after dark frightened me, but my
mother had asked, and to refuse a deathbed request
was a sin long before Mother Church arrived to par-
cel up and name the rights and wrongs of life. I left
Ulca at my mother's side and hurried across the
rainy, nightbound castle.

The woman Xanippa had once been a whore, but
as she had become older and fatter she had decided
she needed another profession, and had developed a
name as an herbwife. Her tumbledown hut, which
stood against the keep's southeast curtain wall, overlooking the Kingswood, was full of smoke and bad
smells. Xanippa had hair like a bird's nest, tied with
what had once been a pretty ribbon. Her face might
have been round and comely once, but years and fat
had turned it into something that looked as though
it had been brought up in a fishing net. She was also
so large she did not move from her stool by the fire
during the time I was there—or on most other oc-
casions, I guessed.

Xanippa was very suspicious of me at first, but

when she found out who I was and what I wanted, and saw my face as proof, she accepted the three small coins I gave her and gestured for me to fetch her splintered wooden chest from the fireplace corner. Like its mistress, the chest had clearly once been in better condition and more prettily painted. She set it on the curve of her belly and began to search through it with a painstaking care that seemed at odds with everything else about her.

"Ah, here," she said at last. "Dragon's claw." She held out her hand to show me the curved, black thing. It was certainly a claw, but far too small to belong to any dragon I could imagine. Xanippa saw my hesitation. "It is an owl's toe, you silly girl. 'Dragon's claw' is just a name." She pointed to a tiny ball of glass over the talon's tip. "Do not pull that off or break it. In fact, do not touch it at all. Do you have a purse?"

I showed her the small bag that hung always on a cord around my neck. Xanippa frowned. "The cloth is very thin." She found some rags in one of the pockets of her shapeless robe and wrapped the claw, then dropped it into my purse and tucked it back in my bodice. As she did so, she squeezed my breast so hard that I murmured in pain, then patted my head. "Merciful Rhiap," she growled, "was I ever so young as this? In any case, be careful, my little sweetmeat. This is heartsbane on the tip of this claw, from the marshes of the Wran. If you are careless, this is one prick that will make sure you die a virgin.'' She laughed. "You don't want that, do you?''

I backed to the door. Xanippa grinned to see my fright. "And you had better give your stepfather a message from me. He will not find what he seeks among the womenfolk here or among the herbwives of the Lake People. Tell him he can believe me, because if I could solve his riddle, I would—and, oh, but I would make him pay dearly for it! No, he will have to find the Witch of the Forest and put his questions to her.''

She was laughing again as I got the door open at last and escaped. The rain was even stronger now, and I slipped and fell several times, but still ran all the way back to the Inner Bailey.

When I reached my mother's bed, the priest had already come and gone, as had my stepfather, who Ulca told me had never spoken a word. My mother had died only a short time after I left on my errand. I had failed her—had left her to suffer and die with no family beside her. The shame and sorrow burned so badly that I could not imagine the pain would ever go away. As the other women prepared her for burial, I could do nothing but weep. The dragon's claw dangled next to my heart, all but forgotten.

I spent weeks wandering the castle, lost and miserable. I only remembered the message Xanippa had given me when my mother had been dead and buried almost a month.

I found my stepfather on the wall overlooking the Kingslake, and told him what Xanippa had said. He did not ask me how I came to be carrying messages for such a woman. He did not even signify he had heard me. His eyes were fixed on something in the far distance—on the boats of the fisher-folk, perhaps, dim in the fog.

The first years in the ruined High Keep were hard ones, and not just for my mother and me. Lord Sulis had to oversee the rebuilding, a vast and endlessly complicated task, as well as keep up the spirits of his own people through the first bleak winter.

It is one thing for soldiers, in the initial flush of loyal indignity, to swear they will follow their wronged commander anywhere. It is another thing entirely when that commander comes to a halt, when following becomes true exile. As the Nabbanai troops came to understand that this cold backwater of Erkynland was to be their home forever, problems began—drinking and fighting among the soldiers, and even more unhappy incidents between Sulis' men and the local people . . . *my* people, although it was hard for me to remember that sometimes. After my mother died, I sometimes felt as if I were the

true exile, surrounded by Nabbanai names and faces and speech even in the middle of my own land.

If we did not enjoy that first winter, we survived it, and continued as we had begun, a household of the dispossessed. But if ever a man was born to endure that state, it was my stepfather.

When I see him now in my memory, when I picture again that great heavy brow and that stern face, I think of him as an island, standing by himself on the far side of dangerous waters, near but forever unvisited. I was too young and too shy to try to shout across the gulf that separated us, but it scarcely mattered—Sulis did not seem like a man who regretted his own solitude. In the middle of a crowded room his eyes were always on the walls instead of the people, as though he could see through stone to some better place. Even in his happiest and most festive moods, I seldom heard him laugh, and his swift, distracted smiles suggested that the jokes he liked best could never truly be explained to anyone else.

He was not a bad man, or even a difficult man, as my grandfather Godric had been, but when I saw the immense loyalty of his soldiers it was sometimes hard for me to understand it. Tellarin said that when he had joined Avalles' company, the others had told him of how Lord Sulis had once carried two of his wounded bondmen from the field, one trip for each, through a storm of Thrithings arrows. If that is true, it is easy to understand why his men loved him, but there were few opportunities for such obvious sorts of bravery in the High Keep's echoing halls.

While I was still young, Sulis would pat me on the head when we met, or ask me questions that were meant to show a paternal interest, but which often betrayed an uncertainty as to how old I was and what I liked to do. When I began to grow a womanish form, he became even more correct and formal, and would offer compliments on my clothes or my stitchery in the same studied way that he greeted the High Keep's tenants at Aedonmansa, when he called each man by his name—learned from the seneschal's accounting books—as he filed past, and wished each a good year.

Sulis grew even more distant in the year after my mother died, as though losing her had finally untethered him from the daily tasks he had always performed in such a stiff, practiced way. He spent less and less time seeing to the matters of government, and instead sat reading for hours—sometimes all through the night, wrapped in heavy robes against the midnight chill, burning candles faster than the rest of the house put together.

The books that had come with him from his family's great house in Nabban were mostly tomes of religious instruction, but also some military and other histories. He occasionally allowed me to look at one, but although I was learning, I still read only slowly, and could make little of the odd names and devices in the accounts of battle. Sulis had other books that he would never even let me glance at, plainbound volumes that he kept locked in wooden boxes. The first time I ever saw one go back into its chest, I found the memory returning to me for days afterward. What sort of books were they, I wondered, that must be kept sealed away?

One of the locked boxes contained his own writings, but I did not find that out for two more years, until the night of Black Fire was almost upon us.

It was in the season after my mother's death, on a day when I found him reading in the gray light that streamed into the throne room, that Lord Sulis truly looked at me for the one and only time I remember.

When I shyly asked what he was doing, he allowed me to examine the book in his lap, a beautiful illuminated history of the prophet Varris with the heron of Honsa Sulis worked in gilt on the binding. I traced with my finger an illustration of Varris being martyred on the wheel. "Poor, poor man," I said. "How he must have suffered. And all because he stayed true to his God. The Lord must have given him sweet welcome to Heaven."

The picture of Varris in his agony jumped a

little—I had startled my stepfather into a flinch. I looked up to find him gazing at me intently, his brown eyes so wide with feelings I could not recognize that for a moment I was terrified that he would strike me. He lifted his huge, broad hand, but gently. He touched my hair, then curled the hand into a fist, never once shifting that burning stare from me.

"They have taken everything from me, Breda." His voice was tight-clenched with a pain I could not begin to understand. "But I will never bend my back. Never."

I held my breath, uncertain and still a little frightened. A moment later my stepfather recovered himself. He brought his fist to his mouth and pretended to cough—he was the least able dissembler I have ever known—and then bade me let him finish his reading while the light still held. To this day I do not know who he believed had taken everything from him—the Imperator and his court in Nabban? The priests of Mother Church? Or perhaps even God and His army of angels?

What I do know was that he tried to tell me of what burned inside him, but could not find the words. What I also know is that at least for that moment, my heart ached for the man.

My Tellarin asked me once, "How could it be possible that no other man has made you his own? You are beautiful, and the daughter of a king.''

But as I have said before, Lord Sulis was not my father, nor was he king. And the evidence of the mirror that had once been my mother's suggested that my soldier overspoke my comeliness as well. Where my mother had been fair and full of light, I was dark. Where she was long of neck and limb and ample of hip, I was made small, like a young boy. I have never taken up much space on the earth—nor will I below it, for that matter. Wherever my grave is made, the digging will not shift much soil.

But Tellarin spoke with the words of love, and love is a kind of spell which banishes all sense.

"How can you care for a rough man like me?" he asked me. "How can you love a man who can bring you no lands but the farm a soldier's pension can buy? Who can give your children no title of nobility?"

Because love does not do sums, I should have told him. Love makes choices, and then gives its all.

Had he seen himself as I first saw him, though, he could have had no questions.

It was an early spring day in my fifteenth year, and the sentries had seen the boats coming across the Kingslake at first light of morning. These were no ordinary fishing craft, but barges loaded with more than a dozen men and their warhorses. Many of the castle folk had gathered to see the travelers come in and to learn their news.

After they had brought all their goods ashore on the lakefront, Tellarin and the rest of the company mounted and rode up the hill path and in through the main gates. The gates themselves had only lately been rebuilt—they were crude things of heavy, undressed timbers, but enough to serve in case of war. My stepfather had reason to be cautious, as the delegation that arrived that day was to prove.

It was actually Tellarin's friend Avalles who was called master of these men, because Avalles was an equestrian knight, one of the Sulean family nephews, but it was not hard to see which of the two truly held the soldiers' loyalty. My Tellarin was barely twenty years old on the first day I saw him. He was not handsome—his face was too long and his nose too impudent to grace one of the angels painted in my stepfather's books—but I thought him quite, quite beautiful. He had taken off his helmet to feel the morning sun as he rode, and his golden hair streamed in the wind off the lake. Even my inexperienced eye could see that he was still young for a fighting man, but I could also see that the men who rode with him admired him too.

His eyes found me in the crowd around my father and he smiled as though he recognized me, although we had never seen each other before. My blood went hot inside me, but I knew so little of the world, I did not recognize the fever of love.

My stepfather embraced Avalles, then allowed Tellarin and the others to kneel before him as each swore his fealty in turn, although I am sure Sulis wanted only to be finished with ceremony so he could return to his books.

The company had been sent by my stepfather's family council in Nabban. A letter from the council, carried by Avalles, reported that there had been a resurgence of talk against Sulis in the imperatorial court at Nabban, much of it fanned by the Aedonite priests. A poor man who held odd, perhaps irreligious beliefs was one thing, the council wrote, but when the same beliefs belonged to a nobleman with money, land, and a famous name, many powerful people would consider him a threat. In fear for my stepfather's life, his family had thus sent this carefully picked troop and warnings to Sulis to be more cautious than ever.

Despite the company's grim purpose, news from home was always welcome, and many of the new troop had fought beside other members of my stepfather's army. There were many glad reunions.

When Lord Sulis had at last been allowed to retreat to his reading, but before Ulca could hurry me back indoors, Tellarin asked Avalles if he could be introduced to me. Avalles himself was a dark, heavy-faced youth with a fledgling beard, only a few years Tellarin's elder, but with so much of the Sulean family's gravity in him that he seemed a sort of foolish old uncle. He gripped my hand too tightly and mumbled several clumsy compliments about how fair the flowers grew in the north, then introduced me to his friend.

Tellarin did not kiss my hand, but held me far more firmly with just his bright eyes. He said, "I will remember this day always, my lady," then bowed. Ulca caught my elbow and dragged me away.

Even in the midst of love's fever, which was to spread all through my fifteenth year, I could not help but notice that the changes which had begun in my stepfather when my mother died were growing worse.

Lord Sulis now hardly left his chambers at all, closeting himself with his books and his writings, being drawn out only to attend to the most pressing of affairs. His only regular conversations were with Father Ganaris, the plain-spoken military chaplain who was the sole priest to have accompanied Lord Sulis out of Nabban. Sulis had installed his old battlefield comrade in the castle's newly built chapel, and it was one of the few places the master of the High Keep would still go. His visits did not seem to bring the old chaplain much pleasure, though. Once I watched them bidding each other farewell, and as Sulis turned and shouldered his way through the wind, heading back across the courtyard to our residence, Ganaris sent a look after him that was grim and sad—the expression, I thought, of a man whose old friend has a mortal illness.

Perhaps if I had tried, I could have done something to help my stepfather. Perhaps there could have been some other path than the one that led us to the base of the tree that grows in darkness. But the truth is that although I saw all these signs, I gave them little attention. Tellarin, my soldier, had begun to court me—at first only with glances and greetings, later with small gifts—and all else in my life shrank to insignificance by comparison.

In fact, so changed was everything that a newer, larger sun might have risen into the sky above the High Keep, warming every corner with its light. Even the most workaday tasks took fresh meaning because of my feelings for bright-eyed Tellarin. My catechisms and my reading lessons I now pursued diligently, so that my beloved might not find me lacking in conversation . . . except on those days when I could scarcely attend to them at all for dreaming about him. My walks in the castle grounds became excuses to look for him, to hope for a shared glance across a courtyard or down a hallway. Even the folktales Ulca told me over our stitchery, which before had been only a means to make the time pass pleasantly, now seemed completely new. The princes and princesses who fell in love were Tellarin and me. Their every moment of suffering burned me like fire, their ultimate triumphs thrilled me so deeply that some days I feared I might actually faint.

After a time, Ulca, who guessed but did not know, refused to tell me any tale that had kissing in it.

But I had my own story by then, and I was living it fully. My own first kiss came as we were walking in the sparse, windy garden that lay in the shadow of the Northmen's tower. That ugly building was ever after beautiful to me, and even on the coldest of days, if I could see that tower, it would warm me.

"Your stepfather could have my head," my soldier told me, his cheek touching lightly against mine. "I have betrayed both his trust and my station."

"Then if you are a condemned man," I whispered, "you may as well steal again." And I pulled him back farther into the shadows and kissed him until my mouth was sore. I was alive in a way I had never been, and almost mad with it. I was hungry for him, for his kisses, his breath, the sound of his voice.

He gifted me with small things that could not be found in Lord Sulis' drab and careful household—flowers, sweetmeats, small baubles he found at the markets in the new town of Erkynchester, outside the castle gates. I could hardly bring myself to eat the honeyed figs he bought for me, not because they were too rich for his purse, although they were—he was not wealthy like his friend Avalles—but because they were gifts from him, and thus precious. To do something as destructive as eat them seemed unimaginably wasteful.

"Eat them slowly, then," he told me. "They will kiss your lips when I cannot."

I gave myself to him, of course, completely and utterly. Ulca's dark hints about soiled women drowning themselves in the Kingslake, about brides sent back to their families in disgrace, even about bastardy as the root of a dozen dreadful wars, were all ignored. I offered Tellarin my body as well as my heart. Who would not? And if I were that young girl once more, coming out of the shadows of her sorrowful childhood into that bright day, I would do it again, with equal joy. Even now that I see the foolishness, I cannot fault the girl I was. When you are young and your life stretches so far ahead of you, you are also without patience—you cannot understand that there will be other days, other times, other chances. God has made us this way. Who knows why He chose it so?

As for me, I knew nothing in those days but the fever in my blood. When Tellarin rapped at my door in the dark hours, I brought him to my bed. When he left me, I wept, but not from shame. He came to me again and again as autumn turned to winter, and as winter crept past we built a warm, secret world all our own. I could not imagine a life without him in it every moment.

Again, youth was foolish, for I have now managed to live without him for many years. There has even been much that was pleasing in my life since I lost him, although I would never have been able to believe such a thing then. But I do not think I have ever again lived as deeply, as truly, as in that first year of reckless discovery. It was as though I somehow knew that our time together would be short.

Whether it is called fate, or our weird, or the will of Heaven, I can look back now and see how each of us was set onto the track, how we were all made ready to travel in deep, dark places.

It was a night in late Feyever-month of that year when I began to realize that something more than simple distraction had overtaken my stepfather. I was reeling back down the corridor to my chamber— I had just kissed Tellarin farewell in the great hall, and was mad with the excitement of it—and I nearly stumbled into Lord Sulis. I was first startled, then terrified. My crime, I felt sure, must be as plain as blood on a white sheet. I waited trembling for him to denounce me. Instead he only blinked and held his candle higher.

"Breda?" he said. "What are you doing, girl?

He had not called me "girl" since before my mother died. His fringe of hair was astrew, as though he had just clambered from some assignation of his own, but if that was so, his stunned gaze suggested it had not been a pleasant one. His broad shoulders sagged, and he seemed so tired he could barely hold up his head. The man who had so impressed my mother on that first day in Godric's hall had changed almost beyond recognizing.

My stepfather was wrapped in blankets, but his legs showed naked below the knee. Could this be the same Sulis, I wondered, who as long as I had known him had dressed each day with the same care as he had once used to set his lines of battle? The sight of his pale bare feet was unspeakably disturbing.

"I . . . I was restless and could not sleep, sire. I wished some air."

His glance flicked across me and then began to rove the shadows again. He looked not just confused but actually frightened. "You should not be out of your chamber. It is late, and these corridors are full of . . ." He hesitated, then seemed to stop himself from saying something. "Full of draughts," he said at last. "Full of cold air. Go on with you, girl."

Everything about him made me uneasy. As I backed away, I felt compelled to say, "Good night, sire, and God bless you."

He shook his head—it almost seemed a shudder—then turned and padded away.

A few days later the witch was brought to the High Keep in chains.

I only learned the woman had been brought to the castle when Tellarin told me. As we lay curled in my bed after lovemaking, he suddenly announced, "Lord Sulis has captured a witch."

I was startled. Even with my small experience, I knew this was not the general run of pillow talk. "What do you mean?"

"She is a woman who lives in the Aldheorte forest," he said, pronouncing the Erkylandish name with his usual charming clumsiness. "She comes often to the market in a town down the Ymstrecca, east of here. She is well known there—she makes herbal cures, I think, charms away warts, nonsense such as that. That is what Avalles said, anyway."

I remembered the message that the once-whore Xanippa had bade me give my stepfather on the night my mother died. Despite the warm night, I pulled the blanket up over our damp bodies. "Why should Lord Sulis want her?" I asked.

Tellarin shook his head, unconcerned. "Because

she is a witch, I suppose, and so she is against God. Avalles and some of the other soldiers arrested her and brought her in this evening.''

''But there are dozens of root peddlers and conjure-women in the town on the lakeshore where I grew up, and more living outside the castle walls. What does he want with her?''

''My lord does not think she is any old harmless conjure-woman,'' Tellarin said. ''He has put her in one of the deep cells underneath the throne room, with chains on her arms and legs.''

I had to see, of course, as much out of curiosity as out of worry about what seemed my stepfather's growing madness.

In the morning, while Lord Sulis was still abed, I went down to the cells. The woman was the only prisoner—the deep cells were seldom used, since those kept in them were likely to die from the chill and damp before they had served a length of term instructive to others—and the guard on duty there was perfectly willing to let the stepdaughter of the castle's master gawk at the witch. He pointed me to the last cell door in the underground chamber.

I had to stand on my toes to see through the barred slot in the door. The only light was a single torch burning on the wall behind me, so the witch was mostly hidden in shadows. She wore chains on wrists and ankles, just as Tellarin had said, and sat on the floor near the back of the windowless cell, her hunched shoulders giving her the shape of a rain-soaked hawk.

As I stared, the chains rattled ever so slightly, although she did not look up. "What do you want, little daughter?" Her voice was surprisingly deep.

"Lord . . . Lord Sulis is my stepfather," I said at last, as if it explained something.

Her eyes snapped open, huge and yellow. I had already thought her shaped like a hunting bird—now I almost feared she would fly at me and tear me with sharp talons. "Do you come to plead his case?" she demanded. "I tell you the same thing I told him—there is no answer to his question. None that I can give, anyway."

"What question?" I asked, hardly able to breathe.

The witch peered at me in silence for a moment, then clambered to her feet. I could see that it was a struggle for her to lift the chains. She shuffled forward until the light from the door slot fell on her squarely. Her dark hair was cut short as a man's. She was neither pretty nor ugly, neither tall nor short, but there was a power about her, and especially in the unblinking yellow lamps of her eyes, that drew my gaze and held it. She was something I had not seen before and did not at all understand. She spoke like an ordinary woman, but she had wildness in her like the crack of distant thunder, like the flash of a deer in flight. I felt so helpless to turn away that I feared she had cast a spell upon me.

At last she shook her head. "I will not involve you in your father's madness, child."

"He is not my father. He married my mother."

Her laugh was almost a bark. "I see."

I moved uneasily from foot to foot, face still pressed against the bars. I did not know why I spoke to the woman at all, or what I wanted from her. "Why are you chained?"

"Because they fear me."

"What is your name?" She frowned but said nothing, so I tried another. "Are you really a witch?"

She sighed. "Little daughter, go away. If you have nothing to do with your stepfather's foolish ideas, then the best you can do is stay far from all this. It does not take a sorceress to see that it will not end happily."

Her words frightened me, but I still could not pull myself away from the cell door. "Is there something you want? Food? Drink?"

She eyed me again, the large eyes almost fever-bright. "This is an even stranger household than I guessed. No, child. What I want is the open sky and my forest, but that is what I will not get from you or anyone. But your father says he has need of me—he will not starve me."

The witch turned her back on me then and shuffled to the rear of the cell, dragging her chains across the stone. I climbed the stairs with my head full to aching—excited thoughts, sorrowful thoughts, frightened thoughts, all were mixed together and full of fluttering confusion, like birds in a sealed room.

My stepfather kept the witch prisoned as Marrismonth turned into Avrel and the days of spring paced by. Whatever he wished from her, she would not give it. I visited her many times, but although she was kind enough in her way, she would speak to me only of meaningless things. Often she asked me to describe how the frost on the ground had looked that morning, or what birds were in the trees and what they sang, since in that deep, windowless cell carved into the stone of the headland, she could see and hear nothing of the world outside.

I do not know why I was so drawn to her. Somehow she seemed to hold the key to many mysteries— my stepfather's madness, my mother's sorrow, my own growing fears that the foundations beneath my new happiness were unsolid.

Although my stepfather did feed her, as she had promised he would, and did not allow her to be mistreated in anything beyond the fact of her imprisonment, the witch woman still grew markedly thinner by the day, and dark circles formed like bruises beneath her eyes. She was pining for freedom, and like a wild animal kept in a pen, she was sickening from her unhappiness. It hurt me to see her, as though my own liberty had been stolen. Each time I found her more drawn and weak than the time before, it brought back to me the agony and shame of my mother's last, horrible days. Each time I left the cells, I went to a spot where I could be alone and I wept. Even my stolen hours with Tellarin could not ease the sadness I felt.

I would have hated my stepfather for what he was doing to her, but he too was growing more sickly with each day, as though he were trapped in some mirror version of her dank cell. Whatever the question was that she had spoken of, it plagued Sulis so terribly that he, a decent man, had stolen her freedom—so terribly that he scarcely slept in the nights at all, but sat up until dawn's first light reading and writing and mumbling to himself in a kind of ecstasy. Whatever the question, I began to fear that both he and the witch would die because of it.

The one time that I worked up the courage to ask my stepfather why he had imprisoned her, he stared over my head at the sky, as though it had turned an entirely new color, and told me, "This place has too many doors, girl. You open one, then another, and you find yourself back where you began. I cannot find my way."

If that was an answer, I could make no sense of it.

I offered the witch death and she gave me a prophecy in return.

The sentries on the wall of the Inner Bailey were calling the midnight watch when I arose. I had been in my bed for hours, but sleep had never once come near. I wrapped myself in my heaviest cloak and slipped into the hallway. I could hear my stepfather through his door, talking as though to a visitor. It hurt to hear his voice, because I knew he was alone.

At this hour, the only guard in the cells was a crippled old soldier who did not even stir in his sleep when I walked past him. The torch in the wall sconce had burned very low, and at first I could not see the witch's shape in the shadows. I wanted to call to her, but I did not know what to say. The bulk of the great, sleeping castle seemed to press down on me.

At last the heavy chains clinked. "Is that you, little daughter?" Her voice was weary. After a while she stood and shuffled forward. Even in the faint light, she had a terrible, dying look. My hand stole to the purse that hung around my neck. I touched my golden Tree as I said a silent prayer, then felt the curve of that other thing, which I had carried with me since the night of my mother's death. In a moment that seemed to have its own light, quite separate from the flickering glow of the torch, I pulled out the dragon's claw and extended it to her through the bars.

The witch raised an eyebrow as she took it from me. She carefully turned it over in her palm, then smiled sadly. "A poisoned owl's claw. Very appropriate. Is this for me to use on my captors? Or on myself?"

I shrugged helplessly. "You want to be free" was all I could say.

"Not with this, little daughter," she said. "At least, not this time. As it happens, I have already surrendered—or, rather, I have bargained. I have agreed to give your stepfather what he thinks he wants in exchange for my freedom. I must see and feel the sky again." Gently, she handed me back the claw.

I stared at her, almost sick with the need to know things. "Why won't you tell me your name?"

Another sad smile. "Because my true name I give to no one. Because any other name would be a lie."

"Tell me a lie, then."

"A strange household, indeed! Very well. The people of the north call me Valada."

I tried it on my tongue. "Valada. He will set you free now?"

"Soon, if the bargain is honored on both sides."

"What is it, this bargain?"

"A bad one for everyone." She saw my look. "You do not want to know, truly. Someone will die because of this madness—I see it as clearly as I see your face peering through the door."

My heart was a piece of cold stone in my breast. "Someone will die? Who?"

Her expression became weary, and I could see that standing with the weight of her shackles was an effort for her. "I do not know. And in my weariness, I have already told you too much, little daughter. These are not matters for you."

I was dismissed, even more miserable and confused. The witch would be free, but someone else would die. I could not doubt her word—no one could, who had seen her fierce, sad eyes as she spoke. As I walked back to my bedchamber, the halls of the Inner Bailey seemed a place entirely new, a strange and unfamiliar world.

My feelings for Tellarin were still astonishingly strong, but in the days after the witch's foretelling I was so beset with unhappiness that our love was more like a fire that made a cold room habitable than a sun which warmed everything, as it had been. If my soldier had not had worries of his own, he would certainly have noticed.

The cold inside me became a chill like deepest winter when I overheard Tellarin and Avalles speaking about a secret task Lord Sulis had for them, something to do with the witch. It was hard to tell what was intended—my beloved and his friend did not themselves know all that Sulis planned, and they were speaking only to each other, and not for the benefit of their secret listener. I gathered that my stepfather's books had shown him that the time for some important thing had drawn close. They would build or find some kind of fire. It would take them on a short journey by night, but they did not say—or perhaps did not yet know—on what night. Both my beloved and Avalles were clearly disturbed by the prospect.

If I had feared before, when I thought the greatest risk was to my poor, addled stepfather, now I was almost ill with terror. I could barely stumble through the remaining hours of the day, so consumed was I with the thought that something might happen to Tellarin. I dropped my beadwork so many times that Ulca took it away from me at last. When dark came, I could not get to sleep for hours, and when I did I woke up panting and shuddering from a dream in which Tellarin had fallen into flames and was burning just beyond my reach.

I lay tossing in my bed all the night. How could I protect my beloved? Warning him would do no

good. He was stubborn, and also saved his deepest
beliefs for those things he could grasp and touch, so
I knew he would put little stock in the witch's
words. In any case, even if he believed me, what
could he do? Refuse an order from Lord Sulis because of a warning from me, his secret lover? No,
it would be hopeless to try to persuade Tellarin not
to go—he spoke of his loyalty to his master almost
as often as he did of his feelings for me.

I was in an agony of fearful curiosity. What did
my stepfather plan? What had he read in those
books, that he now would risk not just his own life,
but that of my beloved as well?

Not one of them would tell me anything, I knew.
Even the witch had said that the matter was not for
me. Whatever I discovered would be by my own
hand.

I resolved to look at my stepfather's books, those
that he kept hidden from me and everyone else.
Once it would have been all but impossible, but
now—because he sat reading and writing and whispering to himself all the night's dark hours—I could
trust that when Sulis did sleep, he would sleep like
the dead.

I stole into my stepfather's chambers early the next
morning. He had sent his servants away weeks before, and the castle-folk no longer dared rap on his

doors unless summoned. The rooms were empty but for my stepfather and me.

He lay sprawled across his bed, his head hanging back over the edge of the pallet. Had I not known how moderate most of his habits were, I would have thought from his deep, rough breathing and the way he had disordered the blankets that he had drunk himself stuporous, but Sulis seldom took even a single cup of wine.

The key to the locked boxes was on a cord around his neck. As I tugged it out of his shirt with as much care as I could, I could not help but see how much happier he appeared with the blankness of sleep on him. The furrows on his brow had loosened, and his jaw was no longer clenched in the grimace of distraction that had become his constant expression. In that moment, although I hated what he had done to the witch Valada, I pitied him. Whatever madness had overtaken him of late, he had been a kind man in his way, in his time.

He stirred and made an indistinct sound. Heart beating swiftly, I hurried to draw the cord and key over his head.

When I had found the wooden chests and unlocked them, I began to pull out and examine my stepfather's forbidden books, leafing quickly and quietly through each in turn, with one ear cocked for changes in his breathing. Most of the plainbound

volumes were written in tongues I did not know, two
or three in characters I could not even recognize.
Those of which I could understand a little seemed
to contain either tales of the fairy-folk or stories
about the High Keep during the time of the Northmen.

A good part of an hour had passed when I discovered a loosely bound book titled *Writings of Var-
gellis Sulis, Seventh Lord of Honsa Sulis, Now
Master of the Sulean House in Exile.* My stepfather's careful hand filled the first pages densely, then
grew larger and more imperfect as it continued, until
the final pages seemed almost to have been scribed
by a child still learning letters.

A noise from the bed startled me, but my stepfather had only grunted and turned on his side. I
continued through the book as swiftly as I could. It
seemed to be only the most recent of a lifetime's
worth of writings—the earliest dates in the volume
were from the first year we had lived in the High
Keep. The bulk of the pages listed tasks to be performed in the High Keep's rebuilding, and records
of important judgments Sulis had made as lord of
the keep and its tenant lands. There were other no-
tations of a more personal nature, but they were brief
and unelaborated. For that terrible day almost three
years earlier, he had written only *"Cynethrith Dead
of Chest Fever. She shall be Buried on the Headland."*

The sole mention of me was a single sentence from several months before—*"Breda happy Today."* It was oddly painful to me that my somber stepfather should have noticed that and made a record of it.

The later pages held almost no mention of the affairs of either home or governance, as in daily life Sulis had also lost interest in both. Instead, there were more and more notes that seemed to be about things he had read in other books—one said *"Plesinnen claims that Mortality is consumed in God as a Flame consumes Branch or Bough. How then . . ."* with the rest smudged—one word might have been *"nails,"* and further on I could make out *"Holy Tree."* Another of his notes listed several *"Doorways"* that had been located by someone named Nisses, with explanations next to each that explained nothing at all—*"Shifted,"* read my stepfather's shaky hand beside one, or *"from a Time of No Occupation,"* or even *"Met a Dark Thing."*

It was only on the last two pages that I found references to the woman in the cell below the throne room.

"Have at Last rec'd Word of the woman called Valada," the scrawl stated. *"No one else Living North of Perdruin has Knowledge of the Black Fire. She must be Made to Speak what she knows."* Below that, in another day's even less disciplined hand,

was written, *"The Witch balks me, but I cannot have another Failure as on the Eve of Elysiamansa. Stoning Night will be next Time of Strong Voices beneath the Keep. Walls will be Thin. She will show me the Way of Black Fire or there is no other Hope. Either she will answer, or Death."*

I sat back, trying to make sense of it all. Whatever my stepfather planned, it would happen soon—Stoning Night was the last night of Avrel, only a few days away. I could not tell from his writings if the witch was still in danger—did he mean to kill her if she failed, or only if she tried to cheat his bargain with her?—but I had no doubt that this search for the thing called Black Fire would bring danger to everyone else, most importantly and most frighteningly my soldier, Tellarin. Again my stepfather murmured in his sleep, an unhappy sound. I locked his books away and stole out again.

All that day I felt distracted and feverish, but this time it was not love that fevered me. I was terrified for my lover and fearful for my stepfather and the witch Valada, but what I knew and how I had discovered it I could not tell to anyone. For the first time since my soldier had kissed me, I felt alone. I was full up with secrets, and unlike Sulis, had not even a book to which they could be confided.

I would follow them, I decided at last. I would

follow them into the place my stepfather spoke of, the place beneath the keep where the walls were thin and the voices strong. While they searched for the Black Fire, I would watch for danger. I would protect them all. I would be their angel.

Stoning Night came around at last.

Even had I not read my stepfather's writings, I think I would have known that the hour had come in which they meant to search for Black Fire, because Tellarin was so distracted and full of shadows. Although he admitted nothing to me as we lay together in my bedchamber, I could feel that he was anxious about what would happen that night. But he was bound to my stepfather by honor and blood, and had no choice.

He snapped at me when I kissed his ear and curled my fingers in his hair. "Give a man some peace, girl."

"Why are you a man and I am a girl?" I teased him, pretending a lightness I did not truly feel. "Is there such a difference in our ages? Have I not given to you already that which makes me a woman?"

My soldier was short-tempered and did not hear the love in what I said. "Anybody who will not leave off when she is asked proves herself still a child. And I am a man because I wear a soldier's badge, and because if my master asks, I must give my life.''

Tellarin was five years my elder, and in those long-ago days I was almost as impressed by the difference as he was, but I think now that all men are younger than their women, especially when their honor has been touched.

As he stared at the ceiling his face turned from angry to solemn, and I knew he was thinking of what he must do that night. I was frightened too, so I kissed him again, softly this time, and apologized.

When he had gone, full of excuses meant to hide his actual task, I prepared for my own journey. I had hidden my thickest cloak and six fat candles where Ulca and the other serving-women would not find them. When I was dressed and ready, I touched my mother's golden Tree where it lay against my heart, and said a prayer for the safety of all who would go with me into darkness.

Stoning Night—the last night of Avrel, on the eve of Maia-month, the black hours when tales say spirits walk until driven back to their graves by dawn and the crowing cock. The High Keep lay silent around me as I followed my beloved and the others through the dark. It did not feel so much that the castle slept as that the great keep held its breath and waited.

THE BURNING MAN

There is a stairwell beneath the Angel Tower, and that was where they were bound. I learned of it for the first time on that night, as I stood wrapped in my dark cloak, listening from the shadows of the wall opposite the tower. Those I followed were four—my stepfather, Tellarin and his friend Avalles, and the woman Valada. Despite the bargain she had made, the witch's arms were still chained. It saddened me to see her restrained like an animal.

The workmen who had been repairing the tower had laid a rough wooden floor over the broken stones of the old one—perhaps to make certain no one fell down one of the many holes, perhaps simply to close off any openings into the castle's deepest places. Some had even suggested that all the old castle floor should be sealed under brick, so that nothing would ever come up that way to trouble the sleep of God-fearing folk.

Because of this wooden floor, I waited a long time before following them through the tower's outer portal, knowing it would take some time for my stepfather and his two bondmen to shift the boards. As I lurked in the shadows by the tower wall while the wind prowled the Inner Bailey, I thought about the Angel who stood at the top of the tower, a figure black with the grime of centuries that no rain could wash away, tipped sideways as though about to lose her balance and fall. Who was she? One of the blessed saints? Was it an omen—did she watch over me as I meant to look over Tellarin and the rest? I looked up, but the tower's high top was invisible in the night.

At last I tried the latch of the tower door and found the bolt had not been shot. I hoped that it meant the Angel was indeed looking out for me.

Inside the tower the moonlight ended, so while still in the doorway I lit my first candle from the hidden touchwood, which had nearly burnt down. My footsteps seemed frighteningly loud in the stony entry hall, but no one appeared from the shadows to demand my business in that place. I heard no sound of my stepfather or the rest.

I paused for a moment in front of the great, upward-winding staircase, and could not help but wonder what the workmen would find when they cleared the rubble and reached the top—as I still wonder all these years later, with the painstaking work yet unfinished. I suppose I will not see it in my lifetime. Will they discover treasures left by the fairy-folk? Or perhaps only those ancient beings' frail bones?

Even were it not for the things that happened on that fateful night, still the Angel Tower would haunt me, as it haunts this great keep and all the lands beneath its long shadow. No mortals, I think, will ever know its all its secrets.

The Burning Man

Once, long ago, I dreamed that my stepfather gave me the Angel herself to clean, but that no matter how I tried, I could not scrub the black muck from her limbs and face. He told me that it was not my fault, that God would have lent me the strength if He truly wanted the Angel's face to be seen, but I still wept at my failure.

I moved from the entry hall to a place where the floor fell away in great broken shards, and tried to imagine what could smash stones so thoroughly and yet leave the tower itself still standing. It was not easy to follow where my stepfather and my beloved had already gone, but I climbed down the rubble, leaning to set my candle before me so that I could have both my hands free. I wished, not for the last time, that I had worn something other than my soft shoes. I clambered down and down, hurting my feet, tearing my dress in several places, until I reached the jumble of smaller broken stones which was the floor, at least a half dozen times my own height below the level of the Inner Bailey. In the midst of this field of shards gaped a great, black hole bigger than the rest, a jagged mouth that waited to swallow me down. As I crunched closer to it, I heard what I knew must be the voices of the others floating up from the depths, although they sounded strange to me.

More stones had been pushed aside to reveal the entrance to the stairwell, a lip of shiny white with steps inside it that vanished into shadow. Another voice floated up, laughing. It belonged to no one I knew.

Even with all that had happened in the previous days, I had never yet felt so frightened, but I knew Tellarin was down there in the dark places. I made the sign of the Tree upon my breast, then stepped onto the stairway.

At first I could find no trace of them.

As I descended, the light of my single candle served only to make the stairwell seem more than ever like a shadowy throat waiting to swallow me, but fear alone could not keep me from my beloved—if anything, it sped my steps. I hurried downward until it seemed I must have gone as far beneath the castle as the Angel Tower loomed above it, but still I had not caught up with them.

Whether it was a trick of sound, or of the winds that are said to blow through the caves of the Kingslake cliffs, I continued to hear unfamiliar voices. Some seemed so close that if I had not had a candle, I would have been certain I could reach out and touch the person who whispered to me, but the flickering light showed me that the stairwell was empty. The voices babbled, and sometimes sang, in a soft, sad tongue I did not understand or even recognize.

I knew I should be too frightened to remain, that I should turn and flee back to moonlight and clean air, but although the bodiless murmurs filled me with dismay, I felt no evil in them. If they were ghosts, I do not think they even knew I was there. It was as though the castle talked to itself, like an old man sitting beside the fire, lost in the memories of days long past.

The stairwell ended in a wide landing with open doorways at either end, and I could not help thinking of the doorways mentioned in my stepfather's book. As I paused to consider which way I should go, I examined the carvings on the walls, delicate vines and flowers whose type I had never seen before. Above one doorframe a nightingale perched on a tree bough. Another tree bough was carved above the far doorway—or rather, I saw as I moved my candle, they were both boughs from one single tree, which had been carved directly above me, spreading across the ceiling of the stairwell as though I myself were the tree's trunk. On the bough above the second doorway twined a slender serpent. I shuddered, and began to move toward the nightingale door, but at that moment words floated up out of the darkness.

"*. . . if you have lied to me. I am a patient man, but . . .*"

It was my stepfather, and even if I had not recognized his faint voice, I would have known him by the words, for that is what he always said. And he spoke the truth—he *was* a patient man. He had always been like one of the stones of the hilltop rings, cool and hard and in no hurry to move, growing warm only after the sun of an entire summer has beat upon him. I had sometimes felt I would like to break a stick upon him, if only to make him turn and truly look at me.

Only once did he ever do that, I had believed—on that day when he told me that "they" had taken everything from him. But now I knew he had looked at me another time, perhaps seen me smile on a day when my lover had given me a gift or a kiss, and had written in his book, *"Breda happy Today."*

My stepfather's words had drifted up through the other doorway. I lit another candle and place it on top of the first, which had burned almost to the holder, then followed the voice of Sulis through the serpent door.

Downward I went, and downward still farther—what seemed a journey of hours, through sloping, long-deserted corridors that twisted like yarn spilled from a sack. The light of the candles showed me stone that, although I knew it was even more ancient, seemed newer and brighter than that which I had seen farther above. In places the passageways opened into rooms choked with dirt and rubble, but which must have been massive, with ceilings as high as any of the greatest halls I have ever heard of in Nabban. The carvings I could see were so delicate, so perfect, that they might have been the actual things of nature—birds, plants, trees—frozen into stone by the sort of magical spells that so often had been part of my mother's and Ulca's stories.

It was astonishing to think that this entire world had lain in its tomb of earth below us as long as we had lived in the High Keep, and for generations before that. I knew I was seeing the ancient home of the fairy-folk. With all the stories, and even with the evidence of the tower itself, I had still never imagined they would have such a way with stone, to make it froth like water and shimmer like ice, to make it stretch overhead in slender arcs like the finest branches of a willow tree. Had the Northmen truly killed them all? For the first time, I understood something of what this meant, and a deep, quiet horror stole over me. The creators of all this beauty, slaughtered, and their houses usurped by their slayers—no wonder the darkness was full of unquiet voices. No wonder the High Keep was a place of haunted sadness for everyone who lived in it. The castle of our day was founded on ancient murder. It was built on death.

It pulled at me, that thought. It became tangled in

my mind with the memory of my stepfather's distracted stare, of the witch in chains. Good could not come from evil, I felt sure. Not without sacrifice. Not without blood and atonement.

My fear was growing again.

The Peaceful Ones might have been gone, but I was learning that their great house remained lively.

As I hurried downward, following the tracks of my stepfather and his company in the dust of centuries, I found suddenly that I had taken a wrong turning. The passage ended in a pile of broken stone, but when I returned to the last cross-corridor, there was no sign of footprints, and the place itself was not familiar, as though the ruins themselves had shifted around me. I closed my eyes, listening for the sound of Tellarin's voice, for I felt sure that my heart would be able to hear him through all the stone in Erkynland. But nothing came to me but the ghost-murmurs, which blew in like an autumn breeze, full of sighing, rustling nonsense.

I was lost.

For the first time it became clear to me what a foolish thing I had done. I had gone into a place where I should not be. Not one person knew I was there, and when my last candle burned out, I would be lost in the darkness.

Tears started in my eyes, but I wiped them away.

Weeping had not brought my father back, or my mother. It would do me no good now.

I did my best to retrace my steps, but the voices flittered around me like invisible birds, and before long I was wandering blindly. Confused by the noises in my head and by the flickering shadows, twice I almost tumbled into great crevices in the passageway floor. I kicked a stone into one that fell without hitting anything until I could not bear to listen any longer.

The darkness seemed to be closing on me, and I might have been lost forever—might have become another part of the whispering chorus—but by luck or accident or the hand of fate, I made a turning into a corridor I did not recognize and found myself standing at the lip of another stairwell, listening to the voice of the witch Valada drift up from the deeps.

"*. . . not an army or a noble household that you can order about, Lord Sulis. Those who lived here are dead, but the place is alive. You must take what you are given . . .*"

It is as though she had heard my very thoughts. Even as I shuddered to hear my forebodings spoken aloud, I hurried toward the sound, terrified that if it faded I would never again hear a familiar voice.

What seemed another hour went by, although I had been so long in the haunted dark that I was no judge.

My lover and the rest seemed almost to have become phantoms themselves, floating ahead of me like dandelion seeds, always just beyond my reach.

The stairs continued to curl downward, and as my third and fourth candles burned I could see glimpses of the great spaces through which we all descended, level upon level, as if making a pilgrimage down the tiers of Heaven. At times, as the candles flickered on the wooden base, I thought I could see even more. From the corner of my eye the ruins seemed to take on a sort of life. There were moments when the ghost-voices swelled and the shadows seem to take on form. If I half-closed my eyes, I could almost see these bleak spaces full of bright, laughing folk.

Why did the Northmen kill such beauty? And how could a people who built such a place be defeated by any mortals, however bloodthirsty and battle-hungry?

A light bloomed in the depths, red and yellow, making the polished stone of the stairwell seem to quiver. For a moment I thought it only another wisp of my imagination, but then, from so close it seemed we could kiss if we wished, I heard my beloved's voice.

"Do not trust her, sire," Tellarin said, sounding more than a little fearful. *"She is lying again."*

Intensely happy, but with my caution abruptly restored, I shaded the candle with my palm and hurried down the stairs as quietly as I could. As their voices grew louder, and I saw that the light blooming in the darkness came from their torches, I pinched the flame to extinguish my candle completely. However glad I was to find them, I guessed they would not feel the same about me.

I crept closer to the light, but could not see Tellarin and the others because something like a cloud of smoke blocked my view. It was only when I reached the base of the curving stair and stepped silently onto the floor of the great chamber that I could actually see the four shapes.

They stood in the middle of a room so cavernous that even the torches my lover and Avalles held could not carry light to its highest corners. Before them loomed the thing I had thought was smoke. I still could not see it clearly, despite the torch flames burning only an arm's length from it, but now it seemed a vast tree with black leaves and trunk. A shadow cloaked it and hid all but the broadest outline, a dark shroud like the mist that hid the hills on a winter morning, but it was not mist in which the tree-shape crouched, I felt sure. It was pure Darkness.

"You must decide whether to listen to me or a young soldier," the witch was saying to my stepfather. "I will tell you again—if you cut so much as a leaf, you will mark yourselves as ravagers and it will not go well with you. Can you not feel that?''

"And I think Tellarin is right," Avalles proclaimed, but his voice was less sure than his words. "She seeks to trick us."

My stepfather looked from the tree-shadow to the witch. "If we may not take any wood, then why have you brought us here?'' he asked slowly, as though it cost great effort just to speak.

I could hear the sour smile in Valada's answer. "You have held me captive in your damp pile of stones for two moons, seeking my help with your mad questions. If you do not believe that I know what I know, why did you shackle me and bring me here?''

"But the wood . . . ?''

"I did not say you could not take anything to burn, I said that you would be a fool to lift axe or knife to the Great Witchwood. There is deadfall beneath, if you are bold enough to search for it.''

Sulis turned to Avalles. "Go and gather some dead wood, nephew.''

The young knight hesitated, then handed his torch to my stepfather and walked a little unsteadily toward the great dark tree. He bent beneath the outer branches and vanished from sight. After an interval of silence, Avalles stumbled back out again.

"It is . . . it is too dark to see," he panted. His

eyes were showing white around the edges. "And there is something in there—an animal, perhaps. I . . . I can feel it breathing." He turned to my stepfather. "Tellarin's eyes are better than mine . . ."

No! I wanted to scream. The tree-thing sat and waited, cloaked in shadows no torchlight could penetrate. I was ready to burst from hiding and beg my beloved not to go near it, but as if he had heard my silent cry, Lord Sulis cursed and thrust the torch back into Avalles' hand.

"By Pelippa and her bowl!" my stepfather said. "I will do it myself."

Just before he stepped through the branches, I thought I heard the leaves whisper, although there was no wind in the chamber. The quiet hiss and rattle grew louder, perhaps because my stepfather was forcing his way beneath the thick branches. Long moments trudged past; then the rustling became even more violent. At last Sulis emerged, staggering a little, with what seemed a long bar of shadow clasped under each arm. Tellarin and Avalles stepped forward to help him but he waved them off, shaking his head as though he had been dealt a blow. Even in the dark room, I could see that he had gone very pale.

"You spoke the truth, Valada," he said. "No axe, no knife."

While I watched, he bade Avalles and my beloved

make a ring on the ground from the broken stones that littered the chamber. He crossed the two pieces of wood he had gathered in the center of the circle, then he used kindling from a pouch on his belt and one of the torches to set the witchwood alight. As the strange fire sputtered into life, the room seemed to become darker, as though the very light from the torches bent toward the firepit and was sucked away. The flames began to rise.

The rustle of the shadowy tree stilled. Everything grew silent—even the flames made no sound. My heart pounded as I leaned closer, almost forgetting to keep myself hidden. It was indeed a Black Fire that burned now in that deep, lost place, a fire that flickered like any blaze, and yet whose flames were wounds in the very substance of the world, holes as darkly empty as a starless sky.

It is hard to believe, but that is what I saw. I could look through the flames of the Black Fire, not to what stood on the other side of the fire, but to *some-where else*—into nothingness at first, but then color and shape began to expand outward in the space above the firepit, as though something turned the very air inside out.

A face appeared in the fire. It was all I could do not to cry out.

The stranger surrounded by the black flames was like no man I had ever seen. The angles of his face were all somehow wrong, his chin too narrow, the large eyes slanted upward at the corners. His hair was long and white, but he did not look old. He was naked from the waist up, and his pale, glossy skin was marked with dreadful scars, but despite the flames in which he lay, his burns seemed old rather than new.

The Black Fire unshaped even the darkness. All that was around it bent, as though the very world grew stretched and shivery as the reflection on a bubble of river water.

The burning man seemed to slumber in the flames, but it was a horribly unquiet sleep. He pitched and writhed, even brought his hands up before his face, as though to protect himself from some terrible attack. When his eyes at last opened, they were dark as shadow itself, staring at things that I could not see, at shadows far beyond the fire. His mouth stretched in a silent, terrible scream, and despite his alien aspect, despite being so frightened I feared my heart would stop, I still ached to see his suffering. If he was alive, how could his body burn and burn without being consumed? If he was a ghost, why had death not ended his pain?

Tellarin and Avalles backed away from the firepit, wide-eyed and fearful. Avalles made the sign of the Tree.

My stepfather looked at the burning man's writhing mouth and blind eyes, then turned to the witch Valada. "Why does he not speak to us? Do something!"

She laughed her sharp laugh. "You wished to meet one of the Sithi, Lord Sulis—one of the Peaceful Ones. You wished to find a doorway, but some doorways open not on elsewhere, but elsewhen. The Black Fire has found you one of the Fair Folk in his sleep. He is dreaming, but he can hear you across the centuries. Speak to him! I have done what I promised."

Clearly shaken, Sulis turned to the man in the flames. "You!" he called. "Can you understand me?"

The burning man writhed again, but now his dark unseeing eyes turned in my stepfather's direction. "Who is there?" he asked, and I heard his voice in the chamber of my skull rather than in my ears. "Who walks the Road of Dreams?" The apparition lifted a hand as though he might reach through the years and touch us. For a moment, astonishment pushed the agony from his odd face. "You are mortals! But why do you come to me? Why do you disturb the sleep of Hakatri of the House of Year-Dancing?"

"I am Sulis." The tremble in my stepfather's voice made him seem an old, old man. "Called by some 'the Apostate.' I have risked everything I own—have spent years studying—to ask a question which only the Peaceful Ones can answer. Will you help me?"

The burning man did not seem to be listening. His mouth twisted again, and this time his cry of pain had sound. I tried to stop my ears, but it was already inside my head. "Ah, it burns!" he moaned. "Still the worm's blood burns me—even when I sleep. Even when I walk the Road of Dreams!"

"The worm's blood . . . ?" My stepfather was puzzled. "A dragon? What are you saying?"

"She was like a great black snake," Hakatri murmured. "My brother and I, we followed her into her deep place and we fought her and slew her, but I have felt her scorching blood upon me and will never be at peace again. By the Garden, it pains me so!" He made a choking sound, then fell silent for a moment. "Both our swords bit," he said, and it was almost a chant, a song, "but my brother Ineluki was the fortunate one. He escaped a terrible burning. Black, black it was, that ichor, and hotter than even the flames of Making! I fear death itself could not ease this agony . . ."

"Be silent!" Sulis thundered, full of rage and misery. "Witch, is this spell for nothing? Why will he not listen to me?"

"There is no spell, except that which opens the doorway," she replied. "Hakatri perhaps came to that doorway because of how the dragon's blood burned him—there is nothing else in all the world like the blood of the great worms. His wounds keep him always close to the Road of Dreams, I think. Ask him your question, Nabban-man. He is as like to answer it as any other of the immortals you might have found.''

I could feel it now—could feel the weird that had brought us here take us all in its grip. I held my breath, caught between a terror that blew like a cold wind inside my head, that screamed at me to leave Tellarin and everything else and run away, and a fierce wondering about what had brought my stepfather to this impossibly strange meeting.

Lord Sulis tilted his chin down toward his chest for a moment, as though now that the time had come, he was uncertain of what he wished to say. At last he spoke, quaveringly at first, but with greater strength as he went on.

''Our Church teaches us that God appeared in this world, wearing the form of Usires Aedon, performing many miracles, singing up cures for the sick and lame, until at last the Imperator Crexis caused him to be hung from the Execution Tree. Do you know of this, Hakatri?''

The burning man's blind eyes rolled toward Sulis again. He did not answer, but he seemed to be listening.

"The promise of Aedon the Ransomer is that all who live will be gathered up—that there will be no death," my stepfather continued. "And this is proved because he was God made flesh in this world, and that is proved because of the miracles he performed. But I have studied much about your own people, Hakatri. Such miracles as Usires the Aedon performed could have been done by one of your Sithi people, or even perhaps by one of only half-immortal blood." His smile was as bleak as a skull's. "After all, even my fiercest critics in Mother Church agree that Usires had no human father."

Sulis bowed his head again for a moment, summoning up words or strength. I gasped for air—I had forgotten to breathe. Avalles and Tellarin still stared, their fear now mixed with astonishment, but the witch Valada's face was hidden from me in shadow.

"Both my wives have been taken from me by death, both untimely," my stepfather said. "My first wife gave me a son before she died, a beautiful boy named Sarellis who died himself in screaming pain because he stepped on a horseshoe nail—a nail!—and caught a death fever. Young men I have commanded were slaughtered in the hundreds, the thousands, their corpses piled on the battlefield like the husks of locusts, and all for a small stretch of land here or there, or sometimes merely over words.

My parents are dead, too, with too much unspoken between us. Everyone I ever truly loved has been stolen from me by death.''

His hoarse voice had taken on a disturbing force, a cracked power, as though he meant to shout down the walls of Heaven itself.

''Mother Church tells me to believe that I will be reunited with them,'' he said. ''They preach to me, saying, 'See the works of Usires our Lord and be comforted, for his task was to show death should hold no fear,' they told me. But I cannot be sure—I cannot simply trust! Is the Church right? Will I see those I love again? Will we all live on? The masters of the Church have called me a heretic and declared me apostate because I would not give up doubting the divinity of the Aedon, but I must know! Tell me, Hakatri, was Usires of your folk? Is the story of his godhood simply a lie to keep us happy, to keep priests fat and rich?'' He blinked back tears, his stolid face transfigured by rage and pain. ''Even if God should damn me forever to hell for it, still I must know—*is our faith a lie?*''

He was shaking so badly now that he took a staggering step back from the fire and almost fell. No one moved except the man in the flames, who followed Sulis with his blank, dark eyes.

I realized that I was weeping too, and silently rubbed the tears away. Seeing my stepfather's true and terrible pain was like a knife twisted inside me, and yet I was angry too. All for this? For such unknowable things he left my mother lonely, and now had nearly destroyed his own life?

After a long time in which all was silent as the stone around us, Hakatri said slowly, "Always you mortals have tortured yourselves." He blinked, and the way his face moved was so alien that I had to turn away and then look at him anew before I could understand what he said. "But you torture yourself most when you seek answers to things that have none."

"No answers?" Sulis was still shaking. "How can that be?"

The burning man raised his long-fingered hands in what I could only guess was a gesture of peace. "Because that which is meant for mortals is not given to the Zida'ya to know, any more than you can know of our Garden, or where we go when we leave this place.

"Listen to me, mortal. What if your messiah were indeed one of the Dawn Children—would that prove somehow that your God had not chosen that to happen? Would that prove your Ransomer's words any the less true?" Hakatri shook his head with the weird, foreign grace of a shorebird.

"Just tell me whether Usires was one of your folk," Sulis demanded raggedly. "Spare me your philosophies and tell me! For I am burning too! I have not been free of the pain in years!''

As the echoes of my stepfather's cry faded, the fairy-lord in his ring of black flames paused, and for the first time he seemed truly to see across the gulf. When he spoke, his voice was full of sadness.

''We Zida'ya know little of the doings of mortals, and there are some of our own blood who have fallen away from us, and whose works are hidden from us as well. I do not think your Usires Aedon was one of the Dawn Children, but more than that I cannot tell you, mortal man, nor could any of my folk.'' He lifted his hands again, weaving the fingers in an intricate, incomprehensible gesture. ''I am sorry.''

A great shudder ran through the creature called Hakatri then—perhaps the pain of his burns returning, a pain that he had somehow held at bay while he listened to my stepfather speak. Sulis did not wait to hear more, but stepped forward and kicked the witchwood fire into a cloud of whirling sparks, then dropped to his knees with his hands over his face.

The burning man was gone.

After a march of silence that seemed endless, the witch called out, ''Will you honor your bargain with me now, Lord Sulis? You said that if I brought you to one of the immortals, you would free me.'' Her voice was flat, but there was still a gentleness to it that surprised me.

My stepfather's reply, when it came, was choked and hard to understand. He waved his hand. "Take off her chains, Avalles. I want nothing more from her."

In the midst of this great bleak wilderness of sorrow, I felt a moment of sharp happiness as I realized that despite my foreboding, the witch, my beloved, even my tortured stepfather, all would survive this terrible night. As Avalles began to unlock the witch's shackles, shivering so that he could hardly hold the key, I had a moment to dream that my uncle would return to health, that he would reward my Tellarin for his bravery and loyalty, and that my beloved and I would make a home for ourselves somewhere far away from this ghost-riddled, wind-swept headland.

My stepfather let out a sudden, startling cry. I turned to see him fall forward onto his belly, his body ashake with weeping. This seizure of grief in stern, quiet Sulis was in some ways the most frightening thing I had yet seen in that long, terrifying night.

Then, even as his cry rebounded in the invisible upper reaches of the chamber and provoked a dim rustle in the leaves of the shadowy tree, something else seized my attention. Two figures were struggling where the witch had stood. At first I thought Avalles and the woman Valada were fighting, but then I saw that the witch had stepped back and was watching the battle, her bright eyes wide with surprise. Instead, it was Avalles and Tellarin who were tangled together, their torches fallen from their hands. Shocked, helpless with surprise, I watched them tumble to the ground. A moment later a dagger rose and fell, then the brief struggle was ended.

I screamed "Tellarin!" and rushed forward.

He stood, brushing the dust from his breeks, and stared at me as I came out of the shadows. The end of his knife was blackened with blood. He had a stillness about him that might have been fear, or simply surprise.

"Breda? What are you doing here?"

"Why did he attack you?" I cried. Avalles lay twisted on the ground in a spreading puddle of black. "He was your friend!"

He said nothing, but leaned to kiss me, then turned and walked to where my stepfather still crouched on the ground in a fit of grief. My beloved put his knee in my stepfather's back, then wrapped his hand in the hair at the back of the older man's head and pulled until his tearstained face was tilted up into the torchlight.

"I did not want to kill Avalles," my soldier explained, in part to me, in part to Sulis. "But he insisted on coming, fearing that I would become closer in his uncle's favor if he were not there too." He shook his head. "Sad. But it is only your death that was my task, Sulis, and I have been waiting long for such a perfect opportunity."

Despite the merciless strain of his position, my stepfather smiled, a ghastly, tight-stretched grin. "Which Sancellan sent you?"

"Does it matter? You have more enemies in Nabban than you can count, Sulis Apostate. You are a heretic and a schismatic, and you are dangerous. You should have known you would not be left here, to build your power in the wilderness."

"I did not come here to build power," my stepfather grunted. "I came here to have my questions answered."

"Tellarin!" I struggled to make sense where there could be none. "What are you doing?"

His voice took on a little of its former gentle tone. "This is nothing to do with you and me, Breda."

"Did you . . . ?" I could scarcely say it. My tears were making the chamber as blurry as the Black Fire ever did. "Did you . . . only pretend love for me? Was it all to help you kill him?"

"No! I had no need of you, girl—I was already one of his most trusted men." He tightened his grip on Sulis then, until I feared my stepfather's neck would break. "What you and I have, little Breda, that is good and real. I will take you back to Nabban with me—I will be rich now, and you will be my wife. You will learn what a true city is, instead of this devilish, backward pile of stone.''

"You love me? Truly, you love me?" I wanted very much to believe him. "Then let my stepfather go, Tellarin!"

He frowned. "I cannot. His death is the task I was given to do before I ever met you, and it is a task that needs doing. He is a madman, Breda! Surely after tonight's horrors, after seeing the demon he called up with forbidden magic, you can see why he cannot be allowed to live."

"Do not kill him, please! I beg you!"

He lifted his hand to still me. "I am sworn to my master in Nabban. This one thing I must do, and then we are both free.''

Even an appeal in the name of love could not stop him. Confused and overwhelmed, unable to argue any longer with the man who had brought me so much joy, I turned to the witch, praying that she would do something—but Valada was gone. She had taken her freedom, leaving the rest of us to murder each other if we wished. I thought I saw a movement in the shadows, but it was only some other phantom, some flying thing that drifted above the stairwell on silent wings.

Lord Sulis was silent. He did not struggle against Tellarin's grip, but waited for slaughter like an old bull. When he swallowed, the skin on his neck pulled so tight that watching it made tears spill onto my cheeks once more. My beloved pressed his knife against my stepfather's throat as I stumbled toward them. Sulis looked at me, but still said nothing. Whatever thought was in his eyes, it had gone so deep that I could not even guess what it might be.

"Tell me again that you love me," I asked as I reached his side. As I looked at my soldier's frightened but exultant face, I could not help thinking of the High Keep, a haunted place built on murder, in whose corrupted, restless depths we stood. For a moment I thought the ghost-voices had returned, for my head was full of roaring, rushing noise. "Tell me again, Tellarin," I begged him. "Please."

My beloved did not move the blade from Sulis' throat, but said, "Of course I love you, Breda. We will be married, and all of Nabban will lie at your feet. You will never be cold or lonely again." He leaned forward, and I could feel the beautiful long muscles of his back tense beneath my hand. He hesitated when he heard the click of the glass ball as it fell to the tiles and rattled away.

"What . . . ?" he asked, then straightened suddenly, grabbing at the spot at his waist where the claw had pricked him. I took a few staggering steps and fell, weeping. Behind me, Tellarin began to wheeze, then to choke. I heard his knife clatter to the stone.

I could not look, but the sound of his last rattling breaths will never leave me.

Now that I am old, I know that this secretive keep will be the place I die. When I have breathed my last, I suppose they will bury me on the headland beside my mother and Lord Sulis.

After that long night beneath the castle had ended, the Heron King, as the Lake People called my step-father, came to resemble once more the man he had been. He reigned over the High Keep for many more years, and gradually even my own brawling, jealous folk acknowledged him as their ruler, although the kingship did not outlive Sulis himself.

My own mark on the world will be even smaller.

I never married, and my brother Aelfric died of a fall from his horse without fathering any children, so although the Lake People still squabble over who should carry the standard and spear of the Great Thane, none of my blood will ever lead them again. Nor, I expect, will anyone stay on in the great castle that Lord Sulis rebuilt after I am dead—there are few enough left of our household now, and those who stay only do so for love of me. When I am gone, I doubt any will remain even to tend our graves.

I cannot say why I chose to keep this bleak place

as my home, any more than I could say why I chose my stepfather's life over that of my beautiful, deceitful Tellarin. Because I feared to build something on blood that should have been founded on something better, I suppose. Because love does not do sums, but instead makes choices, and then gives its all.

Whatever the reasons, I have made those choices.

After he carried me out of the depths and back to daylight, my stepfather scarcely ever mentioned that dreadful night again. He was still distant to the end of his days, still full of shadows, but at times I thought I sensed a peace in him that he had not had before. Why that might be, I could not say.

As he lay at last on his deathbed, breath growing fainter and fainter, I sat by his side for hours of every day and spoke to him of all that happened in the High Keep, talking of the rebuilding, which still continued, and of the tenants, and the herds, as if at any moment he might rise to resume his stewardship. But we both knew he would not.

When the last moment came, there was a kind of quiet expectancy on his face—no fear, but something more difficult to describe. As he strained for his final breath of air, I suddenly remembered something I had read in his book, and realized that I had made a mistake on that night so long ago.

"... *She will show me the Way of Black Fire or*

there is no other Hope,'' he had written. *''Either she will answer, or Death.''*

He had not meant that he would kill her if she did not give him what he needed. He had meant that if she could not help him find an answer, then he would have to wait until death came for him before he could learn the truth.

And now he would finally receive an answer to the question that had tormented him for so long.

Whatever that answer might be, Sulis did not return to share it with me. Now I am an old, old woman, and I will find it soon enough myself. It is strange, perhaps, but I find I do not much care. In one year with Tellarin, in those months of fierce love, I lived an entire lifetime. Since then I have lived another one, a long, slow life whose small pleasures have largely balanced the moments of suffering. Surely two lives are enough for anyone—who needs the endless span of the immortals? After all, as the burning man made clear, an eternity of pain would be no gift.

And now that I have told my tale, even the ghosts that sometimes still startle me awake at midnight seem more like ancient friends than things to be feared.

I have made my choices.

I think I am content.

DISCWORLD

Terry Pratchett

Granny Weatherwax

Discworld is a flat world supported by four elephants standing on top of a huge turtle swimming endlessly through space. Using this classic mythological concept as his starting point, Pratchett cheerfully lampoons a vast range of targets—Shakespeare, Creationism theory, heroic fantasy, etc., etc.—and ventures into such far-flung realms as ancient Egypt, the Aztec Empire, and Renaissance Italy for further raw material. When he is not satirizing historical periods or cultures, Pratchett allows much of the action to center around Ankh-Morpork, a melting pot of a fantasy city that's a mix of Renaissance Florence, Victorian London, and present-day New York.

The series uses fantasy as a fairground mirror, reflecting back at us a distorted but recognizable image of twentieth-century concerns. (For example, equal-opportunity and affirmative-action laws take on new dimensions when you've got vampires, werewolves, and zombies among your citizens. . . .)

The books can be roughly divided into four groups:

In the Rincewind series (*The Colour of Magic, The Light Fantastic, Sourcery, Eric, Interesting Times*), the protagonist is an incompetent, cowardly (or very clear-thinking) magician who is constantly trying to escape some danger only to run into something ten times worse. However unfortunate his misadventures become, in the end he manages to triumph and to restore Discworld to a semblance of order, as order is understood there. The primary satiric target of these books is heroic fantasy, complete with all the genre staples—trolls, wizards, and similar fauna. *Sourcery*, for example, is a parody of the Lovecraftian netherworlds; *Eric* is a spoof of the Faustian deal-with-the-devil theme.

The Granny Weatherwax group (*Equal Rites*, *Wyrd Systers*, *Witches Abroad*, *Lords and Ladies*, *Maskerade*) introduces one of the most popular characters in the series, a witch of iron constitution, steel morals, and reinforced-concrete pride who takes charge in any situation; like a Western hero, she's technically a bad witch who does good. A rewriting of *The Phantom of the Opera* forms the basis for *Maskerade*, and *A Midsummer Night's Dream* is lampooned in *Lords and Ladies* with Shakespeare's more genteel fairies replaced by haughty, vicious elves from Celtic folklore.

The four books composing the Death series (*Mort*, *Reaper Man*, *Soul Music*, *Hogfather*) follow the trials of Death, a humorless entity who secretly harbors a soft spot for humanity, and whose inability to understand these same humans creates real pathos. In *Mort*, Death takes a vacation, leaving his even more softhearted apprentices to carry on while he's gone.

Reaper Man follows Death when he becomes—temporarily—mortal, and learns what humanity *really* means.

The City Watch books *(Guards! Guards!, Men at Arms, Feet of Clay)* combine fantasy with elements of the police-procedural mystery novel, with appropriately lively results. *Guards! Guards!* finds the grubby but honest Ankh-Morpork Night Watch battling a dragon who wants to assassinate the city's Patrician and install a new puppet ruler. *Men at Arms* tracks a serial killer running amok with Discworld's only gun (designed by Discworld's equivalent of Leonardo da Vinci).

The stand-alone novel *Pyramids* injects some modern thinking into a version of Egypt of the Pharaohs. *Moving Pictures* uses the Discworld toolbox to examine the real magic of the movies. *Small Gods* provides a darkly humorous look at the rise of a religion whose one "truth" is that the Discworld is actually spherical instead of flat.

In "The Sea and Little Fishes" Pratchett offers a new adventure of Granny Weatherwax, a highly competitive spirit who believes that "coming in second" is another term for losing. . . .

THE SEA AND LITTLE FISHES

⟨᷽᷽᷽⟩

Terry Pratchett

Trouble began, and not for the first time, with an apple.

There was a bag of them on Granny Weatherwax's bleached and spotless table. Red and round, shiny and fruity, if they'd known the future they should have ticked like bombs.

"Keep the lot, old Hopcroft said I could have as many as I wanted," said Nanny Ogg. She gave her sister witch a sidelong glance. "Tasty, a bit wrinkled, but a damn good keeper."

"He *named* an *apple* after *you*?" said Granny. Each word was an acid drop on the air.

"'Cos of my rosy cheeks," said Nanny Ogg. "An' I cured his leg for him after he felt off that ladder last year. An' I made him up some jollop for his bald head.''

"It didn't work, though," said Granny. "That wig he wears, that's a terrible thing to see on a man still alive."

"But he was pleased I took an interest."

Granny Weatherwax didn't take her eyes off the bag. Fruit and vegetables grew famously in the mountains' hot summers and cold winters. Percy Hopcroft was the premier grower and definitely a keen man when it came to sexual antics among the horticulture with a camel-hair brush.

"He sells his apple trees all over the place," Nanny Ogg went on. "Funny, eh, to think that pretty soon thousands of people will be having a bite of Nanny Ogg."

"Thousands more," said Granny, tartly. Nanny's wild youth was an open book, although only available in plain covers.

"Thank you, Esme." Nanny Ogg looked wistful for a moment, and then opened her mouth in mock concern. "Oh, you ain't *jealous*, are you, Esme? You ain't begrudging me my little moment in the sun?"

"Me? Jealous? Why should I be jealous? It's only an *apple*. It's not as if it's anything important."

"That's what I thought. It's just a little frippery to humor an old lady," said Nanny. "So how are things with you, then?"

"Fine. Fine."

"Got your winter wood in, have you?"

"Mostly."

"Good," said Nanny. "Good."

They sat in silence. On the windowpane a butterfly, awoken by the unseasonable warmth, beat a little tattoo in an effort to reach the September sun.

"Your potatoes . . . got them dug, then?" said Nanny.

"Yes."

"We got a good crop off ours this year."

"Good."

"Salted your beans, have you?"

"Yes."

"I expect you're looking forward to the Trials next week?"

"Yes."

"I expects you've been practicing?"

"No."

It seemed to Nanny that, despite the sunlight, the shadows were deepening in the corners of the room. The very air itself was growing dark. A witch's cottage gets sensitive to the moods of its occupant. But she plunged on. Fools rush in, but they are laggards compared to little old ladies with nothing left to fear.

"You coming over to dinner on Sunday?"

"What're you havin'?"

"Pork."

"With apple sauce?"

"Yes—"

"No," said Granny.

There was a creaking behind Nanny. The door had swung open. Someone who wasn't a witch would have rationalized this, would have said that of course it was only the wind. And Nanny Ogg was quite prepared to go along with this, but would have added: *Why* was it only the wind, and how come the wind had managed to lift the latch?

"Oh, well, can't sit here chatting all day," she said, standing up quickly. "Always busy at this time of year, ain't it?"

"Yes."

"So I'll be off, then."

"Goodbye."

The wind blew the door shut again as Nanny hurried off down the path.

It occurred to her that, just possibly, she might have gone a bit too far. But only a bit.

The trouble with being a witch—at least, the trouble with being a witch as far as some people were concerned—was that you got stuck out here in the country. But that was fine by Nanny. Everything she wanted was out here. Everything she'd *ever* wanted was here, although in her youth she'd run out of men a few times. Foreign parts were all right to visit but they weren't really serious. They had interestin' new drinks and the grub was fun, but foreign parts was where you went to do what might need to be done and then you came back here, a place that was real. Nanny Ogg was happy in small places.

Of course, she reflected as she crossed the lawn, she didn't have this view out of her window. Nanny lived down in the town, but Granny could look out across the forest and over the plains and all the way to the great round horizon of the Discworld.

A view like that, Nanny reasoned, could probably suck your mind right out of your head.

They'd told her the world was round and flat, which was common sense, and went through space on the back of four elephants standing on the shell of a turtle, which didn't have to make sense. It was all happening Out There somewhere, and it could continue to do so with Nanny's blessing and disinterest so long as she could live in a personal world about ten miles across, which she carried around with her.

But Esme Weatherwax needed more than this little kingdom could contain. She was the *other* kind of witch.

And Nanny saw it as her job to stop Granny Weatherwax getting bored. The business with the apples was petty enough, a spiteful little triumph when you got down to it, but Esme needed something to make every day worthwhile and if it had to be anger and jealousy then so be it. Granny would now scheme for some little victory, some tiny humiliation that only the two of them would ever know about, and that'd be that. Nanny was confident that she could deal with her friend in a bad mood, but not when she was bored. A witch who is bored might do *anything*.

People said things like "we had to make our own amusements in those days" as if this signaled some kind of moral worth, and perhaps it did, but the last thing you wanted a witch to do was get bored and start making her own amusements, because witches sometimes had famously erratic ideas about what was amusing. And Esme was undoubtedly the most powerful witch the mountains had seen for generations.

Still, the Trials were coming up, and they always set Esme Weatherwax all right for a few weeks. She rose to competition like a trout to a fly.

Nanny Ogg always looked forward to the Witch Trials. You got a good day out and of course there was a big bonfire. Whoever heard of a Witch Trial without a good bonfire afterward?

And afterward you could roast potatoes in the ashes.

The afternoon melted into the evening, and the shadows in corners and under stools and tables crept out and ran together.

Granny rocked gently in her chair as the darkness wrapped itself around her. She had a look of deep concentration.

The logs in the fireplace collapsed into the embers, which winked out one by one.

The night thickened.

The old clock ticked on the mantelpiece and, for some length of time, there was no other sound.

There came a faint rustling. The paper bag on the table moved and then began to crinkle like a deflating balloon. Slowly, the still air filled with a heavy smell of decay.

After a while the first maggot crawled out.

Nanny Ogg was back home and just pouring a pint of beer when there was a knock. She put down the jug with a sigh, and went and opened the door.

"Oh, hello, ladies. What're you doing in these parts? And on such a chilly evening, too?"

Nanny backed into the room, ahead of three more witches. They wore the black cloaks and pointy hats traditionally associated with their craft, although this served to make each one look different. There is nothing like a uniform for allowing one to express one's individuality. A tweak here and a tuck there are little details that scream all the louder in the apparent, well, uniformity.

Gammer Beavis' hat, for example, had a very flat

brim and a point you could clean your ear with. Nanny liked Gammer Beavis. She might be a bit too educated, so that sometimes it overflowed out of her mouth, but she did her own shoe repairs and took snuff and, in Nanny Ogg's small worldview, things like this meant that someone was All Right.

Old Mother Dismass's clothes had that disarray of someone who, because of a detached retina in her second sight, was living in a variety of times all at once. Mental confusion is bad enough in normal people, but much worse when the mind has an occult twist. You just had to hope it was only her underwear she was wearing on the outside.

It was getting worse, Nanny knew. Sometimes her knock would be heard on the door a few hours before she arrived. Her footprints would turn up several days later.

Nanny's heart sank at the sight of the third witch, and it wasn't because Letice Earwig was a bad women. Quite the reverse, in fact. She was considered to be decent, well-meaning, and kind, at least to less-aggressive animals and the cleaner sort of children. And she would always do you a good turn. The trouble was, though, that she would do you a good turn for your own good even if a good turn wasn't what was good for you. You ended up mentally turned the other way, and that wasn't good.

And she was married. Nanny had nothing against

witches being married. It wasn't as if there were *rules*. She herself had had many husbands, and had even been married to three of them. But Mr. Earwig was a retired wizard with a suspiciously large amount of gold, and Nanny suspected that Letice did witchcraft as something to keep herself occupied, in much the same way that other women of a certain class might embroider kneelers for the church or visit the poor.

And she had money. Nanny did not have money and therefore was predisposed to dislike those who did. Letice had a black velvet cloak so fine that it looked as if a hole had been cut out of the world. Nanny did not. Nanny did not *want* a fine velvet cloak and did not aspire to such things. So she didn't see why other people should have them.

"Evening, Gytha. How are you keeping, in yourself?" said Gammer Beavis.

Nanny took her pipe out of her mouth. "Fit as a fiddle. Come on in."

"Ain't this rain dreadful?" said Mother Dismass. Nanny looked at the sky. It was frosty purple. But it was probably raining wherever Mother's mind was at.

"Come along in and dry off, then," she said kindly.

"May fortunate stars shine on this our meeting," said Letice. Nanny nodded understandingly. Letice always sounded as though she'd learned her witchcraft out of a not very imaginative book.

"Yeah, right," she said.

There was some polite conversation while Nanny prepared tea and scones. Then Gammer Beavis, in a tone that clearly indicated that the official part of the visit was beginning, said:

"We're here as the Trials committee, Nanny."

"Oh? Yes?"

"I expect you'll be entering?"

"Oh, yes. I'll do my little turn." Nanny glanced at Letice. There was a smile on that face that she wasn't entirely happy with.

"There's a lot of interest this year," Gammer went on. "More girls are taking it up lately."

"To get boys, one feels," said Letice, and sniffed. Nanny didn't comment. Using witchcraft to get boys seemed a damn good use for it as far as she was concerned. It was, in a way, one of the fundamental uses.

"That's nice," she said. "Always looks good, a big turnout. But."

"I beg your pardon?" said Letice.

"I said 'but,' " said Nanny. " 'Cos someone's going to say 'but,' right? This little chat has got a big 'but' coming up. I can tell."

She knew this was flying in the face of protocol. There should be at least seven more minutes of small talk before anyone got around to the point, but Letice's presence was getting on her nerves.

"It's about Esme Weatherwax," said Gammer Beavis.

"Yes?" said Nanny, without surprise.

"I suppose she's entering?"

"Never known her stay away."

Letice sighed.

"I suppose you . . . couldn't persuade her to . . . not to enter this year?" she said.

Nanny looked shocked.

"With an axe, you mean?" she said.

In unison, the three witches sat back.

"You see—" Gammer began, a bit shamefaced.

"Frankly, Mrs. Ogg," said Letice, "it is very hard to get other people to enter when they know that Miss Weatherwax is entering. She always wins."

"Yes," said Nanny. "It's a competition."

"But she *always* wins!"

"So?"

"In *other* types of competition," said Letice, "one is normally only allowed to win for three years in a row and then one takes a backseat for a while."

"Yeah, but this is witching," said Nanny. "The rules is different."

"How so?"

"There ain't none."

Letice twitched her skirt. "Perhaps it is time there were," she said.

"Ah," said Nanny. "And you just going to go up and tell Esme that? You up for this, Gammer?"

Gammer Beavis didn't meet her gaze. Old Mother Dismass was gazing at last week.

"I understand Miss Weatherwax is a very proud woman," said Letice.

Nanny Ogg puffed at her pipe again.

"You might as well say the sea is full of water," she said.

The other witches were silent for a moment.

"I daresay that was a valuable comment," said Letice, "but I didn't understand it."

"If there ain't no water in the sea, it ain't the sea," said Nanny Ogg. "It's just a damn great hole in the ground. Thing about Esme is . . ." Nanny took another noisy pull at the pipe. "She's *all* pride, see? She ain't just a proud *person*."

"Then perhaps she should learn to be a bit more humble . . ."

"What's she got to be humble about?" said Nanny sharply.

But Letice, like a lot of people with marshmallow on the outside, had a hard core that was not easily compressed.

"The woman clearly has a natural talent and, really, she should be grateful for—"

Nanny Ogg stopped listening at this point. *The woman*, she thought. So that was how it was going.

It was the same in just about every trade. Sooner or later someone decided it needed organizing, and the one thing you could be sure of was that the organizers weren't going to be the people who, by general acknowledgment, were at the top of their craft. *They* were working too hard. To be fair, it generally wasn't done by the worst, neither. They were working hard, too. They had to.

No, it was done by the ones who had just enough time and inclination to scurry and bustle. And, to be fair again, the world *needed* people who scurried and bustled. You just didn't have to like them very much.

The lull told her that Letice had finished.

"Really? Now, me," said Nanny, "I'm the one who's *nat'rally* talented. Us Oggs've got witchcraft in our blood. I never really had to sweat at it. Esme, now . . . she's got a bit, true enough, but it ain't a lot. She just makes it work harder'n hell. And you're going to tell her she's not to?"

"We were rather hoping you would," said Letice.

Nanny opened her mouth to deliver one or two swearwords, and then stopped.

"Tell you what," she said, "*you* can tell her tomorrow, and I'll come with you to hold her back."

* * *

Granny Weatherwax was gathering Herbs when they came up the track.

Everyday herbs of sickroom and kitchen are known as simples. Granny's Herbs weren't simples. They were complicateds or they were nothing. And there was none of the airy-fairy business with a pretty basket and a pair of dainty snippers. Granny used a knife. And a chair held in front of her. And a leather hat, gloves, and apron as secondary lines of defense.

Even she didn't know where some of the Herbs came from. Roots and seed were traded all over the world, and maybe farther. Some had flowers that turned as you passed by, some fired their thorns at passing birds, and several were staked, not so that they wouldn't fall over, but so they'd still be there next day.

Nanny Ogg, who never bothered to grow any herb you couldn't smoke or stuff a chicken with, heard her mutter, "Right, you buggers—"

"Good morning, Miss Weatherwax," said Letice Earwig loudly.

Granny Weatherwax stiffened, and then lowered the chair very carefully and turned around.

"It's Mistress," she said.

"Whatever," said Letice brightly. "I trust you are keeping well?"

"Up till now," said Granny. She nodded almost

imperceptibly at the other three witches.

There was a thrumming silence, which appalled Nanny Ogg. They should have been invited in for a cup of something. That was how the ritual went. It was gross bad manners to keep people standing around. Nearly, but not quite, as bad as calling an elderly unmarried witch "Miss."

"You've come about the Trials," said Granny. Letice almost fainted.

"Er, how did—"

" 'Cos you look like a committee. It don't take much reasoning," said Granny, pulling off her gloves. "We didn't used to need a committee. The news just got around and we all turned up. Now suddenly there's folk *arrangin'* things." For a moment Granny looked as though she was fighting some serious internal battle, and then she added in throwaway tones, "Kettle's on. You'd better come in."

Nanny relaxed. Maybe there were some customs even Granny Weatherwax wouldn't defy, after all. Even if someone was your worst enemy, you invited them in and gave them tea and biscuits. In fact, the worser your enemy, the better the crockery you got out and the higher the quality of the biscuits. You might wish black hell on 'em later, but while they were under your roof you'd feed 'em till they choked.

Her dark little eyes noted that the kitchen table gleamed and was still damp from scrubbing.

After cups had been poured and pleasantries exchanged, or at least offered by Letice and received in silence by Granny, the self-elected chairwoman wriggled in her seat and said:

"There's such a lot of interest in the Trials this year, Miss—Mistress Weatherwax."

"Good."

"It does look as though witchcraft in the Ramtops is going through something of a renaissance, in fact."

"A renaissance, eh? There's a thing."

"It's such a good route to empowerment for young women, don't you think?"

Many people could say things in a cutting way, Nanny knew. But Granny Weatherwax could *listen* in a cutting way. She could make something sound stupid just by hearing it.

"That's a good hat you've got there," said Granny. "Velvet, is it? Not made local, I expect."

Letice touched the brim and gave a little laugh.

"It's from Boggi's in Ankh-Morpork," she said.

"Oh? Shop-bought?"

Nanny Ogg glanced at the corner of the room, where a battered wooden cone stood on a stand. Pinned to it were lengths of black calico and strips of willow wood, the foundations for Granny's spring hat.

"*Tailor-made*," said Letice.

"And those hatpins you've got," Granny went on. "All them crescent moons and cat shapes—"

"You've got a brooch that's crescent-shaped, too, ain't that so, Esme?" said Nanny Ogg, deciding it was time for a warning shot. Granny occasionally had a lot to say about jewelry on witches when she was feeling in an acid mood.

"This is true, Gytha. I have a brooch what is shaped like a crescent. That's just the truth of the shape it happens to be. Very practical shape for holding a cloak, is a crescent. But I don't *mean* nothing by it. Anyway, you interrupted just as I was about to remark to Mrs. Earwig how fetchin' her hatpins are. Very *witchy*."

Nanny, swiveling like a spectator at a tennis match, glanced at Letice to see if this deadly bolt had gone home. But the woman was actually *smiling*. Some people just couldn't spot the obvious on the end of a ten-pound hammer.

"On the subject of witchcraft," said Letice, with the born chairwoman's touch for the enforced segue, "I thought I might raise with you the question of your *participation* in the Trials."

"Yes?"

"Do you . . . ah . . . don't you think it is unfair to other people that you win every year?"

Granny Weatherwax looked down at the floor and then up at the ceiling.

"No," she said, eventually. "I'm better'n them."

"You don't think it is a little dispiriting for the other contestants?"

Once again, the floor-to-ceiling search.

"No," said Granny.

"But they start off knowing they're not going to win."

"So do I."

"Oh, no, you surely—"

"I *meant* that I start off knowing they're not goin' to win, too," said Granny witheringly. "And they ought to start off knowing *I'm* not going to win. No wonder they lose, if they ain't getting their minds right."

"It does rather dash their enthusiasm."

Granny looked genuinely puzzled. "What's wrong with 'em striving to come second?" she said.

Letice plunged on.

"What we were hoping to persuade you to do, Esme, is to accept an emeritus position. You would perhaps make a nice little speech of encouragement, present the award, and . . . and possibly even be, er, one of the judges . . ."

"There's going to be judges?" said Granny. "We've never had *judges*. Everyone just used to know who'd won."

"That's true," said Nanny. She remembered the scenes at the end of one or two trials. When Granny

Weatherwax won, everyone knew. "Oh, that's very true."

"It would be a very nice gesture," Letice went on.

"Who decided there would be judges?" said Granny.

"Er . . . the committee . . . which is . . . that is . . . a few of us got together. Only to steer things . . ."

"Oh. I see," said Granny. "Flags?"

"Pardon?"

"Are you going to have them lines of little flags? And maybe someone selling apples on a stick, that kind of thing?"

"Some bunting would certainly be—"

"Right. Don't forget the bonfire."

"So long as it's nice and safe."

"Oh. Right. Things should be nice. And safe," said Granny.

Mrs. Earwig perceptibly sighed with relief. "Well, that's sorted out nicely," she said.

"Is it?" said Granny.

"I thought we'd agreed that—"

"Had we? Really?" She picked up the poker from the hearth and prodded fiercely at the fire. "I'll give matters my consideration."

"I wonder if I may be frank for a moment, Mistress Weatherwax?" said Letice. The poker paused in mid-prod.

"Yes?"

"Times are changing, you know. Now, I think I know why you feel it necessary to be so overbearing and unpleasant to everyone, but believe me when I tell you, as a friend, that you'd find it so much easier if you just relaxed a little bit and tried being nicer, like our sister Gytha here."

Nanny Ogg's smile had fossilized into a mask. Letice didn't seem to notice.

"You seem to have all the witches in awe of you for fifty miles around," she went on. "Now, I daresay you have some valuable skills, but witchcraft isn't about being an old grump and frightening people anymore. I'm telling you this as a friend—"

"Call again whenever you're passing," said Granny.

This was a signal. Nanny Ogg stood up hurriedly.

"I thought we could discuss—" Letice protested.

"I'll walk with you all down to the main track," said Nanny, hauling the other witches out of their seats.

"Gytha!" said Granny sharply, as the group reached the door.

"Yes, Esme?"

"You'll come back here afterward, I expect."

"Yes, Esme."

Nanny ran to catch up with the trio on the path. Letice had what Nanny thought of as a deliberate walk. It had been wrong to judge her by the floppy jowls and the overfussy hair and the silly way she waggled her hands as she talked. She was a witch, after all. Scratch any witch and . . . well, you'd be facing a witch you'd just scratched.

"She is not a nice person," Letice trilled. But it was the trill of some large hunting bird.

"You're right there," said Nanny. "But—"

"It's high time she was taken down a peg or two!"

"We-ell . . ."

"She bullies you most terribly, Mrs. Ogg. A married lady of *your* mature years, too!"

Just for a moment, Nanny's eyes narrowed.

"It's her way," she said.

"A very petty and nasty way, to my mind!"

"Oh, yes," said Nanny simply. "Ways often are. But look, you—"

"Will you be bringing anything to the produce stall, Gytha?" said Gammer Beavis quickly.

"Oh, a couple of bottles, I expect," said Nanny, deflating.

"Oh, homemade wine?" said Letice. "How nice."

"Sort of like wine, yes. Well, here's the path," said Nanny. "I'll just . . . I'll just nip back and say goodnight—"

"It's belittling, you know, the way you run around after her," said Letice.

"Yes. Well. You get used to people. Good night to you."

When she got back to the cottage Granny Weatherwax was standing in the middle of the kitchen floor with a face like an unmade bed and her arms folded. One foot tapped on the floor.

"She married a wizard," said Granny, as soon as her friend had entered. "You can't tell me that's right."

"Well, wizards *can* marry, you know. They just have to hand in the staff and pointy hat. There's no actual law says they can't, so long as they gives up wizarding. They're supposed to be married to the job."

"I should reckon it's a job being married to *her*," said Granny. Her face screwed up in a sour smile.

"Been pickling much this year?" said Nanny, employing a fresh association of ideas around the word "vinegar," which had just popped into her head.

"My onions all got the screwfly."

"That's a pity. You like onions."

"Even screwflies've got to eat," said Granny. She glared at the door. "*Nice*," she said.

"She's got a knitted cover on the lid in her privy," said Nanny.

"Pink?"

"Yes."

"Nice."

"She's not *bad*," said Nanny. "She does good work over in Fiddler's Elbow. People speak highly of her."

Granny sniffed. "Do they speak highly of me?" she said.

"No, they speaks *quietly* of you, Esme."

"Good. Did you see her hatpins?"

"I thought they were rather . . . nice, Esme."

"That's witchcraft today. All jewelry and no drawers."

Nanny, who considered both to be optional, tried to build an embankment against the rising tide of ire.

"You could think of it as an honor, really, them not wanting you to take part," she said.

"That's nice."

Nanny sighed.

"Sometimes nice is worth tryin', Esme," she said.

"I never does anyone a bad turn if I can't do 'em a good one, Gytha, you know that. I don't have to do no frills or fancy labels."

Nanny sighed. Of course, it was true. Granny was an old-fashioned witch. She didn't do good for people, she did right by them. But Nanny knew that people don't always appreciate right. Like old Pollitt the other day, when he fell off his horse. What he

wanted was a painkiller. What he *needed* was the
few seconds of agony as Granny popped the joint
back into place. The trouble was, people remembered the pain.

You got on a lot better with people when you
remembered to put frills round it, and took an interest and said things like "How are you?" Esme
didn't bother with that kind of stuff because she
knew already. Nanny Ogg knew too, but also knew
that letting on you knew gave people the serious
willies.

She put her head on one side. Granny's foot was
still tapping.

"You planning anything, Esme? I know you.
You've got that look."

"What look, pray?"

"That look you had when that bandit was found
naked up a tree and crying all the time and going
on about the horrible thing that was after him. Funny
thing, we never found any paw prints. *That* look."

"He deserved more'n that for what he done."

"Yeah   well, you had that look just before ole
Hoggett was found beaten black and blue in his own
pigsty and wouldn't talk about it?"

"You mean old Hoggett the wife beater? Or old
Hoggett who won't never lift his hand to a woman
no more?" said Granny. The thing her lips had
pursed into might have been called a smile.

"And it's the look you had the time all the snow slid down on ole Millson's house just after he called you an interfering old baggage . . ." said Nanny.

Granny hesitated. Nanny was pretty sure that had been natural causes, and also that Granny knew she suspected this, and that pride was fighting a battle with honesty—

"That's as may be," said Granny, noncommittally.

"Like someone who might go along to the Trials and . . . do something," said Nanny.

Her friend's glare should have made the air sizzle.

"Oh? So that's what you think of me? That's what we've come to, have we?"

"Letice thinks we should move with the times—"

"Well? I moves with the times. We ought to move with the times. No one said we ought to give them a *push*. I expect you'll be wanting to be going, Gytha. I want to be alone with my thoughts!"

Nanny's own thoughts, as she scurried home in relief, were that Granny Weatherwax was not an advertisement for witchcraft. Oh, she was one of the *best* at it, no doubt about that. At a certain kind, certainly. But a girl starting out in life might well say to herself, Is this it? You worked hard and denied yourself things and what you got at the end of it was hard work and self-denial?

Granny wasn't exactly friendless, but what she

commanded mostly was respect. People learned to respect storm clouds, too. They refreshed the ground. You needed them. But they weren't nice.

Nanny Ogg went to bed in three flannelette nightdresses, because sharp frosts were already pricking the autumn air. She was also in a troubled frame of mind.

Some sort of war had been declared, she knew. Granny could do some terrible things when roused, and the fact that they'd been done to those who richly deserved them didn't make them any the less terrible. She'd be planning something pretty dreadful, Nanny Ogg knew.

She herself didn't like winning things. Winning was a habit that was hard to break and brought you a dangerous status that was hard to defend. You'd walk uneasily through life, always on the lookout for the next girl with a better broomstick and a quicker hand on the frog.

She turned over under the mountain of eiderdowns.

In Granny Weatherwax's worldview was no place for second place. You won, or you were a loser. There was nothing *wrong* with being a loser except for the fact that, of course, you weren't the winner. Nanny had always pursued the policy of being a good loser. People *liked* you when you *almost* won, and bought you drinks. "She only just lost" was a much better compliment than "She only just won."

Runners-up had more fun, she reckoned. But it wasn't a word Granny had much time for.

In her own darkened cottage, Granny Weatherwax sat and watched the fire die.

It was a gray-walled room, the color that old plaster gets not so much from dirt as from age. There was not a thing in it that wasn't useful, utilitarian, earning its keep. Every flat surface in Nanny Ogg's cottage had been pressed into service as a holder for ornaments and potted plants. People gave Nanny Ogg things. Cheap fairground tat, Granny always called it. At least, in public. What she thought of it in the privacy of her own head, she never said.

She rocked gently as the last ember winked out.

It's hard to contemplate, in the gray hours of the night, that probably the only reason people would come to your funeral would be to make sure you're dead.

Next day, Percy Hopcroft opened his back door and looked straight up into the blue stare of Granny Weatherwax.

"Oh my," he said, under his breath.

Granny gave an awkward little cough.

"Mr. Hopcroft, I've come about them apples you named after Mrs. Ogg," she said.

Percy's knees began to tremble, and his wig started to slide off the back of his head to the hoped-for security of the floor.

"I should like to thank you for doing it because it has made her very happy," Granny went on, in a tone of voice which would have struck one who knew her as curiously monotonous. "She has done a lot of fine work and it is about time she got her little reward. It was a very nice thought. And so I have brung you this little token—" Hopcroft jumped backward as Granny's hand dipped swiftly into her apron and produced a small black bottle. "—which is very rare because of the rare herbs in it. What are rare. Extremely rare herbs."

Eventually it crept over Hopcroft that he was supposed to take the bottle. He gripped the top of it very carefully, as if it might whistle or develop legs.

"Uh . . . thank you ver' much," he mumbled.

Granny nodded stiffly.

"Blessings be upon this house," she said, and turned and walked away down the path.

Hopcroft shut the door carefully, and then flung himself against it.

"You start packing right now!" he shouted to his wife, who'd been watching from the kitchen door.

"What? Our whole life's here! We can't just run away from it!"

"Better to run than hop, woman! What's *she* want

from me? What's she *want*? She's never *nice*!"

Mrs. Hopcroft stood firm. She just got the cottage looking right and they'd bought a new pump. Some things were hard to leave.

"Let just stop and think, then," she said. "What's in that bottle?"

Hopcroft held it at arm's length. "Do *you* want to find out?"

"Stop shaking, man! She didn't actually threaten, did she?"

"She said 'blessings be upon this house'! Sounds pretty damn threatening to *me*! That was Granny Weatherwax, that was!"

He put the bottle on the table. They stared at it, standing in the cautious leaning position of people who were ready to run if anything began to happen.

"Says 'Haire Reſtorer' on the label," said Mrs. Hopcroft.

"I ain't using it!"

"She'll ask us about it later. That's her way."

"If you think for one moment I'm—"

"We can try it out on the dog."

That's a good cow."

William Poorchick awoke from his reverie on the milking stool and looked around the meadow, his hands still working the beast's teats.

There was a black pointy hat rising over the

hedge. He gave such a start that he started to milk into his left boot.

"Gives plenty of milk, does she?"

"Yes, Mistress Weatherwax!" William quavered.

"That's good. Long may she continue to do so, that's what I say. Good day to you."

And the pointy hat continued up the lane.

Poorchick stared after it. Then he grabbed the bucket and, squelching at every other step, hurried into the barn and yelled for his son.

"Rummage! You get down here right now!"

His son appeared at the hayloft, pitchfork still in his hand.

"What's up, Dad?"

"You take Daphne down to the market right now, understand?"

"What? But she's our best milker, Dad!"

"*Was*, son, was! Granny Weatherwax just put a curse on her! Sell her now before her horns drop off!"

"What'd she say, Dad?"

"She said . . . she said . . . 'Long may she continue to give milk' . . ." Poorchick hesitated.

"Doesn't sound *awfully* like a curse, Dad," said Rummage. "I mean . . . not like your gen'ral curse. Sounds a bit hopeful, really," said his son.

"Well . . . it was the way . . . she . . . said . . . it . . ."

"What sort of way, Dad?"

"Well . . . like . . . cheerfully."

"You all right, Dad?"

"It was . . . the way . . ." Poorchick paused. "Well, it's not right," he continued. "It's not right! She's got no right to go around being cheerful at people! She's never cheerful! And my *boot* is *full* of *milk*!"

Today Nanny Ogg was taking some time out to tend her secret still in the woods. As a still it was the best kept secret there could be, since everyone in the kingdom knew exactly where it was, and a secret kept by so many people must be very secret indeed. Even the king knew, and knew enough to pretend he didn't know, and that meant he didn't have to ask her for any taxes and she didn't have to refuse. And every year at Hogswatch he got a barrel of what honey might be if only bees weren't teetotal. And everyone understood the situation, no one had to pay any money, and so, in a small way, the world was a happier place. And no one was cursed until their teeth fell out.

Nanny was dozing. Keeping an eye on a still was a day-and-night job. But finally the sound of people repeatedly calling her name got too much for her.

No one would come into the clearing, of course. That would mean admitting that they knew where it

was. So they were blundering around in the surrounding bushes. She pushed her way through and
was greeted with some looks of feigned surprise that
would have done credit to any amateur dramatic
company.

"Well, what do you lot want?" she demanded.

"Oh, Mrs. Ogg, we though you might be . . . taking a walk in the woods," said Poorchick, while a
scent that could clean glass wafted on the breeze.
"You got to do something! It's Mistress Weatherwax!"

"What's she done?"

"You tell 'er, Mr. Hampicker!"

The man next to Poorchick took off his hat
quickly and held it respectfully in front of him in
the ai-señor-the-banditos-have-raided-our-villages
position.

"Well, ma'am, my lad and I were digging for a
well and then she come past—"

"Granny Weatherwax?"

"Yes'm, and she said—" Hampicker gulped.
" 'You won't find any water there, my good man
You'd be better off looking in the hollow by the
chestnut tree'! An' we dug on down anyway and *we
never found no water!*"

Nanny lit her pipe. She didn't smoke around the
still since that time when a careless spark had sent
the barrel she was sitting on a hundred yards into

the air. She'd been lucky that a fir tree had broken her fall.

"So . . . *then* you dug in the hollow by the chestnut tree?" she said mildly.

Hampicker looked shocked. "*No*'m! There's no telling *what* she wanted us to find there!"

"And she cursed my cow!" said Poorchick.

"Really? What did she say?"

"She said, may she give a lot of milk!" Poorchick stopped. Once again, now that he came to say it . . .

"Well, it was the way she said it," he added, weakly.

"And what kind of way was that?"

"Nicely!"

"Nicely?"

"Smilin' and everything! I don't dare drink the stuff now!"

Nanny was mystified.

"Can't quite see the problem—"

"You tell that to Mr. Hopcroft's dog," said Poorchick. "Hopcroft daren't leave the poor thing on account of her! The whole family's going mad! There's him shearing, his wife sharpening the scissors, and the two lads out all the time looking for fresh places to dump the hair!"

Patient questioning on Nanny's part elucidated the role the Haire Reftorer had played in this.

"And he gave it—?"

"Half the bottle, Mrs. Ogg."

"Even though Esme writes 'A right small spoonful once a week' on the label? And even then you need to wear roomy trousers."

"He said he was so nervous, Mrs. Ogg! I mean, what's she playing at? Our wives are keepin' the kids indoors. I mean, s'posin' she smiled at them?"

"Well?"

"She's a witch!"

"So'm I, an' I smiles at 'em," said Nanny Ogg. "They're always runnin' after me for sweets."

"Yes, but . . . you're . . . I mean . . . she . . . I mean . . . you don't . . . I mean, well—"

"And she's a good woman," said Nanny. Common sense prompted her to add, "In her own way. I expect there *is* water down in the hollow, and Poorchick's cow'll give good milk, and if Hopcroft won't read the labels on bottles then he deserves a head you can see your face in, and if you think Esme Weatherwax'd curse kids you've got the sense of a earthworm. She'd cuss 'em, yes, all day long. But not curse 'em. She don't aim that low."

"Yes, yes," Poorchick almost moaned, "but it don't *feel* right, that's what we're saying. Her going round being *nice*, a man don't know if he's got a leg to stand on."

"Or hop on," said Hampicker darkly.

"All right, all right, I'll see about it," said Nanny.

"People shouldn't go around not doin' what you expect," said Poorchick weakly. "It gets people on edge."

"And we'll keep an eye on your sti—" Hampicker, and then staggered backward grasping his stomach and wheezing.

"Don't mind him, it's the stress," said Poorchick, rubbing his elbow. "Been picking herbs, Mrs. Ogg?"

"That's right," said Nanny, hurrying away across the leaves.

"So shall I put the fire out for you, then?" Poorchick shouted.

Granny was sitting outside her house when Nanny Ogg hurried up the path. She was sorting through a sack of old clothes. Elderly garments were scattered around her.

And she was humming. Nanny Ogg started to worry. The Granny Weatherwax she knew didn't approve of music.

And she smiled when she saw Nanny, or at least the corner of her mouth turned up. That was *really* worrying. Granny normally only smiled if something bad was happening to someone deserving.

"Why, Gytha, how nice to see you!"

"You all right, Esme?"

"Never felt better, dear." The humming continued.

"Er . . . sorting out rags, are you?" said Nanny. "Going to make that quilt?"

It was one of Granny Weatherwax's firm beliefs that one day she'd make a patchwork quilt. However, it is a task that requires patience, and hence in fifteen years she'd got as far as three patches. But she collected old clothes anyway. A lot of witches did. It was a witch thing. Old clothes had personality, like old houses. When it came to clothes with a bit of wear left in them, a witch had no pride at all.

"It's in here somewhere . . ." Granny mumbled. "Aha, here we are . . ."

She flourished a garment. It was basically pink.

"Knew it was here," she went on. "Hardly worn, either. And about my size, too."

"You're going to *wear* it?" said Nanny.

Granny's piercing blue cut-you-off-at-the-knees gaze was turned upon her. Nanny would have been relieved at a reply like "No, I'm going to eat it, you daft old fool." Instead her friend relaxed and said, a little concerned:

"You don't think it'd suit me?"

There was lace around the collar. Nanny swallowed.

"You usually wear black," she said. "Well, a bit more than usually. More like always."

"And a very sad sight I look too," said Granny robustly. "It's about time I brightened myself up a bit, don't you think?"

"And it's so very . . . pink."

Granny put it aside and to Nanny's horror took her by the hand and said earnestly, "And, you know, I reckon I've been far too dog-in-the-manger about this Trials business, Gytha—"

"Bitch-in-the-manger," said Nanny Ogg, absent-mindedly.

For a moment Granny's eyes became two sapphires again.

"What?"

"Er . . . you'd be a bitch in the manger," Nanny mumbled. "Not a dog."

"Ah? Oh, yes. Thank you for pointing that out. Well, I thought, it *is* time I stepped back a bit, and went along and cheered on the younger folks. I mean, I have to say, I . . . really haven't been very nice to people, have I . . ."

"Er . . ."

"I've tried *being* nice," Granny went on. "It didn't turn out like I expected, I'm sorry to say."

"You've never been really . . . *good* at nice," said Nanny.

Granny smiled. Hard though she stared, Nanny was unable to spot anything other than earnest concern.

"Perhaps I'll get better with practice," she said.

She patted Nanny's hand. And Nanny stared at her hand as though something horrible had happened to it.

"It's just that everyone's more used to you being . . . firm," she said.

"I thought I might make some jam and cakes for the produce stall," said Granny.

"Oh . . . good."

"Are there any sick people want visitin'?"

Nanny stared at the trees. It was getting worse and worse. She rummaged in her memory for anyone in the locality sick enough to warrant a ministering visit but still well enough to survive the shock of a ministering visit by Granny Weatherwax. When it came to practical psychology and the more robust type of folk physiotherapy Granny was without equal; in fact, she could even do the latter at a distance, for many a pain-wracked soul had left their bed and walked, nay, run at the news that she was coming.

"Everyone's pretty well at the moment," said Nanny diplomatically.

"Any old folk want cheerin' up?"

It was taken for granted by both women that *old people* did not include them. A witch aged ninety-seven would not have included herself. Old people happened to other people.

"All fairly cheerful right now," said Nanny.

"Maybe I could tell stories to the kiddies?"

Nanny nodded. Granny had done that once before, when the mood had briefly taken her. It had worked pretty well, as far as the children were concerned. They'd listened with openmouthed attention and apparent enjoyment to a traditional old folk legend. The problem had come when they'd gone home afterward and asked the meaning of words like "disemboweled."

"I could sit in a rocking chair while I tell 'em," Granny added. "That's how it's done, I recall. And I could make them some of my special treacle toffee apples. Wouldn't that be nice?"

Nanny nodded again, in a sort of horrified reverie. She realized that only she stood in the way of a wholesale rampage of niceness.

"Toffee," she said. "Would that be the sort you did that shatters like glass, or that sort where our boy Pewsey had to have his mouth levered open with a spoon?"

"I reckon I know what I did wrong last time."

"You know you and sugar don't get along, Esme. Remember them all-day suckers you made?"

"They *did* last all day, Gytha."

"Only 'cos our Pewsey couldn't get it out of his little mouth until we pulled two of his teeth, Esme. You ought to stick to pickles. You and pickles goes well."

"I've got to do *something*, Gytha. I can't be an old grump all the time. I know! I'll help at the Trials. Bound to be a lot that needs doing, eh?"

Nanny grinned inwardly. So *that* was it.

"Why, yes," she said. "I'm sure Mrs. Earwig will be happy to tell you what to do," she said. *And more fool her if she does,* she thought, *because I can tell you're planning something.*

"I shall talk to her," said Granny. "I'm sure there's a million things I could do to help, if I set my mind to it."

"And I'm sure you will," said Nanny heartily. "I've a feelin' you're going to make a big difference."

Granny started to rummage in the bag again.

"You are going to be along as well, aren't you, Gytha?"

"Me?" said Nanny. "I wouldn't miss it for the world."

Nanny got up especially early. If there was going to be any unpleasantness she wanted a ringside seat.

What there was was bunting. It was hanging from tree to tree in terrible brightly colored loops as she walked toward the Trials.

There was something oddly familiar about it, too. It should not technically be possible for anyone with a pair of scissors to be unable to cut out a triangle, but someone had managed it. And it was also obvious that the flags had been made from old clothes, painstakingly cut up. Nanny knew this because not many real flags have collars.

In the Trials field people were setting up stalls and falling over children. The committee were standing uncertainly under a tree, occasionally glancing up at a pink figure at the top of a very long ladder.

"She was here before it was light," said Letice, as Nanny approached. "She said she'd been up all night making the flags."

"Tell her about the cakes," said Gammer Beavis darkly.

"She made *cakes?*" said Nanny. "But she can't cook!"

The committee shuffled aside. A lot of the ladies contributed to the food for the Trials. It was a tradition and an informal competition in its own right. At the center of the spread of covered plates was a large platter piled high with . . . things, of indefinite color and shape. It looked as though a herd of small cows had eaten a lot of raisins and then been ill. They were Ur-cakes, prehistoric cakes, cakes of great weight and presence that had no place among the iced dainties.

"She's never had the knack of it," said Nanny weakly. "Has anyone tried one?"

"Hahaha," said Gammer solemnly.

"Tough, are they?"

"You could beat a troll to death."

"But she was so . . . sort of . . . *proud* of them," said Letice. "And then there's . . . the jam."

It was a large pot. It seemed to be filled with solidified purple lava.

"Nice . . . color," said Nanny. "Anyone tasted it?"

"We couldn't get the spoon out," said Gammer.

"Oh, I'm sure—"

"We only got it in with a hammer."

"What's she planning, Mrs. Ogg? She's got a weak and vengeful nature," said Letice. "You're her friend," she added, her tone suggesting that this was as much an accusation as a statement.

"I don't know what she's thinking, Mrs. Earwig."

"I thought she was staying away."

"She said she was going to take an interest and encourage the young 'uns."

"She is planning something," said Letice, darkly. "Those cakes are a plot to undermine my authority."

"No, that's how she always cooks," said Nanny. "She just hasn't got the knack." *Your authority, eh?*

"She's nearly finished the flags," Gammer reported. "Now she's going to try to make herself useful again."

"Well . . . I suppose we could ask her to do the Lucky Dip."

Nanny looked blank. "You mean where kids fish around in a big tub full of bran to see what they can pull out?"

"Yes."

"You're going to let *Granny Weatherwax* do that?"

"Yes."

"Only she's got a funny sense of humor, if you know what I mean."

"Good morning to you all!"

It was Granny Weatherwax's voice. Nanny Ogg had known it for most of her life. But it had that strange edge to it again. It sounded nice.

"We was wondering if you could supervise the bran tub, Miss Weatherwax."

Nanny flinched. But Granny merely said, "Happy to, Mrs. Earwig. I can't wait to see the expressions on their little faces as they pull out the goodies."

Nor can I, Nanny thought.

When the others had scurried off she sidled up to her friend.

"Why're you doing this?" she said.

"I really don't know what you mean, Gytha."

"I seen you face down terrible creatures, Esme. I once seen you catch a unicorn, for goodness' sake. What're you plannin'?"

"I still don't know what you mean, Gytha."

"Are you angry 'cos they won't let you enter, and now you're plannin' horrible revenge?"

For a moment they both looked at the field. It was beginning to fill up. People were bowling for pigs and fighting on the greasy pole. The Lancre Volunteer Band was trying to play a medley of popular tunes, and it was only a pity that each musician was playing a different one. Small children were fighting. It was going to be a scorcher of a day, probably the last one of the year.

Their eyes were drawn to the roped-off square in the center of the field.

"Are you going to enter the Trials, Gytha?" said Granny.

"You never answered my question!"

"What question was that?"

Nanny decided not to hammer on a locked door. "Yes, I am going to have a go, as it happens," she said.

"I certainly hope you win, then. I'd cheer you on, only that wouldn't be fair to the others. I shall merge into the background and be as quiet as a little mouse."

Nanny tried guile. Her face spread into a wide pink grin, and she nudged her friend.

"Right, right," she said. "Only . . . you can tell me, right? I wouldn't like to miss it when it happens.

So if you could just give me a little signal when you're going to do *it*, eh?''

"What's it you're referring to, Gytha?"

"Esme Weatherwax, sometimes I could really give you a bloody good slap!''

"Oh dear.''

Nanny Ogg didn't often swear, or at least use words beyond the boundaries of what the Lancrastrians thought of as "colorful language.'' She *looked* as if she habitually used bad words, and had just thought up a good one, but mostly witches are quite careful about what they say. You can never be sure what the words are going to do when they're out of earshot. But now she swore under her breath and caused small brief fires to start in the dry grass.

This put her in just about the right frame of mind for the Cursing.

It was said that once upon a time this had been done on a living, breathing subject, at least at the start of the event, but that wasn't right for a family day out and for several hundred years the Curses had been directed at Unlucky Charlie, who was, however you looked at it, nothing more than a scarecrow. And since curses are generally directed at the mind of the cursed, this presented a major problem, because even "May your straw go moldy and your carrot fall off'' didn't make much impression on a pumpkin. But points were given for general style and inventiveness.

There wasn't much pressure for those in any case. Everyone knew what event counted, and it wasn't Unlucky Charlie.

One year Granny Weatherwax had made the pumpkin explode. No one had ever worked out how she'd done it.

Someone would walk away at the end of today and everyone would know that person was the winner, whatever the points said. You could win the Witch with the Pointiest Hat prize and the broomstick dressage, but that was just for the audience. What counted was the Trick you'd been working on all summer.

Nanny had drawn last place, at number nineteen. A lot of witches had turned up this year. News of Granny Weatherwax's withdrawal had got around, and nothing moves faster than news in the occult community, since it doesn't just have to travel at ground level. Many pointy hats moved and nodded among the crowds.

Witches are among themselves generally as sociable as cats but, as also with cats, there are locations and times and neutral grounds where they meet at something like peace. And what was going on was a sort of slow, complicated dance. . . .

The witches walked around saying hello to one another, and rushing to meet newcomers, and innocent bystanders might have believed that here was a meeting of old friends. Which, at one level, it probably was. But Nanny watched through a witch's eyes, and saw the subtle positioning, the careful weighing-up, the little changes of stance, the eye contact finely tuned by intensity and length.

And when a witch was in the arena, especially if she was comparatively unknown, all the others found some excuse to keep an eye on her, preferably without appearing to do so.

It *was* like watching cats. Cats spend a lot of time carefully eyeing one another. When they have to fight, that's merely to rubber-stamp something that's already been decided in their heads.

Nanny knew all this. And she also knew most of the witches to be kind (on the whole), gentle (to the meek), generous (to the deserving; the undeserving got more than they bargained for), and by and large quite dedicated to a life that really offered more kicks than kisses. Not one of them lived in a house made of confectionery, although some of the conscientious younger ones had experimented with various crispbreads. Even children who deserved it were not slammed into their ovens. Generally they did what they'd always done—smooth the passage of their neighbors into and out of the world, and help them over some of the nastier hurdles in between.

You needed to be a special kind of person to do that. You needed a special kind of ear, because you saw people in circumstances where they were inclined to tell you things, like where the money was buried or who the father was or how come they'd got a black eye again. And you needed a special kind of mouth, the sort that stayed shut. Keeping secrets made you powerful. Being powerful earned you respect. Respect was hard currency.

And within this sisterhood—except that it wasn't a sisterhood, it was a loose assortment of chronic non-joiners; a group of witches wasn't a coven, it was a small war—there was always this awareness of position. It had nothing to do with anything the other world thought of as status. Nothing was ever said. But if an elderly witch died the local witches would attend her funeral for a few last words, and then go solemnly home alone, with the little insistent thought at the back of their minds: *I've moved up one.*

And newcomers were watched very, very carefully.

" 'Morning, Mrs. Ogg,'' said a voice behind her. "I trust I find you well?"

"How'd'yer do, Mistress Shimmy,'' said Nanny, turning. Her mental filing system threw up a card: Clarity Shimmy, lives over toward Cutshade with her old mum, takes snuff, good with animals. "How's your mother keepin'?''

"We buried her last month, Mrs. Ogg.''

Nanny Ogg quite liked Clarity, because she didn't see her very often.

"Oh dear . . ." she said.

"But I shall tell her you asked after her, any way," said Clarity. She glanced briefly toward the ring.

"Who's the fat girl on now?" she asked. "Got a backside on her like a bowling ball on a short see-saw."

"That's Agnes Nitt."

"That's a good cursin' voice she's got there. You know you've been cursed with a voice like that."

"Oh yes, she's been blessed with a good voice for cursin'," said Nanny politely. "Esme Weather-wax an' me gave her a few tips," she added.

Clarity's head turned.

At the far edge of the field, a small pink shape sat alone behind the Lucky Dip. It did not seem to be drawing a big crowd.

Clarity leaned closer.

"What's she . . . er . . . doing?"

"I don't know," said Nanny. "I think she's de-cided to be nice about it."

"Esme? *Nice* about it?"

"Er . . . yes," said Nanny. It didn't sound any better now she was telling someone.

Clarity stared at her. Nanny saw her make a little sign with her left hand, and then hurry off.

The pointy hats were bunching up now. There were little groups of three or four. You could see the points come together, cluster in animated conversation, and then open out again like a flower, and turn toward the distant blob of pinkness. Then a hat would leave that group and head off purposefully to another one, where the process would start all over again. It was a bit like watching very slow nuclear fission. There was a lot of excitement, and soon there would be an explosion.

Every so often someone would turn and look at Nanny, so she hurried away among the sideshows until she fetched up beside the stall of the dwarf Zakzak Stronginthearm, maker and purveyor of occult knickknackery to the more impressionable. He nodded at her cheerfully over the top of a display saying LUCKY HORSESHOES $2 EACH.

"Hello, Mrs. Ogg," he said.

Nanny realized she was flustered.

"What's lucky about 'em?" she said, picking up a horseshoe.

"Well, I got two dollars each for them," said Stronginthearm.

"And that makes them lucky?"

"Lucky for me," said Stronginthearm. "I expect you'll be wanting one too, Mrs. Ogg? I'd have fetched along another box if I'd known they'd be so popular. Some of the ladies've bought two."

There was an inflection to the word "ladies."

"*Witches* have been buying lucky horsehoes?" said Nanny.

"Like there's no tomorrow," said Zakzak. He frowned for a moment. They *had* been witches, after all. "Er . . . there will be . . . won't there?" he added.

"I'm very nearly certain of it," said Nanny, which didn't seem to comfort him.

"Suddenly been doing a roaring trade in protective herbs, too," said Zakzak. And, being a dwarf, which meant that he'd see the Flood as a marvelous opportunity to sell towels, he added, "Can I interest you, Mrs. Ogg?"

Nanny shook her head. If trouble was going to come from the direction everyone had been looking, then a sprig of rue wasn't going to be much help. A large oak tree'd be better, but only maybe.

The atmosphere was changing. The sky was a wide pale blue, but there was thunder on the horizons of the mind. The witches were uneasy and with so many in one place the nervousness was bouncing from one to another and, amplified, rebroadcasting itself to everyone. It meant that even ordinary people who thought that a rune was a dried plum were beginning to feel a deep, existential worry, the kind that causes you to snap at your kids and want a drink.

She peered through a gap between a couple of stalls. The pink figure was still sitting patiently, and a little crestfallen, behind the barrel. There was, as it were, a huge queue of no one at all.

Then Nanny scuttled from the cover of one tent to another until she could see the produce stand. It had already been doing a busy trade but there, forlorn in the middle of the cloth, was the pile of terrible cakes. And the jar of jam. Some wag had chalked up a sign beside it: GET THEE SPOON OUT OF THEE JAR, 3 TRIES FOR A PENNEY!!!

She thought she'd been careful to stay concealed, but she heard the straw rustle behind her. The committee had tracked her down.

"That's your handwriting, isn't it, Mrs. Earwig?" she said. "That's cruel. That ain't . . . nice."

"We've decided you're to go and talk to Miss Weatherwax," said Letice. "She's got to stop it."

"Stop what?"

"She's doing something to people's heads! She's come here to put the 'fluence on us, right? Everyone knows she does head magic. We can all feel it! She's spoiling it for everyone!"

"She's only sitting there," said Nanny.

"Ah, *yes*, but *how* is she sitting there, we may ask?"

Nanny peered around the stall again.

"Well . . . like normal. You know . . . bent in the middle and the knees . . ."

Letice waved a finger sternly.

"Now you listen to me, Gytha Ogg—"

"If you want her to go away, you go and tell her!" snapped Nanny. "I'm fed up with—"

There was the piercing scream of a child.

The witches stared at one another, and then ran across the field to the Lucky Dip.

A small boy was writhing on the ground, sobbing.

It was Pewsey, Nanny's youngest grandchild.

Her stomach turned to ice. She snatched him up, and glared into Granny's face.

"What have you done to him, you—" she began.

"Don't*wanna*dolly! Don't*wanna*dolly! Wanna-*soljer!* Wannawanna-wanna*SOLJER!*"

Now Nanny looked down at the rag doll in Pewsey's sticky hand, and the expression of affronted tearful rage on such of his face as could be seen around his screaming mouth—

"Oi*wannawannaSOLJER!*"

—and then at the other witches, and at Granny Weatherwax's face, and felt the horrible cold shame welling up from her boots.

"I said he could put it back and have another go," said Granny meckly: "But he just wouldn't listen."

"—*wannawannaSOL*—"

"Pewsey Ogg, if you don't shut up right this min-ute Nanny will—" Nanny Ogg began, and dredged up the nastiest punishment she could think of: "Nanny won't give you a sweetie ever again!"

Pewsey closed his mouth, stunned into silence by this unimaginable threat. Then, to Nanny's horror, Letice Earwig drew herself up and said, "Miss Weatherwax, we would prefer it if you left."

"Am I being a bother?" said Granny. "I hope I'm not being a bother. I don't *want* to be a bother. He just took a lucky dip and—"

"You're . . . upsetting people."

Any minute now, Nanny thought. Any minute now she's going to raise her head and narrow her eyes and if Letice doesn't take two steps backward she'll be a lot tougher than me.

"I can't stay and watch?" Granny said quietly.

"I know your game," said Letice. "You're planning to spoil it, aren't you? You can't stand the thought of being beaten, so you're intending something nasty."

Three steps back, Nanny thought. Else there won't anything left but bones. Any minute now . . .

"Oh, I wouldn't like anyone to think I was spoiling anything," said Granny. She sighed, and stood up. "I'll be off home . . ."

"No you won't!" snapped Nanny Ogg, pushing her back down onto the chair. "What do *you* think of this, Beryl Dismass? And you, Letty Parkin?"

"They're all—" Letice began.

"I weren't talking to you!"

The witches behind Mrs. Earwig avoided Nanny's gaze.

"Well, it's not that . . . I mean, we don't think . . ." began Beryl awkwardly. "That is . . . I've always had a lot of respect for . . . but . . . well, it *is* for everyone . . ."

Her voice trailed off. Letice looked triumphant.

"Really? I think we *had* better be going after all, then," said Nanny sourly. "I don't like the comp'ny in these parts." She looked around. "Agnes? You give me a hand to get Granny home . . ."

"I really don't need . . ." Granny began, but the other two each took an arm and gently propelled her through the crowd, which parted to let them through and turned to watch them go.

"Probably the best for all concerned, in the circumstances," said Letice. Several of the witches tried not to look at her face.

There were scraps of material all over the floor in Granny's kitchen, and gouts of congealed jam had dripped off the edge of the table and formed an immovable mound on the floor. The jam saucepan had been left in the stone sink to soak, although it was clear that the iron would rust away before the jam ever softened.

There was a row of empty pickle jars beside them.

Granny sat down and folded her hands in her lap.

"Want a cup of tea, Esme?" said Nanny Ogg.

"No, dear, thank you. You get on back to the Trials. Don't you worry about me," said Granny.

"You sure?"

"I'll just sit here quiet. Don't you worry."

"I'm not going back!" Agnes hissed, as they left. "I don't like the way Letice smiles . . ."

"You once told me you didn't like the way Esme *frowns*," said Nanny.

"Yes, but you can trust a frown. Er . . . you don't think she's losing it, do you?"

"No one'll be able to find it if she has," said Nanny. "No, you come on back with me. I'm *sure* she's planning . . . something." *I wish the hell I knew what it is*, she thought. *I'm not sure I can take any more waiting*.

She could feel the mounting tension before they reached the field. Of course, there was *always* tension, that was part of the Trials, but this kind had a sour, unpleasant taste. The sideshows were still going on but ordinary folk were leaving, spooked by sensations they couldn't put their finger on which nevertheless had them under their thumb. As for the witches themselves, they had that look worn by actors about two minutes from the end of a horror movie, when they know the monster is about to make its final leap and now it's only a matter of which door.

Letice was surrounded by witches. Nanny could hear raised voices. She nudged another witch, who was watching gloomily.

"What's happening, Winnie?"

"Oh, Reena Trump made a pig's ear of her piece and her friends say she ought to have another go because she was so nervous."

"That's a shame."

"And Virago Johnson ran off 'cos her weather spell went wrong."

"Left under a bit of a cloud, did she?"

"And I was all thumbs when I had a go. You could be in with a chance, Gytha."

"Oh, I've never been one for prizes, Winnie, you know me. It's the fun of taking part that counts."

The other witch gave her a skewed look.

"You almost made that sound believable," she said.

Gammer Beavis hurried over. "On you go, Gytha," she said. "Do your best, eh? The only contender so far is Mrs. Weavitt and her whistling frog, and it wasn't as if it could even carry a tune. Poor thing was a bundle of nerves."

Nanny Ogg shrugged, and walked out into the roped-off area. Somewhere in the distance someone was having hysterics, punctuated by an occasional worried whistle.

Unlike the magic of wizards, the magic of witches did not usually involve the application of much raw power. The difference is between hammers and levers. Witches generally tried to find the small point where a little change made a lot of result. To make an avalanche you can either shake the mountain, or maybe you can just find exactly the right place to drop a snowflake.

This year Nanny had been idly working on the Man of Straw. It was an ideal trick for her. It got a laugh, it was a bit suggestive, it was a lot easier than it looked but showed she was joining in, and it was unlikely to win.

Damn! She'd been relying on that frog to beat her. She'd heard it whistling quite beautifully on the summer evenings.

She concentrated.

Pieces of straw rustled through the stubble. All she had to do was use the little bits of wind that drifted across the field, allowed to move *here* and *here*, spiral up and—

She tried to stop her hands from shaking. She'd done this a hundred times, she could tie the damn stuff in *knots* by now. She kept seeing the face of Esme Weatherwax, and the way she'd just sat there, looking puzzled and hurt, while for a few seconds Nanny had been ready to kill—

For a moment she managed to get the legs right,

and a suggestion of arms and head. There was a smattering of applause from the watchers. Then an errant eddy caught the thing before she could concentrate on its first step, and it spun down, just a lot of useless straw.

She made some frantic gestures to get it to rise again. It flopped about, tangled itself, and lay still.

There was a bit more applause, nervous and sporadic.

"Sorry . . . don't seem to be able to get the hang of it today," she muttered, walking off the field.

The judges went into a huddle.

"I reckon that frog did *really well*," said Nanny, more loudly than was necessary.

The wind, so contrary a little while ago, blew sharper now. What might be called the psychic darkness of the event was being enhanced by real twilight.

The shadow of the bonfire loomed on the far side of the field. No one as yet had the heart to light it. Almost all of the non-witches had gone home. Anything good about the day had long drained away.

The circle of judges broke up and Mrs. Earwig advanced on the nervous crowd, her smile only slightly waxen at the corners.

"Well, *what* a difficult decision it has been," she said brightly. "But what a marvelous turnout, too! It really *has* been a *most* tricky choice—"

Between me and a frog that lost its whistle and got its foot stuck in its banjo, thought Nanny. She looked sidelong at the faces of her sister witches. She'd known some of them for sixty years. If she'd ever read books, she'd have been able to read the faces just like one.

"We all know who won, Mrs. Earwig," she said, interrupting the flow.

"What *do* you mean, Mrs. Ogg?"

"There's not a witch here who could get her mind right today," said Nanny. "And most of 'em have bought lucky charms, too. Witches? Buying lucky charms?" Several women stared at the ground.

"I don't know why everyone seems so afraid of Miss Weatherwax! I certainly am not! You think she's put a spell on you, then?"

"A pretty sharp one, by the feel of it," said Nanny. "Look, Mrs. Earwig, no one's won, not with the stuff we've managed today. We all know it. So let's just all go home, eh?"

"Certainly not! I paid ten dollars for this cup and I mean to present it—"

The dying leaves shivered on the trees.

The witches drew together.

Branches rattled.

"It's the *wind*," said Nanny Ogg. "That's all . . ."

And then Granny was simply *there*. It was as if

they'd just not noticed that she'd been there all the time. She had the knack of fading out of the foreground.

"I jus' thought I'd come to see who won," she said. "Join in the applause, and so on . . ."

Letice advanced on her, wild with rage.

"Have you been getting into people's heads?" she shrieked.

"An' how could I do that, Mrs. Earwig?" said Granny meekly. "Past all them lucky charms?"

"You're lying!"

Nanny Ogg heard the indrawn breaths, and hers was loudest. Witches lived by their words.

"I don't lie, Mrs. Earwig."

"Do you *deny* that you set out to ruin my day?"

Some of the witches at the edge of the crowd started to back away.

"I'll grant my jam ain't to everyone's taste but I never—" Granny began, in a modest little tone.

"You've been putting a 'fluence on everyone!"

"—I just set out to help, you can ask anyone "

"You did! Admit it!" Mrs. Earwig's voice was as shrill as a gull's.

"—and I certainly didn't do any—"

Granny's head turned as the slap came.

For the moment no one breathed, no one moved. She lifted a hand slowly and rubbed her cheek.

"You know you could have done it easily!"

It seemed to Nanny that Letice's scream echoed off the mountains.

The cup dropped from her hands and crunched on the stubble.

Then the tableau unfroze. A couple of her sister witches stepped forward, put their hands on Letice's shoulders, and she was pulled, gently and unprotesting, away.

Everyone else waited to see what Granny Weatherwax would do. She raised her head.

"I hope Mrs. Earwig is all right," she said. "She seemed a bit . . . distraught."

There was silence. Nanny picked up the abandoned cup and tapped it with a forefinger.

"Hmm," she said. "Just plated, I reckon. If she paid ten dollars for it, the poor woman was robbed." She tossed it to Gammer Beavis, who fumbled it out of the air. "Can you give it back to her tomorrow, Gammer?"

Gammer nodded, trying not to catch Granny's eye.

"Still, we don't have to let it spoil everything," Granny said pleasantly. "Let's have the proper ending to the day, eh? Traditional, like. Roast potatoes and marshmallows and old stories round the fire. And forgiveness. And let's let bygones be bygones."

Nanny could feel the sudden relief spreading out like a fan. The witches seemed to come alive, at the breaking of the spell that had never actually been there in the first place. There was a general straightening up and the beginnings of a bustle as they headed for the saddlebags on their broomsticks.

"Mr. Hopcroft gave me a whole sack of spuds," said Nanny, as conversation rose around them. "I'll go and drag 'em over. Can you get the fire lit, Esme?"

A sudden change in the air made her look up. Granny's eyes gleamed in the dusk.

Nanny knew enough to fling herself to the ground.

Granny Weatherwax's hand curved through the air like a comet and the spark flew out, crackling.

The bonfire exploded. A blue-white flame shot up through the stacked branches and danced into the sky, etching shadows on the forest. It blew off hats and overturned tables and formed figures and castles and scenes from famous battles and joined hands and danced in a ring. It left a purple image on the eye that burned into the brain—

And settled down, and was just a bonfire.

"I never said nothin' about *forgettin'*," said Granny.

When Granny Weatherwax and Nanny Ogg walked home through the dawn, their boots kicked up the mist. It had, on the whole, been a good night.

After some while, Nanny said, "That wasn't nice, what you done."

"I done nothin'."

"Yeah, well . . . it wasn't nice, what you didn't do. It was like pullin' away someone's chair when they're expecting to sit down . . ."

"People who don't look where they're sitting should stay stood up," said Granny.

There was a brief pattering on the leaves, one of those very brief showers you get when a few raindrops don't want to bond with the group.

"Well, all right," Nanny conceded. "But it was a little bit cruel."

"Right," said Granny.

"And some people might think it was a little bit nasty."

"Right."

Nanny shivered. The thoughts that'd gone through her head in those few seconds after Pewsey had screamed—

"I gave you no cause," said Granny. "I put *nothin'* in anyone's head that weren't there already."

"Sorry, Esme."

"Right."

"But . . . Letice didn't *mean* to be cruel, Esme. I mean, she's spiteful and bossy and silly, but—"

"You've known me since we was girls, right?" Granny interrupted. "Through thick and thin, good and bad?"

"Yes, of course, but—"

"And you never sank to sayin' 'I'm telling you this as a friend,' did you?"

Nanny shook her head. It was a telling point. No one even remotely friendly would say a thing like that.

"What's empowerin' about witchcraft anyway?" said Granny. "It's a daft sort of a word."

"Search me," said Nanny. "I *did* start out in witchcraft to get boys, to tell you the truth."

"Think I don't know that?"

"What did you start out to get, Esme?"

Granny stopped, and looked up at the frosty sky and then down at the ground.

"Dunno," she said, at last. "Even, I suppose."

And that, Nanny thought, was that.

Deer bounded away as they arrived at Granny's cottage.

There was a stack of firewood piled up neatly by the back door, and a couple of sacks on the doorstep. One contained a large cheese.

"Looks like Mr. Hopcroft and Mr. Poorchick have been here," said Nanny.

"Hmph." Granny looked at the carefully yet badly written piece of paper attached to the second sack: " 'Dear Miſtreſſ Weatherwax, I woud be moſt grateful if you woud let me name thiſ new championſhip Variety "Eſme Weatherwax." Yours in hopfully good health, Percy Hopcroft.' Well, well, *well*. I wonder what gave him that idea?"

"Can't imagine," said Nanny.

"I would just bet you can't," said Granny.

She sniffed suspiciously, tugged at the sack's string, and pulled out an Esme Weatherwax.

It was rounded, very slightly flattened, and pointy at one end. It was an onion.

Nanny Ogg swallowed. "I *told* him not—"

"I'm sorry?"

"Oh . . . nothing . . ."

Granny Weatherwax turned the onion round and round, while the world, via the medium of Nanny Ogg, awaited its fate. Then she seemed to reach a decision she was comfortable with.

"A very useful vegetable, the onion," she said, at last. "Firm. Sharp."

"Good for the system," said Nanny.

"Keeps well. Adds flavor."

"Hot and spicy," said Nanny, losing track of the metaphor in the flood of relief. "Nice with cheese—"

"We don't need to go that far," said Granny Weatherwax, putting it carefully back in the sack. She sounded almost amicable. "You comin' in for a cup of tea, Gytha?"

"Er . . . I'd be getting along—"

"Fair enough."

Granny started to close the door, and then stopped and opened it again. Nanny could see one blue eye watching her through the crack.

"I was *right* though, wasn't I," said Granny. It wasn't a question.

Nanny nodded.

"Right," she said.

"That's nice."

Short Novels By Bestselling Masters

In Three Spectacular Volumes

"Microcosmic glimpses of broadly imagined worlds and their larger-than-life characters distinguish this hefty volume of heavyweight fantasy.... There's enough color, vitality, and bravura displays of mythmaking in this rich sampler to sate faithful fans and nurture new readers on the stuff of legends still being created." —*Publishers Weekly* (starred review)

Legends 1

Stephen King tells a tale of Roland the Gunslinger, in the world of The Dark Tower, with "The Little Sisters of Eluria."

Robert Silverberg returns to Majipoor and to Lord Valentine's adventure in an ancient tomb, in "The Seventh Shrine."

Orson Scott Card spins a yarn of Alvin and his apprentice from the *Tales of Alvin Maker,* in "Grinning Man."

Raymond E. Feist's *Riftwar Saga* is the setting of the tale of "The Wood Boy."

Legends 2

Terry Goodkind tells of the origin of the Border between the lands in the world of *The Sword of Truth,* in "Debt of Bones."

George R. R. Martin sets his piece a generation before his epic, *A Song of Ice and Fire,* in the adventure of "The Hedge Knight."

Anne McCaffrey, the poet of *Pern,* returns once again to her world of romance and adventure in "Runner of Pern."